Stars Above

Stars Above

A Lunar Chronicles Collection

WRITTEN BY

Marissa Meyer

Feiwel and Friends

NEW YORK

A FEIWEL AND FRIENDS BOOK
An Imprint of Macmillan

Our books may be purchased in bulk for promotional, educational,
or business use. Please contact your local bookseller or the Macmillan Corporate
and Premium Sales Department at (800) 221-7945 ext. 5442 or by e-mail at
MacmillanSpecialMarkets@macmillan.com.

Library of Congress Cataloging-in-Publication Data Available

ISBN: 978-1-250-09184-0 (hardcover) / 978-1-250-09185-7 (ebook)
978-1-250-10445-8 (international)

Feiwel and Friends logo designed by Filomena Tuosto

First Edition: 2016

10   9   8   7   6   5   4   3   2

fiercereads.com

For Sloane and Delaney

Contents

The Keeper

MICHELLE SLID HER FINGERTIP ACROSS THE PORTSCREEN, flipping through the album of photos her granddaughter had sent that morning. Luc had taken Scarlet to see the ruins of the Musée du Louvre, and Scarlet had taken dozens of pictures of the crumbling statues and still-standing wreckage. There was even a photo of Luc and Scarlet together, huddled in enormous wool coats beside a statue with one missing arm. The stone woman looked like a third member of their party.

Michelle kept coming back to this picture, the only one of the album that had both Luc and Scarlet in it. Though Luc wore his usual detached expression—always trying so hard to look sophisticated—Scarlet's grin was effervescent. Her eyes sparkling, one of her front teeth missing, her curly red hair half tucked into the collar of her jacket. She seemed happy.

For once, Luc was trying, and that warmed Michelle to her core. It was a welcome change from the usual comms she received from her granddaughter. Home life had been difficult for the child since her mother had left ... no, Michelle knew it had been difficult long before that. She had known from the beginning that her son was ill-suited to parenthood. Too vain and selfish, and his young wife had been every bit as bad. Their relationship had been passionate and dramatic and doomed from the start. They'd been arguing since practically the moment they started dating—big arguments, with screaming and smashed dishes and law enforcement called by the neighbors more than once. When the pregnancy had been announced, Michelle had struggled to feign joy for them. The disastrous end to their marriage had been inevitable and she'd known that the poor child would be the victim of it.

Usually she was forced to read between the lines of Scarlet's comms, as Luc certainly never told her anything. *"I'm bored and waiting for Papa to get home"* translated to "Luc is out at the bars again and his six-year-old daughter is home alone." Or, *"Thank you for the birthday gift. Papa said he's going to take me to a theme park to celebrate once the weather is better"* translated to "Luc forgot his daughter's birthday again and hopes she'll forget all about his promise by the time spring rolls around." Or, *"The neighbor brought ratatouille for dinner again—the third this week. She uses too much eggplant and I HATE eggplant, but Papa said I was being rude and sent me to my room"* translated to "Luc gambled away their food budget this week, but at least this kindly neighbor is paying attention—unless she's been charmed by Luc's smile and hasn't yet figured out that he's a spineless rascal."

Michelle sighed. She loved her son, but she had lost respect for him a long while ago. She knew she had to accept part of the blame herself, though. She had raised him, after all. Maybe she had spoiled him too much, or maybe not enough. Maybe he'd needed a father in his life to guide him. Maybe—

A knock startled her. She lifted her gaze away from the portscreen, where she'd been staring into the shadowed face of the son she hadn't spoken more than a dozen sentences to this year. Probably one of the neighbor kids hosting a fund-raiser, or someone from town wanting a few eggs from her hens.

Setting the port on the table beside her favorite reading chair, she pulled herself to her feet and ducked out of her bedroom, down the narrow stairs that creaked familiarly every time, into the small foyer of the farmhouse. She didn't bother to look, just opened the door on its ancient hinges.

Her heart stalled. The entire world seemed to hesitate.

Michelle took half a step back, bracing herself on the door. "*Logan.*"

His name struck her with the full force of an asteroid collision, stealing the air from her lungs.

Logan stared back at her. *Logan.* Her Logan. His eyes searched her, every bit as rich and fathomless as she remembered, though they were lined with wrinkles that hadn't been there before. More than thirty years before.

"Hello, Michelle." His voice was a wearier version of the one she had adored all those years ago, but it still filled her with memories and loneliness and warmth. "I am so sorry to intrude on you like this," he said, "but I am in desperate need of your help."

SHE HAD BEEN BOTH PROUD AND TERRIFIED WHEN SHE'D BEEN invited to attend the Earthen diplomats on a visit to Luna—the first in generations. She was one of four pilots for the mission, and the youngest by nearly ten years. It had been an honor, even though most of the people she'd mentioned the mission to prior to departure looked at her like she was crazy for even considering it.

"Luna?" they would ask in disbelief. "You're going to Luna... willingly? But...they'll *murder* you. They'll brainwash you and turn you into an Earthen slave. You'll never come back!"

She laughed and ignored their warnings, confident that the horror stories surrounding Lunars were based on superstitious nonsense more than solid facts. She believed there would be good Lunars and bad Lunars, just like there were good and bad Earthens. Surely they couldn't all be monsters.

Besides, she was only a pilot. She wouldn't be involved in any of the political discussions or important meetings. She didn't even know what the mission was meant to accomplish. She would spend the monthlong visit enjoying the famed luxuries of Artemisia and she would return home with plenty of stories to tell. She wasn't about to let some absurd urban legends keep her from being part of such a historic event.

She was given leave almost as soon as they reached Artemisia, and she soon discovered that the white city was everything she expected it to be and more. Lush gardens and courtyards filled the spaces between white-stone buildings. Trees towered over sprawling mansions—some reaching nearly to the domed enclosure that covered the city. Music poured out of every alleyway and no glass was left empty of wine and everyone she met was carefree and full of laughter. Somehow they all knew she was Earthen without her having to say so, and it seemed that every wealthy merchant and aristocrat in the city made it their personal obligation to show her the grandest time she could imagine.

It was only the fourth day since her arrival and she was in the central square of the city, dancing around an enormous sundial with a strikingly handsome man, when she stepped too close to the edge and tumbled off. She cried out in pain, knowing instantly that her ankle was sprained. Her dancing partner called for a magnetic levitating contraption—similar to a gurney—and took her to the nearest med-clinic.

That was where she met Logan.

He was a doctor, a few years older than she was, and Michelle had known instantly that he was different from the other Lunars she'd met. He was more serious. His eyes more thoughtful. But more than that, he was ... *imperfect.* She studied him while he studied her ankle. Average build. Light brown, untidy hair. There was a mole on his cheek and his mouth drooped on one side, even when he smiled. He was still good-looking, at least by Earthen standards, but on Luna ...

Only when it occurred to her that he was *not* using a glamour did she realize that everyone else she'd met had been.

He offered to let her rest in a suspension tank, but she shook her head.

"It will heal quicker," he said, confused by her refusal.

"I don't like being confined to small spaces," she replied.

"Then you must hate being trapped under the biodome here."

He didn't press her as he began to wrap her ankle the old-fashioned way. For years to come, when she thought of Logan, she would remember his gentle hands and how deftly they had worked.

"It's so beautiful here," she said. "I hardly feel trapped at all."

"Oh, yes. It's a very pretty prison we've built."

It was the first unpleasant comment she'd heard about Luna from a Lunar.

"You think of your home as a prison?"

His gaze flickered up, clashing with hers. He was silent for a long, long time. Instead of answering her question, he finally asked in a hushed whisper, "Is it true that the sky on Earth is the color of a blue jay's wings?"

After that day, Michelle no longer had eyes for the aristocrats and their flashy clothes (especially once Logan told her that the man she'd been dancing with on the sundial was in fact old enough to be her grandfather). She and Logan spent every possible moment together during her stay on Luna. They both knew it was a temporary affair. There was a ticking clock for when she would return to Earth, and she never entertained hope that he might be able to return with her. The rules against Lunar emigration were strict—Luna didn't like its citizens leaving, and Earth didn't want them coming.

Perhaps their romance was more intense for its brevity. They talked about everything—politics and peace and Earth and Luna and constellations and history and mythology and childhood rhymes. He told her horrifying rumors about how the Lunar crown treated the impoverished citizens of the outer sectors, forever ruining the glittering allure that Artemisia had first cast over her. She told him about her dream to someday retire from the military and buy a small farm. He showed her the best place in the city to see the Milky Way, and there was a meteor shower on the night they first made love.

When it was time for her to leave, there were no parting gifts. No tears and no good-byes. He had kissed her one last time and she had boarded the ship to return to Earth and that was the last she had ever seen of Dr. Logan Tanner.

When she'd discovered her pregnancy nearly two months later, it had not even occurred to her to try and find a way to inform him of his child. She was sure that it would not have mattered anyway.

"WE WERE TOLD OF HER DEATH MONTHS AGO," MICHELLE said, pressing her palm flat against the glass lid of the suspended animation tank that had been hidden beneath a pile of old horse blankets in the back of a rented hover. She was trying to keep from heaving. She was not easily disturbed, but never had she been so close to something so sad and horrific. Judging from the size of the body, the child was only three or four years old. She looked more like a corpse—disfigured and covered in burn marks. It was unbelievable that she was alive at all. "There have been rumors . . . conspiracy theorists have speculated that she may have survived and Levana is trying to cover it up. But I didn't believe them."

"Good," said Logan. "We want people to believe she's dead, especially the queen. It's the only way she'll be safe."

"Princess Selene," Michelle whispered. It didn't seem real. None of this seemed real.

Logan was on Earth. Princess Selene was alive. He'd brought her *here.*

"A fire did this?"

"Yes. It happened in the nursery. Levana claims it was an accident, but . . . I believe it was planned. I believe Levana wanted her dead so she could have the throne for herself."

Michelle shook her head in disgust. "Are you sure?"

His dark eyes stared at the form of the princess encapsulated beneath the glass. "Matches and candles are rare on Luna. Under the domes, any sort of air pollution is a concern we take seriously. I don't see how or why a nanny would have had one, or why she would have had it lit in the middle of the day, in a child's playhouse." He sighed and met Michelle's eyes. "Also, there was a peer of mine. Dr. Eliot. She was the first doctor to examine the princess, and the one to proclaim her as dead and have her body removed from the palace. Her quick thinking saved the princess's life." His gaze slipped. "Two weeks ago, she was accused of being a traitor to the crown, though details of her crime were never released. I believe she was tortured for information and then killed. That's when I knew I had to run. That Selene and I had to run."

"Who else knows?"

"I . . . I'm not sure. There's one other man, Sage Darnel, who worked in bioengineering. He was beginning to act suspicious of me before I left. Asking questions that hinged too close to the truth, but . . . I don't know if he figured anything out, or was only guessing. Or maybe I'm being paranoid."

"If he does know, would he . . . is he an ally, or . . ."

He shook his head. "I don't know. We're all so caught up in the mind games of Artemisia, I can never tell who's happy under the regime and who hates Levana as much as I do." He released a frustrated breath. "There's nothing I can do about it now. They'll no doubt be suspicious that I disappeared, but I couldn't stay there. *She* couldn't stay there." The tank made a low gurgling noise, as if in agreement.

"What if they come looking for you?" Michelle's heart was starting to pound. The burden of it was settling over her shoulders. Queen Levana was the most powerful woman in the galaxy. If Logan's theories were true, then she wouldn't stop looking for the princess. And anyone who helped the princess was in danger.

"I don't think they can trace me here," Logan said, though his expression was unconvincing. "I've changed spaceships and hover cars six times since arriving on Earth and manipulated everyone I've seen so that they wouldn't be able to recognize me."

"But what about our . . ." She stumbled over the word *relationship*. ". . . connection? We weren't discreet before."

"It was a long time ago, and affairs happen so frequently on Luna, I doubt anyone was paying attention to us."

Affairs. He said the word too casually, and Michelle was surprised at the sting of hurt it caused.

Logan's expression softened. He looked exhausted and too gaunt, but he was still handsome to her. Maybe even more handsome now than when they were young. "You're the only person I trust, Michelle. I don't know where else to take her."

It was the right thing to say. Her pain diffused. She inhaled deeply and looked down at the child again. "My house is small," she said. "I couldn't hide her if I—"

She hesitated. The house had been built in the second era. It had survived the Fourth World War. She swallowed.

"The bomb shelter," she said. "There's a bomb shelter under the hangar, wired for a generator and everything."

Logan pressed his lips together until they turned white. There was regret etched into his face, but also hope. It took him a while, but eventually he nodded. "You understand the danger you'll be in if you keep her here? She is the most valuable person on this planet."

For some reason, this comment made Michelle think of Scarlet, her granddaughter. Only a couple of years older than the princess before her.

Scarlet—*Logan's* granddaughter.

She opened her mouth, but shut it again.

"I'm sorry," said Logan, misinterpreting her hesitation. "I'm sorry to ask this of you."

"What are you going to do?" she said.

"I will help you until I know the princess is stable and you're confident in caring for her. Then I'll go into hiding until ... until she's old enough to be removed from stasis."

She wanted to ask him where he would hide, and how, and when he would return. But she didn't say any of those things. Instinct told her that it was better not to know. *Safer* not to know.

"And once she's awoken from stasis?"

His gaze became distant, like he was trying to peer into the future. Trying to imagine the woman this child might become.

"Then I will tell her the truth," he said, "and help her reclaim her throne."

THOUGH SCARLET HAD TAKEN THE MAGLEV TRAIN BETWEEN Paris and Toulouse a dozen times before, she'd underestimated how different it would be traveling by herself. Her body had been wound tight from the moment she'd boarded the train. She hadn't had much money for her ticket, so she was in the cheapest car and the seats were uncomfortable, especially for such a long trip. She dreaded the idea that someone would sit next to her and ask where she was going and where were her parents and did she need help. She already had a speech rehearsed in case it happened. She was going to visit her grandmother, who would be picking her up from the station. Of course her parents knew where she was. Of course she was expected.

But of course she wasn't.

The train entered a new station and she squeezed her backpack against her side and tried to look grouchy as new passengers boarded. She exuded her best "leave me alone" vibes.

It worked. No one sat next to her, and she exhaled in relief as the train rose on its magnets again.

Unzipping the top pocket of her pack, she pulled out her portscreen and stuck a pair of wireless headphones into her ears. Maybe some music would help her forget about what she was doing.

She had left Paris. She was never going back again. She was going to live with her grand-mère and no one could stop her.

She wondered if her father had even realized she was gone yet. Probably not. He was probably still drunk and unconscious.

She shut her eyes and tried to relax as the music blasted into her ears, but it was no use. She was hyperaware of the movements of the train, the chatting of passengers, the announcements of upcoming stops. She was waiting for the chime of her portscreen—a comm from her father demanding to know where she was. Or a nervous, worried comm, begging her to come home. Or even a missing child alert from the police.

She listened to the entire album and no alerts came.

She watched the cities come and go, the fields and vineyards disappear over the hills, the sun sink toward the horizon, and no alerts came.

The car became more crowded as time passed. A man in a suit eventually sat next to her and her whole body tensed, but he didn't try to talk or ask any questions. He busied himself reading a newsfeed on his port and eventually dozed off, but Scarlet had heard enough stories about bag snatchers and child-nappings that she dared not let down her guard.

The album started over. The notice board at the front of the car announced that the next stop was Toulouse, and an entirely new bout of nerves writhed in her stomach. She had to wake the man up to get past him, and he startled and said something about almost missing his stop again. He laughed. Scarlet ducked past him without meeting his gaze, clutching the straps of her backpack.

"Hey, kid."

She clomped down the steps to the platform.

"Kid!"

She quickened her pace, panic and adrenaline rushing through her veins. She looked around for someone who would help her if she needed it. Someone in uniform or an android or—

"Kid, wait!" A hand landed on Scarlet's shoulder and she spun around, ready to scream.

It was the man in the suit. "You left this on the bench," he said, holding out her water bottle.

Her pulse immediately subsided and she grabbed the bottle away without a thank-you. Turning, she jogged across the platform and up the escalators. She felt embarrassed for her overreaction, but still unnerved. She was alone and no one knew where she was or that she was even missing. She doubted she would feel safe until she reached her grandmother's house, and even then she'd have to persuade Grand-mère to let her stay.

She found an empty taxi hover and climbed inside, giving her grandmother's address. The screen asked her to approve the cost of travel, and the price blinking at her made her stomach drop. It would almost deplete her savings.

Swallowing hard, she scanned her wrist and approved the payment.

MICHELLE HAD BEEN CARING FOR THE PRINCESS FOR ALMOST two years, and the regular ministrations had become second nature. Just another chore to check off her daily list. Feed the animals. Gather the eggs. Milk the cow. Check the princess's diagnostics and adjust the tank's fluid levels as needed.

The child was growing. She would have been five years old now—*was* five years old, Michelle reminded herself. Even after all these months it was hard not to think of the girl as a corpse she kept locked up beneath her hangar.

She wasn't a corpse, but she wasn't exactly alive, either. The machines did everything for her. Breathed. Pumped blood. Sent electrical signals to her brain. Logan had told her it was important to keep her brain stimulated so that when she awoke she wouldn't still have the mind of a three-year-old. Supposedly she was being fed knowledge and even life experiences as she lay there, unmoving. Michelle didn't understand how it worked. She couldn't imagine how this child could sleep for her entire life and then be expected to become a queen upon her return to society.

But that would be Logan's job, whenever he returned. There were years still before anyone would know who this child was going to become.

Michelle finished recording Selene's vital statistics and flipped off the generator-powered lights. The bomb shelter, which had been converted into a makeshift hospital room and scientific laboratory, remained lit by the pale blue light from the suspension tank. Michelle clipped her portscreen to her belt and climbed the ladder to the hangar above. She grabbed one of the storage crates that she shuffled between the hangar and the barn—a useful excuse in case anyone ever saw her coming and going. The bomb shelter and its occupant were a secret, a dangerous one, and she could never allow herself to lose caution.

This was the direction of her thoughts when she stepped onto the gravel drive and saw the taxi hover waiting there. She wasn't expecting visitors. She never had visitors to expect.

She squared her shoulders and settled the crate on one hip. The pebbles crunched beneath her feet. She glanced into the hover's windows as she passed, but it was empty, and no one was waiting on the porch, either.

Setting down the crate, Michelle grabbed the only weapon she passed—a pair of rusted gardening shears—and shoved open her front door.

She froze.

Scarlet was sitting on the bottom step of the foyer's staircase, a backpack tucked under her legs. She was bundled up in the same wool coat that Michelle remembered from the Louvre photos, but now it was fraying at the shoulder seams and looked two sizes too small for a growing girl.

"Scarlet?" she breathed, setting the shears on the entry table. "What are you doing here?"

Scarlet's cheeks reddened, making her freckles even more pronounced. She looked like she was on the verge of crying, but the tears didn't come. "I came to live with you."

"THIS IS JUST ANOTHER ONE OF HER CRIES FOR ATTENTION!" Luc spat. His nose and cheeks were tinged red, his words slurred. He was outside and on the screen Michelle could see the puffs of his breaths in the night air. "Just put her back on the train and let her figure it out."

"She is seven years old," Michelle said, aware of how thin the walls around her were. No doubt Scarlet could hear her father's raised voice, even from downstairs. "It's a wonder she made it here safely at all, being all by herself like that."

"And what do you expect me to do? Fly down there to pick her up? I have work in the morning. I *just* got this new job and—"

"She is your *daughter*," Michelle said. "I expect you to be a father, to show that you care about her."

Luc snorted. "You're lecturing me on how to be a good parent? That's rich, Maman."

The comment struck her straight between the ribs. Michelle stiffened. The knot of tension in her stomach wound so tight it threatened to cripple her.

It was her biggest regret, not being there for her son when he was little. She'd been a single mother trying to balance a newborn son with a military career—a career that had been full of potential. She had long ago realized how badly she'd failed in balancing anything. If she could do it all over again . . .

But she couldn't. And while Luc's flaws were partially her doing, she wasn't about to see the same neglect happen to her darling Scarlet.

She looked away from the portscreen. "She can stay the night, of course. I'm not sending her back on a train by herself."

Luc grunted. "Fine. I'll figure out what to do with her tomorrow."

Michelle shut her eyes and squeezed them tight. She pictured the secret door to the bomb shelter. The half-alive girl in that glowing blue tank. She pictured a faceless woman—*Dr. Eliot*—being tortured for information on what had happened to Princess Selene.

She gulped.

"Maybe she should stay here," she said, and pried her eyes open again. Her mind was already made up by the time she looked back at the screen. "Maybe I should take care of her, at least until . . . until you're on your feet again." Even as she said it, she wasn't confident it would ever be a reality.

Scarlet deserved more. More than a nonexistent mother and a careless father. Scarlet deserved more than Luc had been given.

"We'll talk about this tomorrow," Luc said. He still sounded angry, but there was also a hint of relief in his voice. Michelle knew he wouldn't fight her on this.

She disconnected the comm link and left the port on her bed before making her way back down the stairs.

Scarlet was at the dining table, curled around a bowl of pea pods—the first of the season. She had a pile of empty shells growing beside her, and a pod open in her fingers.

Scarlet popped a pea into her mouth when Michelle entered. It crunched between her teeth.

She was pretending to be unconcerned, a look Michelle recognized immediately. It was an expression she herself wore more often than she cared to admit.

"You can stay," said Michelle.

The crunching stopped. "Forever?"

Michelle sat down opposite Scarlet. "Maybe. Your father and I have more to discuss, but . . . for now, at least, you can stay with me."

A smile—the first Michelle had seen since Scarlet's arrival—broke across her face, but Michelle raised a hand. "Listen carefully, Scar. This is a farm, and there is a lot of work that needs to be done here. I'm getting older, you know, and I will expect you to help out."

Scarlet nodded eagerly.

"And I don't just mean the fun stuff, like gathering eggs. There's manure to shovel and fences to paint . . . This isn't an easy life."

"I don't care," said Scarlet, still beaming. "I want to be here. I want to be with you."

"HAPPY BIRTHDAY, DEAREST SCARLET," GRAND-MÈRE SANG, carrying the lemon cake to the table. Eleven candle flames flickered and danced over the white frosting. "Happy birthday, my dear."

Scarlet closed her eyes for a moment of consideration. She had been waiting for this moment all day. Well, mostly she'd been waiting for the delicious lemon cake that her grandmother had made for her birthday every year since she'd come to live with her, but there was something special about making a wish, too.

She wasn't superstitious, but she loved the sense of possibilities that came with wishing.

I wish...

Even having thought of it all day, though, she hadn't made up her mind. It was a struggle to come up with a decent wish. A worthy wish.

That they wouldn't lose any more chickens to whatever predator had gotten into the coop last week? That her father wouldn't forget her birthday again, like he had last year, and the year before that? That Padgett Dubois would stop making fun of her freckles, or that Gil Lambert would actually notice her at school one of these days?

No. None of those were worthy enough.

She knew it was a long shot, but ...

I wish that Grand-mère would teach me how to fly.

Opening her eyes, she leaned forward and blew out the candles in one impressive breath. Grand-mère applauded. "Well done! You get those powerful lungs from me, you know." She winked and pushed two wrapped presents across the table. "Go ahead and open these while I dish up the cake."

"Thank you, Grand-mère." She pulled the larger gift toward her. It was heavier than she expected, and she took care as she untied the ribbon and peeled open the worn pillowcase it had been wrapped in.

Scarlet opened the box. Stared. Lifted one eyebrow.

She looked up at her grandmother, who was licking the frosting off each burnt candle. She couldn't tell if the "present" was a joke. Sure, her grandmother was eccentric, but . . .

"A . . . gun?" she said.

"A Leo 1272 TCP 380 personal handgun," said her grandmother, picking up a carving knife and making the first cut into the cake. A moment later she lifted a perfect slice from the pan and deposited it onto Scarlet's plate. She passed it across the table along with a fork, the layers of yellow cake and white buttercream as flawless as any bakery dessert Scarlet had ever seen.

Her grandmother's skills in the kitchen weren't nearly as wide praised as they should have been. Mostly, when people talked about Michelle Benoit, they joked about the slightly crazy woman who never wanted any help running her farm. Who chased off unwanted solicitors with a shotgun. Who sang when she gardened and claimed that it made the vegetables sweeter.

Scarlet loved her grandmother for her quirks, but even she found it a little off-putting to receive a weapon—an actual, deadly weapon—for her eleventh birthday. Sure, she'd used the shotgun before to chase away wild wolves or shoot clay pigeons when she was bored. But a handgun? This wasn't for hunting. This was for . . . protection.

"Don't look so disappointed," Grand-mère said with a laugh, cutting herself a slice of cake. "It's an excellent model. Just like the one I've carried for years. I'll show you how to load it and empty it when we're done eating. Once you're comfortable carrying it, you'll find that you never want to be without it again."

Scarlet licked her lower lip and nudged the box away with the gun still sitting inside. She was hesitant to touch it. She wasn't even sure if it was legal for someone her age to carry a gun. "But . . . why? I mean, it's a little . . ."

"Unorthodox?" Grand-mère chuckled. "What were you expecting? A baby doll?"

Scarlet made a face at her. "A new pair of tennis shoes would be nice."

Her grandma pulled a bit of cake off her fork with her teeth. Though she was still grinning, there was a heavy seriousness in her gaze when she set the fork down and reached over to remove the gun from the box. Her movements were confident, controlled. She looked like she had picked up a thousand guns in her life, and maybe she had.

"Don't worry, Scar," she said, not looking up. "I'll teach you how to use it, although I hope you never have to." She gave a little shrug and set the gun on the table between them, the barrel pointing toward the kitchen window. "I just want you to know how to defend yourself. After all, you just never know when a stranger will want to take you somewhere you don't mean to go."

Her words were foreboding and Scarlet found herself eyeing the gun as goose bumps scrabbled down her arms. "Thank you?" she said uncertainly.

Her grandmother swallowed another bite of cake and pointed her fork toward the second box. "Open your other present."

Scarlet was more hesitant with this one. The gift was small enough to fit in the palm of her hand and wrapped in a clean dish towel. Maybe it was poison darts, she thought. Or a taser. Or—

She lifted the box's lid.

Her grandmother's pilot pin sat on a bed of tissue paper— a star with a yellow gemstone in its center and gold-plated wings spanning to either side. Scarlet took it into her palm and looked up.

"That was given to me on the day I was promoted to pilot," her grandmother said, smiling at the memory. "And now I want you to have it."

Scarlet curled her fingers around the pin. "Thank you."

"You're welcome. I hope it will protect you in flight as much as it protected me."

Her heart began to throb. She almost dared not hope . . .

"In flight?"

Her grandmother's cheeks dimpled with mischievous glee. "Tomorrow morning, I'm going to start teaching you how to fly the podship."

"THE MULCH WILL PROTECT THE GARDEN OVER THE WINTER," Michelle said, raking a layer of straw over the cutting garden.

Hollow stems and wilted leaves still jutted from the dirt, mere remnants of the colorful dahlias and lilies that had filled the bed throughout the summer. "You want to make sure it's thick, like a heavy winter quilt."

"I *know*," said Scarlet. She was perched on top of the wooden fence, her face cupped in both hands. "I know what mulch is. We do this every year."

Michelle's mouth bunched to one side. She straightened and thrust the rake toward her granddaughter. "If you're such an expert, you can finish the job."

With a saucy eye roll that seemed reminiscent of every thirteen-year-old girl Michelle had ever met, Scarlet hopped off the fence and took the rake from her. The straw rustled and crackled under Scarlet's worn tennis shoes. Michelle took a step back to watch and, pleased that Scarlet did indeed seem to know what she was doing, she grabbed the pitchfork from the stack of dwindling straw and went to turn the compost pile.

The low hum of an approaching hover made Michelle's heart skitter—a reaction that had become common over the past eight years. Her farm was situated on a little-used country road, with only two neighbors beyond her on the lane, and they mostly used podships like she did, even for short trips into town. Hovers were a rarity, and her paranoia had grown worse with every week and month that passed. Maybe she should have relaxed over the years, when no one had come asking questions about Logan, when no one had inquired about her connection to the Lunars or her knowledge of a missing princess. Clearly, after all this time, no one suspected that she was involved—in fact, most people believed that the princess was dead, just as they'd been told years before, and that rumors of her faked death were nothing but fanciful gossip, especially as an eventual war with Luna seemed more and more inevitable.

None of this calmed her, though. Rather, with every day that passed without any retribution coming her way for her decision to harbor Selene, the more certain she became that someday, *someday*, her secret would be discovered.

"Is that a hover?" Scarlet asked, leaning into the rake and squinting at the black speck rolling over the farthest hill.

"Probably just another obnoxious escort salesman," said Michelle. She jerked her head toward the house. "Go inside, Scarlet."

Scarlet scowled at her. "If it's just a salesman, why do I have to go inside?"

Michelle fisted a hand on her hip. "Must you always argue with me? Just go inside."

With another eye roll, Scarlet dropped the rake onto the half-covered garden bed and stomped off toward the house.

Michelle didn't release her grip on the pitchfork as the hover came closer. For a moment, she thought it would pass by them and continue on to the neighbors, but at the last moment it slowed and turned into her driveway. Michelle was by no means a connoisseur of hovers, yet she could tell this was an old model. Old, but well maintained. Its windows glinted under the late autumn sun as it came closer.

She glanced back once as she heard the house's back door clamor shut, then went to greet the newcomer, holding the pitchfork horizontally like a javelin. She had no qualms about being called crazy. She had no fear of frightening off a solicitor or some hapless city dweller who had gotten turned around on the unfamiliar country roads. She didn't mind her reputation so long as it kept curious strangers off her property.

It wasn't a stranger, though, who opened the door.

He had hardly changed in the years since he'd helped her set up the bomb shelter for the safekeeping of Selene. The same wrinkles, the same graying hair.

Until he met her gaze and she was forced to reconsider.

Maybe he had changed, after all. There was something in his eyes. A panic of sorts that was even more anxious than it had been ages ago. A wide-eyed haunting, a barely discernible twitch at the end of one brow.

He opened his mouth to speak, but Michelle beat him to it, yelling, "Whatever you're selling, we're not interested!"

Logan hesitated, his mouth still open. It took him a long, long, long time to recover from her unexpected rejection. This, too, was a change. He had always been so quick before, so sharp-witted, so clever.

"I . . . I am sorry to bother you . . . ," he stammered. His eyes darted past Michelle to the windows of the farmhouse, and she saw them stall for a moment. Just as she'd expected, Scarlet was watching. "I need your help," he started again. "I . . . I think I'm lost?"

Michelle lowered the tines of the pitchfork to the soil. "Is something wrong with your vehicle? It was making a strange noise when you pulled up."

Logan's attention turned back to her, and his expression cleared somewhat. "Yes, I fear so. Unfortunately, I'm a regular dunce when it comes to fixing ... things." He gestured hopelessly at the hover.

Feigning annoyance, Michelle turned toward the hangar. "Sounded like some old cooling gel. I have some in here, and I can draw you a map to wherever it is you're trying to get to."

She didn't look back, but she could hear Logan's shoes crunching on the hard, cold soil as they crossed to the hangar. She didn't look at Scarlet in the window, either, though she could feel her granddaughter's suspicious gaze following them.

Suspicious, because that's just how Michelle had raised her to be. She would have felt guilty about it, but Logan's arrival reminded her how dangerous their situation was, no matter how much time had passed. Until the princess was no longer in her care, she and Scarlet would never be completely safe.

The second she heard the hangar door shut, she spun around to face Logan. "What's happened?"

Logan's face had that sense of nervousness again. "I'm sorry. I didn't know you were ... I didn't think you would have ..." He was struggling to think of what to call Scarlet, but Michelle didn't inform him. To tell him she had a granddaughter would teeter too close to telling him that *he* had a granddaughter, and she had years ago made the decision that it was better—safer—for everyone if he never found out.

"Why are you here?" she said instead, leaning the pitchfork against a row of wooden cabinets that were peeling with old paint. "You told me you wouldn't be back until the child was at least fifteen years old. I wasn't expecting you for years still."

"I know. But we can't wait . . . I can't wait any longer. We must complete her operations. We must wake her up, soon, before it's too late."

Michelle frowned. When he had first brought the princess to her, he'd explained at length what would need to happen when she was older. When her body was almost full grown, they would outfit her with what physical features would be necessary for her to walk and breathe and speak and be the queen that Luna needed. It had taken Michelle a long while to comprehend that he meant to turn the princess into a cyborg, which on some levels seemed a travesty, but she'd long ago come to the understanding that it was the only way. She was not one to pass judgment on cyborgs, anyway. Just one more misunderstood group, like so many others.

Still, Logan had always insisted that the cyborg operation be conducted once the child was older. To outfit an immature body with cyborg limbs as extensive as she would require would be clunky and inefficient, and perhaps even incompatible with her growing organic tissue in the long term.

"Why?" she finally said. "She's still so young. Why wake her now?"

Logan's face fell and he leaned against the podship that she used for local deliveries. "I have Lunar sickness." His voice cracked. It sounded like a confession of some shameful crime. Michelle's expression must have conveyed her confusion, though, because his eyes softened at her. "I am going mad, Michelle. When I first came to Earth, I was able to use my gift in small ways, simple ways, to avoid detection. But over the years, even small manipulations have begun to feel dangerous. I've been afraid some other Lunar might be near, might recognize my use of the gift. Or that an Earthen might pick up on the manipulation. Even if it was something harmless, they might know ..." He swallowed. A deep crease had formed between his brows. "So I stopped. I haven't used my gift for years, and now ... now I am paying the price. It is driving me insane, and I don't think I could stop it now, even if I tried. It's happened fast. So much faster than I thought it would ..." He dragged his palms down his face and groaned into them.

Michelle stared. She wasn't sure if she understood half of what he said, but she was only a pilot and a farmer. Logan was the Lunar, the doctor, the one who had left his home and risked everything to keep the child safe. If he believed she needed to be woken up sooner, then Michelle didn't think she could argue with him.

"Will she be ready?" she asked.

Logan's arms dropped to his sides. "She must be." He opened his mouth to say something else but stopped. Then, after a long moment, he said, "She will not be staying with you once she is stable and awake. I have endangered you for long enough."

This was the topic they had always skipped around before. The *after*. It had been difficult enough trying to keep her alive, hidden, secure. It had seemed too distant and complicated to imagine what would become of her once the operation was complete. But now they had no choice but to think of it.

Soon, she would not be a body in a tank. She would be a child.

An eleven-year-old girl, who would no doubt be frightened and confused.

"Where will you take her?"

"I've found a man who lives in the Eastern Commonwealth, just outside of New Beijing. His name is Garan Linh, and he's an intelligent man with a vast knowledge of android systems and artificial intelligence, which will be useful given her cyborg... additions. But he's also an inventor, and he's created this marvelous device that attaches to a person's nervous system. In an Earthen, it can keep them from ever being manipulated by the Lunar gift. But in a Lunar, it can ensure that they are unable to use their gift at all, whilst also protecting them from developing the hallucinations associated with Lunar sickness."

Michelle was frowning again as she tried to take in everything he was telling her. "Well...good, then. That will help you, won't it? Prevent you from ... er, going mad?"

"No, no. I will not take one. He has only two in the prototype stage. One must be for the princess, of course. She will eventually have to be taught how to control her gift, and until then, we can't risk her revealing her identity. The other prototype is for you."

"Me?"

"Just in case." Logan fixed an intense look on her. "Just in case anything should ever happen to you. Just in case any Lunar should find you and ... try to manipulate you into giving up the princess's location."

Her jaw tensed. There were other ways to get information out of a person. More old-fashioned ways. But Logan wished to protect her mind, at least, and she had heard tales of Queen Levana and her thaumaturges' creative methods before. She was grateful that Logan wanted to protect her in this small way. She recognized his sacrifice, even if she knew he would never admit that it was such.

"All right," she said, wiping her sweating palms down the sides of her jeans. "You've found this inventor, and the child will receive this device of his. Then what?"

"Then she will go to live with him. He's already agreed to care for her as his legal ward, and he has two children of his own. It will be a good fit."

She cocked her head. "Does he know who she is?"

"Not yet." Logan inhaled a sharp breath. "But I will have to tell him. He must know the full extent of the danger he's putting himself and his family in if he's to agree to this. And . . . and he must know how valuable she is. I'll try to keep an eye on her for as long as I can, but I'm not sure I will still be lucid enough to tell her the truth once she's ready. It's possible that responsibility will fall to him."

It sounded so certain. So final. It dawned on Michelle how terrified Logan was of whatever was happening inside his own head.

Logan had always prided himself on his thinking mind. How horrible it must be to know he was losing it now.

His mouth quirked unexpectedly. "I will not take your pity now, Michelle. All my decisions have been my own, and I am still convinced that they were the right ones."

"Of course they were," she said. "You have changed the course of history."

"Not yet. But someday, perhaps." He rubbed his temple and glanced at the secret door that led down to Selene's room. "How is she?"

"Much the same. Getting taller. She's grown like a tadpole this year."

He nodded. "I will need at least a week to complete the operations. We'll have to conduct them in stages. Can you be ready in a month?"

A month. After so many years of nothing, nothing, nothing, it was so sudden, like a maglev train screeching toward her.

"I will have to send Scarlet away," she whispered, mostly to herself. "Perhaps she can stay with her father for a while."

Logan peered at her. She peered back and waited for him to ask. *Scarlet. Who is Scarlet? Who is her father? Who is . . . ?*

He lowered his gaze first, and she couldn't read him. She couldn't tell if he guessed the truth or not. They were together for such a short time, and so long ago. There was no reason for him to suspect . . .

But he'd always been good at interpreting her silences.

He didn't ask. Just nodded and said, "I will tell Garan to make his travel arrangements."

IT ALL SEEMED PAINFULLY FAMILIAR.

Scarlet's anger had cooled somewhat during the maglev ride from Paris back to Toulouse, but she still had a furious knot in her stomach. She never wanted to see her lousy father again. She'd told herself as much when she'd run away the first time, back when she was seven, but this time she meant it. That drunken, arrogant, condescending jerk was nonexistent to her.

She couldn't believe she'd agreed to stay with him for a whole month. Looking back, all of Grand-mère's encouraging words about how it would be a good bonding opportunity and give her father a chance to see what a strong young woman she was becoming and blah blah blah—*gag*. Instead, all he'd done from the moment she'd arrived was pawn her off on his fawning "lady friends" while he left her for hours, only to come back stinking of cognac. And when he *was* around, he was criticizing her clothing choices, or blaming Grand-mère for filling her head with too many opinions, or accusing Scarlet of idolizing "the crazy old bat."

That comment had been the last straw. The last straw *ever.*

After a ten-minute screaming fit, Scarlet had repacked her bag and stormed out of his apartment, slamming the door satisfyingly behind her. She'd headed straight to the train station. Her father hadn't even tried to stop her, and she really didn't care.

She'd lasted nine days.

She thought that was an impressive feat on its own.

She was going to the farm. To her grandmother. To her home.

The moment she stepped off the train and back onto the platform in Toulouse, the angry knot began to dissolve. She inhaled a long breath, looking forward to the familiar scent of hay and manure that had once been disgusting to her, but had developed into something comforting and almost pleasant. Soon she would be drinking a cup of thick, decadent hot chocolate while she vented all her frustrations to Grand-mère. Soon she would be snuggled under her favorite winter quilts, listening to the serene hoots of the barn owl that had taken up residence on the farm earlier that year.

This time, the ride in the taxi hover wasn't full of anxiety. Every moment that passed, taking her farther away from Paris and her un-father, filled her with the tranquil, pleasant sensation of coming home. When the hover turned onto their narrow road and she spotted their house settled amid the snow drifts, the relief she felt nearly overwhelmed her.

Home.

She was out of the hover before it had come to a complete stop, launching herself over the gravel drive and yanking open the front door. But she had taken only a few steps into the entryway when she felt the silent stillness of the house.

She paused.

No clanging of pots in the kitchen. No creaking floorboards overhead. No familiar humming.

Her grandmother wasn't here.

"Grand-mère?" she attempted anyway.

"Scarlet!"

She spun around, a grin bursting across her face. Her grandmother was rushing toward her across the drive, her face contorted in worry.

"I heard the hover pull up," she said, panting for breath. "What are you doing here?"

"I came home early," Scarlet said. "I couldn't stand it there. Oh, Grand-mère, it was horrible, absolutely horrible!" She moved to meet her grandmother on the front steps but hesitated.

Her grandmother's hair was wild and uncombed and the circles under her eyes were extra dark, as if she hadn't slept since Scarlet had left.

And she was not smiling.

"You can't be here!" her grandmother cried, then flinched at the shrill tone of her own voice.

Scarlet frowned. "What?"

"That isn't—" Her grandmother let out a groan. She didn't stop when she reached the front step—not to give Scarlet a hug or a kiss on the cheek, nothing. After more than a week of separation, all her grandmother did was shove her inside the house.

Scarlet dropped her backpack on the floor with a heavy thud. "What's going on?"

Her grandma took a moment to compose herself, but her face was still twisted into a scowl. "You weren't supposed to be home for weeks. Didn't you think to send me a comm and let me know you were coming back early?"

"I wanted to surprise you," Scarlet snapped. It was easy to switch back into her angry mode—after all, she'd been angry for the past week. "Why are you yelling?"

"I'm not—!" Her grandmother growled and crossed her arms over her chest.

Scarlet mimicked the pose, glaring up at her. It wouldn't be long now before they were the same height.

After a moment, her grandmother released a frustrated breath and rubbed the bridge of her nose. "Fine," she said. "Fine. Nothing can be done about it now. But, since you're home . . ." Her voice changed, taking on a short, businesslike tone. She still sounded angry, but now Scarlet could see that she was frazzled, too. "I haven't been able to get into town yet this week." She pivoted on her heels and marched into the kitchen. "We'll call back that taxi and you can go run some errands for me. I need you to go to the bakery and the hardware store, and you can take the drapes in to the cleaners and—"

"Excuse me?" said Scarlet from the doorway. She gaped at her grandmother bustling around the kitchen, pulling together a list of groceries. "That's it? I have had a horrible, horrible week, and now you're going to send me out to run some stupid errands without . . ." Her voice warbled. "Without even saying 'welcome home'?"

Her grandmother paused and turned to face her. A flash of guilt crossed over her face, but she whisked it away and squared her shoulders. "If you wanted a party, you should have commed to tell me you were on your way back. I have things I need to get done, Scarlet. You have to . . . I need you to run into town for these things, today. After all, if you're old enough to take the train all the way from Paris by yourself, you're clearly old enough to run a few errands."

"Fine, I'll stop the hover," said Scarlet, gritting her teeth and blinking back her tears before they could fall. "Just comm me the list when you have it, as I wouldn't want to take up any more of your *valuable* time." She stormed back to the entryway. "By the way," she yelled over her shoulder, "I missed you, too!"

She slammed the door so hard it made the house's gables shake overhead, but this time there was nothing satisfying about it.

MICHELLE WAS CHOKING ON GUILT. SCARLET HAD HARDLY spoken to her since she returned home yesterday afternoon. Or maybe Michelle was avoiding talking to her, unable to explain why she'd been so upset, unable to apologize in any meaningful way. It seemed easier to be silent. To move around the small house and ignore the other's existence until this was all over.

She knew it wasn't right. She wanted to tell Scarlet the truth. But how did you tell your granddaughter that she'd been sent to Paris for a month so you could help a Lunar doctor conduct the delicate operations to turn a missing princess into a cyborg? How did you explain to her that some inventor was coming from the Eastern Commonwealth today to install a device into your nervous system and adopt the girl who's been secretly kept underneath your hangar for the past eight years? How do you make her understand that if she tells *anyone* about this, if she lets this humongous secret slip, it could lead to both of you being hunted and tortured and killed?

No, she couldn't tell Scarlet anything. So she had to go on

pretending that she was annoyed that Scarlet had come home early, when normally she would have welcomed her with adoring arms.

She was sick to her stomach over it all.

But it was almost over, she told herself again. Soon, the princess would be gone, and she and Scarlet would be safe, and they could go on with their lives as if this had never happened.

She checked the time on her portscreen. Linh Garan was scheduled to arrive soon. If she'd had more time to think yesterday, she would have waited and sent Scarlet into town with a long list of errands today, but it was too late for that now.

Climbing the creaky stairs, she knocked at Scarlet's bedroom door. She heard rustling inside before Scarlet opened the door a crack and glared out at her.

Michelle pretended to still be angry with her, too, though she despised herself for it.

Lifting her chin, she said, "This cold is making my arthritis act up and I wasn't able to do most of the chores this morning. I need you to go do them. The cow will be growing uncomfortable if she isn't milked soon."

Scarlet propped open the door a bit more and drew her brows together. "Since when do you have arthritis?"

Michelle met her glare for glare. "You know that I don't like to complain, Scarlet. I don't speak of it much."

"Or ever," she shot back.

Michelle sighed. She didn't want to fight. "I know you don't like milking the cow, but could you please just do it?"

Scarlet threw up her hands. "You could just ask, you know. This is my farm, too. I haven't complained about doing chores in years, but you still treat me like some spoiled city kid who's going to throw a tantrum every time you ask me to do something. All I want is to belong here, and for you to *treat me* like I belong here."

Michelle's eyes began to water. She tried to respond, but was rendered speechless.

Scarlet sighed and turned away, the disappointment obvious on her face. Michelle hadn't thought it was possible to feel worse than she already did.

"You're right," Michelle finally whispered. Scarlet glanced back at her, and Michelle gave her a weakened smile. "I'll try to be better." She cleared her throat. "So, will you . . ."

"Of course I'll go do the chores," muttered Scarlet, looking only slightly appeased. "Just let me change my clothes."

She swallowed, watching as her granddaughter pulled her red hair up into a messy bun.

Stars, she loved this child. This child who was becoming a young woman before her eyes.

She couldn't wait until she could tell her so.

"Thank you," she said, and made her way back down the stairs.

Minutes later, she heard Scarlet's footsteps pounding down the stairs. The back door creaked and shut—not a slam, but not particularly gently, either.

No sooner had she started a pot of coffee than she heard a

quiet knock at the front door. She tensed. He was early. She hoped Scarlet hadn't noticed his arrival.

Wiping her clammy hands on a towel, Michelle went to answer the door.

"Bonjour," she said to the dark-haired man on her stoop. "You must be Monsieur Linh."

He was fidgeting with the collar of a heavy winter coat, and he didn't stop fidgeting even when he took her hand. His smile was big, though. Big and eager and nervous and impressed. "And you are Michelle Benoit," he said. "The keeper of the greatest secret of the third era. It is a most profound honor to meet you."

Still reeling from the fight with Scarlet, Michelle found it difficult to smile back, so she just stepped aside and offered to take his coat. "My granddaughter lives with me, and I'm afraid she doesn't know about any of this, so I'll appreciate your discretion."

"Of course. If I could not be discreet, I'm sure Logan would not have considered me for this momentous responsibility."

"I'm sure that's true. Please, come into the kitchen. My granddaughter is out taking care of some chores. We should have about half an hour to discuss the girl and the procedure before she returns."

FAMOUS LAST WORDS, MICHELLE THOUGHT, REPEATING THE catastrophe of her meeting with Garan over in her head again and again. She sat at the foot of her bed, a box settled on her lap. She was staring through the window at a half-moon partially obscured by wispy winter clouds and wondering how the politics and mysteries of a world so very far away had managed to take such a toll on her own life.

She had hardly slept. Though she and Scarlet had certainly had their spats since Scarlet had come to live with her, never had their fights been like this. Never had they felt like they *mattered*. Never had Michelle felt hopeless to make things right.

She hadn't given Scarlet enough credit with the chores. She'd completed them almost as quickly as Michelle herself could do them, and Michelle had still been talking with Garan when Scarlet had come back in. *Sneaked* back in. She'd eavesdropped on their conversation, and though Michelle wasn't sure exactly what she'd heard, it was clear that Scarlet hadn't figured out anything about Princess Selene. Rather, she'd misinterpreted the conversation and now seemed to be under the impression that Michelle was going to send her away. That Garan was adopting *her*.

And Michelle didn't know how to explain otherwise. She didn't know how to make this right.

"Soon," she whispered. Soon this would be behind them. Soon she would find a way to make this up to Scarlet.

She looked down at the box in her lap and unfolded the flaps. A red hooded sweatshirt was folded neatly inside—the cotton soft and still smelling of newness. It was by no means a fancy gift, but it would transition nicely into spring once the snow melted, and Scarlet loved wearing red. She treated it like an act of defiance given her red hair.

Michelle looked forward to giving it to her once this whole mess was over.

The alarm chimed on her portscreen. Two hours past midnight. It was time.

She tucked the box beneath her bed. Opening her bedroom door, she hesitated for a moment in the narrow hallway, listening until she could detect Scarlet's heavy breathing from the other bedroom. She took a step closer and laid her palm against the closed wooden door.

"I love you, my Scarlet," she whispered to the still night air. Then she turned and slipped down the stairs, careful to skip over the stair that creaked.

Logan and Garan were already working when she arrived in the secret room that housed Selene's body. Over the last week the princess had been transformed from the mutilated child Michelle had been keeping watch over to a cyborg with metal plating and a complicated software system integrated with her brain. Michelle had acted as Logan's assistant, getting supplies and tools and monitoring vital statistics, but for the most part she'd tried to keep her eyes averted. She had a strong spirit, but even this intrusion was a bit much for her to handle.

Logan glanced up when Michelle's feet hit the concrete floor. He nodded in greeting. He and Garan were each wearing masks, and Michelle grabbed an extra one and slipped it on over her mouth before approaching the operating table.

The child had been turned onto her side. Logan was holding a medical portscreen over her neck, letting a laser gently meld together the incision in the back of her neck. They'd already finished installing Garan's prototype onto her spinal column. That meant it couldn't have taken them more than forty minutes.

Michelle was comforted by the knowledge. After all, her turn would be next.

"How is she?" she asked, glancing at the shiny metal hand and leg.

"Surprisingly well," said Logan. "Her body has adapted to the new prostheses and wiring even better than I hoped. I'm optimistic that the worst is behind us." He checked the incision—almost invisible now but for a pale white scar that would fade with time. "There. Let's get her back into the tank."

They worked together to move her. Though she was still of slight build, the new leg added a surprising amount of heft to her body.

"Are we putting her back into stasis?" Michelle asked.

"No." Logan's eyes glimmered as he looked up at her. "We're waking her up."

She stiffened. "What? Tonight? I thought it was still going to be a week or more before she's ready."

"A week before she's ready for long-distance travel," said Logan. He bent down to connect a set of sensors to the child's head. He'd been removing and reapplying those sensors all week, after every operation. "But we'll begin the awakening process tonight.

I want to make it slow and gradual. Her system has gone through enough shocks—I'll do my best to make this as smooth a transition as possible."

"She's going to be conscious, then?" said Michelle. "For the next week?"

She hadn't been expecting this. She couldn't keep an awake, sentient girl down in this dungeon, but she couldn't bring her into the house, either, and—

Logan shook his head. "Awake, but still heavily medicated. It will be a couple of days before she's cognizant of her surroundings, and Garan has agreed to stay with her and begin working with her to build up her muscle tissue. If the tank has done its job correctly, and the new wiring has synthesized properly with her system, then I hope she will be capable of walking out of here in a week's time."

Walking. After all these years, the princess was about to be walking, and speaking, and *awake.*

Michelle stepped closer and peered into the girl's face. Her brown hair was slick with the gel that had harbored her since she was only three years old. Her face was gaunt and her frame lithe, almost bone-thin. She hoped Garan would feed her a big meal when he welcomed her into his family.

She was only a child, and there were already so many hopes and expectations heaped on her shoulders. Michelle suddenly pitied her.

More than that, she realized she was going to miss her, this child who had caused her so much worry. Who had been a constant fixture in her life for so long, and who would leave now and never even know Michelle's name. Never know who had cared for her for so long.

"All right," Logan murmured. He had attached a portscreen to the side of the tank and was staring at it. "I'm going to initiate the procedure. It will be a few moments, but we should soon begin to see signs of life independent of the machinery."

There was a hum from the base of the suspension tank.

The girl didn't move. Not a breath, not a flinch.

Michelle glanced up at Garan, who was watching the child with eager curiosity. "What are you going to call her?" she asked.

Garan turned to her. "Call her?"

"You can't very well call her Selene. I was wondering if you'd chosen another name."

He stood up straighter. His expression took on a look of bewilderment. "I honestly hadn't given it any consideration."

"Michelle is right," said Logan, still inspecting the portscreen. "We will need to give her an ID chip, too, if we expect her to fit in here on Earth. It will require some history for her—a family, and a believable story for how she became a cyborg. Enough to keep away any suspicion. I have some ideas already, but you are welcome to assign her a name, as her guardian."

Garan's gaze dropped to the child again. His brow was furrowed. "I'm not good with naming things. My wife chose the names for our daughters. I don't think it even occurred to me that I might have a say in it."

Michelle licked her lips behind the face mask. "I have a thought."

Both men glanced at her.

"What about . . . *Cinder*?"

There was a hesitation, and she could tell they were doubtful about the name. She lifted her chin and explained, "It's an unassuming name, but also . . . powerful. Because of where she came from. She survived that fire. She was reborn from the cinders."

They turned as one to look at the girl again.

"Cinder," said Logan, rolling the name over on his tongue. "*Cinder.* I like it, actually."

"Me too," said Garan. "Linh Cinder."

Michelle smiled, glad they had been easily swayed. A child's name was not a decision to be made lightly, but she felt it was the perfect name for her. And now the princess would have a token to take with her. A name that Michelle had given to her, like a parting gift, even if she never knew it.

Cinders. Embers. Ashes. Michelle hoped that whatever strength had allowed this child to survive the fire all those years ago was a strength that still burned inside her. That it would go on burning, hotter and hotter, until she was as bright as the rising sun.

She would need that strength for what lay ahead.

Michelle pressed her palm to the top of the tank, near where the girl's heart was, just as a screen pulsed.

A heartbeat.

Then, seconds later, another. And another.

Nerves tingling, Michelle leaned closer and let her breath fog the glass. "Hello, Cinder," she whispered. "I'm so pleased to finally meet you."

As if she'd heard her name being spoken, the child opened her eyes.

Glitches

"ARE YOU READY TO MEET YOUR NEW FAMILY?"

She tore her gaze away from the window, where snow was heaped up on bamboo fences and a squat android was clearing a path through the slush, and looked at the man seated opposite her. Though he'd been kind to her throughout their trip, two full days of being passed between a hover, a maglev train, two passenger ships, and yet another hover, he still had a nervous smile that made her fidget.

Plus, she kept forgetting his name.

"I don't remember the old family," she said, adjusting her heavy left leg so that it didn't stick out quite so far between their seats.

His lips twisted awkwardly into an expression that was probably meant to be reassuring, and this ended their conversation. His attention fell down to a device he never stopped looking at, with a screen that cast a greenish glow over his face. He wasn't a very old man, but his eyes always seemed tired and his clothes didn't fit him right. Though he'd been clean-cut when he first came to claim her, he was now in need of a razor.

She returned her gaze to the snow-covered street. The suburb struck her as crowded and confused. A series of short one-story shacks would be followed by a mansion with a frozen water fountain in its courtyard and a red-tiled roof. After that, a series of clustered town houses and maybe a run-down apartment complex before more tiny shacks took over. It all looked like someone had taken every kind of residence they could think of and spilled them across a grid of roads, not caring where anything landed.

She suspected that her new home wasn't anything like the rolling farmland they'd left behind in Europe, but she'd been in such a foggy-brained daze at the time that she couldn't remember much of anything before the train ride. Except that it had been snowing there, too. She was already sick of the snow and the cold. They made her bones ache where her fleshy parts were connected to her steel prosthetics.

She swiveled her gaze back toward the man seated across from her. "Are we almost there?"

He nodded without looking up. "Almost, Cinder."

Enfolding her fingers around the scar tissue on her wrist, she waited, hoping he would say something else to ease her nerves, but he didn't seem the type to notice anyone's anxiety above his own. She imagined calling him *Dad*, but the word was laughably unfamiliar, even inside her head. She couldn't even compare him with her real father, as her memory had been reduced to a blank slate during the intrusive surgeries, and all she had left of her parents were their sterile identity profiles, with plain photos that held no recognition and a tag at the top labeling them as DECEASED. They'd been killed in the hover crash that had also claimed her leg and hand.

As confirmed by all official records, there was no one else. Cinder's grandparents were also dead. She had no siblings. No aunts or uncles or friends—at least, none willing to claim her. Perhaps there wasn't a human being in all of Europe who would have taken her in, and that's why they'd had to search as far as New Beijing before they found her a replacement family.

She squinted, straining to remember who *they* were. The faceless people who had pulled her from the wreckage and turned her into *this*. Doctors and surgeons, no doubt. Scientists. Programmers. There must have been a social worker involved, but she couldn't recall for sure. Her memory gave her only dizzy glimpses of the French countryside and this stranger sitting across from her, entranced by the device in his hands.

Her new stepfather.

The hover began to slow, drifting toward the curb. Its nose hit a snowbank and it came to a sudden shuddering stop. Cinder grabbed the bar overhead, but the hover had already settled down, slightly off-kilter in the packed snow.

"Here we are," said the man, eyes twinkling as the hover door slid open.

She stayed plastered to her seat, her hand still gripping the bar, as a gust of icy wind swirled around them. They'd arrived at one of the tiny shack houses, one with peeling paint and a gutter that hung loose beneath the weight of the snow. Still, it was a sweet little house, all white with a red roof and enough dead branches sticking up from the ground that Cinder could almost imagine a garden come springtime.

The man paid the hover with a swipe of his wrist, then stepped out onto a pathway that had been plowed down to a sheet of ice. The door to the house opened before he'd taken a step and two girls about Cinder's own age came barreling down the front steps, squealing. The man crouched down on the pathway, holding out his arms as the girls launched themselves into him.

From her place inside the hover, Cinder heard the man laugh for the first time.

A woman appeared inside the doorway, belting a quilted robe around her waist. "Girls, don't suffocate your father. He's had a long trip."

"Don't listen to your mother, just this once. You can suffocate me all you like." He kissed his daughters on the tops of their heads, then stood, keeping a firm grip on their hands. "Would you like to meet your new sister?" he asked, turning back to face the hover. He seemed surprised at the empty pathway behind him. "Come on out, Cinder."

She shivered and pried her hand away from the safety bar. Sliding toward the door, she tried to be graceful stepping out onto the curb, but the distance to the ground was shorter than she'd expected and her heavy leg was inflexible as it crunched through the compacted ice. She cried out and stumbled, barely catching herself on the hover's doorframe.

The man hurried back toward her, holding her up as well as he could by the arm, one hand gripping her metal fingers. "It's all right, perfectly natural. Your muscles are weak right now, and it will take time for your wiring to fully integrate with your nervous system."

Cinder stared hard at the ground, shivering from both cold and embarrassment. She couldn't help finding irony in the man's words, though she dared not laugh at them—what did integrated wiring have to do with being perfectly natural?

"Cinder," the man continued, coaxing her forward, "this is my eldest daughter, Pearl, and my youngest, Peony. And that is their lovely mother, Adri. Your new stepmother."

She peered up at his two daughters from behind a curtain of fine brown hair.

They were both staring openly at her metal hand.

Cinder tried to shrink away, but then the younger girl, Peony, asked, "Did it hurt when they put it on?"

Steady on her feet again, Cinder pried her hand out of the man's hold and tucked it against her side. "I don't remember."

"She was unconscious for the surgeries, Peony," said the man.

"Can I touch it?" she asked, her hand already inching forward.

"That's enough, Garan. People are watching."

Cinder jumped at the shrill voice, but when she looked up, her "stepmother" was not looking at them, but at the house across the street.

Garan. That was the man's name. Cinder committed it to memory as she followed Adri's gaze and saw a man staring at her through his front window.

"It's freezing out here," said Adri. "Pearl, go find the android and have her bring in your father's luggage. Peony, you can show Cinder to her room."

"You mean *my* room," said Pearl, her lip curling as she began to shuffle back toward the house. "I'm the oldest. I shouldn't have to share with Peony."

To Cinder's surprise, the younger girl turned and latched on to her arm, tugging her forward. She nearly slipped on the ice and would have been embarrassed again, except she noticed that Peony's feet were slipping around too as she pulled Cinder ahead. "Pearl can take the room," she said. "I don't mind sharing with Cinder."

Adri's face was taut as she looked down at their intertwined elbows. "Don't argue with me, either of you."

Condensation sprang up on Cinder's steel hand as she went from the chilled air to the house's warm entryway, but Peony didn't seem to notice as she led her toward the back of the house.

"I don't know why Pearl's upset," she said, shouldering open a door. "This is the smallest room in the house. Our bedroom is much nicer." Releasing Cinder, she went to pull open the blinds on the single small window. "But look, you can see the neighbor's cherry tree. It's really pretty when it blooms."

Cinder didn't follow her to the window, instead casting her gaze around the room. It seemed small, but it was larger than the sleeper car on the maglev train, and she had no prior bedrooms to compare it with. A mattress sat in the corner with blankets tucked neatly around its sides, and a small dresser stood empty on the nearest wall.

"Pearl used to have a netscreen in here, but Mom moved it into the kitchen. You can come watch mine whenever you want to, though. Do you like *Nightmare Island*? It's my favorite drama."

"*Nightmare Island*?" No sooner had Cinder said it than her brain started streaming data across her vision. A POPULAR DRAMA AIMED AT TEENAGE GIRLS THAT INCLUDES A CAST OF THIRTY-SIX YOUNG CELEBRITIES WHO ARE CAUGHT UP IN LIES, BETRAYAL, ROMANCE, AND THE SCHEME OF A CRAZED SCIENTIST WHO—

"Don't tell me you've never heard of it!"

Cinder scrunched her shoulders beside her ears. "I've heard of it," she said, blinking the data away. She wondered if there was a way to get her brain to stop doing that every time she heard an unfamiliar phrase. It had been happening almost nonstop since she'd woken up from the surgery. "That's the show with the crazed scientist, right? I've never seen it, though."

Peony looked relieved. "That's fine, I have a subscription to the whole feed. We'll watch it together." She bounced on her feet and Cinder had to tear her gaze away from the girl's excitement. Her gaze landed on a box half-tucked behind the door. A small pronged hand was hanging over the edge.

"What's this?" she said, leaning forward. She kept her hands locked behind her back.

"Oh, that's Iko." Abandoning the window, Peony crouched down and scooted the box out from the wall. It was filled with random android parts all jumbled together—the spherical body took up most of the space, along with a glossy white head, a sensor lens, a clear bag filled with screws and program chips. "She had some sort of glitch in her personality chip, and Mom heard that she could get more money for her if she sold her off in pieces rather than as a whole, but nobody wanted them. Now she just sits here, in a box."

Cinder shuddered, wondering how common glitches were in androids. Or cyborgs.

"I really liked Iko when she was working. She was a lot more fun than that boring garden android." Peony picked up the thin metal arm with the three prongs and held it up so that the fingers clicked together. "We used to play dress-up together." Her eyes lit up. "Hey, do *you* like playing dress-up?"

Adri appeared in the doorway just as Cinder's brain was informing her that "dress-up" was A GAME OFTEN PLAYED BY CHILDREN IN WHICH COSTUMES OR ADULT CLOTHES ARE USED TO AID IN THE PROCESS OF IMAGINATION . . .

Obviously, she thought, sending the message away.

"Well, Cinder?" said Adri, tightening her robe's belt again and surveying the small room with a pinched face. "Garan told me you wouldn't require much. I hope this meets your expectations?"

She looked around again, at the bed, the dresser, the branches that would someday bloom in the neighbor's yard. "Yes, thank you."

Adri rubbed her hands together. "Good. I hope you'll let me

know if you need anything. We're glad to share our home with you, knowing what you've been through."

Cinder licked her lips, thinking to say thank you again, but then a small orange light flickered in her optobionics and she found herself frowning. This was something new and she had no idea what it meant.

Maybe it was a sign of a brain malfunction. Maybe this was a glitch.

"Come along, Peony," said Adri, stepping back into the hall. "I could use some help in the kitchen."

"But Mom, Cinder and I were going to—"

"*Now*, Peony."

Scowling, Peony thrust the android arm into Cinder's hand and followed after her mother.

Cinder held up the limb and shook it at their backs, making the lifeless fingers wave good-bye.

SIX NIGHTS AFTER SHE'D ARRIVED AT HER NEW HOME, CINDER awoke on fire. She cried out, tumbling off the mattress and landing in a heap with a blanket wrapped like a tourniquet around her bionic leg. She lay gasping for a minute, rubbing her hands over her arms to try and smother the flames until she finally realized that they weren't real.

A warning about escalating temperatures flashed in her gaze and she forced herself to lie still long enough to dismiss it from her vision. Her skin was clammy, beads of sweat dripping back into her hair. Even her metal limbs felt warm to the touch.

When her breathing was under control, she pulled herself up onto weak legs and hobbled to the window, thrusting it open and drinking in the winter air. The snow had started to melt, turning into slush in the daytime before hardening into glistening ice at night. Cinder stood for a moment, reveling in the frosty air on her skin and entranced by how a nearly full moon turned the world ghostly blue. She tried to remember the nightmare, but her memory gave her only fire and, after a minute, the sensation of sandpaper in her mouth.

She shut the window and crept toward her bedroom door, careful not to trip on the bag of secondhand clothes Pearl had begrudgingly given to her the day before, after her father had lectured her about charity.

She heard Adri's voice before she reached the kitchen and paused, one hand balancing her on the wall as her body threatened to tip toward its heavier left side.

As she strained to hear, Adri's voice grew steadily louder, and Cinder realized with a jolt that Adri wasn't *speaking* louder, but rather something in her own head was adjusting the volume on her hearing. She rubbed her palm against her ear, feeling like there was a bug in it.

"Four months, Garan," Adri said. "We're behind by four months, and Suki-jiě has already threatened to start auctioning off our things if we don't pay her soon."

"She's not going to auction off our things," said Garan, his voice a strange combination of soothing and strained. Garan's voice had already become unfamiliar to Cinder's ear. He spent his days out in a one-room shed behind the house, "tinkering," Peony said, though she didn't seem to know what exactly he was tinkering with. He came in to join his family for meals, but hardly ever talked, and Cinder wondered how much he heard, either. His expression always suggested his mind was very far away.

"Why *shouldn't* she sell off our things? I'm sure I would in her place!" Adri said. "Whenever I have to leave the house, I come home wondering if this will be the day our things are gone and our locks are changed. We can't keep living on her hospitality."

"It's going to be all right, love. Our luck is changing."

"Our luck!" Adri's voice spiked in Cinder's ear and she flinched at the shrillness, quickly urging the volume to decrease again. It obeyed her command, through sheer willpower. She held her breath, wondering what other secrets her brain was keeping from her.

"*How* is our luck changing? Because you won a silver ribbon at that fair in Sydney last month? Your stupid awards aren't going to keep food on this table, and now you've brought home one more mouth—and a *cyborg* at that!"

"We talked about this . . ."

"No, *you* talked about this. I want to support you, Garan, but these schemes of yours are going to cost us everything. We have our own girls to think about. I can't even afford new shoes for Pearl, and now there's this creature in the house who's going to need . . . what? A new *foot* every six months?"

Shriveling against the wall, Cinder glanced down at her metal foot, the toes looking awkward and huge beside the fleshy ones— the ones with bone and skin and toenails.

"Of course not. She'll be fine for a year or two," said Garan.

Adri stifled a hysterical laugh.

"And her leg and fingers can be adjusted as she grows," Garan continued. "We shouldn't need replacements for those until she reaches adulthood."

Cinder lifted her hand into the faint light coming down the hallway, inspecting the joints. She hadn't noticed how the knuckles were fitted together before, the digits nestled inside each other. So this hand could grow, just like her human hand did.

Because she would be stuck with these limbs forever. She would be cyborg forever.

"Well, how *comforting*," said Adri. "I'm glad to see you've given this so much thought."

"Have faith, love."

Cinder heard a chair being pushed back. She retreated into the hallway, but all that followed was the sound of running water from the faucet. She pressed her fingers over her mouth, trying to feel the water through psychokinesis, but even *her* brain couldn't quench her thirst on sound alone.

"I have something special to reveal at the Tokyo Fair in March," Garan said. "It's going to change everything. In the meantime, you must be patient with the child. She only wants to belong here. Perhaps she can help you with the housework, until we can get that android replaced?"

Adri scoffed. "Help me? What can she do, dragging that monstrosity around?"

Cinder cringed. She heard a cup being set down, then a kiss. "Give her a chance. Maybe she'll surprise you."

She ducked away at the first hint of a footstep, creeping back into her room and shutting the door. She felt that she could have wept from thirst, but her eyes stayed as dry as her tongue.

"HERE, YOU PUT ON THE GREEN ONE," SAID PEONY, TOSSING A bundle of green-and-gold silk into Cinder's arms. She barely caught it, the thin material slipping like water over her hands. "We don't have any real ball gowns, but these are just as pretty. This is my favorite." Peony held up another garment, a swath of purple-and-red fabric decorated with soaring cranes. She strung her bony arms through the enormous sleeves and pulled the material tight around her waist, holding it in place while she dug through the pile of clothes for a long silver sash and belted it around her middle. "Aren't they beautiful?"

Cinder nodded uncertainly—although the silk kimonos were perhaps the finest things she'd ever felt, Peony looked ridiculous in hers. The hem of the gown dragged a foot on the floor, the sleeves dangled almost to her knees, and street clothes still peeked out at her neck and wrists, ruining the illusion. It almost looked like the gown was trying to eat her.

"Well, put yours on!" said Peony. "Here, this is the sash I usually put with that one." She pulled out a black-and-violet band.

Cinder tentatively stuck her hands into the sleeves, taking extra care that no screws or joints caught the fine material. "Won't Adri be mad?"

"Pearl and I play dress-up all the time," said Peony, looping the sash around Cinder's waist. "And how are we supposed to go to the ball if we don't have any beautiful dresses to wear?"

Cinder raised her arms, shaking the sleeves back. "I don't think my hand goes with this one."

Peony laughed, though Cinder hadn't meant it to be funny. Peony seemed to find amusement in almost everything she said.

"Just pretend you're wearing gloves," said Peony. "Then no one will know." Grabbing Cinder by the hand, she pulled her across the hall and into the bathroom so they could see themselves in the mirror.With her fine, mousy hair hanging limp past her shoulders and awkward metal fingers poking out of the left sleeve, Cinder looked no less absurd than Peony.

"Perfect," said Peony, beaming. "Now we're at the ball. Iko used to always be the prince, but I guess we'll have to pretend."

"What ball?"

Peony stared back at her in the mirror as if Cinder had just sprouted a metal tail. "The ball for the peace festival! It's this huge event we have every year—the festival is down in the city center and then in the evening they have the ball up at the palace. I've never gone for real, but Pearl will be thirteen next year, so she'll get to go for the first time." She sighed and spun out into the hallway. Cinder followed, her walking made even more cumbersome than usual by the kimono trailing on the ground.

"When I go for the first time, I want a purple dress with a skirt so big I can hardly fit through the door."

"That sounds uncomfortable."

Peony wrinkled her nose. "Well, it has to be spectacular, or else Prince Kai won't notice me, and then what's the point?"

Cinder was almost hesitant to ask as she followed flouncing Peony back into her bedroom—"Who's Prince Kai?"

Peony spun toward her so fast, she tripped on the skirts of Adri's kimono and fell, screaming, onto her bed. "*Who's Prince Kai?*" she yelled, struggling to sit back up. "Only my future husband! Honestly, don't girls in Europe know about him?"

Cinder teetered between her two feet, unable to answer the question. After twelve whole days living with Peony and her family, she already had more memories of the Eastern Commonwealth than she had of Europe. She hadn't the faintest idea what—or who—the girls in Europe obsessed over.

"Here," said Peony, scrambling across her messy blankets and grabbing a portscreen off the nightstand. "He's my greeter."

She turned the screen on and a boy's voice said, "Hello, Peony." Cinder shuffled forward and took the small device from her. The screen showed a boy of twelve or thirteen years old wearing a tailored suit that seemed ironic with his shaggy black hair. He was waving at someone—Cinder guessed the photo was from some sort of press event.

"Isn't he gorgeous?" said Peony. "Every night I tie a red string around my finger and say his name five times because this girl in my class told me that will tie our destinies together. I know he's my soul mate."

Cinder listed her head, still staring at the boy. Her optobionics were scanning him, finding the picture in some database in her head, and, this time, she expected the stream of text that began to filter through her brain. His ID number, his birth date, his full name and title. Prince Kaito, Crown Prince of the Eastern Commonwealth.

"His arms are too long for his body," she said after a while, finally picking up on what didn't feel right about the picture. "They're not proportionate."

"What are you talking about?" Peony snatched the port away and stared at it for a minute before tossing it onto her pillow. "Honestly, who cares about his arms?"

Cinder shrugged, unable to smother a slight grin. "I was only saying."

Harrumphing, Peony swung her legs around and hopped off the bed. "Fine, whatever. Our hover is here. We'd better get going or we'll be late for the ball, where *I* am going to dance with His Imperial Highness, and *you* can dance with whoever you would like to. Maybe another prince. We should make one up for you. Do you want Prince Kai to have a brother?"

"What are you two doing?"

Cinder spun around. Adri was looming in the doorway—again her footsteps had gone unnoticed, and Cinder was beginning to wonder if Adri was really a ghost that floated through the hallways rather than walked.

"We're going to the ball!" Peony said.

Adri's face flushed as her gaze dropped to the silk kimono hanging off Cinder's shoulders. "Take that off this instant!"

Shrinking back, Cinder instantly began undoing the knot that Peony had tied around her waist.

"Peony, what are you thinking? These garments are expensive, and if she got snagged—if the lining—" Stepping forward, she grabbed the collar of the dress, peeling it off Cinder as soon as the sash was free.

"But you used to let Pearl and me—"

"Things are *different* now, and you are to leave my things alone. Both of you!"

Scowling, Peony started unwrapping her own dress. Cinder bit the inside of her cheek, feeling oddly vulnerable without the heavy silk draped around her and sick to her stomach with guilt, though she wasn't sure what she had to be guilty about.

"Cinder."

She dared to meet Adri's gaze.

"I came to tell you that if you are to be a part of this household, I will expect you to take on some responsibilities. You're old enough to help Pearl with her chores."

She nodded, almost eager to have something to do with her time when Peony wasn't around. "Of course. I don't want to be any trouble."

Adri's mouth pursed into a thin line. "I won't ask you to do any dusting until I can trust you to move with a bit of grace. Is that hand water-resistant?"

Cinder held out her bionic hand, splaying out the fingers. "I ... I think so. But it might rust ... after a while ..."

"Fine, no dishes or scrubbing, then. Can you at least cook?"

Cinder racked her brain, wondering if it could feed her recipes as easily as it fed her useless definitions. "I never have before, that I can remember. But I'm sure ..."

Peony threw her arms into the air. "Why don't we just get Iko fixed and then *she* can do all the housework like she's supposed to?"

Adri's eyes smoldered as she looked between her daughter and Cinder. "Well," she said finally, snatching up the two kimonos and draping them over her arm. "I'm sure we'll be able to find *some* use for you. In the meantime, why don't you leave my daughter alone so she can get some of her schoolwork accomplished?"

"What?" said Peony. "But we haven't even gotten to the ball yet."

Cinder didn't wait to hear the argument she expected to follow. "Yes, Stepmother," she murmured, ducking her head. She slipped past Adri and made her way to her own room.

Her insides were writhing but she couldn't pinpoint the overruling emotion. Hot anger, because it wasn't her fault that her new leg was awkward and heavy, and how was she to know Adri wouldn't want them playing in her things?

But also mortification, because maybe she really was useless. She was eleven years old, but she didn't know anything, other than the bits of data that seemed to serve no purpose other than to keep her from looking like a complete idiot. If she'd had any skills before, she had no idea what they had been. She'd lost them now.

Sighing, she shut her bedroom door and slumped against it.

The room hadn't changed much in the almost two weeks since she'd come to call it home, other than the cast-off clothes that had been put into the dresser drawers, a pair of boots tossed into a corner, the blankets bundled up in a ball at the foot of her bed.

Her eyes landed on the box of android parts that hadn't been moved from its spot behind the door. The dead sensor, the spindly arms.

There was a bar code printed on the back of the torso that she hadn't noticed before. She barely noticed it now, except that her distracted brain was searching for the random numbers, downloading the android's make and model information. Parts list. Estimated value. Maintenance and repair manual.

Something familiar stirred inside her, like she already knew this android. How its parts fit together, how its mechanics and programming all functioned as a whole. Or no, this wasn't familiarity, but ... a connectedness. Like she knew the android intimately. Like it was an extension of her.

She pushed herself off the door, her skin tingling.

Perhaps she had one useful skill after all.

IT TOOK THREE DAYS, DURING WHICH SHE EMERGED FROM her room only to sit for meals with her new family and, once, to play in the snow with Peony while Adri and Pearl were at the market. Her metal limbs had frosted over with cold by the time they were done, but coming inside to a pot of green tea and the flush of shared laughter had quickly warmed her back up.

Adri had not asked Cinder to take on any household chores again, and Cinder imagined it seemed a lost cause to her step-mother. She stayed hopeful, though, as the jumble of android pieces gradually formed into something recognizable. A hollow plastic body atop wide treads, two skinny arms, a squat head with nothing but a cyclops sensor for a face. The sensor had given her the most trouble, and she had had to redo the wiring twice, triple-checking the diagram that had downloaded across her eye-sight, before she felt confident she'd gotten it right.

If only it worked. If only she could show to Adri, and even Garan, that she wasn't a useless addition to their family after all. That she was grateful they'd taken her in when no one else would. That she wanted to belong to them.

She was sitting cross-legged on her bed with the window open behind her, allowing in a chilled but pleasant breeze, when she inserted the final touch. The small personality chip clicked into place and Cinder held her breath, half expecting the android to perk up and swivel around and start talking to her, until she remembered that she would need to be charged before she could function.

Feeling her excitement wane from the anticlimactic finale, Cinder released a slow breath and fell back onto her mattress, mentally exhausted.

A knock thunked against the door.

"Come in," she called, not bothering to move as the door creaked open.

"I was just wondering if you wanted to come watch—" Peony fell silent, and Cinder managed to lift her head to see the girl gaping wide-eyed at the android. "Is that ... Iko?"

Grinning, Cinder braced herself on her elbows. "She still needs to be charged, but I think she'll work."

Jaw still hanging open, Peony crept into the room. Though only nine years old, she was already well over a foot taller than the squat robot. "How ... *how?* How did you fix her?"

"I had to borrow some tools from your dad." Cinder gestured to a pile of wrenches and screwdrivers in the corner. She didn't bother to mention that he hadn't been in his workshop behind the house when she'd gone to find them. It almost felt like theft, and that thought terrified her, but it wasn't theft. She wasn't going to keep the tools, and she was sure Garan would be delighted when he saw she'd fixed the android.

"That's not ..." Peony shook her head and finally looked at Cinder. "You fixed her by yourself?"

Cinder shrugged, not sure if she should be proud or uncomfortable from the look of awe Peony was giving her. "It wasn't that hard," she said. "I had ... I can download ... information. Instructions. Into my head. And I figured out how to get the android's blueprint to go across my vision so I could ..." She trailed off, realizing that what she'd been sure was a most useful skill was also one more strange eccentricity her body could claim. One more side effect of being cyborg.

But Peony's eyes were twinkling more by the minute. "You're kidding," she said, picking up one of Iko's hands and waggling it around. Cinder had been sure to thoroughly grease it so the joints wouldn't seize up. "What else can you do?"

"Um." Cinder hunched her shoulders, considering. "I can ... make stuff louder. I mean, not really, but I can adjust my hearing so it seems louder. Or quieter. I could probably mute my hearing if I wanted to."

Peony laughed. "That's brilliant! You'd never have to hear Mom when she's yelling! Aw, I'm so jealous!" Beaming, she started to drag Iko toward the door. "Come on, there's a charging station in the hallway."

Cinder hopped off the bed and followed her to a docking station at the end of the hall. Peony plugged Iko in and, instantly, a faint blue light started to glow around the plug.

Peony had raised hopeful eyes to Cinder when the front door opened and Garan stumbled into the hallway, his hair dripping. He wasn't wearing his coat.

He started when he saw the girls standing there. "Peony," he said, short of breath. "Where's your mother?"

She glanced over her shoulder. "In the kitchen, I thi—"

"Go fetch her. Quickly, please."

Peony stalled, her face clouding with worry, before hurrying toward the kitchen.

Intertwining her fingers, Cinder slid in closer to the android. It was the first time she'd been alone with Garan since their long trip, and she expected him to say something, to ask how she was getting along or if there was anything she needed—he'd certainly asked that plenty of times while they were traveling—but he hardly seemed to notice her standing there.

"I fixed your android," she said finally, her voice squeaking a little. She grabbed the android's limp arm, as if to prove it, though the hand did nothing but droop.

Garan turned his distraught gaze on her and looked for a moment like he was going to ask who she was and what she was doing in his house. He opened his mouth, but it took a long time for any words to form.

"Oh, child."

She frowned at the obvious pity. This was not a reaction she'd expected—he was not impressed, he was not grateful. Thinking he must not have heard her correctly, she went to repeat herself—no, she'd *fixed* the android—when Adri came around the corner, wearing the robe she always wore when she wasn't planning on going out. She had a dish towel in her hand and her two daughters trailing in her wake.

"Garan?"

He stumbled back, slamming his shoulder hard into the wall, and everyone froze.

"Don't—" he stammered, smiling apologetically as a droplet of water fell onto his nose. "I've called for an emergency hover."

The curiosity hardened on Adri's face. "Whatever for?"

Cinder pressed herself as far as she could into the wall, feeling like she was pinned between two people who hadn't the faintest idea she was standing there.

Garan folded his arms, starting to shiver. "I've caught it," he whispered, his eyes beginning to water.

Cinder glanced back at Peony, wondering if these words meant something to her, but no one was paying Cinder any attention.

"I'm sorry," said Garan, coughing. He shuffled back toward the door. "I shouldn't even have come inside. But I had to say . . . I had to . . ." He covered his mouth and his entire body shook with a cough, or a sob, Cinder couldn't tell which. "I love you all so much. I'm so sorry. I'm so, so sorry."

"Garan." Adri took half a step forward, but her husband was already turning away. The front door shut a second later, and Pearl and Peony cried out at the same time and rushed forward, but Adri caught them both by their arms. "*Garan!* No—you girls, stay here. Both of you." Her voice was trembling as she pulled them back before chasing after Garan herself, her night robe swishing against Cinder's legs as she passed.

Cinder inched forward so she could see the door being swung open around the corner. Her heart thumped like a drum against her ribs.

"GARAN!" Adri screamed, tears in her voice. "What are you— you can't go!"

Cinder was slammed against the wall as Pearl tore past her, screaming for her father, then Peony, sobbing.

No one paused. No one looked at Cinder or the android in their hurry for the door. Cinder realized after a moment that she was still gripping the android's skeletal arm, listening. Listening to the sobs and pleas, the *No*s, the *Daddy*s. The words echoed off the snow and back into the house.

Releasing the android, Cinder hobbled forward. She reached the threshold that overlooked the blindingly white world and paused, staring at Adri and Pearl and Peony, who were on their knees in the pathway to the street, slush soaking into their clothes. Garan was standing on the curb, his hand still over his mouth as if he'd forgotten it was there. His eyes were red from crying. He looked weak and small, as if the slightest wind would blow him over into the snowdrifts.

Cinder heard sirens.

"What am I supposed to do?" Adri screamed, her arms covered in goose bumps as they gripped her children against her. "What will I do?"

A door slammed and Cinder looked up. The old man across the street was on his doorstep. More neighbors were emerging—at doors and windows, their gazes bright with curiosity.

Adri sobbed louder, and Cinder returned her attention to the family—her new family—and realized that Garan was watching *her*.

She stared back, her throat burning from the cold.

The sirens became louder and Garan glanced down at his huddled wife, his terrified daughters. "My girls," he said, trying to smile, and then a white hover with flashing lights turned the corner, screaming its arrival.

Cinder ducked back through the doorway as the hover slid up behind Garan and settled into the snow. Two androids rolled out of its side door with a gurney hovering between them. Their yellow sensors flashed.

"A comm was received at 17:04 this evening regarding a victim of letumosis at this address," said one of the androids in a sterile voice.

"That's me," Garan choked—his words instantly drowned out by Adri's screaming, "NO! Garan! You can't. You can't!"

Garan attempted a shaken smile and held out his arm. He rolled up his sleeve, and even from her spot on the doorstep Cinder could see two dark spots on his wrist. "I have it. Adri, love, you must take care of the girl."

Adri pulled back as if he'd struck her. "*The girl?*"

"Pearl, Peony," Garan continued, as if she hadn't spoken, "be good for your mother. Never forget that I love you so, so very much." Releasing the hard-won smile, he perched himself uncertainly on the floating gurney.

"Lie back," said one of the androids. "We will input your identification into our records and alert your family immediately of any changes in your condition."

"No, Garan!" Adri clambered to her feet, her thin slippers sliding on the ice and nearly sending her onto her face as she struggled to rush after her husband. "You can't leave me. Not by myself, not with . . . not with this *thing!*"

Cinder shuddered and wrapped her arms around her waist.

"Please stand back from the letumosis victim," said one of the androids, positioning itself between Adri and the hover as Garan was lifted into its belly.

"Garan, no! NO!"

Pearl and Peony latched back on to their mother's sides, both screaming for their father, but perhaps they were too afraid of the androids to go any closer. The androids rolled themselves back up into the hover. The doors shut. The sirens and the lights filled up the quiet suburb before fading slowly away. Adri and her daughters stayed clumped together in the snow, sobbing and clutching one another while the neighbors watched. While Cinder watched, wondering why her eyes stayed so dry—stinging dry—when dread was encompassing her like slush freezing over.

"What is happening?"

Cinder glanced down. The android had woken up and disconnected herself from the charging station and now stood before her with her sensor faintly glowing.

She'd done it. She'd fixed the android. She'd proven her worth.

But her success was drowned out by their sobs and the memory of the sirens. She couldn't quite grasp the unfairness of it.

"They took Garan away," she said, licking her lips. "They called him a letumosis victim."

A series of clicks echoed inside the android's body. "Oh, dear . . . not Garan."

Cinder barely heard her. In saying the words, she realized that her brain had been downloading information for some time, but she'd been too caught up in everything to realize it. Now dozens of useless bits of information were scrolling across her vision. LETUMOSIS, ALSO CALLED THE BLUE FEVER OR THE PLAGUE, HAS CLAIMED THOUSANDS OF LIVES SINCE THE FIRST KNOWN VICTIMS OF THE DISEASE DIED IN NORTHERN AFRICA IN MAY OF 114 T.E....Cinder read faster, scanning until she found the words that she feared, but had somehow known she would find. TO DATE, THERE HAVE BEEN NO KNOWN SURVIVORS.

Iko was speaking again and Cinder shook her head to clear it. "—can't stand to see them cry, especially lovely Peony. Nothing makes an android feel more useless than when a human is crying."

Finding it suddenly hard to breathe, Cinder deserted the doorway and slumped back against the inside wall, unable to listen to the sobs any longer. "You won't have to worry about me, then. I don't think I can cry anymore." She hesitated. "Maybe I never could."

"Is that so? How peculiar. Perhaps it's a programming glitch."

She stared down into Iko's single sensor. "A programming glitch."

"Sure. You have programming, don't you?" Iko lifted a spindly arm and gestured toward Cinder's steel prosthetic. "I have a glitch, too. Sometimes I forget that I'm not human. I don't think that happens to most androids."

Cinder gaped down at Iko's smooth body, beat-up treads, three-fingered prongs, and wondered what it would be like to be stuck in such a body and not know if you were human or robot.

She raised the pad of her finger to the corner of her right eye, searching for wetness that wasn't there.

"Right. A glitch." She feigned a nonchalant smile, hoping the android couldn't detect the grimace that came with it. "Maybe that's all it is."

The Queen's Army

THEY CAME AT THE END OF THE LONG NIGHT, WHEN THE MIN-
ing sector had not seen sunlight for almost two weeks. Z had
crossed his twelfth birthday some months ago, and just enough
time had passed that he'd stopped imagining glimpses of gold
embroidery on black coats. He'd just stopped questioning every
thought that flickered through his brain. He had just begun to
hope that he would not be chosen.

But he was not surprised when he was awoken by a tap at the
front door. It was so early that his father hadn't left for the plant,
one sector over, where he assembled engines for podships and
tractors. Z stared at the dark ceiling and listened to his parents'
whisperings through the wall, then to his father's footsteps padding past his door.

Muffled voices in the front room.

Z balled up his blanket between his fists and tried to pour all
his fears into it and then release them all at once. He had to do it
three times to keep from hyperventilating. He didn't want his

brother, still asleep on the other side of the room, to be afraid for him.

He had known this was inevitable.

He was at the top of his class. He was stronger than some of the men his father worked with in the plant. Still, he'd thought that maybe his instructors would overlook him. Maybe he would be skipped.

But those thoughts were always fleeting. Since he was a little boy, he had been raised to expect a visit from the queen's thaumaturges during his twelfth year, and knew if he was deemed worthy, he would be conscripted into the new army she was building. It was a great honor to serve the crown. It would bring pride to his family and his sector.

"You should get dressed."

He lifted his head to find his brother's eyes shining in the darkness. So he wasn't asleep after all.

"They'll ask for you soon. You don't want to make them wait."

Not wanting his brother to think he was scared, he swung his legs out of the bed.

He met his mother in the hallway. Her cropped hair was sticking up on one side and she had pulled on a cotton dress, though the static of her slip had it clinging around her left thigh. She paused from adjusting the material, and, for one crushing second, he saw the despair that she'd always hidden when they talked about the soldier conscription. Then it was gone and she was licking her fingers and desperately trying to smooth down Z's unkempt hair. He flinched, but didn't fidget or complain, until his father appeared beside them.

"Ze'ev." His voice was thick with an emotion that Z didn't recognize. "Don't be afraid."

His father took his hand and guided him to the front of the house where not one but two thaumaturges were waiting for him. They both wore the traditional uniform of the queen's court—high-collared coats that swept down to their thighs with wide, elaborately embroidered sleeves. However, the woman wore black, denoting a third-level thaumaturge, while the man wore red. Second level. Z didn't think there were more than a dozen second-level thaumaturges on all of Luna, and now one was standing in his house.

He couldn't help picturing his home as it must look through the eyes of such high officials. The front room was large enough for only a worn sofa and a rocking chair, and his mom kept a vase of dusty faux flowers on the side table. If they'd bothered to look through the second doorway, they would have seen a sink piled with dishes where flies were buzzing, because his mother had been too tired to clean last night and Ran and Z had decided to play kicks with the other sector kids rather than do their chores. He regretted that now.

"Ze'ev Kesley?" said the man, the second level.

He nodded, clutching his father's hand and using all his will not to duck behind him.

"I am pleased to inform you that we have reviewed your aptitude tests and chosen you to receive the physical modifications and training in order to become one of the great soldiers of Her Majesty's army. Your enrollment is effective immediately. There is no need to pack any belongings—you will be provided with all that you need. As it is expected that henceforth you will have no more contact with your biological family, you may now say your good-byes."

His mother sucked in a breath behind him. Z didn't realize he was shaking until his father turned and grasped him by both shoulders.

"Don't be afraid," he said again. A faint smile flickered, then disappeared. "Do what they ask, and make us proud. This is a great honor."

His voice was strained. Z couldn't tell if his father believed what he was saying, or if it was only a show for the thaumaturges.

His chest constricted. "But . . . I don't want to go."

His father's face became stern. "Ze'ev."

Z looked at his mother. Her dress was still clinging to her slip but she'd stopped fidgeting. The tears hadn't yet spilled over onto her cheeks. There were wrinkles around her eyes that he'd never noticed before.

"Please," he said, wrapping his arms around her waist. He knew how strong he was. If he held on tight enough, they could never force him to let go. He clamped his eyes shut as the first hot tears slipped out. "Please don't let them—"

Just as a sob tore at his throat, a shadowy new thought slipped to the forefront of his mind.

This was a small, pathetic house in an inconsequential mining sector.

The people here were miserable and unimportant. His parents were weak and stupid—but *he*, he was destined for greatness. He was one of the few selected to serve the queen herself. It was an honor. The thought of lingering here a moment longer made him sick.

Z gasped and pulled away from his mother. Heat was crawling up his neck—spurred by mortification and shame. How could he think such things?

Worse yet, he was still thinking them, somewhere in his head. He couldn't shake them entirely, no matter how much guilt they stirred up.

He turned to gape at the thaumaturges. The woman had a smile toying around her mouth. Though he'd first thought she was pretty, this new expression made him shudder.

"You will be given a new family soon enough," she said, in a voice that lilted like a nursery rhyme. "We have means of making you accept this and come willingly, should we be inclined to use them."

Z cringed, repulsed by the knowledge that she had seen these horrible thoughts. Not only seen them—she had created them. She had been manipulating him, and it had been so seamless, had intertwined with his own emotions so effortlessly. When his peers practiced mind control on one another or an instructor prodded him with thoughts of obedience, it felt like a new idea being etched into his brain. It was recognizable and, often, he found that with enough focus he could defy it.

This was a different level of manipulation, one that he couldn't resist so easily. He knew it then. He would be forced to go with them, and he would become a puppet of Her Majesty, with no more willpower than a trained dog.

Behind him, he heard his bedroom door opening.

Ran had come out to watch—pulled by his curiosity.

Z tightened his jaw and tried his best to stifle his mounting despair. He would be brave—so his brother would not see his fear. He would be strong for him.

Some of the terror and dread did begin to fade once the decision was reached. Empowered by the knowledge that it was his choice—that the thaumaturges had not made it for him—he faced his mother and stood on his tiptoes to kiss her cheek. She grabbed at him before he could pull back and crushed him against her, pressing a frantic kiss against his hair. When she released him, just as quickly, the tears had begun to fall and she had to turn her face away to hide them.

He embraced his father too, just as briefly and just as fiercely so he would know how much love was put into it.

Then he squared his shoulders and stepped toward the thaumaturges.

The woman's grin returned. "Welcome to the queen's army."

THEY SAID THE ANESTHESIA WOULD GIVE HIM SUCH A DEEP, empty sleep that there would be no dreams, but they were wrong. He dreamed of needles burrowing into his skin. He dreamed of pliers gripping his teeth. He dreamed of hot ashes and smoke in his eyes. He dreamed of a white tundra, a cold he had never known, and a hunger barely satiated by dripping meat in his jaws.

Mostly, he dreamed of howls in the distance. Forlorn cries that went on and on and on.

The waking came slowly, like being pulled up from a pit of mud. The howls began to dim as he pried open his eyes. He was in the same room that he'd been in when the nameless nurse had stuck the needle into his arm, but he knew instantly that he was changed. The walls around him were a brighter, crisper white than he'd ever known. The sound of every machine and contraption reverberated in his skull. The scent of chemicals and ammonia invaded his nostrils, making him want to gag, but he was too weak.

His limbs were heavy on the exam table, his joints aching. He wore an oversize shirt that made him feel vulnerable and cold. There was a lump beneath his neck. Forcing his fumbling arm to move, he reached behind his head to find bandages there.

As his awareness sharpened, he struggled to recall what little information the nurse had given him.

All soldiers were modified to increase their effectiveness as members of the queen's army. He would wake up *improved*.

He took in another breath and this time picked up on a new scent. No, two scents.

Two individual odors made up of pheromones and sweat and soap and chemicals. Coming closer.

The door opened and a man and a woman entered. The woman wore a white lab jacket and had spiky auburn hair.

The man was a thaumaturge, but not one who had taken

Z from his home. He had dark, wavy hair that he'd tucked back behind both ears and eyes that were as black as the sky. They matched his tailored third-level thaumaturge coat.

And Z could pick out every unique odor on them—lotions and cosmetics and hormones.

"Good," said the woman, pressing her finger against a pad on the wall. The exam table began to hum and Z was raised to a seated position. He grasped at the thin blanket around his chest. "Your monitor informed me that you were awake. I am Dr. Murphy. I presided over your surgeries. How are you feeling?"

Z squinted at her. "I'm not . . . am I—"

He hesitated as his tongue met something foreign in his mouth. He clasped his hand over his lips, then reached inside. The pad of his thumb found the sharp point of a fang and he jerked it away.

"Careful," said the woman. "Your new implants will serve as some of your most effective weapons. May I?"

He didn't resist as she pulled his jaw open and examined his teeth. "Your gums are healing nicely. We replaced all of your teeth, otherwise there wouldn't be room for the canines. We've also re-inforced your jaw for additional leverage and pressure. You'll likely be sore for another ten to fourteen days, especially as we wean you off the painkillers. How are your eyes?" She pulled a contraption out of her pocket and flicked a light across his pupils. "You'll likely notice increased pigmentation—it's nothing to concern yourself with. Once your optic nerves adapt, you'll find that your eyesight has become optimized to detect and pinpoint motion.

Do let your thaumaturge know if you experience any dizziness, blurred vision, or dark spots. I trust you're already experiencing heightened senses of hearing and smell?"

It took him a moment to realize it was a question, and he gave a shaky nod.

"Excellent. The rest of your modifications will evolve over the next eight to twelve months. As your body adapts to the genetic alterations, you'll notice new muscle strength, agility, flexibility, and stamina. All this will come with increased metabolism, so you'll find yourself eating more in the coming months. Even more than a normal twelve-year-old boy, that is." Her eyes twinkled.

Z's pulse began to pound against his temples.

"But we've prepared for all that," she continued when he didn't laugh. "Soldiers are provided a high-protein diet that we've created for your specific needs. Do you have any questions before I hand you off to Thaumaturge Jael?"

His breathing was becoming more and more difficult to soothe. "What's going to happen to me? In the next . . . eight to twelve months?"

She flashed a braggart's smile. "You'll become a soldier, of course." She held up the small device again. With a tap, a holograph emerged, showing two rotating images.

One, a young male, perhaps in his late teens.

The other, a white wolf.

"Based on years of research and trials, we have perfected our methods of genetic engineering, allowing us to combine select genes of Her Majesty's prized *Canis lupus arctos* with those of still-developing Lunar males." She tapped another button and the two holographs merged. Z sucked in a breath. This new creature had rounded shoulders, and enormous hands that were covered with a fine layer of fur, and fangs that jutted from a grotesquely twisted mouth. More fur covered his face, surrounding severe yellow eyes.

Z pushed himself back into the exam table.

"Using this method," continued the doctor, "we have created the ultimate soldier. Strong and fearless, with the instincts of one of nature's greatest predators. Most important, he is a soldier who is entirely subject to the will of his thaumaturge." She shut off the holograph. "But Thaumaturge Jael will be able to explain all that to you in due time."

"Th-that's going to happen to me?"

The doctor opened her mouth to speak, but the thaumaturge cleared his throat and took a step toward the bed. "Perhaps, or perhaps not. You have undergone the modifications to give you the skills all soldiers require. But we chose to withhold the more *animalistic* changes. For now."

"Though we can complete the necessary mutations at any time," added the doctor.

"But—why not . . ."

"You have been selected as one of only five hundred conscripts to receive special training," said the thaumaturge. "Your aptitude tests suggest you could be valuable to us as more than a member of the infantry, and Her Majesty is preparing a unit of soldiers to play a very specific role." He listed his head. "Whether or not you are admitted into that program will ultimately depend on the potential you display during your training."

The threatening look the thaumaturge pinned on him wasn't necessary. Z never wanted to be back on this exam table. He never wanted another needle beneath his skin. He never wanted to wake up with fur on his face and eyes that had no humanity behind them.

The queen was making a different kind of soldier, and he had already decided that he would be one of them.

HE WAS KEPT IN THE FACILITY FOR ANOTHER TWENTY-FOUR hours, so that the doctor could monitor how his body was reacting to the surgeries. He discovered that what had seemed like a few hours of nightmares had, in reality, been twenty-six days of being kept comatose in a suspended animation tank while his body underwent the surgeries and adapted to the mutations. Twenty-six days, gone, while his DNA melded with that of a white wolf, while nameless doctors and scientists turned him into a beast to serve his queen. In that time, the sun had come and gone, plunging the great city of Artemisia into another long night.

The next day, he found a pile of clothes left beside his bed—soft brown pants, a black T-shirt, and plain boots. They fit him perfectly.

He had just finished dressing when he smelled someone coming—the thaumaturge from the day before. His nausea from his new heightened sense of smell had been quelled during the night, but a new sinking, crawling feeling settled in Z's gut as the thaumaturge entered the room.

Because another sense was missing.

The telltale vibration of energy that his people could perceive and manipulate. It was gone.

His throat clamped. "Something's wrong with me," he said before the thaumaturge could speak. "My gift. It's ... I think something's wrong."

The thaumaturge stared blankly for a moment, before his expression softened into kindness. The look eased Z's growing panic. "Yes, I know," he said. "That is an unfortunate result of the modifications. You see, wild animals do not have the abilities that we do; therefore we must hinder your awareness of bioelectricity so that your Lunar instincts will not interfere with your new wolfish instincts. Don't be alarmed—you are not powerless. We have simply given you a new tool with which to take advantage of your gift. It will be my job to ensure that all of your instincts and abilities are functioning properly when you're called on to use them."

Z licked his lips, finding it awkward to maneuver around his new teeth. He had to shut his eyes to force the wash of bile back down his throat.

They had taken away his Lunar gift. He was as vulnerable as an Earthen now. As useless as a shell. And yet they wanted him to be a soldier?

"We were not properly introduced yesterday," the thaumaturge continued. "You are to call me Master Jael. You will be known as Beta Kesley until and unless your ranking changes. I am glad to see you dressed. Come then."

He left the room, and it took Z a scrambling minute to realize he was meant to follow.

"The candidates for special operative status have been given their own training grounds beneath AR-3," Master Jael said as they left the research facility. Z caught only the briefest glimpse of the glittering white buildings of Artemisia—Luna's major city—before Jael led him down into the lava tubes beneath the surface. A personal shuttle was waiting for them. "The training grounds consist of separate barracks for each pack, a community dining hall, and a series of training rooms in which you will perform formations and learn fighting techniques. This is also where you will decide your placement in the pack."

"The pack?"

"Your new family. We have found that your instincts react best when we mimic the hierarchy of wolves in their natural habitat, and so each pack consists of six to fifteen operatives, depending on the mental strength of their thaumaturge." His grin widened. "You are my fourteenth pack member."

Z turned away to watch the black regolith walls pass by the shuttle window and tried to pretend that he understood what Master Jael was talking about.

The training grounds were in enormous caverns carved into the lava tubes. When they walked into the main room, Jael's heels clipping with each step, Z saw that thirteen soldiers were already lined up to greet them, dressed exactly as he was. He guessed their ages ranged from twelve to eighteen or older, and though they stood in perfect posture in a straight line, with their heels together and arms stiff at their sides, Z knew instantly who was their leader. The tallest and the largest and the one whose eyes flashed when they met his.

"Master Jael," he said, and in unison, all the soldiers clasped a fist to their hearts.

"Alpha Brock. You have a new member joining you today. This is Beta Ze'ev Kesley."

Z could feel the scrutiny of the soldiers cutting into him. He forced himself to stand up straighter, though it pinched the muscles between his shoulder blades. He took the time to meet each of their gazes, thinking that, though there was a proliferation of unfamiliar aromas in this hall, he could pick out which scents belonged to each of them.

"Beta Kesley," said Master Jael, "join your pack."

Z glanced at the thaumaturge and his pulse skipped. There was something eager in the look, but Z didn't know what he was expected to do. Did Jael want him to bow? Or clasp his hand to his heart like the others had?

Before he could decide, Z felt a jolt through his nerves, like an electric shock. And then he was pacing toward the line of soldiers, his feet no longer under his control.

Blood rushed to his face.

Mind control.

A surge of defiance crawled up from the base of his throat. Z scrunched his face up, and, with every bit of concentration he had, he forced his legs to freeze. He found himself in an awkward stance, his legs caught midstep, his hands fisted at his sides. He was already panting with the effort.

He pried open his eyes and looked at Master Jael. He was surprised to find amusement, not anger, in the thaumaturge's expression. Through his teeth, he said, "Thank you, *Master*, but I can walk without your help."

Jael grinned, and with a snap Z felt the hold on his mind release.

"But of course," Jael said. "Please, join the line."

Letting out a breath, Z turned toward his new pack.

He gasped. The leader—Alpha Brock—was now less than an arm's distance away, a snarl showing the points of his canines.

Before Z could think, a fist collided with his jaw, knocking him onto the floor and shoving the wind out of him. For a moment his lungs burned with the need for air and his head rang from the punch. The pain in his jaw was the worst, his gums still sore from the surgery. The throbbing brought tears to his eyes.

"Don't ever disrespect Master Jael again," said Alpha Brock. With a grunt, he landed a kick to Z's ribs.

Z cried out and crunched into a ball, trying to protect his stomach, but another kick didn't follow. Tasting blood, he spit onto the chalky ground. He was glad that none of his new teeth came with it.

Shaking, he risked a glance at Master Jael, but the thaumaturge was standing calmly back, his hands in his sleeves. When he caught Z's gaze, his eyebrows rose without mercy and he said, very slowly, "Get up and join your pack."

Standing seemed impossible. The world was spinning and he wondered if that one kick hadn't broken a rib.

But more afraid of the repercussions of ignoring an order than of the pain, Z pulled himself to all fours and, with a grunt, pushed himself onto wobbly legs. The Alpha stared down at him as Z stumbled to the end of the line. The other soldiers had not moved.

"You will soon learn," said Master Jael, "that your placement in this pack is determined by strength, courage, and the ability to defend yourself. You will not see such mercy again."

Z BEGAN TO LOSE TRACK OF TIME. FIRST THE DAYS AND THEN the weeks and months merged into constant training. Formations. Strategies and tactics. And fights—so many fights. Like wolves in the wild sometimes fight for dominance, these soldiers fought all the time. Constantly trying to best one another, to show off, to prove their worth, to improve their station. Almost all of them seemed to have a thirst for violence that Z couldn't claim, though he often pretended to desire the taste of blood and the crunch of bones as much as any of them. There wasn't much choice.

He didn't win all his fights, but he didn't lose them all, either. After a year and a half—or what he guessed was close to a year and a half, with neither the long days nor the long nights to judge by—he found himself solidly in the middle of his pack. An average beta. After that one punch from Alpha Brock, he had never again allowed himself to be caught by surprise, and he had developed a knack for parrying and blocking. Offensive tactics didn't come as naturally, but he could often avoid being hit for long enough to tire out his opponent.

It would never make him Alpha, but it kept him from becoming the tormented Omega.

Alpha Brock, on the other hand, remained ever on top of the pack. Undefeated, he picked more fights than any of them, as though he had to constantly remind himself and everyone else how much better he was. Z tried to stay out of his way, but it was impossible to avoid him entirely, and when Brock wanted to fight, there was no denying him. Z had received more bruises and scars from those fists than he could count.

The pack was standing around watching an impromptu brawl between Betas Wynn and Troya on an otherwise unremarkable afternoon when Z caught the scent of Master Jael approaching, along with another scent. Familiar and strange at the same time.

Z tore his eyes from the fight as the others picked up on the scents. The two fighters took another moment, but in a breath, they had released each other, and together they all rushed to line up for Jael's entrance. Z recognized the cadence of Jael's footsteps beside something awkward and shuffling. Jael had not brought anyone new to their barracks since Z himself had joined the pack.

Master Jael stepped out of the cave and into the training cavern, a new conscript at his side.

Z couldn't keep back a gasp. Beside him, Wynn flinched at the noise, and he was sure they'd all noticed his reaction. He wasn't the only one with advanced hearing.

The new conscript was his brother. Taller now, but otherwise not much had changed.

Ran took longer to notice him. Standing half a step behind Master Jael, dressed in uniform, pale and wide-eyed, he was busy scanning the faces of his new family.

Until his eyes landed on Z, and he froze.

"Alpha Brock," said Jael, "this is the final recruit for your pack, Beta Ran Kesley."

Together with the rest of the pack, Z clasped his fist to his chest.

"Beta Kesley, you may join your pack."

Z gulped, waiting for the moment when Ran's legs would betray him and recognition would flash across his face.

And it came, and Ran's eyes did widen, but then he bowed his head and put up no resistance as his body joined the others at the end of the line and his balled fist hit his chest.

Z found that his heart was thundering. He wondered if the others could hear it.

He heard Ran's breathing, three bodies away from him, as Jael released his control.

"Welcome to your new family. Training will commence at 06:00 tomorrow. You have much to be caught up on." Jael spun on his heels and left them without ceremony.

No one moved until both the sound of his footsteps and the scent of his cologne had dissipated.

Then Alpha Brock snorted. The noise sent ice rushing through Z's veins.

The pack broke formation and within seconds had Ran surrounded.

"Well," said Alpha Brock. "You did better on your induction than your arrogant brother, at least."

Ran's gaze flickered to Z, a look of fear and uncertainty, before flying back to Alpha Brock.

"I honestly didn't think Master Jael could handle one more member," Alpha Brock continued, smirking. "You must be pretty weak-minded for him to have taken you on."

Ran took half a step away. Z could see he was still dazed from the surgeries, his pupils dilated and a sheen of sweat on his brow.

"Leave him alone, Brock," said Z, stepping into the circle. It was the only time he could recall addressing him directly.

Brock turned and peered at Z from the corner of his eye. "What's that, Kesley?"

"Give him some time. We all know you're Alpha—you don't have to bully every twelve-year-old kid who comes in here to prove it."

He thought he heard a snicker behind him, but it was stifled as Brock's expression darkened. He turned toward him fully and Z was surprised at the relief that rushed into him. At least Brock wasn't targeting Ran anymore.

But then Brock spun so fast, his leg lifted for a roundhouse kick, that Z wasn't sure *he* could have blocked it. Brock's foot smashed into Ran's head, hurtling him into Beta Rafe.

White spots flashed in Z's vision, and he didn't realize what he was doing until a roar emerged from his throat and his fist collided with Brock's jaw.

Brock stumbled back, surprised, but it was short-lived.

Snarling, he flew back at Z and used the leverage of Z's second punch to spin him around, catching Z's head in the crook of his elbow. With one arm pinned at his side, Z growled and tried to toss Brock over him, like he'd learned to throw others when they had him in such a position, but Brock was too big. Z's free hand beat uselessly, pathetically against Brock's ear.

"This is my pack," Brock said. "Don't you ever tell me how to treat them."

The second he was released, Z pushed himself away. But Brock still gripped his wrist. As Z mindlessly sought to put distance between them, he felt something sharp puncture the flesh beneath his elbow. He cried out and yanked his arm away, and the sting ripped down his skin, cutting his flesh from elbow to wrist.

Z stumbled away and clutched his arm against his chest. Brock grinned. He'd taken to filing his nails into knife-sharp points, a trend quickly picked up by the other pack members.

Now Z understood why.

Trying to ignore the pain and the blood dripping down between his fingers, he raised his fists for the next attack.

But Brock merely wiped Z's blood off on his pants and turned away, unconcerned about retribution as the rest of the pack watched.

Z's stomach sank as Brock turned and spat at his brother, who was still on the ground. Brock's spit landed on his shoulder. Ran didn't back away or bother to wipe it off.

"Lesson number one," said Brock. "Never let someone else take your fights for you."

Z didn't let his fists down until Brock had led the rest of the pack away. Then he whipped off his shirt and wrapped the fabric around the wound. It didn't take long for the blood to soak through.

"Ran—are you all right? Is your jaw broken?" He stumbled toward his brother and held a hand toward him. But when Ran met his gaze, it was not with gratitude, but anger.

"Why did you do that?" he said, rubbing his cheek. "Did you have to embarrass me on my first day?"

Z drew back. "Ran . . ."

Ignoring the extended hand, Ran climbed to his feet. "You always have to show me up. I thought this was my chance to prove myself, but of all the soldiers, I have to be grouped with *you*. Stuck in your shadow, again." He shook his head, and Z thought maybe there was wetness in his eyes before he spun away. "Just leave me alone, Z. Just . . . forget we were ever brothers at all."

IT HAD BEEN NEARLY FIVE YEARS SINCE Z HAD UNDERGONE the genetic modifications. Five years without seeing his parents. Five years spent underground—fighting and brawling and training. Not another word had ever been spoken about the possibility of being chosen for the queen's special soldiers, but it was never far from his mind. He frequently awoke from dreams of long syringes and fur covering his body.

There were fifty packs that had been held back from the full surgeries, and they gathered daily for an hour-long feast in the dining hall. It was during the feasts that Z felt most like the animal they wanted him to be. The stench was overwhelming—sweat and blood from all five hundred soldiers mixed with rare cuts of meat that were presented on slabs of wood and stone. They often fought over the choicest bits, resulting in yet more brawls. One more test. One more way to stake your place among your brothers.

There had been a time when Z had sat back and waited for the leftovers, living like a scavenger, rather than join the flying fists and gnashing teeth. But his hunger was as strong as any of theirs— the kind of hunger that was never satisfied—and a few years into his training he had made the decision that he would never again be served last. After only a few victories, his pack brothers had stopped challenging him.

He still avoided Alpha Brock's wrath, despite having grown taller than him in the last year. Z did notice that even Brock hadn't seemed eager to pick any fights with him for a while, instead directing the majority of his cruelty toward mocking and manipulating Ran.

Or, Omega Kesley.

It had been clear from the start that Ran was the weakest. Z had hoped it was only because of his age and size, but soon it was obvious that his brother simply didn't have the fortitude necessary to carve out a place of respect among the pack.

Worst of all, he didn't seem to understand why he remained at the bottom of the chain. He idolized Brock, mimicking the way he talked and attempting to duplicate his fight moves, though he didn't have the upper-body strength to pull off most of them. He had even begun sharpening his nails.

It made Z sick to see it. At times, he wanted to pull his brother aside and shake him and explain that he wasn't helping himself. By cowing to everything Brock did, he was only making himself an easier target.

And yet, Ran had never given any indication that he wanted Z's help, and so Z had let him be. Had watched as his brother clung pathetically to Brock's side, hoping for recognition and receiving only table scraps.

Z was watching his brother gnaw on one of Brock's abandoned bones, the meal whittled down now to pools of blood and shreds of charred flesh, when he caught the scents.

So many aromas. Jael among them, but the others were unknown. Forty . . . maybe fifty . . .

He whipped his head toward the main door of the dining hall, his brow furrowed.

It took a few moments of rowdy talk and chewing before the soldiers around him hushed. A hesitation—thaumaturges never came to the dining hall—before they all pushed back from the tables and jostled around one another to form their lines, wiping juice from their chins.

Jael entered, along with the forty-nine other thaumaturges, all in black coats. They spread out so that they formed a funnel from the entryway. Jael's gaze found his pack and narrowed. A subtle warning.

Z drew his shoulders back until the muscles began to complain.

The silence was startling after the feast's chaos. Z found a piece of meat stuck in a molar and tried to work it out without moving his jaw too much.

They waited.

And then, a new scent. Something floral and warm that reminded him of his mother.

A woman stepped out from the wide cavern, wearing a gauzy dress that billowed around her feet and a sheer veil that covered her face and drifted past her elbows. On top of the veil sat a delicate white crown, carved from shimmering regolith stone.

Z was glad that he was not the only one who gasped. He instantly peeled his gaze away from Her Majesty and stared straight ahead, at the black cavern wall. His palms began to sweat, but he resisted the urge to wipe them on his pants or check his face for remnants of his meal.

The piece of meat blissfully relinquished its hold on his tooth, and he swallowed.

"Gentlemen," said the queen. "I am here to congratulate you on the progress you've all made as soldiers in my formidable new army. I have been monitoring your training sessions for many months now, and I am pleased with what I've seen."

A low rustle slipped through them—the faintest of fidgets. Z did not know how she could have watched them without their knowing. Maybe their training sessions had been recorded.

"You are all aware," the queen continued, "that you are among the soldiers being considered for a unique mission that will aid in the hostilities between Luna and Earth. This is a role of honor, reserved for those who have risen above the confines of their past, the limitations of their bodies, and the fear of the unknown. They will be my most prized soldiers, chosen not only for their strength and bravery, but also for their intelligence, cunning, and adaptability. My court and I will be making our final selections soon."

Her words were blurred in Z's thoughts and he could think of nothing past a bead of sweat making its way down his temple and how his fingers were beginning to twitch with too much energy and no outlet.

The queen, who had been as still as the soldiers until now, a faceless sheet speaking to them, lifted one arm and gestured to the thaumaturges. "I'm sure that I do not need to remind your thaumaturges that those who are in control of the selected packs will receive instant advancement in their court status."

Z dared a glance at Jael and saw that his dark eyes had gone fierce, his jaw set.

"Gentlemen."

Z snapped his gaze back to the wall.

"Your thaumaturges have asked for the opportunity to showcase some of their brightest soldiers. I look forward to the demonstration." She swirled her fingers through the air and the thaumaturges spread out into the crowd.

Jael's walk was tense as he reached them. "Alpha Brock," he snapped, "you will be fighting. No teeth, no claws—I want to show your skill. Understood?"

Brock fisted his hand against his chest. "Yes, Master Jael. Who will be my opponent?"

Jael's gaze swept to Beta Wynn. Though technically all Betas had the same rank in the pack, everyone kept a mental record of wins and losses, of victories and failures, and everyone knew that Wynn wasn't far behind Brock in his abilities.

But then Jael let out a slow breath. "Ze'ev."

Z's eyes widened, and he glanced at Master Jael, heat flooding his face. But Jael showed no humor or uncertainty, only a stern determination as he paced past the others and came to stand before him. Their gazes clashed, and it was with some shock that Z realized he was now taller than Master Jael too.

"She wants a show," he said. "This time, don't hold back."

Z's brow twitched, but he tried to remain neutral as he saluted his thaumaturge.

His thoughts were frenzied as they were marched into the largest training room. Her Majesty had been escorted onto a platform on one end and placed atop a throne so that she could watch the proceedings in comfort.

Fifty packs. Fifty fights.

Z's stomach was roiling as they began. He couldn't focus on the brawls. He was only seeing Jael's dark eyes, hearing his words over and over again. *This time, don't hold back.*

Did Jael think he faked his losses? Did Jael believe he was capable of defeating Brock, or did he only want to ensure that he lasted as long as he could?

Only once did he dare to glance over at his opponent and saw that Brock had a furious scowl. He obviously didn't think Z was a worthy opponent, not in front of the queen herself.

Ran, too, looked sullen, and although not a person in the room would have expected Ran to be chosen as one of Jael's examples, Z sensed that Ran had fantasized about such a chance to prove himself more than once.

Finally, their turn came.

Jael bowed to Her Majesty and introduced them—Alpha Brock fighting Beta Kesley.

Z could smell the blood from the previous fights, still warm and salty, mingling with the regolith dust. He and Brock trekked to the fighting circle and stared at each other.

Only when he sank into his fighting stance did he feel the panic and confusion subside.

He didn't win all his fights, but he won more than he lost. He had become strong and fast. He would not make a fool of himself in front of Her Majesty.

And if they impressed her, perhaps she would choose their pack for her special mission. He would never have to go through the rest of the surgeries. He would never become a mindless beast in her army.

Brock's eyes flashed. There was a burning in his gaze that Z didn't recognize, but he was sure it carried a promise of pain.

Brock came at him first with a right hook aimed at his jaw. Z ducked easily—too easily. Brock feinted at the last moment and drove his other fist into Z's side. Z clenched his teeth and pushed himself back, retaliating with a front kick to Brock's stomach.

They backed away from each other, bouncing on the balls of

their feet, hands poised in front of their faces. A trickle of sweat dropped down Z's spine.

He squinted, watching the way Brock's body swayed, noticing how he briefly clenched his left fist.

A roundhouse kick was coming.

No sooner had he thought it than Brock whipped forward, aiming his foot at Z's head.

He caught it and pulled, throwing Brock onto his side.

Z danced out of Brock's reach, panting. Salt was beginning to sting his eyes. Brock didn't stay down long. He flashed his sharp teeth and rushed forward—

Jab to the ribs. Elbow to the face. Sideswipe kick.

He saw them all happening an instant before they did. *Block. Block. Jump. Attack.*

Teeth snapped as he landed an uppercut to Brock's jaw. A left hook to his side.

Brock withdrew, face contorted in fury. It was difficult for Z to hide his own surprise at this newfound skill.

But it wasn't new. It was from years of sitting on the sidelines, watching and studying and inspecting every fight, every brawl, every punch thrown, every victory won. He knew how Brock fought.

And he suspected that if he were pitted against any one of his pack members, he would have seen the same signs, recognized the same tricks and tells.

He could beat them.

He could beat all of them.

Brock stretched his neck to one side and Z heard the sound of his spine popping. Brock shook it out like a dog, then sank into his stance again.

His eyes glinted.

Bolstered, Z shot forward.

Jab. Blocked.

Cross. Blocked.

Uppercut. Blocked.

Knee—

Z gasped, pain ripping through his abdomen as five nails dug into his side, piercing the flesh above his hip bone. Brock squeezed, digging his fingers deeper into the flesh. Z nearly collapsed, catching himself on Brock's shoulder with a strangled grunt.

"I will kill you before I let you win this fight," Brock breathed against him.

He let go all at once and stepped away. Without his support, Z fell to one knee. He pressed his hand against the wounds, not daring to look at Jael or the queen, to see if anyone noticed or cared that Brock had disobeyed the rules Jael had laid out for them.

But no. They were wild animals. Predators who ran on instinct and bloodthirst.

Who would expect a fair fight from such monsters?

All she wanted was a show.

He heard a low growl and didn't at first realize that it was coming from his own throat. He dared to look up. Brock's stance had relaxed. There was blood up to the first knuckles of his fingers.

Flashes of red sparked in the corners of Z's vision. His side throbbed.

"Best just to stay down," Brock said.

Z snarled. "You'll have to kill me."

He pushed himself off the ground and lunged forward. For a moment, Brock seemed startled, but then he was blocking again, knocking away every advance. But Z was fast, and finally a punch landed against Brock's cheek.

With a roar, Brock reached toward Z's wound, but Z dodged away and grasped Brock by the wrist, pulling him so close he could smell the meat lingering on his breath. With his free hand, he grabbed Brock's throat. Hesitated.

Kill him.

The words stole into his head like the long night came upon the cities—sly, but complete. They possessed him, their command working their way into his desires and hunger and desperation and crawling down into his pulsing fingertips.

I want to see how you would do it.

He gritted his teeth.

Brock's nostrils widened. His eyes glowed with disdain as he sensed Z's indecision.

Z felt the shift in his opponent's weight and he knew it was coming. Fingernails in his side, the blinding pain, the white spots in his vision.

With a roar, he let go of Brock's wrist and grabbed the back of his head.

Snap.

He dropped the body to the ground before the light went out in Brock's eyes.

Z's heart was thumping painfully, his blood a tsunami rushing through his ears.

But outside of him there was silence. Complete and endless silence.

Licking his salted lips, he tore his gaze away from Brock and the way his neck was bent all wrong.

His pack was watching him with disbelief and awe, but to his surprise, there did not seem to be any hatred there.

His gaze continued. They were *all* gaping at him. The other packs, the thaumaturges. All except Jael, who didn't look exactly pleased, and yet didn't seem surprised, either.

Only when the queen stood did he dare to look at her. Her head was listed to the side, and he imagined a pensive expression behind the veil.

"Clean and efficient," she said, bringing her hands together for three solid claps. She had not applauded any of the other fights. He did not know what it meant. "Well done ... Alpha."

His stomach flipped, but the queen was already gesturing for the body to be removed, for the fights to continue, and Z had to stumble off toward his pack before she retracted her praise. Her words followed him, as kind and gentle as a bell.

Well done, *Alpha*.

He had killed Brock, and in the law of the pack, he was now to take his place as the undisputed leader.

He was the new Alpha.

He paused in front of his pack brothers. None of them seemed surprised by the queen's words. They had all known it the moment Brock hit the ground.

As he watched, they each brought their fists to their chests in mute respect. In silent acceptance of his victory. Even his brother saluted him, but there alone was bitterness. There alone was anger over Z's success.

Z nodded twice—once to acknowledge the show of respect, and once at his brother, so that Ran would know that he saw his disappointment.

Then he slipped past them all and headed toward the barracks. He did not care if Jael would be furious or if rumors of his insolence would spread throughout all of Luna by the time he emerged again.

He knew that Jael's pack would be chosen for the queen's mission because of him. They would become her special, prized soldiers. Their bodies would not be tampered with again.

With that one kill, he had ensured that she would never turn him into a monster.

He knew it as sure as, somewhere on the surface, the long, long day was coming.

Carswell's Guide to Being Lucky

CARSWELL DUNKED THE COMB BENEATH THE FAUCET AND
slicked it through his hair, tidying the back so that it was neat and
pristine, and the front spiked up just right. Boots sat on the
counter, watching him with her yellow slitted eyes and purring
heavily, even though it had been nearly ten minutes since he'd
stopped petting her.

"Today's goal," he said—to the cat, he supposed, or maybe the
mirror, "is eighteen univs. Think I can do it?"

The cat blinked, still purring. Her tail twitched around
her paws as Carswell turned off the water and set the comb beside her.

"I've never made that much in one lunch hour before," he said,
pulling a skinny blue tie over his head and cinching the knot
against his neck, "but eighteen Us will put us at a total of fifteen
hundred. Which means"—he flipped down the shirt collar—"the
bank will upgrade my account to 'young professional' and increase
the monthly interest rate by two percent. At this rate, that would
trim nearly sixteen weeks off my five-year plan." Carswell reached

for the tie tack that lived in the small crystal dish beside the sink. The school uniform only allowed for personal tastes to show through in the tiniest of accessories, which had led to a trend among the girls of tying little gems onto their shoes, and the boys of splurging on diamond-stud earrings. But Carswell had only this tie tack, which he'd dipped into his own savings for rather than ask his parents, because he knew his mom would insist he buy something tasteful (code: *designer*) instead. It hadn't been much of a setback. The tiny steel tack had cost merely three univs, and it had since become his signature piece.

A tiny spaceship. A 214 Rampion, to be exact.

His mother, as expected, had hated the tie tack when she'd noticed it for the first time nearly two weeks later. "Sweetheart," she'd said in that sweet tone that just bordered on condescending, "they have a whole display of spaceship accessories at Tiff's. Why don't we go down there after school and you can pick out something nice? Maybe a racer, or a fleet ship, or one of those vintage ones you used to like? Remember all those posters you had on your walls when you were little?"

"I like the Rampions, Mom."

She'd grimaced. Literally grimaced. "What under the stars is a Rampion ship, anyway?"

"Cargo ship," his father had jumped in. "Mostly military, aren't they, son?"

"Yes, sir."

"A cargo ship!" Exasperated, his mom had set her hands on her hips. "Why would you want a tie tack of a cargo ship, of all things?"

"I don't know," he'd said, shrugging. "I just like them."

And he did. A Rampion had the bulk of a whale but the sleekness of a shark, and it appealed to him. Also, there was something nice about a ship that was purely utilitarian. Not flashy, not overdone, not luxurious. Not like every single thing his parents had ever purchased.

It was just ... useful.

"Presentable?" he said, scruffing Boots on the back of her neck. The cat ducked her head in a way that was almost realistic and purred louder.

Grabbing the gray uniform blazer off the door handle, he headed downstairs. His parents were both at the breakfast table (as opposed to the formal dining room table in the next room), all eyes glued to their portscreens, while Janette, one of the maids, refilled their coffee mugs and added two sugars to his mom's.

"Good morning, young captain," Janette said, pulling his chair out from the table.

"Don't call him that," said Carswell's father without looking up. "You can call him 'captain' after he earns it."

Janette only winked at Carswell while she took the blazer from him and hung it on the back of his chair.

Carswell smiled back and sat down. "Morning, Janette."

"I'll bring your pancakes right out." She finished with a silently mouthed *captain* and another wink before drifting toward the kitchen.

Without bothering to look up at his otherwise-engaged parents, Carswell pulled his book bag toward him on the floor and removed his own portscreen. Just as he was turning it on, though, his father cleared his throat.

Loudly.

Intimidatingly.

Carswell glanced up through his eyelashes. He probably should have noticed an extra layer of frost sitting over them this morning, but really, who could tell anymore?

"Would you like a glass of water, sir?"

As a response, his dad tossed his portscreen onto the table. His coffee cup rattled.

"The school forwarded your status reports this morning," he said, pausing for dramatic effect before adding, "They are not up to standards."

Not up to standards.

If Carswell had a univ for every time he'd heard something wasn't up to standards, his bank account would be well into "beginning investor" status by now.

"That's unfortunate," he said. "I'm sure I almost tried this time."

"Don't be smart with your father," said his mom in a rather disinterested tone, before taking a sip of her coffee.

"Math, Carswell. You're failing *math*. How do you expect to be a pilot if you can't read charts and diagrams and—"

"I don't want to be a pilot," he said. "I want to be a captain."

"Becoming a captain," his dad growled, "starts with becoming a great pilot."

Carswell barely refrained from rolling his eyes. He'd heard that line a time or two, also.

A warm body bumped into his leg and Carswell glanced down to see that Boots had followed him and was now nudging his calf with the side of her face. He was just reaching down to pet her when his dad snapped, "Boots, go outside!"

The cat instantly stopped purring and cuddling against Carswell's leg, turned, and traipsed toward the kitchen—the fastest route to their backyard.

Carswell scowled as he watched the cat go, its tail sticking cheerfully straight up. He liked Boots a lot—sometimes even felt he might love her, as one does any pet they grew up with—but then he would be reminded that she wasn't a pet at all. She was a robot, programmed to follow directions just like any android. He'd been asking for a real cat since he was about four, but his parents just laughed at the idea, listing all the reasons Boots was superior. She would never get old or die. She didn't shed on their nice furniture or climb their fancy curtains or require a litter box. She would only bring them half-devoured mice if they changed her settings to do so.

His parents, Carswell had learned at a very young age, liked things that did what they were told, when they were told. And that didn't include headstrong felines.

Or, as it turned out, thirteen-year-old boys.

"You need to start taking this seriously," his dad was saying, ripping him from his thoughts as the cat-door swung closed behind Boots. "You'll never be accepted into Andromeda at this rate."

Janette returned with his plate of pancakes, and Carswell was grateful for an excuse to look away from his dad as he slathered them with butter and syrup. It was better than risking the temptation to say what he really wanted to say.

He didn't want to go to Andromeda Academy. He didn't want to follow in his dad's footsteps.

Sure, he wanted to learn how to fly. *Desperately* wanted to learn how to fly. But there were other flight schools—less prestigious ones maybe, but at least they didn't require selling six years of his life to the military so he could be ordered around by more men who looked and sounded like his dad, and cared about him even less.

"What's wrong with you?" his dad said, swiveling a finger at Janette. She began to clear his place setting. "You used to be good at math."

"I am good at math," Carswell said, then shoved more pancake into his mouth than he probably should have.

"Are you? Could have fooled me."

He chewed. And chewed. And chewed.

"Maybe we should get him a tutor," said his mother, flicking her finger across her portscreen.

"Is that it, Carswell? Do you need a tutor?"

Carswell swallowed. "I don't need a tutor. I know how to do it all; I just don't feel like doing it."

"What does that mean?"

"It means that I have better things to do. I understand all the concepts, so why should I waste whole days of my life working through those stupid worksheets? Not to mention"—he gestured wildly, at everything, at nothing. At the light fixture that changed automatically based on the amount of sunlight that filtered in through the floor-to-ceiling windows. At the sensors in the wall that detected when a person entered a room and set the thermostat to their own personal preferences. At that brainless robotic cat—"we are surrounded by computers *all* the time. If I ever need help, I'll just have one of them figure it out. So what does it matter?"

"It matters because it shows *focus. Dedication. Diligence.* Important traits that, believe it or not, are usually found in *spaceship captains.*"

Scowling, Carswell sawed at the pancake stack with the side of his fork. If his mother had noticed, she would have reminded him to use a knife, but she was far too busy pretending to be at a different table altogether.

"I have those traits," he muttered. And he did, he knew he did. But why waste focus and dedication and diligence on something as stupid as math homework?

"Then prove it. You're grounded until these grades come up to passing."

His head snapped up. "Grounded? But mid-July break starts next week."

Standing, his dad snapped his portscreen onto the belt of his own uniform—the impeccably pressed blue-and-gray uniform of Colonel Kingsley Thorne, American Republic Fleet 186.

"Yes, and you will spend your break in your bedroom doing *math homework* unless you can show me, and your teacher, that you're going to start taking this seriously."

Carswell's stomach sank, but his dad had marched out of the breakfast room before he could begin to refute him.

He couldn't be grounded for mid-July break. He had big plans for those two weeks. Mostly, they involved an entrepreneurial enterprise that began with sending Boots up into the fruit trees on his neighbors' property and ended with him selling baskets of perfectly ripe lemons and avocados to every little old lady in the neighborhood. He'd been charming his neighbors out of their bank accounts since he was seven, and had become quite good at it. Last summer, he'd even managed to get the Santos family to pay him sixty-five univs for a box of "succulent, prize-winning" oranges, having no idea that he'd picked the fruits off their own tree earlier that day.

"He's not serious, is he?" Carswell said, turning back to his mom. "He won't keep me grounded for the whole break?"

His mom, for maybe the first time that morning, tore her eyes away from her portscreen. She blinked at him and he suspected that she had no idea what his father's doled-out punishment was for his low grades. Maybe she didn't even realize what the argument had been about.

After a moment, just long enough to let the question dissolve in the air between them, she said, "Are you all ready for school, sweetheart?"

Huffing, Carswell nodded and shoved two more quick bites into his mouth. Snatching up his book bag, he pushed away from the table and tossed his blazer over one shoulder.

His dad wanted to see an improvement of grades? Fine. He would find a way to make it happen. He would come up with some solution that gave him the freedom he required during his break but didn't include laboring away over boring math formulas every evening. He had more important things to do with his time. Things that involved business transactions and payment collections. Things that would one day lead to him buying his own spaceship. Nothing fancy. Nothing expensive. Just something simple and practical, something that would belong to him and to him alone.

Then his dad would know just how focused and dedicated he was, right as he was getting the aces out of here.

JULES KELLER HAD HIT HIS GROWTH SPURT EARLY, MAKING him a full head taller than anyone else in the class, and he was even sporting the start of peach-fuzz whiskers on his chin. Unfortunately, he still had a brain capacity equivalent to that of a pelican.

That was Carswell's first thought when Jules slammed his locker shut and Carswell barely managed to get his fingers out of the way in time.

"Morning, Mr. Keller," he said, calling up a friendly smile. "You look particularly vibrant this morning."

Jules stared down the length of his nose at him. The nose on which a sizable red pimple seemed to have emerged overnight. That was one other thing about Jules. In addition to the height and the brawn and the fuzz, his growth spurt had given him a rather tragic case of acne.

"I want my money back," said Jules, one hand still planted on Carswell's locker.

Carswell tilted his head. "Money?"

"Stuff doesn't work." Reaching into his pocket, Jules pulled out a small round canister labeled with exotic ingredients that promised clean, spot-free skin in just two weeks. "And I'm sick of looking at your smug face all day, like you think I don't know better."

"Of course it works," said Carswell, taking the canister from him and holding it up to inspect the label. "It's the exact same stuff I use, and look at me."

Which was not entirely true. The canister itself had been emptied of its original ridiculously expensive face cream when he'd dug it out of the trash bin beside his mother's vanity. And though he'd sometimes sneaked uses of the high-quality stuff before, the canister was now full of a simple concoction of bargain moisturizer and a few drops of food coloring and almond extract that he'd found in the pantry.

He didn't think it would be *bad* for anyone's skin. And besides, studies had been showing the benefit of placebos for years. Who said they couldn't cure teenage acne just as effectively as they could cure an annoying headache?

But Jules, evidently unimpressed with the evidence Carswell had just presented, grabbed him by his shirt collar and pushed him against the bank of lockers. Carswell suspected it wasn't to get a better look at his own flawless complexion.

"I want my money back," Jules seethed through his teeth.

"Good morning, Carswell," said a chipper voice.

Sliding his gaze past Jules's shoulder, Carswell smiled and nodded at the freckled brunette who was shyly fluttering her lashes at him. "Morning, Shan. How'd your recital go last night?"

She giggled, already flustered, and ducked her head. "It was great. I'm sorry you couldn't make it," she said, before turning and darting through the crowd toward a group of friends who were waiting near the water fountain. Together they broke into a fit of teasing chatter as they proceeded down the hallway.

Jules pushed Carswell into the lockers again, pulling his attention back. "I *said*—"

"You want your money back, yeah, yeah, I heard you." Carswell held up the canister. "And that's fine. No problem. I'll transfer it over during lunch."

Harrumphing, Jules released him.

"Of course, you'll lose all the progress you've made so far."

"What progress?" Jules said, bristling again. "Stuff doesn't work!"

"Sure it works. But it takes two weeks. Says so right here." He pointed at the label, and Jules snarled.

"It's been *three*."

Rolling his eyes, Carswell tossed the canister from hand to hand. "It's a *process*. There are *steps*. The first step is"—he respectfully lowered his voice, in case Jules didn't want the sensitive nature of their conversation to be overheard—"you know, clearing away the first layer of dead skin cells. Exfoliation, as it were. But a really deep, intense, *all-natural* exfoliation. That takes two weeks. In step two, it unlocks all the grease and dirt that's been stuck in the bottom of your pores—that's the step you're in the middle of right now. In another week, it'll move on to step three. Hydrating your skin so that it has a constant, healthy glow." He quirked his lips to one side and shrugged. "You know, like me. I'm telling you, it does work. And if there's one thing I know, it's skin-care products." Unscrewing the cap, he took a long sniff of the cream. "Not to mention . . . no, never mind. You don't want it. It's not worth mentioning at all. I'll just take this back and—"

"Not to mention what?"

Carswell cleared his throat and dipped forward, until Jules had lowered his own head into their makeshift huddle. "The scent is proven to make you more attractive to girls. It's practically an aphrodisiac, in aromatherapy form."

A crease formed in between Jules's brows, and Carswell recognized confusion. He was about to explain what an aphrodisiac was when a third form sidled up beside them.

"Hey, Carswell," said Elia, the pep squad captain, slipping her hand into the crook of his elbow. She was easily one of the prettiest girls in school, with thick black hair and a persistent dimple in one cheek. She was also a year older and about four inches taller than Carswell, which wasn't particularly uncommon these days. Unlike Jules, Carswell hadn't seen even a glimmer of a growth spurt yet, and he was really starting to get fed up with waiting, even though none of the girls seemed bothered that they'd been outpacing him in the height department since their sixth year.

"Morning, Elia," Carswell said, slipping the canister of facial cream into his pocket. "Perfect timing! Could you do me a favor?"

Her eyes widened with blatant enthusiasm. "Of course!"

"Could you tell me, what does my good friend Jules here smell like to you?"

Instant redness flushed over Jules's face and, with a snarl, he pushed Carswell into the lockers again. "What are you—!"

But then he froze. Carswell's teeth were still vibrating when Elia leaned forward so that her nose was almost, almost touching Jules's neck, and sniffed.

Jules had become a statue.

Carswell lifted an expectant eyebrow.

Elia rocked back on her heels, considering for a moment as her gaze raked over the ceiling. Then—"Almonds, I think."

"And ... do you like it?" Carswell ventured.

She laughed, the sound like an inviting wind chime. Jules's blush deepened.

"Definitely," she said, although it was Carswell she was smiling at. "It reminds me of one of my favorite desserts."

Jules released him and, once again, Carswell smoothed his jacket. "Thank you, Elia. That's very helpful."

"My pleasure." She tucked a strand of hair behind her ear. "I was wondering if you're going to the Peace Dance next week?"

His smile was both practiced and instinctual. "Undecided. I may be cooking dinner for my sick grandmother that night." He waited expectantly as Elia's gaze filled with swooning. "But if I do end up going to the dance, you'll be the first I ask to go with me."

She beamed and bounced on her toes for a moment. "Well, I'd say yes," she said, looking suddenly, briefly bashful. "Just in case you weren't sure." Then she turned and practically skipped down the hall.

"Well," said Carswell, pulling the canister back out of his pocket. "I guess our business is all concluded, then. Like I said, I'll return your payment in full by second period. Of course, the retail price on this stuff just went up twenty percent, so if you change your mind later, I'm afraid I'm going to have to charge—"

Jules snatched the canister out of his hand. His face was still bright red, his brow still drawn, but the anger had dissolved from his eyes. "If nothing's changed in another three weeks," he said, low and threatening, "I'll be shoving the rest of this cream down your throat."

Well, *most* of the anger had dissolved from his eyes, anyway.

But Carswell merely smiled and gave Jules a friendly pat on the chest just as the anthem of the American Republic began to blare through the school speakers. "So glad I could clear things up for you."

Turning, Carswell waved his wrist over his locker to unlock the ID-coded mechanism and gathered up his things, as polite a dismissal as he could give.

HE WALKED INTO LITERATURE CLASS FOUR MINUTES LATE, HIS book bag over one shoulder as he deftly buttoned up his blazer. He slid into the only remaining seat—front row, dead center.

"So nice of you to join us, Mr. Thorne," said Professor Gosnel.

Crossing his ankles, Carswell tipped back in his chair and flashed a bright smile at the teacher. "The pleasure is all mine, Professor Gosnel."

She sighed, but he could see the corner of her mouth twitch as she punched something into her portscreen. Within moments, the screens built into the classroom desks lit up with the day's assignment. *Great dramatists of the first century, third era*, was emblazoned across the top, followed by a list of names and which of the six Earthen countries each dramatist had hailed from.

"For today, I want everyone to select one artist from this list," said the teacher, pacing in front of the classroom, "and choose a drama from their body of work that appeals to you. At half past, we'll split into pairs and you can take turns reading the dramas you've found with your partner and discussing how the themes in them relate to our world today."

A finger tapped Carswell gently at the base of his neck, the universal symbol for "I choose you." Carswell struggled to remember who had been sitting behind him when he took this seat, and if it was someone he wouldn't mind being partnered with. Had it been Destiny? Athena? Blakely? Spades, he hoped it wasn't Blakely. Once she started talking, it was difficult to remember what peace and quiet sounded like.

He slid his gaze to the side, hoping he could catch his mystery partner's reflection in the windows before committing to the partnership, when his gaze caught on the girl sitting in the seat beside him.

Kate Fallow.

His gaze narrowed thoughtfully.

Despite having been in the same grade since toddler primaries, he doubted that he and Kate had spoken more than fifty words to each other their whole lives. He didn't think it was anything personal. Their paths just hadn't crossed much. As evidenced at that moment, she preferred to sit in the front of class, whereas he did his best to end up somewhere near the back. Instead of coming out to sporting events or school festivals, Kate always seemed to rush straight home when classes were over. She was at the top of their class and well liked, but by no means popular, and she spent most lunch hours with her nose buried in her portscreen. Reading.

This was only the second time Carswell Thorne had stopped to ponder one Kate Fallow. The first time, he had wondered why she liked books so much, and if it had anything to do with why he liked spaceships. Because they could take you somewhere far, far away from here.

This time, he was wondering what her math score was.

There was a thud as Carswell settled his chair legs back on the floor and leaned across the aisle. "You probably know who all these writers are, don't you?"

Kate's head whipped up. She blinked at him for a moment before her startled eyes glanced at the person behind her, then back to Carswell.

He grinned.

She blinked. "Ex-excuse me?"

He inched closer, so that he was barely seated on the edge of his chair, and dragged the tip of his stylus down her screen. "All these dramatists. You read so much, 1 bet you've already read them all."

"Um." She followed the tip of his stylus before . . . there it was, that sudden rush of color to her cheeks. "No, not all of them. Maybe . . . maybe half, though?"

"Yeah?" Settling an elbow on his knee, Carswell cupped his chin. "Who's your favorite? 1 could use a recommendation."

"Oh. Well, um. Bourdain wrote some really great historical pieces . . ." She trailed off, then swallowed. Hard. She lifted her eyes to him and seemed surprised when he was still paying attention to her.

For his part, Carswell was feeling a little surprised too. It had been a long time since he'd really looked at Kate Fallow, and she seemed prettier now than he'd remembered, even if it was the kind of pretty that was overshadowed by the likes of Shan or Elia. Kate was softer and plumper than most of the girls in his class, but she also had the largest, warmest brown eyes he thought he'd ever seen.

Plus, there was also something endearing about a girl who seemed entirely floored by no more than a moment's worth of attention from him. But maybe that was just his ego speaking.

"Is there a certain type of drama you like?" Kate whispered.

Carswell twisted his lips up in thought. "Adventure stories, 1 guess. With lots of exotic places and daring escapades . . . and swashbuckling space pirates, naturally." He followed this up with a wink and watched, preening inside, as Kate's mouth turned into a small, surprised O.

Then Professor Gosnel cleared her throat. "This is supposed to be *individual* study, Mr. Thorne and Miss Fallow. Twenty more minutes, and then you can partner up."

"Yes, Professor Gosnel," said Carswell without missing a beat, even as the redness stretched to Kate's hairline and a few students snickered near the back. He wondered if Kate had ever been reprimanded by a teacher in her life.

He slid his gaze back to Kate and waited—five seconds, six—until her gaze darted uncertainly upward again. Though she caught *him* staring, she was the one who instantly turned back to her desk, flustered.

Feeling rather accomplished, Carswell took to scanning through the names. A few sounded familiar, but not enough that he could have named any of their works. He racked his brain, trying to remember what, exactly, he was supposed to be doing for this assignment anyway.

Then Kate Fallow leaned over and tapped her stylus against a name on the list. Joel Kimbrough, United Kingdom, born 27 T.E. His list of works spilled down the screen, with titles like *Space Ranger on the Ninth Moon* and *The Mariner and the Martians.*

Carswell beamed up at Kate, but she had already returned her attention to her own screen, without any sign of her blush receding.

The next twenty minutes were spent scanning through Joel Kimbrough's extensive body of work, while his mind churned through different scenarios in which he could get Kate Fallow to help him with his math homework—preferably, just to let him copy off her so he wouldn't need to put any more time into that wasteful venture.

When Professor Gosnel finally told them to choose a partner, Carswell scooted his desk closer to Kate's without hesitation. "Would you like to work together?"

She gaped at him again, no less surprised than the first time. "*Me?*"

"Sure. You like histories, I like adventures. Match made in heaven, right?"

"Um..."

"Carswell?" hissed a voice behind him. He glanced around. Blakely was seated behind him, leaning so far over her desk that her nose was practically on his shoulder. "I thought you and I could be partners."

"Er—one second." He lifted a finger to her, then turned back to Kate and plowed on. "Actually, there's something I've kind of been meaning to ask you for a while now."

Kate's jaw hung, as Carswell feigned a sudden onslaught of uncertainty and scooted his chair a bit closer. "You know how we're in the same math class?"

She blinked, twice. Nodded.

"Well, I was thinking, if you're not busy, and if you wanted to, maybe we could study together one of these days. Maybe after school." He followed this up with his easiest smile—practiced and precise.

Kate could not have looked any more stunned if he'd just proposed that they move to Colombia State together and become coffee bean farmers. "You want to ... study? With me?"

"Yeah. Math, specifically." He rubbed the back of his neck. "I'm not doing that great in it. I could really use your help." He added a drop of pleading to his expression and watched as Kate Fallow's eyes widened and softened simultaneously. Those pretty, enormous brown eyes.

Carswell was surprised to feel a jolt behind his sternum, and suddenly he was almost looking forward to his studying time with Kate Fallow, which was a rather unexpected twist.

Because, of course, she would say yes.

Although it was Blakely who spoke next. "*Carswell.* We should get started on this assignment, don't you think?" There was an edge to her tone that Kate must have noticed. Something that hinted at jealousy.

With a glance back at Blakely, Kate looked more flustered than ever. But then she nodded and gave an awkward shrug. "Sure. All right."

Carswell beamed. "Great. And also—I hate to ask this—but would you mind if I took a look at today's assignment? I tried to do it last night but was completely lost. All those equations . . ."

"Mr. Thorne," said Professor Gosnel, suddenly hovering between him and Kate, "this is literature class. Perhaps you could use your time to discuss *literature.*"

He tilted his head back to meet her gaze. "Oh, we are discussing literature, Professor." Clearing his throat, he tapped the screen, pulling up Kimbrough's thirty-ninth published work, *Marooned in the Asteroid Labyrinth.* "As you can see, dramatist Joel Kimbrough often played on themes of loneliness and abandonment, in which the protagonist is forced to overcome not only external obstacles like space monsters and malfunctioning spaceship engines, but also the internal devastation that comes with complete solitude. His works often employ the vast emptiness of space as a symbol of loneliness and the battles each of us face against our own personal demons. In the end, his protagonists overcome their feelings of insecurity only *after* they accept the help of an unlikely assistant, such as an android or an alien or"—his mouth quirked to one side—"a pretty girl who happens to be a skilled marksman when she's handed a high-powered ray gun."

A wave of tittering rolled through the class, confirming Carswell's suspicions that he now had an audience.

"So, you see," he said, gesturing again at the screen, "I was just telling Miss Fallow that the themes in Kimbrough's works relate to my own personal struggles with math homework. I so often feel lost, confused, completely hopeless . . . but, by joining forces with a pretty girl who understands the problems I currently have to work through, I may yet overcome the obstacles laid out before me and achieve my ultimate goal. Namely, high marks in math class." He gave a one-shouldered shrug and added, for good measure, "And literature class, naturally."

Professor Gosnel stared down at him with her lips pursed and he could tell that she was still annoyed, although simultaneously trying to hide a twinge of amusement. She sighed. "Just *try* to stay on task, Mr. Thorne."

"Yes, Professor Gosnel." He glanced at Kate, and though she wouldn't meet his eyes, she was nibbling at her bottom lip and almost smiling.

The rest of the class was still chuckling as Professor Gosnel turned back to her own screen and began listing some of the literary terms students should be using to discuss their assignments— words like *themes, obstacles*, and *symbolism*. Carswell smirked.

Then a voice broke out of the mild chatter, loud enough to reach Carswell, but quiet enough to make it seem like it wasn't intentional. "If it's a pretty girl that he needs to help with his 'problems,' he's out of luck if Kate Fallow is the best he can find."

Someone else guffawed. A few girls giggled before putting their hands over their mouths.

Carswell glanced back to see Ryan Doughty smirking at him—a friend of Jules's. He shot him a glare before turning back to Kate. Her smile had vanished, her eyes filling with mortification.

Carswell curled his hand into a tight fist, having the sudden, unexpected urge to punch Ryan Doughty in the mouth. But instead, as the class quieted down, he ignored the feeling and once again scooted his chair closer to Kate's.

"So, like I was saying before," he said, teetering on the line between casual and nervous, "maybe we could eat lunch together today, out in the courtyard." He would have to cancel the afternoon's card game, which would put him behind schedule, but if he could submit today's homework during math—complete and on time—it would be the fastest way to start turning around his marks. And he only had a week to show his dad that things were improving before mid-July break started. "What do you say?"

Kate's jaw was hanging again, her blush having returned full force.

"*Carswell?*"

Sighing, he didn't hide his glare as he turned back to Blakely. "Yes, Blakely?"

Her glower put his to shame. "I thought you and I were going to be partners today."

"Uh—I'm not sure, Blakely. I'm afraid I already asked Kate, but . . ." He grinned shyly in Kate's direction. "I guess she hasn't given me an answer yet."

Blakely harrumphed. "Well then, maybe we should call off our date to the dance too. Then you two can go fight obstacles and achieve goals together."

He sat up straighter. "Huh?"

"Last week," Blakely said, curling her fingers around the edge of her desk, "I asked if you were going to the Peace Dance and you said I'd be the girl you asked if you did. I've been planning on it ever since."

"Oh, *right.*" Carswell was losing track of how many girls he'd said some version of this line to, which was probably bad planning on his part, but at the time Blakely had asked, he'd been hoping to get her to invest in his Send Carswell to Space Camp fund.

"Unfortunately," he said, "it's looking like I may be babysitting my neighbors' toddlers that day. Two-year-old triplets." He shook his head. "They're a handful, but so blasted cute, it's impossible not to love them."

Blakely's anger fizzled into warm adoration. "Oh."

Carswell winked. "But if they end up not needing me, you'll be the first to know."

She squinched her shoulders up from the flattery. "But do you want to work together today?"

"Ah, I'd love to, Blakely, but I did ask Kate already . . . er, Kate?"

Kate had her head down, her hair falling over her face so that he could only see the tip of her nose. Her body had taken on a new tenseness, her knuckles whitening as she gripped the stylus.

"It's all right," she said, without looking up at him. "I'm sure the teacher will let me work on my own. You can work with your girl-friend."

"Oh—she's not—we're not—"

Blakely grabbed his arm. "See, Kate doesn't mind. You said that you chose Joel Kimbrough?"

Clearing his throat, Carswell looked first at Blakely, then back up at Kate, now hidden behind an invisible wall.

"Um, fine." He leaned toward Kate again. "But are we still on for lunch? So I can, you know, check out that homework assignment?"

Kate tucked her hair behind her ear and leveled a look at him that was both annoyed and intelligent. It told him that she knew exactly what he was doing, or trying to do. To her. To Blakely. To every girl he'd ever asked a favor from. Carswell was surprised to feel a tingle of shame down his spine.

Her jaw twitched. "I don't think so. And we probably shouldn't study together after all."

Turning away, she fitted a pair of speaker-plugs into her ears, and the conversation was over. In its wake was a feeling of disappointment that Carswell couldn't quite place, but he didn't think had very much to do with math.

"SEVEN CARD ROYALS," SAID CARSWELL, DEALING ANOTHER hand of cards. "Aces are wild. Triplets beat the house."

"Why don't we ever play that doubles beat the house?" asked Anthony, picking up his cards and rearranging them in his hands.

Carswell shrugged. "We can play that way if you want. But it means the pots will be smaller. Not as much risk, not as big a payout."

"Triplets are fine," said Carina, needling Anthony in the side with her elbow. "Anthony's just afraid he's going to lose *again.*"

Anthony scowled. "It just seems like the odds are a little biased toward Carswell, that's all."

"What do you mean?" Carswell waved his hand over the pot. "I've lost the last three hands in a row. You guys are bleeding me dry over here."

Carina raised her eyebrows at Anthony as if to say, *See? Do the math.* Anthony duly fell quiet and tossed his ante into the pot. They were playing with markers scavenged from the school's lunch bar—olives were micro-univs, potato crisps were singles, and jalapeño slices made for fivers. The trick was to keep Chien—who was seated on Carswell's left and had the appetite of a whale—from eating them in between games.

At the end of every school day, Carswell—as "the house"— would divvy up the wins and losses between the players' real savings accounts. He'd based his system on the same odds that the casinos in the valley used, allowing him to win about 60 percent of the time. It was just enough to turn a consistent profit but also give players frequent enough wins that they kept coming back. It had turned out to be one of his more profitable ventures to date.

Carina took the next hand without much competition, but that was followed by a round in which no one could beat the house's required triplets-or-better, ending Carswell's losing streak. He kept the grin from his face as he raked the pot of food scraps into his dwindling pile.

He quickly did the math in his head. He was up from where he'd started the lunch period, nearly eleven univs. Just seven more would put him at his goal for the day and push him into the next bracket of his savings account.

Seven univs. Such a small thing to just about anyone in this school, just about anyone in the entire city of Los Angeles. But to him, they equaled sixteen weeks of freedom. Sixteen weeks of being away from his parents. Sixteen weeks of total independence.

He brushed his thumb over his Rampion tie tack for good luck and dealt another hand.

As the betting began, he glanced up and caught sight of Kate Fallow sitting on the low stone wall that surrounded the courtyard, the pleated skirt of her uniform pulled snugly around her knees. She was reading from her portscreen—no surprise there—but it was odd to see her out here at all. Carswell had no idea where she normally spent her lunch hour, but he was pretty sure it wasn't in this courtyard, where *he* could always be found.

The betting ended and Carswell began to dole out replacement cards, but now he was distracted. His gaze kept flicking back to Kate. Watching how she smiled at something on the screen. Mindlessly tugged at her earlobe and tapped her heels against the wall. Seemed to sigh with a hint of longing.

Maybe she came to the courtyard every day and he'd never noticed. Or maybe she'd come here today because he'd suggested it, even if the offer had ultimately been declined.

Either way, it was clear from the faraway look in her eyes that she wasn't in the courtyard right now, not really, and he couldn't help wondering where she was.

Holy spades. Was he developing a crush on *Kate Fallow?* Of all the girls who smiled and swooned and giggled, all the girls who would have handed over their math homework for nothing more than a flirtatious compliment, and he suddenly couldn't keep his eyes off one of the most awkward, isolated girls in the school?

No, there had to be more to this. He was probably just confusing his desperation to raise his math grades and lift his dad's punishment with something that bordered on romantic interest. He didn't like Kate Fallow. He just wanted Kate Fallow to like *him* so he could swindle her out of her math homework.

Just like he swindled everyone.

There it was again. That peculiar tingle of shame.

"Ha! Suited triplets!" said Chien, laying out his cards. The other players groaned, and it took Carswell a moment to scan the hands and determine that, indeed, Chien had taken the round. Usually he could pick out the winning hand in half a glance, but he'd been too distracted.

As Chien scooped up his winnings, Carswell determined that he probably should have quit while he was ahead after all. He was back down to eight univs won for the day, ten behind his goal.

Boots would not be impressed.

"Well done, Chien," he said. "One more hand?"

"There won't be time for it if our dealer goes out to space again," said Anthony. "What's wrong with you?"

He cringed, the words reflecting his father's question from just that morning. "Nothing," he said, shuffling the cards. "Just had something on my mind."

"Oh, I see what he was looking at," said Carina. "Or should I should say *who*."

Chien and Anthony followed Carina's gesture. "Kate Fallow?" said Anthony, with a curled lip that said he highly doubted *she* was the person who had caught Carswell's interest.

Ducking his head, Carswell redistributed a new round of cards, but no one picked them up.

"He was flirting with her in lit class this morning," said Carina. "Honestly, Carswell. Everyone knows you're a hopeless flirt, but do you really have to get every girl in the whole school to fall under your spell? Is this some sort of manly conquest you're on or something?"

It was easy for Carswell to slip back into his most comfortable role. Cupping his chin in one hand, he leaned toward Carina with a suggestive smirk. "Why? Are you feeling left out?"

Groaning, Carina shoved him away, at the same time that the speakers announced the end of lunch hour. A groan rose up from the courtyard but was hastily followed by the sounds of footsteps padding back into the buildings and friends bidding each other good-bye for the whole ninety minutes they were about to be separated.

Carswell gathered up the cards he'd just dealt and slipped them back into his bag. "I'll tally the winnings," he said, shooing away a fly that was buzzing around the pile of food.

"How do we know you won't take a little extra for yourself?" asked Chien, with unhidden distrust.

Carswell only shrugged. "You can stay and count up your own if you'd prefer, but then we'll both be late to class."

Chien didn't argue again. Of course, a lost univ or two was nothing to any of them, so what did it matter if Carswell skimmed a little off the top?

By the time he'd entered the balances into his portscreen and put in a reminder to shuffle the money between their accounts when he got home, the courtyard had emptied but for him and the seagulls that were creeping in to pick at the scraps of abandoned food. Carswell slipped his portscreen back into his bag beside the deck of cards and heaved it over one shoulder.

The second announcement blared. The halls were abandoned as Carswell made his way to second-era history. He would be a couple of minutes late for the second time that day, but the teacher liked him, so he couldn't bring himself to be worried about it.

And then, through the quiet that was laced with the padding of his own footsteps and the hushed conversations behind closed classroom doors, he heard a frustrated cry.

"Stop it! Give it back!"

Carswell paused and traced his steps back to the hallway that led off to the tech hall.

Jules Keller was holding a portscreen over his head, grinning, with Ryan Doughty and Rob Mancuso surrounding him.

And then there was Kate Fallow, her face flushed and her hands on her hips in a semblance of anger and determination, even though Carswell could tell from here that she was shaking and trying not to cry.

"What do you keep on this thing, anyway?" said Jules, peering up at the screen and scrolling through her pages with his thumbs. "Got any naughty pictures on here?"

"She sure does stare at it a lot," said Rob with a snort.

Carswell's shoulders sank, first with embarrassment for Kate, then with that inevitable feeling that something bad was about to happen. Bracing himself, he started down the hall. No one seemed to have noticed him yet.

Kate squeezed her shoulders against her neck and held out a hand. "It's just a bunch of books. Now give it back. *Please.*"

"Yeah, sleazy books, probably," said Jules. "Not like you could ever get a real date."

Kate's bottom lip began to quiver.

"Seriously, there aren't any games on here or anything," said Jules with apparent disgust. "It's the most boring portscreen in L.A."

"We should just keep it," said Ryan. "She's obviously not using it right."

"No—it's mine!"

"Hello, gentlemen," said Carswell, at the same moment that he reached up and snatched the portscreen out of Jules's hand. He had to get on his tiptoes to do it, which he hated, but seeing the flash of surprise and bewilderment that crossed Jules's face made it worthwhile.

Of course, the look didn't last long.

Carswell took a few steps back as Jules's hand flexed into a fist. "What a coincidence," he said. "I was just coming to look for Kate. So glad you found her for me." He raised his eyebrows at Kate, then quirked his head back down the hallway. "Come on."

She swiped at the first tear that started down her cheek. Wrapping her arms around her waist, she dodged around the boys to come stand beside him, but Carswell hadn't taken two steps away before Jules grabbed him by the shoulder and turned him back around.

"What, is she your girlfriend now or something?" he said, nostrils flaring with, if Carswell hadn't known better, a hint of jealousy.

Which just blasted figured. Mocking and bullying a girl *would* be the way that Jules attempted to show affection. It somehow seemed to fit with that completely messed-up head of his.

Carswell stifled a sigh. Maybe he could start an after-school Flirting 101 class. There were a lot of people in this school who could really use the help.

What could he charge for that? he wondered.

"Right now," he said, drawing his attention back to the numb-skull in front of him and placing a hand on Kate's arm, "she's the girl that I'm escorting back to class. Feel free to spread whatever rumors you want from that."

"Yeah? How about the rumor that I gave you a black eye because you wouldn't mind your own business?"

"I'm honestly not sure people are going to buy that one, given that—"

The fist collided with Carswell's eye faster than he'd have thought possible, sending him reeling back against the row of lockers with a resounding clang.

The world tilted and blurred and he thought Kate may have screamed and something clattered on the ground—her portscreen, falling from his own hand—but all he could think was, *Spades and aces and stars, that hurt.*

He'd never been punched before. He'd always assumed it would be easy to bounce back from, but now he had the instinctive desire to curl up into a ball and cover his head with both arms and play dead until they all went away.

"Carswell!" yelled Kate, seconds before Rob grabbed him by the elbow and yanked him away from the lockers, and then Jules's fist was in his stomach and he'd probably broken a rib and Carswell was on his knees and Ryan was kicking him and all his senses were made up of pain and grunts and Kate's shrieks and he really would have thought that he'd have lasted a lot longer than this, but . . .

A gruff voice bulleted through the haze of fists and feet and

Carswell was left blessedly alone, curled up on the school's tiled floor. He tasted blood in his mouth. His entire body was throbbing.

As his senses began to register his surroundings again, he realized that Vice Principal Chambers had broken up the fight, but Carswell was too woozy to make sense of his angry words.

"Carswell?" said a sweet, soft, horrified voice.

His left eye was already swelling shut, but he peeled open the right to see that Kate was now crouched over him. Her fingers were hovering just off his shoulder, like she was afraid to touch him.

He tried to smile, but felt it probably looked more like a grimace. "Hey, Kate."

Her eyes were filled with sympathy, her face still flushed, but she wasn't crying anymore, and Carswell liked to think he'd put an end to that, at least.

"Are you all right? Can you stand?"

Bracing himself, he sat up, which was a start. Kate helped a little, although she still seemed hesitant.

"Ow," he muttered. His entire abdomen was throbbing and bruised. He wondered if they'd broken a rib after all.

Aces, how embarrassing. He would be investing in some good martial arts simulators after this. Or maybe boxing. He'd never be on the losing side of a fistfight again if he could help it, outnumbered or not.

"Are you all right, Mr. Thorne?" said Mr. Chambers.

Squinting upward, Carswell saw that they'd been joined by two of the tech professors, who were standing with their arms folded over Jules and his friends. Everyone was scowling. Rob even looked a tiny bit guilty, or maybe he just hated that they'd been caught.

"I'm grand," said Carswell. "Thank you for asking, Mr. Chambers." Then he flinched and rubbed at the spot on his side where the jolt of pain had originated from.

Mr. Chambers sighed heavily. "You know that all fighting is against school policy, Mr. Thorne. I'm afraid this calls for a one-week suspension. For all four of you."

"Wait—no!" said Kate. Then, to Carswell's surprise, she laced their fingers together. He blinked at their hands, then up at her profile, and doubted she even realized she was doing it. "Carswell was defending me. They'd taken my portscreen and wouldn't give it back. It's not his fault!"

The vice principal was shaking his head, and though Carswell could tell he felt bad about the decision, he also had an expression that suggested there was nothing he could do about it. "School rules, Miss Fallow."

"But that isn't fair. He didn't do anything wrong!"

"It's a no-tolerance policy. I'm sorry, but we can't make exceptions." Mr. Chambers glanced back at the other boys. "Mr. Keller, Mr. Doughty, Mr. Mancuso—you can follow me to my office so we can comm your parents. Miss Fallow, why don't you assist Mr. Thorne to see the med-droid." He attempted sympathy when he met Carswell's one-eyed gaze again. "We'll comm your parents later."

Chin falling to his chest, Carswell cursed under his breath.

This was also against school policy, but Mr. Chambers blessedly ignored it.

"Miss Fallow, I'll alert your teacher to forgive your absence for this period."

"Thank you, Mr. Chambers," she murmured, full of resignation.

As Jules and his friends were escorted away, Carswell allowed himself to lean against Kate and push himself onto his wobbly legs, with another handful of curses and groans.

"I'm so sorry," she whispered as he draped an arm around her shoulders and she began escorting him toward the med-droid office.

"Not your fault," he said through his teeth. Although, now that he had the strenuous effort of walking to focus on, the pain almost seemed to be dulling. Almost. "You get your portscreen?"

"Yes. Thank you. And I got your bag." Then she huffed angrily. "I can't believe they're suspending you. It isn't fair."

He tried to shrug, but it came out as a more general flopping of his free arm. "I was already grounded for mid-July break. A suspension can't make it that much worse."

"Grounded? For what?"

His gaze flickered to her, and he couldn't avoid a wry smile, even though it pinched his throbbing cheekbone. "Poor math grade."

She flushed. "Oh."

Carswell pressed a hand against his ribs, finding that by applying a slight amount of pressure he could relieve some of the jarring as they walked. "Yep, I'm grounded until I bring my score back up. Of course, that's not going to happen now that I can't even go to class." He tried to laugh as if it didn't bother him, but quickly realized what a bad idea that was, and the sound turned into something of a pained cough. "Oh well. Just more time to catch up on my Joel Kimbrough reading, I guess."

She tried to giggle, maybe to make him feel better, but it didn't sound any more authentic than his laugh had.

"When you're done," she said, "I'm sure you could write an amazing paper that explores the parallels between the dangers of space travel as compared to navigating school hallways and social status and … and …"

"And parents."

Her laugh was less forced this time. "And parents, of course."

"I suspect that Martians have pretty much always symbolized parents in those books."

"They must, being that they're so … otherworldly."

"And terrifying."

This time, her laugh wasn't forced at all, and it gave Carswell a warm, tender feeling somewhere under all the bruising. He wished he could have laughed with her without it causing a flash of pain in his skull.

"Think Professor Gosnel would give me extra credit?"

"I'm sure she would," said Kate. But then her sympathy was back. "It wouldn't help with your math grade, though."

"True. If only studying algebra formulas was half as much fun as corny space adventures."

"If only." Pursing her lips, Kate glanced up at him through her cascade of hair. Then she took in a deep breath. "I'll let you copy my math homework."

He raised an eyebrow.

"Until . . . until your grade is up. And when we come back from break, I can help you study, if you still want me to."

"Thank you." He smiled, and he didn't even have to fake his gratitude, though the relief came with that peculiar undercurrent of shame again. He knew that she felt guilty, that she felt as though she owed him something. He knew he was taking advantage of those feelings.

But he didn't argue, and he didn't reject her offer. Because in the back of his head, he was already counting up the hours this would save him, the money he could earn with that time. He was already moving past Kate and her portscreen and her gentle laugh and the lingering pain from his first fistfight.

Already, he was moving on to the next goal, the next dream, the next obstacle. Carswell grinned, just to the point where it started to hurt, and rubbed a thumb over his tie tack.

For luck.

After Sunshine Passes By

AT NINE YEARS OLD, CRESCENT MOON WAS THE YOUNGEST
infantry soldier in Luna's great warrior army. She stood at perfect
attention in the front line of her platoon—back straight as a pin
and arms locked at her sides. She was proud of her service to the
queen. Already she had been hailed for her bravery and even
honored with a medal of courage from Commander-General Sybil
Mira after the battle of—

"Crescent."

Mistress's voice interrupted the fantasy, and Cress snapped
a fist to her heart in salute. "Yes, Commander—um, I mean, Mistress?"

Some of the older kids snickered down the line and Cress felt
her cheeks flame. Though she had pinned her gaze respectfully to
the bunk beds against the opposite wall, she tore them away now
to look at Mistress Sybil, who stood at the end of the long, narrow
dormitory. Her lips were thinned and white.

Cress swallowed hard and lowered her hand. Her body shrank,

mimicking the same meek posture the other kids had when they lined up for the monthly blood withdrawals. Of course, she wasn't really a soldier. She wasn't even sure what the word *infantry* meant. But that didn't keep her from fantasizing, from imagining herself somewhere better than here. *Anywhere* but here.

She couldn't understand why the other shells were so content to accept their stifled existence, why they mocked her for trying to escape, even if the escape was only in her own mind. Yet mock her they did. At least, until they wanted something from her; then they were sweet as syrup.

Sybil's nostrils flared as she inhaled an impatient breath. "Did you hear what I said, Crescent?"

Cress racked her brain, even though she knew it was useless. Her face grew hotter as she shook her head.

"I was just telling the rest of your peers that we have received evidence that someone recently hacked into the feed of the educational programming intended for Luna's most promising youth." Her gray eyes narrowed at Cress. "I was unsurprised to find that the feed had been copied, and was now being broadcast *here*, in the shell dormitories. Can you explain this, Crescent?"

She swallowed and shrank back again, and her shoulder bumped into the boy beside her. "I . . . um . . ."

"It was my idea," said Calista, who stood near the front of the line. Sybil's piercing eyes shifted to her. "Don't be mad at Cress. I put her up to it. I just thought . . . *we* just thought . . ."

Sybil waited, expressionless, but Calista seemed to have lost her gumption. A silence filled the dormitory, and though the temperature was static, Cress began to shiver.

Finally, Arol spoke. "We thought it could teach us how to read." He cleared his throat. "I mean, those of us who don't know how ..."

Which was most of them. Cress had managed to download a Beginning Readers app to their shared holograph node a few years ago, and she and a couple others had made it through the entire course before Sybil had found out and blocked it from them. They had tried to teach the others—those who wanted to learn—but without paper or portscreens it was a slow, tedious process.

Most of them wanted to know, though. There was something liberating about it. Something powerful.

She thought Sybil knew that too; otherwise she wouldn't have been opposed to it.

Sybil began to pace down their line, eyeing each of them in turn, though most of the kids dropped their stares as she passed. She moved like a cat. A proud, spoiled one, who hunted for sport, not survival. The guard who had accompanied her waited by the door, attention pinned on the distant wall, ignoring them all.

"If it was important for you to have the skill of reading," said Sybil, "do you not think I would have ensured that you were taught? But you are not here to be educated. You are here because we have hopes of *curing* you. You are here to supply us with shell blood so that we might study your deficiencies and, perhaps, someday we will know how to fix you. When that day comes, you will be reintroduced as full citizens of Luna." Her words turned sharp. "But until that day, you have no place in civilized society, and no purpose beyond the blood that runs through your veins. *Reading* is a privilege that you have not earned."

She stopped in front of Cress and turned to face her. Cress cowered, though she wished that she hadn't. There would be no medal of bravery today.

Reading was a privilege she had not earned. Except . . . she felt that she had. She had learned the language of computers and networks and she had learned the language of letters and sounds and she had done it all on her own. Wasn't that *earning* it?

It didn't matter now. Knowledge was something that Sybil could never take away from her.

"Crescent."

She shuddered and forced herself to look up. She braced herself for a reprimand—Sybil certainly looked angry enough.

But instead, Sybil said, "You will have your blood taken first today, and then you will prepare for a departure. I have a new assignment for you."

CRESS HELD THE BANDAGE AGAINST HER ELBOW AS SHE FOLlowed Mistress through the underground tunnels that connected the shell dormitories to the rest of Luna's capital city. The shells were kept separated from the rest of society because supposedly they were *dangerous*. They couldn't be manipulated by the Lunar gift, which meant they posed a threat to the queen and the rest of the aristocracy, those Lunars who were able to manipulate the minds of people around them. It had, in fact, been an enraged shell who had assassinated the previous king and queen, leading to the banishment of shells in the first place.

Cress had heard the story a hundred times—this *proof* that people like her weren't fit to be around other Lunars. That they needed to be fixed before they could be trusted. But still she couldn't understand it.

She knew that she wasn't dangerous, and most of the other shells were children like her. Almost all of them had been taken from their families when they were newborns.

How could someone as powerful as Queen Levana be afraid of someone like *her*?

But no matter how many times she tried to get a better explanation from Sybil, she was rebuked. *Don't argue. Don't ask questions. Give me your arm.*

At least, since Sybil had learned of Cress's affinity for computers, she had started to pay a bit more attention to her. Some of the other kids were starting to get frustrated. They said that Cress was becoming a favorite. They were jealous that Sybil kept taking her out of the dorms—no one else *ever* left the dorms, and Cress had even gotten to go to the palace a few times, a story that the younger kids never tired of hearing about, even though Cress had only gone in through the servants' passages and been taken straight to the security control center. She hadn't seen the throne room or anything interesting like that, and she certainly hadn't seen the queen herself. Still, it was more than most anyone else in the dormitories had seen, and they loved to hear her tell the tale, over and over again.

She suspected that Sybil was taking her to the palace again this time, until Mistress took a turn that she had never taken before. Cress almost tripped over her own feet in surprise. The guard, pacing an arm's reach from her (because, again, she was *danger-ous*), cast her a cool glare.

"Where are we going, Mistress?"

"The docks," Sybil answered without pretense.

The docks.

The *spaceship* docks?

Cress furrowed her brow. She hadn't been to the docks before. Did Sybil need her to program special surveillance equipment into one of the royal ships? Or update the parameters for the ships that could enter and exit Artemisia?

Or . . .

Her heart started to thump, although she did her best to temper it. She should not hope. She should not let herself be excited. Because the thought that Sybil might be taking her on a ship . . . that she might be going into *space* . . .

Her eagerness was almost too much to bear. She knew that she shouldn't let herself wish for it, but she wished anyway. Oh, the stories she would tell. The little kids would crowd around her to hear all about her space adventure. She started looking around the corridor with new eyes, trying to mentally record every last detail that she could take back to them later.

But these corridors were so bland, with their polished-smooth stone walls, that there wasn't much to tell. Not yet.

"Mistress," she ventured to ask, "what will you have me do at the docks?"

Sybil was silent for so long that Cress began to regret asking. Maybe she'd angered her. Sybil didn't like being asked rudimentary questions. She didn't like it much when Cress talked at all, other than *Yes, Mistress* and *Of course, Mistress* and *I would be happy to complete this task for you, Mistress.*

And though Cress had never been fond of Sybil—had, in fact, been terrified of her since before she could remember—she still wanted Sybil to be fond of *her.* She wanted Mistress to be proud. She imagined Sybil bragging about her to the queen, telling Her Majesty of the young prodigy in her care, who could be so much more useful to the crown if she weren't trapped in those awful dormitories all the time. Cress hoped that if she could impress Sybil enough, someday the queen would have to take notice of her. Maybe she would be offered a job and she could prove that shells weren't dangerous after all. That they want to belong and be good, loyal Lunars just like anyone. Maybe, just maybe, the queen would listen to her.

"Do you remember," said Sybil, jolting Cress from a daydream in which Queen Levana herself was praising Cress for her brilliance and essential service to the crown, "when I asked you about conducting more extensive surveillance on the leaders of the Earthen Union?"

"Yes, Mistress."

"You told me then that our current software was unsuited for the surveillance we had in mind. That the feeds were too easily disrupted or dropped. That the very act of obtaining live audio feeds from Earth would no doubt be noticed, and likely traced back to us. Is that correct?"

"Yes, Mistress."

Sybil nodded. "Your work has been invaluable to me of late, Crescent."

Cress's lips parted. It was rare to hear anything remotely re-sembling praise from Sybil, and her chest warmed at her words. They turned a corner and the corridor ended at an enormous set of double doors.

"I believe," Sybil continued, not looking at Cress as she pressed her fingertips to a scanner on the wall, "that I have resolved all of the dilemmas that were keeping us from achieving our objectives."

The doors slid open. Cress followed Sybil onto a wide platform that encircled a cavernous domed space, filled with the shimmer-ing white bodies of royal spaceships. The floor beneath them was glowing, casting the shadows of the ships onto black ceilings. At the far end of the dock, the massive barrier between the atmosphere-controlled area and outer space was sealed tight.

What was more—there were *people.*

Not many, but a dozen at least, mingling around one of the larger ships. They were too far to see clearly, but Cress could make out vibrant-colored clothing, and one of the men was wearing an enormous hat and—

Sybil grabbed Cress's elbow and yanked her in the opposite direction. Cress gasped and stumbled after her.

"Do not look at them," said Sybil.

Cress frowned. Her arm was stinging but she resisted the urge to rip it out of Sybil's grip. "Why? Who are they?"

"They are members of Artemisia's families, and they would not appreciate being gawked at by a *shell.*" She dragged Cress down a ramp to the dock's main floor, releasing her elbow once they were separated from the aristocrats by the svelte forms of the spaceships. It was disconcerting to be walking on the glowing floor. It felt like walking on a star. Cress was so distracted that she crashed into Sybil when she came to an abrupt stop.

Sybil looked down at her, lip twitching, and didn't respond to Cress's hasty apology. She just turned and nodded to the guard, who opened the door to a small podship. It couldn't have fit more than three or four passengers, but while it was small, it was also luxurious. A faint strip of lights curled around the ceiling. A holograph node was projecting the image of a burbling water fountain in one corner. The benches behind the pilot were covered in a fabric that made the blankets in the dormitories look like animal feed sacks.

Sybil gestured for Cress to get in, and the invitation was so unexpected that Cress could only stand and stare at the podship's interior in disbelief. "Really?" she whispered. "I'm . . . we're leaving Artemisia?" She felt momentarily dizzy—with elation, but perhaps also a bit because of the blood taken before.

"We are leaving Luna," said Sybil. "Now get in."

Cress's mouth ran dry. *Leaving Luna?* It was more than she had dared to hope. A ride in a spaceship. A real trip into space. The other shells would be so jealous.

Pulse hammering, she climbed into the ship and settled into the farthest seat. Sybil sat facing her and immediately switched off the fountain holograph, as if she found the sound annoying. The guard took the pilot's seat, and within moments Cress could feel the subtle hum of the engine vibrating through the soles of her feet.

Her mounting excitement was met with almost equal amounts of anxiety as the ship lifted, hovering over the other stationary vehicles. It began to glide toward the massive exit. Mistress Sybil still hadn't given her any indication as to what this new job was that she was meant to do. Though she had managed to successfully complete every task given to her before, she could sense that something was different about this one. Bigger. More important.

This could be her chance to prove to Sybil—to everyone—that she was more than just a shell. She was valuable. She deserved to be a citizen of Luna.

She couldn't fail.

With a shaky breath, she pulled her hair over one shoulder and began twisting the ends around her wrists. She'd thought of cutting it a year ago, but the other girls had talked her out of it. They told her how beautiful it was, how lucky she was that it grew so thick and strong. They said she would be crazy to cut it, so she didn't. Now she supposed it had become a sort of security blanket for her. She often caught herself fidgeting with it when she was nervous.

The massive doors had opened, making the entire dock rumble, and now they were sitting in a holding chamber, waiting for the doors to seal closed again before they could be released into space. The anticipation was choking her.

She was leaving Luna. Leaving *Luna.* Never in all her dreams had she thought that *she,* a lowly, forgotten shell, would have the chance to see life beyond Luna's protective biodomes.

But here she was, only nine years old and setting off on her first great adventure.

The enormous, ancient metal doors cracked open and slowly, slowly peeled back. They revealed the barren white landscape of Luna first, crater-pocked and desert-still. And beyond them ... beyond the horizon ... beyond Luna ...

Stars.

Stars like she had never seen, had never imagined seeing. The sky was alive with them. And in their midst, proud and beautiful and right before her eyes, was planet Earth.

Their ship began to coast forward again, gradually at first, but picking up speed as they abandoned Luna's weak gravitational pull and soared away from its surface.

Cress didn't realize she'd put her hands on the windows until her breath fogged against the surface. She pulled back, revealing two handprints that perfectly framed the blue planet.

Sybil's cryptic words churned in her head. Was she taking Cress to *Earth?*

It would indeed solve all the issues Cress had pointed out with regards to spying on the Earthens. She had to get closer. She needed better equipment and more time, but mostly she needed to close the physical distance between them.

Was Sybil asking her to be a spy? Earthens wouldn't suspect a child like her, and she was a shell—perfectly suited to fit in with the ungifted Earthens. She could infiltrate government databases. She could commandeer every media feed on the planet. She could obtain secrets from every government official and private comms from every citizen. She could be the best spy in Lunar history.

And best of all, she would no longer be just a shell, trapped in a dormitory and forced to give blood every four weeks. She would have a blue sky. She would walk with bare feet on real grass. She would splash through ocean water and climb to the tops of skyscrapers and go to the theater and dance in the rain and—

She noticed Sybil watching her, and only then did she realize she had an enormous grin on her face. She smothered it as quickly as she could.

"How long will it take to get there?" she asked.

"Hours," said Sybil, unclipping a portscreen from her white thaumaturge coat. "Your first objective will be to access the notes from the weekly meetings between Emperor Rikan and his advisory cabinet. I suggest you begin planning how you will accomplish this."

Cress pressed her lips together and nodded eagerly, her thoughts already churning with ideas. No doubt the meeting had an android secretary recording the notes, possibly even taking an audio or video recording, and as long as that android had net connectivity . . .

She leaned her head against the bench and turned to look at the planet again while she mulled it over—coding and security hacks buzzing through her thoughts.

Stars, but the planet was beautiful. More breathtaking than she'd imagined it. The projected images from the holograph nodes didn't begin to do it justice. How it sparkled and glowed and moved, always moving, the wisps of clouds always churning. It was as though the planet itself were a living organism.

She started to hum as she thought and dreamed and planned. She hummed a lot when she was working. It helped her channel her thoughts sometimes, but today her thoughts were too disjointed to be focused. How different her life looked from just this morning. How quickly everything had changed.

The journey passed in silence but for the quiet tap of Sybil's fingers on the portscreen and Cress humming to herself. The pilot never spoke. It was almost as if he weren't even there, but then, that's how all the guards acted. Invisible. She didn't blame them. Working for Mistress Sybil often made her wish she were invisible too.

Her gaze reattached to Earth. It reminded her of a lullaby one of the older girls had taught her years ago, one that Cress still loved to sing to the children at lights-out.

Sweet Crescent Moon, up in the sky,
Won't you sing your song to Earth as she passes by?
Your sweetest silver melody, a rhythm and a rhyme,
A lullaby of pleasant dreams as you make your climb.
Send the forests off to bed, the mountains tuck in tight,
Rock the ocean gently, and the deserts kiss good night.
Sweet Crescent Moon, up in the sky,
You sing your song so sweetly after sunshine passes by.

Cress caught sight of the guard peering at her in the window's reflection. She stiffened, realizing she'd been singing aloud. He quickly looked away, but Sybil was watching her now too.

Not just watching. *Glowering.*

Cress gulped. "Sorry."

Sybil set her portscreen on her lap, fixing her attention more fully on Cress. "You probably don't realize how old that song is. A lullaby that's been sung on Luna perhaps as far back as colonization."

"I did know that," Cress said before she could stop herself. It was her favorite song. She'd researched it once.

Sybil's eyes narrowed, almost imperceptibly. "Then you must know that the song was written at a time when Earth and Luna were allies. Some consider it to be a song symbolizing peace between the two planets. Some feel that it is unpatriotic today—that it suggests Earthen sympathizing."

Heat rushed to Cress's cheeks again and she sat straighter, shaking her head. "That's not why I like it," she said. "I just like . . . I mean, it has my name in it. *Crescent Moon.* Sometimes I think . . . I wonder if maybe my parents named me for the song."

The thaumaturge gave an abrupt snort, startling Cress. "That is highly unlikely," Sybil said, looking out the window. "From what I recall of your parents, they were not given to such flights of fancy."

Cress stared at her. "You knew my parents?"

Sybil was quiet for a time. Expressionless but for a smug tilt of her mouth. Finally, she slid her attention back to Cress. "The only thing you need to know of your parents was that they willingly gave you up to be killed in the shell infanticide." Her eyes glinted, pleased with her own cruelty. "Your mother herself put you into my arms. All she said was, 'A shell. How mortifying.'"

The words struck Cress harder than they should have. Of

course she'd known that her parents had given her up to be killed. That was the law—even though shells weren't actually killed, just hidden away, but most civilians didn't know that. Her parents would have believed she was dead, and Sybil never tired of reminding the shells how *unwanted* they were. That if it wasn't for her saving them, they would all be dead, and no one would mourn them.

But Sybil had never told her that part before. *Mortifying.*

She sniffed and turned away before Sybil could see the tears building in her eyes.

Out the window, Cress saw that they were approaching something—another spaceship? She squinted and leaned forward. It was spherical, with three enormous winglike appendages tilted away from it.

"What's that?"

Sybil barely turned her head. "It's a satellite."

Cress squeezed both fists around her hair. "We're going to crash into it."

A wisp of a smile flitted over Sybil's mouth.

The podship began to slow. Cress watched, enraptured, as the satellite grew larger in the window until it was taking up her entire view. There was a clamp on one side, pre-extended. The guard latched onto it on his first attempt, and the podship shuddered around them. A cacophony of noises followed—thumps and rattles and whirring machinery and hisses and thuds. A hatch was extending from the satellite and suctioning against the side of the podship, creating a tunnel for them to exit into.

Cress furrowed her brow. Were they stopping to refuel? To pick up supplies? To outfit her with her new secret Earthen identity?

The podship door opened, and Sybil stepped out into the tunnel, beckoning for Cress to follow. The guard kept his distance behind her.

The hatch was narrow and smelled of metal and recirculating air. A second door was closed at the end of the corridor, but opened upon their approach.

Cress found herself in a small round room. A desk circled the space, and the walls above it were covered in invisi-screens, angled to be seen from anywhere in the room. Only one wall was empty—noticeably empty.

A sense of dread settled in Cress's stomach, but she couldn't tell what it meant. Sybil had stepped aside and was watching Cress, waiting, but Cress didn't know what she was waiting for.

There was a second door identical to the one they had just entered through—perhaps another hatch for a second ship, she thought. And a third door led to . . .

She stepped forward uncertainly.

It was a bathroom. A sink. A toilet. A tiny shower.

She turned back. Goose bumps covered her skin.

"There is a recirculating water system," said Sybil, speaking as if they'd been in the middle of a conversation. She opened a tall cabinet. "And enough nonperishable food to last for six to eight weeks, though I will replenish your supplies every two to three weeks, or as needed, as I come to check on your progress. Her Majesty is hopeful that you'll be making great forward strides in our Earthen surveillance now that you've been so meticulously outfitted with the exact requirements you specified. If you find you need anything more for your work, I will obtain it for you."

Cress's stomach was knotting itself now, her breaths coming in shorter gasps as she took in the invisi-screens again. The holograph nodes. The processors and receivers and data boards.

State-of-the-art. All of it.

It was exactly what she needed to spy on Earth.

"I'm . . . to live here?" she squeaked. "Alone?"

"For a time, yes. You said you needed to be closer to Earth, Crescent. I've given you what you requested in order to serve Her Majesty. That is what you want, isn't it?"

She started nodding without realizing it. Tears were gathering in her eyes, but she brushed them away with the palm of her hand. "But where will I sleep?"

Sybil paced to the too-empty wall and hit a switch. A bed lowered out of the wall. It was larger than the bunk Cress had in the dormitories, but that did little to cheer her.

Alone. She was being left here, *alone*.

"You have your first orders," said Sybil. "Is there anything else you require?"

Cress couldn't remember what her first orders had been. She'd been so focused on going to Earth. So excited about trees and oceans and cities . . .

And now she didn't have any of that. She didn't even have the dormitory or the other shells anymore.

"How long?" she asked, her voice wavering. "How long do I have to stay here?"

When Sybil was silent, Cress forced herself to look up and meet her gaze. She hoped for sympathy, kindness, *anything.*

She shouldn't have hoped. If anything, Sybil looked only irritated at Cress's weakness.

"You will stay here until your work is done." Then, after a moment, her features softened. "Of course, if your work is satisfactory, then perhaps when you are finished we can discuss your return to Artemisia . . . as a true citizen of Luna."

Cress sniffed loudly and tilted her head back as much as she dared to hold in the tears.

A true citizen of Luna. Not just a shell. Not a prisoner. Not a secret.

She looked around the room again. She was still horrified, but also more determined than she had ever been.

"All right, Mistress. I will do my best to please Her Majesty."

A glimmer of approval shone in Sybil's eyes. She nodded and gestured at the guard, who turned without ceremony and marched back toward the podship.

"I know you will, Crescent." She turned to follow him out the door. There were no parting words, no reassuring smile, no comforting embrace.

The door slammed and Mistress Sybil was gone and that was that.

Cress was alone.

She gasped and exhaled and moved toward one of the small

windows, intending to watch them debark from the satellite and return to Luna.

A glow in the opposite window caught her eye. She turned and drifted to the other side of the tiny room instead.

Earth was so big it nearly filled up the entire frame.

Her whole body was trembling as she crawled up onto the desk and curled against the cabinet, staring at the blue planet. Blue and green and gold. She would sing for a while before she began her work. It would calm her. Singing always made her feel better.

Sweet Crescent Moon, up in the sky . . .

That was all she could get through before the tears came in earnest, drowning out everything else.

The Princess
and the Guard

"HELP ME, SIR CLAY! SAVE ME!" WINTER COWERED BEHIND THE
fort of pillows. Though their fortress was strong, she knew it would
not keep out the villains forever.

Luckily, at the most opportune of moments, Sir Jacin Clay
leaped to her defense, brandishing the legendary Earthlight
Saber—in reality, a wooden training sword he'd gotten from his
father for his seventh birthday.

"You'll never have the princess!" Jacin yelled. "I'll protect her
with my life, you Earthen fiend!" He swung and jabbed at the air,
while Winter abandoned the wall of pillows and scurried beneath the bed.

"Sir Clay! Behind you!"

Jacin pivoted to face her at the same time that Winter sprang
upward.

"Princess?" he asked, his eyes twitching with uncertainty.

Winter grinned a wicked grin and tackled him around the
middle, sending them both crashing onto the mattress. "A-ha!"

she bellowed. "I have lured you into my trap! You believed I was your beloved princess, but it was only my glamour tricking you. I am none other than Vile Velamina, the infamous space pirate!"

"Not Vile Velamina," said Jacin, with a feigned gasp of horror. "What have you done with my princess?"

"She is being held prisoner aboard my spaceship. You will never see her again. *Bwa-ha-ha!*"

"No! I will rescue her!"

Jacin—who was starting to leave Winter behind in the height department—tossed her easily off the bed. She screeched and landed on the floor with a thump. It wasn't a hard throw, but her knee burned where it hit the rug.

Jacin climbed to his feet, steadying himself on the plush mattress, and thrust the point of the sword at her. "Actually, it is I who have lured *you* into a trap, you stinking pirate. You are now precisely where I want you." Reaching up, he grabbed onto one of the tassels that hung from the canopy on Winter's bed. "With a yank on this rope, a trapdoor will open beneath you, and you will plummet straight into . . ." He hesitated.

"Oh—the menagerie!" Winter suggested, eyes brightening. "Ryu's cage. And the wolf is very, very hungry and will no doubt gobble the pirate up!"

Jacin scowled at her. "Are you plotting your own demise?"

"That was the princess speaking. I was implanting the thought directly into your brain. Velamina has me tied up, but not unconscious."

Jacin started to laugh. "What she said, then." He made a great show of pulling on the tassel. The curtains didn't budge, but Winter played along, screaming in anguish and rolling around on the carpet as if she'd just been thrown into a den with the most dangerous feral wolf of all time.

Jacin held the sword toward the ceiling. "Now I must find my princess and return her safely to the palace, where I will be rewarded with great honor."

"*Honor?*" Winter sneered. "Aren't you going to ask for riches, or something? Like a mansion in AR-4?"

Shaking his head, Jacin stared dreamily toward outer space. "Seeing my princess's smile when she is returned safely home is all the reward that I need."

"Ew, gross." Winter threw a pillow at his head, but Jacin dodged it and hopped down from the bed.

"Now then—with the pirate vanquished I have only to find her spaceship."

Winter pointed at the glass doors that opened out onto her balcony. "It's out there."

Chest puffed like a proud hero, Jacin strutted to the doors.

"Hold on!" Winter jumped to her feet and grabbed a belt from her wardrobe. She fluffed her thick curls around her face, trying to leave Vile Velamina behind and return to her sweet, demure princess role instead.

On the balcony, she made a great show of tying herself to the rail.

"You do realize," Jacin said, watching apprehensively, "that if anyone looked up here right now, they'd think you really were in trouble."

"Pffft. No one would believe that *you* could manipulate me so easily."

His jaw twitched, just a little, and Winter felt a sting of guilt. Though he pretended otherwise, she knew Jacin was sensitive about how poorly his Lunar gift was developing. At almost eight years old he should have been starting glamour practice and emotional manipulation, but it was becoming apparent that Jacin had inherited his father's lack of skill. He was almost as ungifted as a shell.

Winter knew it was bad—shameful, even—to have so little talent, especially here in the capital city of Artemisia.

On the other hand, *her* gift had started developing when she was only four, and was becoming stronger every day. She was already meeting once a week with a tutor, Master Gertman, who said she was growing up to be one of the most talented pupils he'd ever had.

"All right, I'm ready," she said, cinching the belt around her wrists.

Jacin shook his head. "You're crazy, is what you are."

She stuck her tongue out at him, then tossed her hair off one shoulder and screwed up her face in distress. "Won't some strong, brave hero come save me from these awful pirates? Help! Help!"

But Jacin's frown remained, his attention caught on something over her shoulder. "Who's that, in the throne room?"

Winter glanced back. Her chambers were in the private wing of Artemisia Palace, where the royal family slept, just down the hall from her father and stepmother's rooms. They were on the third floor, with a marvelous view of Lake Artemisia below, and she could see most of the opposite wing of the palace, which wrapped around the lake's far side.

At the very center of the palace was the throne room. It was the only room that had a balcony jutting far out over the lake's waters—with no rail or barrier to provide protection if anyone stepped too close to the edge.

And there was a woman standing there, peering into the waters below.

Winter didn't recognize her, but the uniform of a palace servant was clear even from far away.

"What's she doing?" she asked.

She had barely finished speaking before Jacin turned and started to run.

Heart thumping, Winter scrambled to undo the belt around her wrists. "Wait—Jacin! Wait for me!"

He did not wait, and it didn't occur to Winter to use her gift to force him to wait until he was already out her bedroom door. Finally she managed to get the belt undone. With one hurried look back toward the throne room, relieved to see that the woman hadn't moved, she bolted after Jacin.

Her guard—her *real* guard—startled when she burst out into the corridor and followed at a fast clip as she flew down the hallway, around the familiar white-stone curves of the palace. No one tried to stop her, though guards and nobility and thaumaturges alike stepped out of her way as she barreled past.

From a distance she watched Jacin's white-blond hair disappear through the enormous black doors of the throne room. The doors had almost shut again when she wedged her arm between them and shoved her way inside.

Jacin stood only a few steps into the room and Winter nearly crashed into him, catching herself on his outstretched arm instead.

"*No!*" the woman gasped. "Take her out of here. Her Highness needn't see this." Her voice was wobbly and cracked, her eyes bloodshot. She was young, maybe in her early twenties, and she was pretty in a natural way. No glamour was creating her rosy skin or thick brown hair, but neither was a glamour hiding the hollowness of her cheeks or the wild panic in her eyes. Everything in her expression suggested a brokenness, a desperation, and a heartbreak later Winter understood.

The woman stood barely half a step from the balcony's edge. She intended to jump.

Of her *own will.*

Winter's jaw hung open. How could anyone wish that for oneself?

"Please," Winter said, taking a hesitant step forward. "Step back now. It'll be all right."

Jacin planted a hand on Winter's shoulder, as if he meant to hold her back, but with a twitch of her thoughts Winter sent his hand right back to his side. She heard his unhappy intake of breath but ignored it as she stepped beyond his reach.

Behind her, she heard the *clomp* of her guards' footsteps as they caught up, the bang of the doors admitting them.

But they were only guards. They had as much talent as Jacin or Winter's father—which is to say, almost none at all. They could not help this poor woman.

She could, though. *She could save her.*

Gulping, Winter took another step.

The woman had started to cry. "Please," she pleaded. "Please go away, Your Highness. Please let me do this." She hid her face behind her hands and Winter noticed a purple-yellow bruise on her arm.

"It will be all right now. You can trust me."

Just come back.

The woman recoiled, and her expression began to change. No longer frightened, but rather dark and determined. She clenched her jaw and looked down at the lapping waves. The lake was unfathomably deep and spread all the way to the horizon, as far as one could see.

Her toe crept back, teetering toward the edge.

Horror expanded in Winter's chest. The woman needed help, needed *her* help . . .

She squeezed her fists and, with her mind, reached for that toe. She was aware of the danger—if she accidentally knocked the woman off-balance, then she might send her off the balcony even while she was trying to save her.

But it was instinctual, as it had been from her first lessons with Master Gertman.

She was careful. She was slow and gentle. She eased her will into the woman's toe and the sole of her foot and her ankle and up to her knee and her thigh.

She brought the woman's foot steadily down.

The woman whimpered. "No. Please. *Please.*"

"It's all right," Winter cooed, urging forward the other leg now. One step.

A second step.

The woman retreated, ever so slowly, from the balcony's edge.

After the third step, she sagged, the strength draining from her, and Winter allowed her to collapse onto the glass floor.

Relief rushed through her and she went to the woman, kneeling beside her and placing a hand on her shoulder. The woman's sobs came harder.

"You're all right now," said Winter. "You're safe."

When the woman only cried harder, Winter did her best to comfort her. She persuaded the woman that it was true, that she *was* safe and everything would be all right. She imprinted pleasant emotions on the surface of her mind. It was the most difficult of the manipulations that Lunars were capable of—to change not only people's vision or to bend their bodies to one's will, but to change the very depth of their own feelings.

But Winter believed she could do it. She had to do it. This was what she'd been practicing for.

She chose happiness. A soft blanket of joy settling over the woman's thoughts. She didn't stop until a grateful smile stretched over the woman's mouth, warming Winter to the core.

"Th-thank you, Princess," the woman said, her voice listless and trembling.

Winter beamed back. "You're welcome."

She had nearly forgotten Jacin and her guards watching them until more footsteps crashed into the room.

"What is the meaning of this?"

She froze, all sense of comfort vanishing at her fingertips. As if a string had been cut, the servant moaned and crumpled onto her side.

Swallowing hard, Winter glanced back. Her stepmother, Queen Levana, along with a handful of guards and her two highest-ranking thaumaturges—Sybil Mira and Aimery Park—all stood scowling at the display. Winter and Jacin and the woman whose smile had already collapsed into an empty look.

Winter's personal guard stammered what explanation he could, and Winter looked away, unable to bear her stepmother's disapproving frown.

"It seems the girl is in need of assistance." This was Thaumaturge Park, his voice like a gentle stream over smooth rocks. He had the loveliest voice of any person in the court, and yet hearing it always sent chills down Winter's spine.

"She *needs* to be put back to work," said Queen Levana. "I will not abide idleness in my palace. If she creates such a disturbance again, she will be dealt with in court. Now—I want everyone out of my throne room this instant."

The servant curled in on herself, limp as a helpless doll.

Winter tried to give the servant a gift of tranquility as the guards dragged her away, but the woman's expression was so desolate that she had no way of knowing if she'd succeeded.

"WHAT HAPPENED IN THE THRONE ROOM TODAY, WINTER?"
Her heart jumped and she craned her head back to look at her father as he set aside the holographic storybook he'd just finished reading. Winter's emotions had been jumbled all afternoon—torn between pride that she had rescued that poor woman and distress that she had needed rescuing in the first place.

Here in the palace, they were always surrounded by a wealth of art and splendor, food and entertainment. Workers, even regular servants, were said to be treated more fairly in Artemisia than any other place on Luna. So what could be so bad that she would consider taking her own life?

"There was a servant who was . . . she was going to jump from the throne room, into the lake," said Winter. "I think . . . I think she wanted to hurt herself. So I stopped her."

Her father nodded, and she could tell he'd already heard the story, probably from the guards who had been on duty at the time. Everyone liked her dad. Despite being married to the queen, the other guards still treated him like a friend, and more than once Winter and Jacin had gotten in trouble when her personal guards had told him of their mischief.

"Are you all right?"

She nodded. "I don't understand why she wanted to do it, though."

Her father was silent for a long time before he tightened his arm around Winter's shoulders, drawing her against his chest. His heartbeat was comforting and steady.

"I'm proud of you for trying to do the right thing," he finally said, though the way he said it made Winter frown. *Trying?* "But I need you to understand that there are often other ways to help someone than by manipulating them with your gift. It's usually best to talk to them first and then figure out how best to help them." He hesitated before adding, "When you use your gift on someone without their permission, you're taking choice and free will away from them, and that isn't fair."

Winter pulled away, no longer comforted by his heartbeat. She turned to stare at him. "She was going to jump. She would have died."

"I understand, Winter. I'm not saying you did anything wrong, and I know you were doing what you felt was the right thing to do. And maybe it was. But . . . it's becoming clear that you're going to be talented, much more talented than I ever was. And while I'm proud of you, I also know that being strong with our gift can sometimes lead to us making poor decisions. Decisions that can hurt the people around us if we aren't careful."

Winter's jaw tightened, and she was surprised at the hurt and anger that began to churn in her stomach. Her father didn't understand. He couldn't possibly understand—after all, he couldn't have helped that woman today. Not like she had.

Winter had saved the woman's life. She was a hero.

Her lip started to tremble, and her father's face softened. He pulled her back against him again and kissed the top of her head.

"You're not in trouble," he said. "I hope that girl will get the help she needs now, and that she'll thank you someday. I just need you to know . . . there are people in this palace, and on all of Luna, who see manipulation as the quickest way to solve every problem. While it might be useful at times, it's rarely the only way, or the best way. And the person you would manipulate . . . they do deserve to have a choice. Do you understand?"

She nodded, but she was pretty sure that he *didn't* understand.

She loved her father with all her heart, but he would never know what it was like to help someone with a mere thought. To give them happiness or to change how they saw the world.

She was going to use her gift to help people. To make Artemisia better.

Saving that servant had been only the beginning.

FOR THE MONTHS THAT FOLLOWED, WINTER FOCUSED MORE on her studies than ever before. Her glamour became stronger. Her thoughts became sharper. She practiced on Jacin when she could, though after that first talk with her father, she made sure to always ask his permission.

She kept her eye out for the servant who was still alive because of her. Winter always reserved a special smile for her, and every time their paths crossed in the palace, she made sure to give her an extra boost of pleasant emotions.

She made sure the woman was proud of the great work she did here in the palace.

She fed her contentment from living in such a beautiful city.

She coaxed her into feeling loved and appreciated, safe and calm—a steady drip of every good emotion Winter could think to give her, so she might never feel tempted to end her life again.

A year passed, then two, then three—but Winter started to notice a change in what she had begun to think of as a quiet companionship between her and the servant. She noticed that when the woman saw Winter coming, she would often change directions before Winter could get close enough to alter her thoughts. She was avoiding her.

Winter couldn't understand why.

Then one afternoon, during her weekly session with Master Gertman, he told Winter that she had become so strong in her gift and so far exceeded his expectations that she might be talented enough to someday become a thaumaturge. It was a great honor. A role reserved for only the most talented Lunars in their entire kingdom.

Winter preened like a peacock all afternoon. She bragged about it to Jacin, and was annoyed when he didn't look nearly as impressed as she thought he ought to.

She went to bed that night with a pleased grin on her lips.

Hours later, she was awoken by the deafening sound of a gunshot coming from her father's room.

She would have nightmares for years to come. Her father's blood. The thaumaturge who had shot him, now lying dead, too, in the room's corner. Winter still standing in her nightgown and the feel of disbelieving tears on her cheeks and how she was unable to move, like her toes had been stitched to the carpet.

It was Selene all over again. One moment the person she loved most in the whole world was there, and then they were gone. Selene, taken by fire and smoke. Her father, by a thaumaturge and a gun.

In the years to come, it would not be the blood or her father's dead eyes or the guards rushing past her that Winter would most remember.

It was her stepmother. The queen. Wracked by such heartbroken sobs that Winter thought they might never stop echoing in her head. Those wails would haunt her nightmares all her life.

At nine years old, Winter had begun to realize that it wasn't normal for a queen to be married to a guard. She had begun to understand that there was something strange about such a match, even embarrassing.

But hearing her stepmother's cries that night, she had understood why Levana had chosen her father. She loved him. In spite of the rumors and the glares and the disapproving frowns, she had loved him.

From that night, Winter had started to fear the thaumaturges. They were not honorable members of the court. They were not her friends or her allies.

She would never be one of them, no matter how much praise her gift brought her.

WINTER GASPED AWAKE, HER STEPMOTHER'S SOBS STILL ECHO-ing in her head, leftover remnants from the nightmare. She was drenched in cold sweat.

It had been years since her father's murder, and months since she'd dreamed of it, but the shock and horror felt the same every time.

Not bothering to wait for her pulse to slow, Winter pushed herself from the bed. She fumbled around in her wardrobe for a pair of soft-soled slippers and pinned back her wild curls before slipping into the corridor.

If the guard who stood watch at her door was surprised to see her up in the middle of the night, he didn't show it. It was not a rare occurrence. There had been a time when she sneaked down nearly every night to the palace wing where the guards and their families lived, back when the nightmare had plagued her in earnest. Those nights when she and Jacin would fix themselves mugs of melted cream-and-chocolate and watch stupid dramas on the holograph nodes. When he would pretend that he didn't notice her crying as she pressed her face against his shoulder.

This night, though, she did not make it all the way to the guards' private wing.

Rather, as she approached the main thoroughfare of the

palace, she heard chatter bouncing off the windows. The *clomp* of booted feet. A pair of maids whispered sadly in an alcove, startling and curtsying when they noticed Winter in their midst.

She followed the commotion and found it centered in one of the libraries.

Thaumaturge Aimery Park stood near a window. He was wearing his crimson coat, even though it was the middle of the night. "Your Highness, what are you doing awake?"

Winter did not like Thaumaturge Park, though she was smart enough not to let it show. She couldn't even pinpoint what it was about him that set her nerves to vibrating when he was nearby.

He always smiled when he saw her, but it was the smile of a vulture.

Not wanting to mention the nightmare, Winter answered him, "I thought I heard something."

He nodded. "Something tragic has occurred, young princess. You do not need to see."

He looked back out the window, and despite his warning, he didn't stop Winter as she made her way to another window, where two guards were looking down toward the gardens.

Winter gasped.

A body was sprawled out in the fountain beneath the window. Blood filling the basin. Limbs turned at odd angles.

She knew, though it was too far to see for sure, that it was the servant woman. The one she'd saved years ago, when she was only a child. The one who Winter had been feeding happiness to for more than half her young life. At least, she thought she had.

Winter stumbled back.

"She was ill, Princess," said Aimery. "It is terrible, but these things do happen."

Unable to speak around the emotion clogging her throat, Winter turned and rushed from the room. Walking at first, then faster, *faster*. Behind her, she heard the familiar *clomp* of boots as her guard chased after her. Let him run. Let him chase.

She ran as fast as she could, arms pumping, feet barely touching the cool floor.

When she reached the wing where the guards lived, she passed Jacin's father, Sir Garrison Clay, on his way to start his next shift. He was a palace guard, like Winter's father had been. They had been in training together years before and had been friends from the start—which is how she'd known Jacin all her life too.

"Highness," said Garrison, eyes widening when he saw her and took in what must have been a look of shock. "What's wrong?"

"Is Jacin awake?"

"I don't think so. Are you all right?"

She nodded and whispered, "Just another nightmare."

His expression was understanding as he turned and headed back to the apartment he shared with Jacin and his wife, along with two other guards and their families, all in about the same amount of space as Winter's private chambers. He let her inside with a fatherly squeeze of her shoulder before leaving—it was not acceptable for a guard to be late for duty, even if it was the princess herself who came knocking on his door.

Jacin was still asleep, but he was a light sleeper, and his eyes snapped open the moment Winter creaked open the door. His mother's heavy breathing could be heard from the cot on the other side of the room. "What is it?" he whispered, pushing himself upward.

Winter took a step forward, but hesitated. For years, it would have felt like the most natural thing in the world for her to crawl into bed beside him. After all, he had comforted her more times than she could count after her father died.

But lately she could sense something changing. Jacin was fourteen now, and no longer the slightly gangly boy she'd grown up with. It seemed like he was taller and stronger every day.

There had been recent changes in herself, too, though she wasn't sure if he'd noticed.

Suddenly, having never before cared about all the court whispers of "propriety" and "decorum," Winter found herself questioning the meaning of her oldest, dearest friendship.

"Winter?"

"She's dead," she stammered. "The servant. She . . . jumped out a window, into the gardens. She—"

She started to cry.

Jacin's face twisted and he held his arms toward her.

All her concerns vanished as she scrambled onto the bed and buried her face in his chest. She was an idiot to think that getting older changed anything. This was, and would always be, the only place she belonged.

"GOOD AFTERNOON, SIR OWEN," WINTER SAID AS SHE STEPPED
out of her quarters the next morning. She gave a curtsy to her guard, guilty for having made him chase her halfway through the palace the night before, but he neither looked at her nor acknowledged her greeting. Which was the way of the guards. They were there to serve and to protect, and to act as a target and a shield for any intruder that might want to harm the royal family. They were not friends. They were not confidants.

But Winter couldn't always bring herself to ignore them as they ignored her.

She glided down the hall on her way to her tutoring session and spotted Jacin waiting for her as soon as she turned the corner into an elevator bank. She smiled—an instinctive reaction—though it fell once she took in his expression. A frown creased Jacin's brow.

He glanced once at her guard, who had followed a respectful distance in her wake, before dipping his head toward her. "They found a note."

"A note?"

"From the servant. The one that ..." He didn't have to finish. "My dad is on the team conducting the investigation. It was found in the servant's quarters. Probably won't be made public, but he read it before it was taken away."

"And it was a ... suicide note?" she asked, her heart pattering. The words chilled her. Suicide was always met with suspicion in their society. Everyone knew, even twelve-year-old princesses, that an apparent suicide could just as easily have been a murder caused through manipulation. That was how almost all of the queen's formal executions were carried out, after all. Hand the convicted perpetrators a sharp blade and let them drain out their own lives.

But the crown did not have a monopoly on the Lunar gift, much as the queen may have wished it so. No death could ever be proven a true suicide, and few murders were ever solved.

"What did it say?" Winter asked.

"It wasn't murder. She definitely meant to do it." Jacin's voice stayed low as they stepped into the elevator, along with her stoic guard, and he said nothing else until they'd stepped out again and left the guard to follow a few paces behind.

Winter frowned. Much as she'd hoped that it was a mis-understanding, she wasn't surprised. No one had been manipu-lating the woman in the throne room before Winter rescued her. Or thought that she'd rescued her. She couldn't help wondering how many attempts the woman had made to take her life before she finally succeeded.

"But why?"

Jacin's gaze darted around the hallway. A few young aristo-crats wandered by, probably having just finished with their own tutoring sessions, and when they noticed the princess they stopped to gawk at her. Winter ignored them. She was used to gawking.

Jacin scowled every time and seemed relieved when they passed.

"Are you sure you want to know?"

She wasn't sure at all, but she nodded anyway. What could drive a person to such a decision? What could make them think there were no other options? Especially when there were doctors and specialists who could ensure you never felt sad or lonely or frightened again.

Jacin swallowed hard. "She was pregnant."

Her feet stalled. Jacin paused with her, his brow drawn tight.

"Pregnant?"

It clarified nothing. She'd only ever known women to be happy upon discovering a pregnancy.

Jacin's jaw tightened. He had gone from looking sorry to angry in half a heartbeat. His blue eyes, normally so bright, were now shadowed with a fury Winter rarely saw. "The note said that Thaumaturge Park is—was the father."

She stared.

"Evidently, he's been manipulating her for a long time." Jacin looked away, seething. "No one knows exactly how long it's been going on. Or ... what methods exactly he'd been using to ..." His face was reddening, his breath erratic and his knuckles white.

What methods.

This was a horror that Winter knew of, yet so few spoke of it. Manipulation of the strong against the weak. You could make a person do *anything*, and though there were laws against it, with the powerful among the elite and the enforcers, who was to stop them?

She recalled the desperation in the woman's eyes, the desperation that had gotten stronger over the years.

Winter pressed a hand against her stomach. Her mouth was suddenly stinging and sour and she couldn't swallow fast enough. She would be sick.

"I'm sorry." Jacin held her elbow. "I didn't know if I should tell you or not. I know . . . I know you have to *see* him . . ."

Only in the court. She would only have to see him among the court.

It would still be far too much. "Will they do anything to him?" she asked.

But Jacin didn't have to answer.

Aimery was a great favorite of the queen. No repercussions would come to him for this crime.

Squeezing her eyes shut, Winter accepted a brief embrace from Jacin before pulling away. He stayed with her for the rest of the walk to her session, but she hardly noticed his presence as her mind sorted through this terrible information.

The woman's desperation.

The bruises that she sometimes noticed on her arms, only half covered by the sleeves of her uniform.

And Aimery looking down at her from the library. *"These things do happen . . ."*

She stopped suddenly beside a potted plant and bent over, heaving into the soil. Jacin and the guard both dropped to her side. Jacin's sure hand on her back, comforting. The guard asking if he should call for a medic.

She shook her head. "Something I ate," she said, spitting as daintily as she could. "But . . . perhaps, if a servant could clean up . . ."

"I'll alert someone straightaway."

Nothing else was said of it, but Winter felt no better. Her stomach was still churning.

She had rescued the woman. She believed she had saved her.

When really she had handed her right back into the grip of her tormenter. She had allowed him to keep abusing her for years, and the woman couldn't even have fought against it—not when Winter was forcing her to be happy, to be content, to *just keep accepting it.*

Winter had not saved her at all.

"YOU ARE DISTRACTED TODAY, YOUR HIGHNESS."

Winter pulled her gaze away from the servant girl who was a constant fixture in her tutoring sessions. The one who kept her eyes lowered and her hands clasped in her lap. Who said nothing. Who was but a tool for Winter's education. Over the past year, Winter had made the girl laugh and swoon, dance and touch her nose, fall into a deep sleep. She still did not know the girl's name.

"Your Highness?" said Master Gertman. "Did you hear me?"

Winter smiled at her instructor. "I apologize. I'm still . . . a little upset, I think, about the servant. The other day."

"Ah, yes. I heard it was the same girl you kept from jumping from the throne room when you were young." Master Gertman laced his fingers together. "It is not for you to worry about, Princess. Tragic things happen sometimes, even here in Artemisia."

Tragic. *Tragic.* Everyone said it as though the word had meaning. But was the woman's death the tragedy, or her life?

She looked again at the servant girl, waiting to be manipulated. She had a good life here in the palace, didn't she? Winter never did anything awful to her during her trainings, never hurt her or forced her to hurt herself. She gave her pretty illusions to see. She fed only happy emotions into her brain.

For her service, the girl and her family were richly rewarded. It was better than anyone in the outer sectors could hope for.

Wasn't it?

But looking at her now, Winter noticed, for the first time, a strained whiteness around the girl's knuckles.

She was tense. Maybe even frightened. Of *Winter?* Of the tutor? Of one of the other pupils who trained here throughout the day?

Winter's entire world was spinning and it occurred to her with sudden clarity that this was wrong. Her training sessions. The thaumaturges. The entire Lunar gift. The power that the strong, like she and the queen and Aimery, held over the weak. Like this servant girl. Like Jacin.

Like Winter's father.

It was exactly what he had tried to tell her all those years ago.

"Try again, Princess," prompted the tutor. "You did so well last week."

She looked at Master Gertman again. "I'm sorry. I'm a little faint. I haven't been feeling well, and ... Could you repeat your instructions, please?"

"Just a basic glamour, Your Highness. Perhaps you could try changing the color of your hair?"

Winter reached up and grabbed a handful of her thick black curls. She could do that. She'd done it plenty of times before.

The servant girl inhaled a bracing breath.

Winter released her hair and ran her fingers over it instead. Beauty was usually the goal of simple glamour, and usually she would call up the glamour of the most beautiful woman she knew, the most beautiful woman *anyone* knew. Her stepmother, Queen Levana. The most beautiful woman on Luna.

The difficult part was making herself seem older. In order for a glamour to be effective, you had to believe that you looked as you wanted others to see you. And while Winter found it easy to change her tight curly hair or the hue of her brown skin or to make herself taller or shorter or thinner or curvier—making herself *mature*, with all the grace and experience of her stepmother, required a mental focus she was still developing.

She was getting better, though. Master Gertman praised her often.

Someday, she would be powerful.

Someday, she could be as strong as a thaumaturge.

She stared at the top of the servant's head.

"I'm sorry," she whispered. "I can't."

The tutor frowned.

Rubbing the back of her neck as if she were embarrassed, Winter gave him a faint smile. "I'm just so tired. And distracted. Perhaps we should try again another day. If that's all right, Master Gertman?"

His frown did not disperse. The servant made no movement, nothing to suggest she had even heard Winter or cared the slightest that the princess would not be manipulating her today. It was as though she weren't there at all.

Finally, Master Gertman leaned back and nodded. "Of course, Your Highness. You should go rest. We'll try again next week."

She stood and smiled as prettily as she could. The tutor looked briefly flustered. "Thank you, Master." She curtsied before leaving his office.

Jacin was still waiting in the hallway, just where she'd left him. He scrambled to his feet in surprise. "Done already?"

Winter shut the tutor's door behind her and held Jacin's gaze. His eyes caught the light of the enormous windows that lined the corridor wall. Her friend was becoming handsome indeed, and he would never need a glamour to improve upon that.

Her palms were suddenly warm and growing damp.

Her unexpected resolve frightened her, but she knew she wouldn't change her mind.

"I've come to a decision, Jacin."

He cocked his head at her.

All the best people—Jacin and her father and Sir Garrison Clay and the servants who smiled kindly in the hallways and did not seem at all bothered that they did not have perfect unblemished skin or dark, thick eyelashes—they did not use glamours. They did not manipulate the people around them.

Winter didn't want to be like her stepmother or the thaumaturges.

She wanted to be like the people she loved.

She stepped close to Jacin, because no one else could hear her now. Because her decision would go against everything their society stood for, everything they valued.

"I will never use my gift," she whispered. "Not ever again."

IT WAS EASIER THAN SHE EXPECTED IT TO BE, ONCE THE DECIsion was made. It required some changes of habits, no doubt. If she wanted a servant to bring something, she had to ask, rather than simply impose the request into their mind. If she wanted to look extra pretty for a party, she would call up a stylist to tint her cheeks and glitter her eyelids, rather than create the illusion in her mind's eye first.

She never once forgot her vow, though. She stayed true to her word.

Master Gertman was confused as all the progress they'd made in the past years dissolved over the course of a single week. Winter was persistent with her excuses. She pretended to try. She was very convincing. But after every fake attempt, the servant would crease her brow and shake her head, as confused as the tutor.

A month after Winter had sworn off her gift, she passed that servant girl in between sessions and, for the first time, the girl smiled at her in a way that suggested a shared secret.

She wondered if the girl knew that Winter was only pretending. She wondered if the girl was grateful for her weekly respites from whatever manipulations were done to her by the rest of the tutor's pupils.

"It's called Lunar sickness," said Jacin as they whiled away an afternoon in Winter's chambers. Though rumors had begun circulating about the two of them and how they spent more time alone with each other than was proper, Winter and Jacin refused to be cowed by the passing scowls and snide remarks from the court. Besides, she knew her guards would never say anything. They respected Jacin's family too much to add fuel to such shameful gossip.

Jacin slid his hand through the medical-studies holograph that shimmered in the center of the room. There had been a time when they would call up adventure stories and virtual reality games using the holograph node, but now more often than not Jacin wanted to study anatomy books and psychology texts instead. In a year he would be applying for an occupation, and his heart had been set on a doctor's internship ever since Winter could remember.

Seeing how excited he got when he talked about it made her heart warm, but she also dreaded to think of the years he would spend away from her. He could be stationed at any med-clinic on all of Luna. There was a slim chance he could end up in Artemisia, at their med-clinic or in one of their laboratories, but it was more likely he'd end up in the less desirable outer sectors, at least for the first few years of his training.

Winter hated the thought of him leaving, even temporarily, but she would never tell him so for fear he would give up his dream in order to stay with her. She wouldn't be able to forgive herself if he did that. "Lunar sickness?" She cupped her cheek in one hand, sitting cross-legged on the carpet and staring up at the holograph. It showed a very dull brain diagram.

"That's the common term. The official name is Bioelectric Suppression Psychosis."

"I've never heard of it."

"It's very rare. It happens whenever a gifted Lunar chooses not to use their gift for an extended period of time. The only cure they know of is . . . well, to start using the gift again." Jacin's jaw was tight as he swiveled the holograph one way and then the other. "It doesn't come up very often, though, because why would a gifted Lunar forgo using their gift?" He glanced at her, and he seemed concerned, but not judgmental. He had never once, since Winter had told him of her conviction, tried to persuade her to change her mind.

"And what will it do?" she said, leaning back against the sofa. "This Lunar sickness?"

His shoulders drooped. "It will make you go crazy."

She tilted her head to one side and refrained from laughing, but only barely. "Well, I'm *already* crazy, so that doesn't sound so bad at all."

His lip twitched, but the smile was halfhearted at best. "I'm serious, Winter. People who suffer from it have frequent hallucinations. Sometimes bad ones. Being chased or attacked. Seeing . . . monsters."

Her playfulness drooped and she inspected the brain diagram, but it was just a brain. How frightening could that be?

"I already have nightmares and I survive them just fine," she said. "I'll survive this too."

Jacin hesitated. "I just want you to be ready. And ..." He fixed his eyes on her. "If ever you change your mind, I'll understand. Everyone would understand. You don't have to do this, Winter. You can manipulate people without being cruel, you know."

She shook her head. "I didn't think I was being cruel when I pulled that woman back from the ledge."

Jacin lowered his eyes.

"It has to be this way," said Winter. "I will accept this side effect. I will accept any amount of monsters my mind wants to give me, but I will not become a monster myself."

SHE WAS BEGINNING TO THINK THAT JACIN HAD ONLY BEEN trying to frighten her with all that sickness and psychosis talk. Five months had passed and she felt more grounded than ever—more in control of her decisions and willpower than she'd felt her whole life. Her thirteenth birthday was on the horizon, and her choice to live only by the skills that did not require manipulation had made her more aware of what those skills were.

Politeness, it turned out, was almost as effective when you wanted someone to do something for you. And kindness went further toward lasting admiration than any amount of mind control.

Word was spreading, too, about her lack of a gift. Though no one could call her a shell, it was becoming apparent that her Lunar abilities were inferior to the other sons and daughters of Artemisia's families. Some thought it a shame that their beloved princess was turning out to be so weak-minded, but others, she sensed, weren't so easily fooled by Winter's failings. The servants had started to give her appreciative smiles whenever she passed them. The looks of fear that she noticed in her stepmother's presence ceased to exist around Winter, and this alone made her happier—and stronger—than any amount of tutoring had ever done.

There were changes, too, in how members of Artemisia's aristocracy acted around her, though Winter sensed it had less to do with her gift and more to do with the growth spurt that had finally arrived, forcing the seamstresses to work overtime to keep her in hemlines that reached the floor and sleeves that didn't ride up her forearms.

"Her Highness is growing into a fine lady indeed," she had heard one of the thaumaturges say in court, and though the queen had snorted her disagreement, Winter had seen multiple conferring nods before she bashfully lowered her head. "Of course, no beauty could ever compete with yours, My Queen," the thaumaturge had continued, "but we will all be proud to have such a beautiful princess in our midst. She does our court proud, I think."

"She will do our court, and this family, proud," Levana had said derisively, "when she learns to control her glamour like a proper member of the gentry. Until then, she is nothing but a disappointment." She'd cut a glower at Winter. "To me, and no doubt to her father."

Winter had squirmed in her seat, embarrassed.

But it had not changed her decision.

Besides, Winter's instincts told her Levana was wrong. Her father *would* have been proud.

As for Levana herself, Winter couldn't help but wonder if it was jealousy that had prompted her to lash out. Except, jealousy of what? That someone had called her beautiful, when everyone knew that Queen Levana was the most beautiful of all?

Absurd.

THE QUEEN—WHO HAD NEVER ACTED WARMLY TOWARD WIN-ter, even when she'd been a child—grew even colder in the weeks that followed. Always watching Winter with wary eyes, her red lips twisted in annoyance. Winter couldn't guess why Levana was inspecting her. She had very little concept of what she looked like, other than what Jacin told her and the compliments others paid. Mirrors had been banned in Artemisia since before her father's death.

"You are looking lovely as ever, Your Highness," said Provost Dunlin, brushing a kiss against Winter's hand. She pulled herself from her thoughts and forced herself not to recoil. Though the gala being held in the great hall was crowded and loud with music and laughter, she knew her stepmother was always near and always watching. She would not be pleased to see Winter spurning the court's respect. No matter how gross and slimy some of them made her feel.

"You are gracious as ever, Provost Dunlin," she said, and though she smiled, it was a reserved one.

"My son has been paying you many compliments since we saw you at your birthday celebration," he said, waving his son over. Alasdair was a little older than Jacin, but shorter and significantly rounder, and he could claim about as much charm as his father.

He grinned at Winter, though, as if he were entirely unaware of this fact, and kissed her hand as well.

"A pleasure to see you again, Alasdair," said Winter.

"The pleasure is *all* mine." Alasdair's gaze slipped down to Winter's chest, and her gut tightened.

She ripped her hand out of his grip—but her disgust was momentary. Another second and she was flushed with satisfaction at the compliment, pleased with the flattery. She *was* maturing, and it was nice to know that the handsome, eligible men of the court were taking notice . . .

Winter had to excuse herself to keep from turning into a stammering fool. She glanced up at her stepmother, who was watching her curiously, even as Head Thaumaturge Sybil Mira prattled on about something or other.

Queen Levana raised her eyebrow, and Winter hastened a curtsy in her direction before slipping out of the hall.

The feelings of flattery fell off her shoulders, slowly at first, then faster and faster until all that was left was a twist of loathing.

That filthy scum had been manipulating her. *Her.* Though she expected glamours from the court, only the queen and her thaumaturges ever dared to influence Winter's emotions. Alasdair hadn't even been particularly subtle about it, which repulsed Winter more, knowing how easily he'd caught her unprepared. She shuddered, feeling more violated than she would have imagined a basic mind trick could make her feel. She knew that some Lunars were able to put up barriers around their minds, but it took practice and a skill that she didn't possess. She *hated* this court. She hated the lies and the fraud of it all.

"*Winter?*"

She halted.

The corridor was quiet here, though not completely deserted as women came and went from the washroom. Palace guards stood statue-like along the walls. She let her gaze travel over the lines of their faces, thinking maybe Jacin's father, Garrison Clay, was among them—but no. She did not know any of these men.

Winter...

She shivered. Her breaths turned to tatters.

"Your Highness, are you all right?" asked one of the servants who stood nearby.

Ignoring her, Winter took off running in the direction of the voice.

It was him. *It was him.*

She skidded around a corner, away from the private wing of the royal family, where she'd last seen him alive, and toward the guard quarters. The place where her father had lived before Winter was born. Before Levana had claimed Evret Hayle as her husband and tied their fates together forever.

Winter...

His voice rumbling and warm, just how she remembered.

Winter...

She saw his open smile. Remembered how tall he was, how

strong. How he could throw her into the air and catch her every time.

Winter… Winter…

"Winter!"

She gasped and spun around just as Jacin grabbed her elbow. She blinked the daze away. Looked back down the corridor, past the guard quarters, toward the servant halls.

Empty.

"What are you doing here?"

She met Jacin's eyes again. He was looking at her gown, frowning. "Why aren't you at the gala?"

"I heard him," she said, taking Jacin's hand into both of hers. Gripping so hard that part of her feared she would crush his fingers, but he didn't even flinch.

"Who?"

"My father." Her voice splintered. "He was here. He was calling to me and I … I followed him and … and …"

Her heart rate began to slow. Realization crept through the bewilderment at the same moment that Jacin's confusion turned to concern.

Releasing him, she pressed a palm to her own forehead. No fever. She wasn't ill.

Before she had time to be frightened of what it meant, he was holding her, telling her that it would be all right. He was there. He would always be there.

That was the first of the hallucinations.

They kept coming.

They got worse.

Hungry beasts crawled out of the shadows in the night, scratching at the floor beneath her bed.

Bodies hung from the chandeliers over the tables in the dining hall.

A necklace of jewels would tighten around her neck, strangling her.

Usually Jacin was there, as he'd been all her life. He would make light of it and force her to laugh about the absurdity of whatever trick her mind was playing. He would talk her through each episode with his steady rationality, leaving no room for her to doubt his words. He would hold her and let her cry, and it was during one of these embraces when Winter realized with all the force and clarity of a solar flare—

She was in love with him. She had always, always been in love with him.

"I BROUGHT YOU SOMETHING," SAID JACIN, SMILING IMPISHLY when he spotted her. He was sprawled out on a bench in the gardens, his legs stretched out before him. It seemed he would never stop growing, even though his legs and arms no longer fit his body.

He was holding a white box that was emblazoned with the seal of Winter's favorite candy maker.

Her eyes widened. "Petites?"

"Mom took me for new boots this morning and I made her stop for some."

Winter hopped up onto the bench, sitting on its back so that her feet were tucked under Jacin's knee. Though the biodomes of Luna were temperature- and climate-controlled, there was always an extra chill beside the lake, warranting the closeness. She did not hesitate, as soon as the box was open, to pop one of her favorite candies into her mouth. The sweet-sour burst of apples melted across her tongue.

"S'pose you wan' one?" she said through her full mouth, pretending resentment as she held the box out for Jacin.

He smirked. "So generous, *Your Highness.*"

She wrinkled her nose at him and took another bite.

There had been a time—right after she'd realized how hopelessly in love with her best friend she was—when she had become awkward and reserved. When she had thought that she must become a lady when she was near him, as she was expected to be in the presence of any suitor ... should she ever *have* a suitor. She smiled demurely when he made a joke and she touched him only timidly and she sat like a proper princess when they were together.

That time had lasted for about three hours, until Jacin had given her a strange look and asked what was wrong with her.

There was no point in pretending to be someone else now. Jacin knew every one of her secrets, every habit and every flaw. There would be no hiding them, and besides, those three hours had served only to make him uncomfortable, not enamored.

A cold voice cut through their candy devouring, shooting a tinge of anxiety along Winter's spine.

"Winter."

A single word, her own name, that brought more dread with it than a thousand threats.

Jacin jumped to his feet, swiping any candy bits off his mouth as he bowed to the queen.

Winter was slower to follow, but she, too, lowered into a curtsy as her tongue dug out bits of candy from between her teeth.

"Hello, Stepmother," she said.

The queen's glare was focused on Jacin. "You are dismissed, Jacin. Go find some way to be useful."

"Yes, Your Majesty," he said, still in his bow, and a second later he was marching away from them, back toward the palace. The stiffness to his stride made Winter curious if he was mirroring the strut of the guards or if Levana was controlling his limbs.

"Did you need something, Stepmother?"

Levana stared at her for a long time.

A very long time.

Winter could read nothing behind her glamour, her placid expression, her breathtaking beauty. She had heard some rumors lately that *she*, Winter, the gangly princess with the unruly hair, might someday surpass the queen's beauty. She laughed every time she heard such nonsense, knowing that it could be only empty flattery.

Finally, one side of Levana's lips curved upward. Maybe it was meant to be comforting, but it failed.

"Come with me, Winter."

She turned and headed back toward the palace without waiting to see if Winter would follow, because of course she would.

"You are spending too much time with that boy," Levana said as they stepped beneath the portico overhang and back into the bright-lit corridors of the palace. "You are getting older. You are no longer a child, and soon you will have suitors and perhaps even requests for marriage. You must be aware of propriety and expectations. That is your role in this family. That is the part you will play on behalf of the crown."

Winter kept her eyes focused on the floor. Nothing the queen was saying was news to her, but she had never broached the subject so openly. She *did* know what was expected of her, and marrying the son of a palace guard wasn't it. She ignored the fact that Levana herself had married a man from the working class when she'd been just a princess. Winter's father. A lowly palace guard himself.

The sneers and derision from the court continued even to this day, thirteen years after their marriage and four years after her father's death. It was a mistake that Winter would not be allowed to make for herself.

She would marry for political gain.

Jacin would go off and become a doctor and she might never see him again.

"Of course, Stepmother," she said. "Jacin is only a friend."

It was the truth. He was a friend, albeit one she would cut out her heart for.

Levana took her to the elevator and they rode it to the top

floor, to the queen's solar. A private place that Winter had rarely entered.

The room was beautiful—the highest place in all of Artemisia. The walls were made of glass and she could see the entire city, all the way to the walls of the dome and beyond into the desolate landscape of Luna. Far off on the horizon, she spotted the glow of the other nearby sectors.

It occurred to Winter for the first time how odd it was that her stepmother was alone. No thaumaturge loitering at her elbow. No simpering member of the court trying to earn her favor. Only a single guard was posted at the solar's door, and Levana sent him away.

Winter's stomach began to churn.

"Master Gertman tells me that you have not been improving in your lessons," said Levana, floating around a desk. "In fact, he says that you have not shown any sign of the Lunar gift in nearly a year."

Winter felt a sting of betrayal, though she knew it wasn't fair. The tutor was doing his job, and keeping the queen apprised of Winter's progress was a part of it.

Her tutor could not be blamed for Winter's choices.

Lowering her gaze, Winter did her best to look embarrassed. "It's true. I don't know what happened. I thought things were going well, but then ... well, there was that suicide. You remember? The servant who threw herself into the fountain?"

"What of it?"

Winter shrugged sadly. "I tried to stop her once before. I used my gift to bring her away from the throne room ledge and it worked. I thought I'd done so well. But then . . . after she died, it was as though my gift began to weaken." She frowned and shook her head. "I don't know what's wrong with me. I try. I try so hard. But it's like . . . it's like my gift is broken."

To her surprise, tears were starting behind her lashes.

Quite the actress she was becoming.

Levana sneered. She did not look even remotely sympathetic. "I had hoped you would progress well and become a useful member of this court, but it seems that you might take after your father after all." She paused. "You are aware that he was not adept at his gift, either."

Winter nodded. "Guards never are."

She had no idea if her mother—her biological mother—had been skilled with her gift. No one ever spoke of her, and she knew better than to ask.

"But we do know, don't we, that you are not as talentless as your father, because Master Gertman tells me that at one point you showed marvelous promise. In fact, he feels that you were once one of his most outstanding students, and he is as baffled as anyone over your current lack of ability. I wonder if this isn't all due to some . . . psychological trauma. Perhaps pertaining to that suicide?"

"Maybe, but I don't know how to fix it. Maybe I need to see a doctor rather than a tutor." Winter barely smothered her own smirk. A *doctor.* What might they prescribe for the girl who was going crazy, who heard monsters clawing at her door nearly every night?

But she would not mention that. She knew what was wrong with her. She knew how to make the visions stop. But she wouldn't give in to them. She was stronger than the monsters.

"No," said Levana. "I have another idea, Princess. A bit of added motivation, to assist with your studies."

She opened a drawer, smiling serenely. Every movement was graceful and precise. The queen moved like a dancer, always. So controlled. So lovely to watch, even now, despite the cruelty that Winter knew lay beneath her beauty.

She waited, expecting a lesson plan or some trivial instructions for practicing her gift.

Instead, the queen produced a knife.

The handle was carved from milky crystal and the blade was obsidian black. Like her stepmother, it was both threatening and exquisite. Winter's stomach dropped. Her head spun with alarm, but her feet were cemented to the carpet. "Stepmother?"

"You will learn to use your gift, Winter. You will not embarrass me and this crown any more than you already have." Pacing toward her, Levana held out the knife, handle first.

It took a while, but finally Winter forced herself to take it. Her hand was shaking, but she knew that she took the knife of her own will. She was not being coerced.

Not yet.

She had seen this scene play out dozens of times in the throne room. Criminals being sentenced to self-inflicted death.

"I don't understand."

"You are a very pretty child." Levana's expression remained

poised. Winter's arm still trembled. "We would not want to ruin that prettiness, now would we?"

Winter swallowed.

"Manipulate me, Winter. Go ahead."

"What?" she squeaked, certain she'd heard wrong. She'd only practiced on malleable servants in the past. She wasn't sure she could manipulate her stepmother even if she tried—and she wasn't going to try. She *couldn't*, not after working so hard to free herself of her Lunar instincts.

But what was the queen planning?

Images of her own throat being slit flashed through Winter's thoughts.

Her heart pounded.

"Prove that you are capable of a simple little manipulation," said Levana. "That you aren't a waste of my time and my protection. That you aren't the mockery of a princess the people of Artemisia believe you are. Just one little tiny manipulation, and ... I will let you go."

Winter looked down at the knife in her hand.

"Or," Levana continued, her tone sharpening, "if you fail, I will give you a new reason to practice your glamour. I will give you something to *hide*. Believe me, I know how strong that motivation can be. Do you understand?"

Winter did not understand.

She nodded anyway.

Her fingers tightened around the cool handle.

"Go on, then. I will even let you choose what manipulation you will perform. A glamour. An emotion. Make me take that knife back from you if you can. I won't fight you." Levana's smile was patient, almost maternal, if Winter had known what a maternal smile looked like.

It took a long, long time for the smile to fade.

A long, long time for Winter to consider her choice.

Her decision.

Her vow.

I will never use my gift. Not ever again.

"I'm sorry," Winter whispered around her dry throat. "I cannot."

The queen held her gaze. Passive at first, before Winter saw fury spark in her eyes, an anger that burned hot with loathing. But it soon faded, smothered with mere disappointment.

"So be it."

Winter flinched as her hand began to move of its own accord. She slammed her eyes shut against Levana's detached expression and saw the vision again. A deep cut in her throat. Blood spilling across the floor.

Her breath caught as the tip of the blade grazed her neck. Her body went rigid.

But the knife didn't cut her throat. It continued up, up, until the sharp point settled against the corner of her right eye.

Her gut twisted. Her pulse thundered.

She gasped as the blade cut into the soft flesh beneath her eye and was dragged slowly down her cheek. She could feel tears welling behind her eyelids from the stinging-hot pain, but she kept her eyes shut and refused to let them fall.

The blade stopped at her jaw and her hand lowered, taking the knife with it.

Winter gulped down a shuddering breath, dizzy with horror, and opened her eyes.

She was not dead. She had not lost an eye. She could feel blood dripping down her cheek and throat and catching on the collar of her dress, but it was only a single cut. It was only blood.

She blinked rapidly, dispelling any tears before they could betray her, and met her stepmother's hardened glare.

"Well?" Levana said through her teeth. "Would you like to try again before your beauty is marred further?"

Beauty, thought Winter. Of course. It meant so much to the queen, and so very little to her. The pain she could tolerate. The scar she could accept.

A new resolve straightened her spine. She would not allow the queen to win this battle. She refused to lose herself to the queen's mind games.

"I cannot," she said again.

The knife came to her face again, drawing another parallel line beside the first. This time, she kept her eyes open. She was no longer afraid of crying, though the blood felt like warm, thick tears on her cheek.

"And now?" Levana said. "Go on, Winter. A simple manipulation. Prove your worth to this court."

Winter held her gaze. Her stepmother's face had lost its calm facade. She was openly livid. Even her shoulders were trembling with restrained rage.

They both knew this was no longer about a princess making a mockery of the royal family. Levana must have sensed the quiet defiance brewing inside her.

The queen could make anyone do *anything*. She had only to think it, and her will was done.

But not this. She could not force Winter to do this.

It was a struggle for Winter to keep a proud smile from her face as she said firmly, "I will not."

Levana snarled and the knife rose again.

WHEN THE QUEEN RELEASED HER, WINTER REFUSED TO RUN back to her chambers. She walked like royalty, head high and feet clipping steadily on the marble. She didn't even consider using her glamour to hide the three gashes and the blood that dripped down her neck, staining her dress. She was proud. Her wound was proof that she had been to battle and survived.

People stopped to stare, but no one asked about the three cuts in her flesh. No one stopped her. Her guards, sworn to defend their princess at all costs, said nothing.

The queen would be proven wrong. Winter's skin would be permanently marred, but she would not let the scars bully her into submission. The wounds would become her armor, and a constant reminder of her victory.

She might be broken. She might be *crazy*. But she would not be defeated.

When she reached the wing to her private quarters, she drew up short.

Jacin was waiting for her outside her chamber doors. Beside him stood Head Thaumaturge Sybil Mira in her pristine white coat.

Jacin was staring at the ground, his face tense.

Sybil was smiling, a hand on Jacin's shoulder. And when they both looked at Winter—

Jacin appeared shocked, first, though it fast turned to horror, while Sybil . . .

Winter shuddered.

Sybil Mira looked not surprised at all, and not the tiniest bit sympathetic. Levana must have told her what she was planning. Maybe it had even been Sybil's idea—Winter knew that the head thaumaturge had a great amount of influence over the queen.

"What happened?" Jacin said, shrugging off Sybil's hand and rushing toward her. He went to place his palm over her bloodied cheek but hesitated. He covered his hand with his sleeve first before pressing the material against her.

"Shall I call for a medic, Your Highness?" said Sybil, folding her hands into her own sleeves.

"I'm fine, thank you. You can step aside so that I might retire to my quarters."

"If you are sure I cannot be of service." Sybil did step aside, even bowed her head, but an amused smile lingered on her lips as Winter brushed past her. Jacin stayed with her, step for step, applying pressure to the cheek that she had not dared touch. It hadn't stopped stinging, and the pain was a persistent reminder of what she had endured and the choices she had made. She would never regret those choices, scars or no.

"Who did this?" Jacin demanded as Winter shoved through her bedroom door, leaving her personal guard outside.

"I did, of course," she said, to which he stared, aghast. She snorted bitterly. "*My hand* did."

His eyes blazed, full of murder. "The queen?"

She had only to stay silent to confirm it.

Rage cascaded over his face, but he turned away too fast for Winter to appreciate the depth of it. He pulled her into the powder room and set her on the edge of the tub. Within minutes, he had cleaned the wounds and applied a generous amount of healing salve.

"I shouldn't have left you," he muttered through gnashed teeth as he applied a makeshift bandage of cotton strips. Winter was impressed that he was able to keep his hands so calm, while his expression was so furious.

He would make a great doctor.

"You had no choice," she said. "Neither of us did."

"Why would she do this to you? Is she jealous?"

She met his flashing gaze. "Why would the queen be jealous of me?"

His anger sizzled. "How does this benefit her?"

"She said that she wanted me to learn to use my gift, so that I would stop making a mockery of the crown. She thought that if I . . . she thought this would motivate me to learn to use my glamour."

Understanding dawned on his face. "To hide the scars."

She nodded. "I also think she wanted to remind me that I'm . . . that I belong to her. That I'm nothing but a pawn in her game, to be used as she sees fit." She slumped, letting go of the composure she'd fought so hard for. "But I am not her pawn. I refuse to be."

Jacin stood with his hands strangling a towel for a long moment, looking like he wanted to keep working, keep cleaning, keep bandaging, but he'd already done all he could. Finally, with a huff, he sat beside her on the tub's edge. His anger was fading, replaced with guilt. "If she thinks you're intentionally not using your gift, she might see it as rebellious." His tone was subdued now, though his fingers showed no mercy to the towel. "I think she is jealous. Because people like you. They respect you. And you don't have to manipulate them for it."

"I'm not trying to do anything," said Winter. "I just . . . I just don't want to be like her. Like them!"

Jacin smiled, but it was tired. "Exactly. What could be more threatening than that?"

She sagged further, settling her face into her hands, careful not to press against her stinging cheek. Then she frowned and peered up at Jacin from the corner of her eye. "What did Thaumaturge Mira want?"

He inhaled sharply. For a moment she thought he wouldn't say anything, but finally he spoke. "She came to tell me that I would need to find new housing accommodations if my plan is to stay in Artemisia until my internship begins next year."

Her brow creased. "New housing? Why wouldn't you stay here in the palace?"

"Because my parents are leaving."

She straightened.

"My father's been transferred to one of the outer sectors, as a security guard."

Her heart thumped. "A demotion? But . . . why?"

Jacin started to shake his head, but then stopped and met her gaze, and instantly Winter knew why.

She was spending too much time with this boy.

She was *in love* with this boy.

And that would not fit into Levana's perfectly constructed plans for her. That could cause problems for the queen and whatever alliance she planned to cement using Winter's hand as the purchase price.

Send his family away, and the boy would leave too.

She pressed a hand over her mouth.

"My parents don't seem to mind," said Jacin. "I think they're both relieved to be getting out of Artemisia. All the politics." *And the manipulations*, he didn't say, but didn't have to.

"You're leaving me," she breathed.

Jacin pursed his lips. He looked terrified as he snaked his hand beneath her arm, entwining their fingers together. Their hands fit like a lock and key. It had been years since they had simply held hands, and she wished they had never stopped.

"No," he said. "I'm not leaving you."

She raised her eyes. There was a determined set to his jaw that surprised her. "But where will you go, if you can't stay here?" she asked. "And besides, when your internship starts you'll have to leave anyway, and then . . ."

"Thaumaturge Mira gave me another option. Or ..." He gulped. "The queen gave me another option. They've invited me to join the palace guard. I could begin training as early as next week."

Her eyes widened and she yanked her hand away. "No. *No.* Jacin, you can't. What about being a doctor? What about—"

"I could stay with you, Winter. I could stay here in the palace."

"Until they send you off to one of the outer sectors, you mean."

"They won't do that."

"How can you be sure?"

"Because I'll be the most loyal guard Her Majesty has ever known."

His expression was withdrawn. Haunted.

Winter's hand went slack in his grip.

Levana would threaten her, maybe even threaten her *life.*

Maybe she already had, which was how they'd gotten Jacin to consider it in the first place.

He would do anything they asked if he thought he was protecting her.

"You know how we all take aptitude tests in year fourteen?" Jacin said, unable to look at her. "I tested high for a potential pilot role. Thaumaturge Mira said she could use me as her personal guard and transporter."

"No, Jacin. You can't. If you do this, you'll never be able to get out."

Releasing her hand, he stood up and began pacing the powder room floor. "I don't know what else to do. I can't leave you here, especially now, after this." He waved a hand toward her cheek and

Winter placed her palm over the washcloth. The blood hadn't yet soaked through.

"I don't want you to be a guard, Jacin. Not after ... what happened to my father ..." Her voice cracked.

Killed by a thaumaturge, with no hope at all of defending himself. Because he was weak. Jacin was weak. *She* was weak.

Against the queen and her court, they had no hope at all.

Pawns. Just pawns.

"I think you should go," she said.

He stared at her, hurt.

"With your parents, I mean. I think you should go with them. In a year, apply for your medical internship and be the doctor you've always wanted to be. This is what you want, Jacin. To help people. To *save* people."

"Winter, I ..."

She gasped, her gaze catching on the wall over Jacin's shoulder. A frosted-glass window was there, letting in enough daylight to make the entire room glow rosy and gold.

But the light was being blotted out.

By blood.

Crimson, thick, sticky blood, oozing from the mortar that held in the glass windowpane, dripping thickly down the sides and pooling on the sill.

She started to tremble. Jacin spun around, following the look. He was silent a long moment before saying, "What? What's wrong?" He looked back at her.

Something splattered on Winter's forearm.

She tilted her head back.

The ceiling.

Covered in it.

Red, everywhere. The tang of iron on her tongue. Her mouth was thick with it.

Her chest convulsed with panic and nausea. She shoved herself to her feet and spun in a full circle, watching as the blood came down from the ceiling, soaking into the gilt wallpaper and wood moldings, puddling on the tile floor.

"Winter. What is it? What are you seeing?"

The blood reached her toes.

She turned and shoved past him, scrambling out of the powder room.

"Winter!"

Her bedroom was no better. She froze in the middle of it. Blood had made a waterfall over her bed, staining the linens in crimson, squishing in the carpet beneath her feet. The door into the corridor had a bloodied curtain dripping from the jamb.

No getting through.

No getting away.

She stumbled and teetered on her weak legs, then tripped toward the only escape—the doors that led to the balcony. She heard Jacin screaming behind her, and she hoped he would follow, hoped he would not get stuck here in the suffocating stench, the incessant dripping—

She threw open the doors.

Her stomach hit the protective barrier. Her hands latched on to the rail. The blood kept coming. Pouring out of the bedroom, spilling over the balcony, dribbling down to the garden.

It was the palace. The whole palace was bleeding.

It would fill up the entire lake.

Gasping for air, she hauled one leg up and threw herself over the rail.

Arms locked around her just as her center of balance tilted forward. Her stomach swooped, but Jacin was hauling her back into the room. She shrieked and clawed, demanding that he let her go. If he didn't, she would drown. They would both be swallowed alive—

He wrestled her to the warm, sticky carpet and pinned her wrists to either side of her head.

"Winter, stop!" he cried, leaning down and pressing his cheek against hers in an attempt to soothe her. "It's all right, Winter. You're all right."

She turned her head and snapped her teeth at him. He pulled back far enough that she barely missed his ear. She screamed in frustration, writhing and kicking, but Jacin refused to yield. "You're all right," he whispered, again and again. "I'm here."

Winter had no idea how long the hallucination lasted. How long she struggled, trying to get away from the blood that cascaded over every surface of the room. A room that had once seemed a sanctuary.

Sanctuary.

There was no safe place. Not in Artemisia. Not on all of Luna.

Except—*Jacin.*

When her screams succumbed to hysterical sobbing, Jacin finally allowed his hold to turn from the grip of a jailer to the embrace of her best friend.

"This is why," he whispered, and it occurred to Winter that, at some point, he'd started crying too. "This is why I can't leave you, Winter. This is why I'll never leave."

THE NIGHTMARE CAME AGAIN. AND AGAIN. WEEKS OF IT, incessant.

Gunshots.

Dead eyes.

Blood sprayed on the bedroom walls.

Only, this time, the queen did not simply curl herself against her dead husband and cry and cry and cry.

This time, she took the knife that she had used to stab the thaumaturge and she carved three straight lines into the cheek of Winter's father.

Winter tried so hard to stay strong, knowing that every time she sought out Jacin's security, it would further cement his decision to stay. So she rocked herself in her bed and tried to whisper comfort into her own blankets.

Until the night she could stand it no longer.

He was the only place that was safe.

Her nightclothes still damp from the terrors, she rushed out of her quarters, pretending not to notice the night guard who followed in her wake.

Jacin would hold her. Jacin would comfort her. Jacin would keep the nightmares at bay.

Except—Jacin was gone.

That's what they told her when she arrived, pounding on the apartment door that the Clays had shared with two other families.

He and his family had been transferred the day before and she hadn't even known, he hadn't even told her, he hadn't said good-bye.

Demoted. Transferred. *Gone.*

Shocked and heartbroken, Winter retreated. She wandered blindly back toward the main corridor of the palace.

Gone.

She'd told him to go. She'd believed it would be for the best. It was the only way for him to have a chance at happiness. He had to get away from Artemisia. Away from the queen. Away from *her.*

And yet, she had not believed he would really go.

Jacin.

Her dearest friend.

Her *only* friend.

Just like Selene. Just like her father.

They all left.

"Win—Princess?"

She froze.

Slowly turned.

It was him, but not him.

A hallucination.

Because this could not be her Jacin wearing the pressed uniform of a guard-in-training, his blond hair tucked behind his ears, not quite long enough to be tied back. He stood with his arms stiff at his sides, like he was waiting to carry out orders.

Not a smile.

Not a teasing glint in his eye.

Barely even recognition.

"Jacin," she whispered to the phantom that looked like her best friend.

His Adam's apple bobbed with what looked to be a painful gulp. Then his jaw set and he clicked his heels together awkwardly. His gaze lifted away from her eyes, staring at the wall in the distance with the same vacant expression that all the guards had. The same emptiness.

"Shall I escort you to your quarters ... Princess?"

Every bit the guard.

Winter, by habit, found herself drawing her shoulders back. A defense. She would hide behind politeness and grace.

Every bit the princess.

It was strange, how quickly it started to feel normal.

They had played this game before, she realized. A hundred times they had played it.

He, the loyal guard. She, the princess he must protect.

"Yes," she said, as loudly as her voice would allow. "Thank you ... Sir ... Clay."

A slight shake of his head. "Squire Clay, Your Highness. Guard-in-training."

"Squire Clay." She gulped and slowly turned her back on him, walking dazedly back through the halls.

He followed behind her. Respectful and distant.

Over her shoulder, she dared a nervous smile. "If you aren't too busy with your training later, Squire Clay, I fear I might need rescuing from a pirate."

His eyelid twitched. He did not look at her and he didn't smile—but she caught it, just for a moment. The light entering his eyes.

"It would be my honor, Princess."

The Little Android

MECH6.0 STOOD AGAINST THE HANGAR'S CHARGING WALL, one of hundreds of mute sentinels watching the passengers flutter by with their hovering luggage carts and excited chatter. Before her, the massive *Triton* hunkered imposingly in the center of the hangar, dwarfing the crowd, as greeters scanned the ID chips of their guests and ushered them aboard. A ship's maiden voyage was always a festive occasion, but this one seemed more vibrant than usual, as the *Triton* was about to set the record for largest cruiser ever to be launched. Waiters were passing glasses of champagne to the passengers as they boarded and had their belongings escorted away, women were donning their finest kimonos and *hanbok* and cocktail gowns, and a live orchestra had even been hired for the entertainment.

Against the festive backdrop, the ship itself appeared menacing to Mech6.0, with its polished metal paneling and small round windows glinting beneath the hangar's lights. It hadn't seemed so big when she'd been working on it, running wires and soldering frame pieces and screwing on protective paneling. At the time, she'd almost felt like she and her brethren were a part of this enormous metal beast. A thousand tiny moving pieces making one efficient machine. But now the result of their labors was ready to set sail, and she no longer felt attached to it at all. Only dwarfed by its magnificence.

And perhaps a little abandoned.

As the guests giggled and chattered and discussed how many space cruises they'd been on before, and the beauty of the new ship, and all the comforts the ads had promised, Mech6.0 watched and listened and felt the thrumming of electricity warming her insides.

"All aboard! *Triton* to debark in ten minutes. *Ten-minute warning!* All aboard!"

The crowd dwindled. The monotonous beep of the ID scanners trickled to an occasional sparse rhythm. One ramp rose up to the ship, closing with a thud that vibrated through the hangar's floors and up Mech6.0's treads—then two ramps, then three.

"Wait!" A woman's voice echoed through the hangar, followed by the hasty padding of feet. "We're coming! We're here," she said, breathlessly dragging a young girl behind her.

"Just in time," said one of the greeters, scanning the woman's wrist. "On up you go."

She thanked him profusely and pushed a lock of messy hair off her face. Retightening her grip on the girl's wrist, she gave her floating hover cart a push and jogged up the ramp.

Mech6.0's scanner caught on something small and flat as it dislodged from the young girl's backpack and fluttered down toward the greeter, who didn't notice. Her programming alerted her to the incongruence, and she shuffled through proper responses.

If she found something that a human had lost, or that had been stolen, she was to return it.

But she was not to interrupt the boarding process, particularly once the captain had called for the ship to be sealed and prepared for takeoff.

As soon as the ramp began to rise off the ground, Mech6.0 knew that her opportunity to return the item to the girl was lost. She kept her scanner pinned to that small card until the ramp tilted up and up and the card slipped off and came spinning and twirling through the air. Past the greeters who were already pulling back the ropes for the ticketing lines, past the statue-like forms of her brothers and sisters, past the hired musicians, until it landed against Mech6.0's own treads and stuck there.

The roar of the ship's engines pulled her attention back toward the *Triton*, and her scanner lifted up and up as the hangar's ceiling began to open. The gears cranked and rumbled, revealing first a teasing hint of moonlight and then a gap filled with stars. Then, slowly, an entire galaxy opened up above the hangar.

It was beautiful. Mech6.0 loved this moment—anticipated it every time they completed a new project and prepared to send it off into the sky. That short glimpse of the galaxy was not like anything else in her world, a world that was normally filled with mechanics and tools and the dark, shadowy spaces inside a quiet, lonely spaceship.

The galaxy, she had come to understand, was vast and bright and endless.

A surge of electricity startled Mech6.0, like a spark straight to the processor that was protected beneath her torso paneling. Startled, she turned her head to peer down the line of identical androids—to her left first and then to her right.

Not only did they not seem to have felt the sudden surge, but none of them were even looking up at the overhead sky. Stiff and uncurious, they remained staring straight ahead.

Mech6.0 returned her attention to the ship as it rose up off the ground and hovered on the magnetic field beneath the hangar's roof. The thrusters burned white-hot for a moment, and the ship rose higher and higher, breaching the ceiling before it swooped gracefully up toward the starry night sky and disappeared.

As the cheers died out and the crowd began to disperse, the musicians began packing up their instruments. The enormous ceiling lowered in on itself and clanged, shutting them in tight again, and not long after the space had cleared, the lights shut off with three loud bangs, plunging the mech-droids into pitch blackness and silence.

Four minutes passed, in which Mech6.0 was still remembering the view of the stars, which she knew were somehow always there and yet always out of her reach, before she remembered the girl's lost card.

Her sensor light flickered on, creating a circle of pale blue light around her. Her neighbors swiveled their heads, perhaps in curiosity, but more likely in disapproval, but she ignored them as she cast the scanner down toward her treads. Extending her arm, she pinched the card between her padded grippers and held it up.

It was thin but stiff, like a sheet of aluminum, and on one side was scrolled in fancy, shiny lettering: *Celebrity Holos, Collector's Set, 39th Edition, 124 T.E.*

She turned the card over and a flickering, pale holograph rose up from it and began to rotate. She was looking at the likeness of a teenage boy who seemed vaguely familiar, with shaggy black hair and a relaxed smile.

Mech6.0 felt her fan stutter in an odd way, and wondered if there might be something wrong with her internals. If this kept up, she was going to have to alert the maintenance mechanic. But this thought was fleeting as she opened the hollow storage compartment on her abdomen and tucked the holographic card inside. Maybe she would return it one day, she considered, although her statistical calculations told her that it would probably never happen.

TWO DAYS PASSED BEFORE MECH6.0 WAS GIVEN A NEW AS-signment, along with fourteen of her fellow mech-droids. She stood in line with the others as Tam Sovann, the shipyard's owner, paced around the project's underside, inspecting the landing gear and discussing the plans with their new client, Ochida Kenji. Ochida-shìfu was a middle-aged man with a little facial hair and a very expensive-looking suit. His ship was a recreational yacht, luxurious and spacious enough for those who could afford luxury and space. Mech6.0 scanned the ship while she waited to receive her instructions, plugging the information into her database. A 94 T.E. Orion Classic, one of the most expensive ships of its day and one of the most popular for refurbishing over the past decade. The name *Child of the Stars* had been painted near its nose, but had faded with time.

"The body is in good shape, Ochida-shìfu," said Tam, "but we're looking at a full engine rebuild to bring it up to code, and remodeling the interior to include all the most modern amenities will require that we take it down to the paneling. I am confident we can meet your deadline, though, while maintaining the ship's original character."

"Your reputation speaks for itself," said Ochida Kenji. "I have no doubt she's in good hands."

"Excellent. Let me introduce you to the engineer who will be heading up your rebuild. This is Wing Dataran, one of our brightest stars."

Like a programmed reflex, Mech6.0's sensor swiveled toward the group. Though Wing Dataran had been working at the shipyard for almost a year, their paths had never crossed. The *Triton* had been much too big, and she had never been assigned to any of his smaller projects.

But she had known about him. She had connected him to the

net database the first time she'd seen him—as she did with all of her human employers—but something about him had kept that profile in the forefront of her memory. A young hardware engineer, he had been hired straight out of tech-university, where he had specialized in spaceship engines with additional concentrations in internal design and mechanical systems.

For reasons that didn't fully compute, she frequently found her sensor seeking him out in the crowd of androids and technicians, and every time she spotted him, her fan did that strange little jump, like it had when she'd seen the holograph. Only now did she realize that there were similarities between Dataran and the holographic figure. Not only in how all humans were similar, with their two eyes and protruding noses and five-fingered, fleshy hands. But Dataran and the boy in the holograph both had pronounced cheekbones and slender frames that suggested a particular grace. And they had both made her fan sputter.

What did that mean?

Dataran unclipped a portscreen from his tool belt after they'd finished their introductions. "I've already begun working up some initial plans," he said, showing something on the screen to Ochida, "but I want to discuss with you any special requests you might have before I finalize them. Particularly those new luxury features, which can put added stress on the engine. I want to make sure it's fully . . ."

He trailed off, eyes snagging on something over Ochida's shoulder. Everyone followed his gaze, including Mech6.0.

A girl had emerged from the ship, wearing an orange-and-white kimono.

"Ah, there you are, my princess," said Ochida, waving her down toward them. "Have you been inside the ship this whole time?"

"Just saying good-bye," said the girl, floating down the ramp. "When I see her again, it will be like meeting an entirely new ship."

"Don't be ridiculous. You and I are going to be involved every step of the way, making sure my little girl is given precisely the ship she wants." Ochida wrapped an arm around her shoulders, before raising an eyebrow at Tam Sovann. "If that isn't a problem?"

"Of course not. We welcome your input and want to make sure you're fully satisfied with the end result."

"Good, good. Gentlemen, this is my daughter, Miko. I may have my opinions and my wallet, but she's the one you really have to please with this rebuild. Think of it as her ship, not mine."

Miko dipped her head respectfully toward the shipyard owner and Dataran, who stood straighter when her eyes met his.

"This is a very busy place," said Miko, glancing around at the ships of varying sizes and states of construction, at all the men and women and androids scurrying around their landing gears and wheeling enormous toolboxes back and forth. "How can you keep it all straight?"

"Each project has a separate crew assigned to it," said Tam, "and they'll stay focused on that one project from beginning to completion. We find it's the most efficient use of our workers."

Her gaze settled on Dataran again. "And you will be on our crew?"

There was a tinge of color in his cheeks, Mech6.0 noticed. Perhaps it was warmer than usual in the hangar, although she didn't come equipped with atmospheric temperature gauges to tell for sure. "Yes, Ochida-mèi," he stammered. "I'll be your engineer. I'll be the one . . . pleasing . . . er . . ." His flush deepened.

"You can call me Miko," she said with a friendly smile. "I know a little about mechanics myself, but perhaps I'll learn something new from you during this process."

He opened his mouth to reply, but no sound came out.

"Why don't we get these androids started on some of the exterior dismantling," said Tam, "and Dataran, perhaps you could give Ochida-mèi a tour of the shipyard while we sign off on some papers?"

"O-of course," he said, fumbling to replace the portscreen on his belt. He dislodged a small, shiny chain, which he quickly tucked back into his pocket. "If you would like that?"

"I would, very much." As her father nudged her forward, Miko reached for the back of her neck to adjust the hair that was bundled there, and Mech6.0's sensor picked up on something small and dark that suggested an abnormality—a birthmark, perhaps, or a tattoo?

As her processor received its first set of instructions, Mech6.0 claimed a spot near the front of the ship, where she could back out screws while keeping her sensor turned toward the bustling hangar. She watched as Dataran pointed out the various machinery and ship models and tried to guess what he might be telling Ochida Miko about. The purpose of the different tools? The history of the ships? How they had the most efficient system of android labor in any shipyard in the Commonwealth?

She saw him introducing the girl to different mechanics and engineers who they passed.

For a while, they disappeared into the almost-completed WindWalker800, and Mech6.0 could only catch glimpses of them through the cockpit windows. She noticed they were both smiling.

Dataran took Miko through parts storage, the painting room, even past the android charging docks, and while Mech6.0 couldn't hear them, she frequently recognized the dimples of his laughter and noticed how his gazes grew more daring, settling on the girl with increased frequency, just as her gazes settled on him.

By the time Dataran was opening the gate and ushering Miko up onto the platforms that hung suspended over the water supply and refueling tanks, Mech6.0 realized that she had stopped working.

She turned her sensor toward the ship's paneling that had only two screws still fastening it to the hull, then glanced at her brethren beside her. They all had at least three panels already taken down.

This was very odd. Not only her strange fascination with the humans, but that it could overpower her need to complete her task. Perhaps something really was wrong with her.

Yes, she would have to check in with maintenance after this shift.

Then, as she was removing her first panel, someone yelled. Mech6.0 turned in time to see one of the enormous cranes tilt beneath a too-heavy load, its outstretched arm swaying danger-ously for a moment that stretched out for ages before it found the tipping point. The enormous metal arm fell toward the suspended platforms, bolts snapping and cables whipping into the air.

Still on the hanging walkway, Miko screamed.

Dataran pushed her out of the way.

The arm of the crane cracked against his head, the sound reverberating right into Mech6.0's hard plastic shell. He was un-conscious before his body fell into the oil vat below.

Miko screamed again, clinging to the walkway railing. The crane landed hard, and one of the cables flew loose from the ceil-ing. The platform careened to one side, but the remaining cables held.

Mech6.0 did not take the time to process the situation or calculate the best course of action—she was already rolling toward the containers. Around her, people yelled and machin-ery screeched and halted, footsteps thundered and the rickety walkway trembled overhead. Someone called for a ladder or a rope, but Mech6.0 already had her magnets activated to collect the panel screws, and with single-minded precision, she found herself climbing the side of the enormous tank, her grippers spread out against its metal sides, heaving her body upward. It was an awkward climb, one her body was not made for, as her treads banged against the tank and her arms flailed for the next purchase. Her joints strained under her weight. But then she was hauling herself up onto the ledge, which was just barely wide enough for her to stand on.

The vat of oil was black as the night sky without stars. Black and terrifying.

Mech6.0 tipped herself over and went in.

She sank fast, and though she immediately turned her sensor light on to full brightness, it did little to help her. Extending her arms as far as they would go, she searched the bottom of the tank, knowing that he was here somewhere, he was here, he was—

Here.

She tightened her grippers and dragged her body toward him through the thick oil. It was seeping through her paneling now, blocking her input plugs, glugging into the charging inlet. But she had him.

She wrapped her arms around his torso and heaved him upward. He was heavier than she expected and it occurred to her that the bolts connecting her arms to their sockets might not hold, but she kept going. Finding the tank's wall, she planted her prongs against the side again and started to climb. There was no light anymore, no senses at all but the sound of her grippers and the tread bumping into the wall and the weight of his body pressing down onto her as she forced both of them up, up, up . . .

They broke through the surface. Sound crashed into her, more screams and gasps. Then someone was lifting him away, and Mech6.0 barely managed to collapse sensor-facedown onto the tank's ledge before her programming recognized self-destructive behavior and killed the power to her limbs.

She lay there, hollow and helpless, as the oil dripped off her sensor. She began to make out human shapes on the platform and her audio picked up on a discussion of towels and air passageways and lungs and blood on his head and it seemed to take so very long, the oil dulling all her senses, but then he was coughing and vomiting and breathing and the humans were rejoicing and when they had finally wiped enough oil from his face that it was safe for him to open his eyes, Dataran looked around at all the humans first. And then, for the very first time, he looked at her.

DATARAN HAD BEEN TAKEN AWAY TO A HOSPITAL AND MECH6.0 was in the android maintenance office, her limbs being rubbed clean—or as clean as possible—by a man in green coveralls who kept shaking his head.

"These won't be salvageable either," he said, clicking his tongue as he inspected her input plugs. He wasn't doing a particularly good job of cleaning her, Mech6.0 thought, and she was feeling more sluggish and drained by the minute.

It began to occur to her that maybe she couldn't be fixed. That maybe he wouldn't even try.

Sighing, the man spun around on his rolling chair so he could enter something into a netscreen on the wall. Mech6.0 glanced down at her body, her joints and the seams of her paneling stained brownish-black from the oil. At least her vision was clear again, and her processor seemed to be working, if slower than usual.

She was surprised to see a collection of screws still clinging to her side from when she'd been removing the panel from the Orion Classic. She reached her grippers toward them, glad to see that her sensor-gripper coordination was functional as she plucked them off one by one and set them on the mechanic's table. She reached for the final screw and tugged.

Then paused. Then tugged some more. It was not a screw at all, but the link of a chain that had wrapped around to her back. She gave the chain a yank and whatever had magnetically sealed itself to her came loose. She found herself staring at a locket, which she suspected would have been gold if it wasn't blackened by the oil.

Her memory saw Dataran tucking a chain back into his pocket.

This belonged to him.

The mechanic spun back toward her and she hid the locket behind her back. He was eyeing her suspiciously and shaking his head again when the office door opened and the shipyard's owner came strolling in.

"Well?"

The mechanic shook his head. "Its body is ruined. I could spend a couple weeks trying to clean it up, but I frankly don't see the point. Better off just getting a new one."

Tam frowned as he looked the android up and down. "What about the processor, the wiring ... Can it be salvaged?"

"There will probably be some parts we can hold on to for later use. I'll start to dismantle it tomorrow, see what we've got. But as for the processor and personality chip ... that much must have been fritzing even before the oil."

"Why do you say that?"

The mechanic brushed his sleeve across his damp forehead. "You saw how all the other androids reacted when Dataran fell in?"

"I don't think they did anything."

"Exactly. That's what they're supposed to do. Just keep working, not get involved with drama and upsets. What this one did . . . it isn't normal. Something's wrong with it."

A spark flickered inside Mech6.0's head. She'd begun to suspect as much, but to have it confirmed was worrisome.

"What do you think it is?"

"Who knows? You hear stories about this once in a while. Androids whose artificial intelligence reaches a point of learning at which they develop almost human-like tendencies. Unpractical reasoning, near-emotional responses. There are plenty of theories for why it happens, but the important thing is, it isn't good."

"I'm not sure I agree." The owner crossed his arms over his chest. "This mech-droid may have saved Dataran's life today."

"I realize that, and thank the stars. But what will it do next time there's a disturbance? The fact is, an unpredictable android is a dangerous one." He shrugged. "My advice: Either send out the computer for reprogramming, or scrap it entirely."

Pressing his lips into a thin line, Tam let his gaze travel over Mech6.0's body. She squeezed the locket tighter in her three-fingered grasp.

"Fine," Tam said. "But let's worry about it tomorrow. I think we could all use the rest of the night off."

They left her on the table in the mechanic's room, and as the lights of the shipyard thudded into blackness, Mech6.0 realized it was the first night in her existence that she hadn't been plugged into the charging dock.

Because charging her wasn't necessary. Because tomorrow she would be dismantled and put on a shelf somewhere, and the bits of her that weren't worth saving would be sent off to the scrap yard.

Tomorrow she would be gone.

She analyzed those words for a long time, her processor whirring and sputtering around them, trying to calculate the hours and minutes left in her existence before there would be only a black hole where her consciousness had been before.

She wondered if Dataran would give a single thought to the malfunctioning android who had saved his life and been destroyed for it.

Dataran. She had something that belonged to him now. It was in her code to return it to him if she could. She brought the locket up in front of her sensor and scanned its dimensions and the small hinge and the tiny unlocking mechanism. It was a challenge to open with her clumsy prongs, but finally she did—

And the galaxy expanded before her.

The holograph filled up the entire office. The sun and the planets, the stars and the nebulas, asteroids and comets and all the beauty of space contained in that tiny, unimpressive little locket.

Mech6.0 clicked it shut, storing the universe away in its small prison once again.

No. She couldn't stay here. She could not stand to be lost to the

darkness forever, when there was still a whole universe she'd
never seen.

MECH6.0 HAD NEVER BEEN OUTSIDE OF THE SHIPYARD BEFORE,
not since she'd been programmed and built and purchased. She
quickly discovered that the world was chaotic and loud and filled
with so much sensory information she worried that her frazzled
synapses would be fried before she ever reached her destination.

But she tried to focus on the map of New Beijing and the profile she'd discovered on the net as she turned into the first street of
market booths, crowded with barrels of spices and woven blankets that hung from wire racks and netscreens chattering from
every surface.

"Robotic cats, two for the price of one, today only! No shed-
ding, just purring!"

"Depression? Low energy? Infertility? What's your ailment—
we have cures! We even have the newest prevention drops for the
blue fever, tried and true!"

"Plum wine, rice wine, come try a free sample!"

"Big sale on serv-droids, now's the time to upgrade! New
models, just in!"

She kept her sensor down and attempted to look inconspicuous. The net was filled with stories of android theft, and she was
worried that being crushed together with so many humans, she
would soon find herself snatched up and saddled with some new

owner, who would no doubt have her dismantled anyway once they discovered her damage.

Finally, she spotted a nondescript booth just where the market directory had said it would be. The walls were lined with shelves that sagged from their jumble of tools and android parts and outdated portscreens stacked three layers deep.

Mech6.0 rolled up to the table that blocked the entrance. A girl was standing near the back of the booth, wearing thick work gloves and cargo pants, scanning something with a portscreen. She paused and tapped her fingers against the screen, then reshuffled some items on the shelf before scanning another item.

"Pardon . . . me," said Mech6.0, her senses crackling at the effort. She did not have many opportunities to speak at the shipyard, and the long trek had already drained her power source.

The girl glanced toward her. "Oh—sorry! I'll be with you in just a minute." She finished entering whatever data she was working on and clipped the portscreen to her belt. "How can I help you?"

"Looking for . . . Linh Cinder."

"You found her." The girl tilted her head to one side, furrowing her brow. "Is your voice box on the fritz?"

"Whole . . . body," said Mech6.0. "Purchase . . . new?"

It took a moment, but then Linh Cinder nodded. "Oh, sure. I can do that. Is your owner around?"

Mech6.0 felt a sudden drop in power, but was relieved when it was only a temporary loss. Now that she'd found the mechanic, she shut off her net database in order to conserve what energy she could. "No owner."

Linh Cinder's brow furrowed. Her eyes darted to the android dealer across the way. "Oh. I see." She reached for her portscreen again and set it on the table between them, before typing in a few commands. "Well. All right, so I can order up a replacement mech body today, but it usually takes about a week to get here, unless the warehouse downtown has some in stock. You're a 6.0, right? It doesn't look like they have any. Do you mind waiting a week?"

"Can I . . . wait here?"

"Uh . . ." Hesitating, Cinder glanced over her shoulder at the booth, cluttered with machines and toolboxes. Then she shrugged. "Sure, I can probably clear a space for you." Tightening her ponytail, she sat down in the chair that had been pushed beneath the table. "But if you don't have an owner . . . how do you plan on paying for this?"

Paying.

Money. Currency. Univs. To give compensation for goods or services.

Androids did not get paid.

"Trade," said Mech6.0.

"Trade?" Cinder dipped her gaze over Mech6.0's battered form. "For what?"

Mech6.0 opened the compartment in her abdomen. Her prongs found the metal locket on its chain first and wrapped around it.

Her fan slowed—almost stopped.

Releasing the locket, she searched again, and her grippers

emerged with the small holographic card instead. She placed it on the table.

Removing the glove from her right hand, Cinder picked up the card and flipped it over, reading the words on the back before turning it so that the holograph projected from the flat surface.

"A Prince Kai holographic trading card," she muttered, rubbing her brow with her gloved hand. "Because that's all I need." Sighing, she peered at Mech6.0 again. "I'm sorry, but this is only worth about twenty micro-univs. It would barely buy you a screw." She looked truly regretful as she handed the card back. Mech6.0 pinched it gently between her prongs.

"Do you have anything else?"

Her processor pulsed. *The locket.*

But it was not hers. It belonged to Dataran, and she was going to return it to him. When she had her new body. When she saw him again.

Her power source dropped low again. The colors of the world dimmed beyond her sensor's eye.

"Nothing . . . else."

Linh Cinder frowned sympathetically. "Then I'm sorry. I can't help you."

Mech6.0 analyzed the situation again, calculating the potential worth of the locket and the importance that she received a new body, and soon. But despite her logical reasoning telling her that the locket might be valued high enough to complete the trade, there was a new factor involved in the calculation. The value of her one possession—something that had been Dataran's. The value of his smile when she returned it to him.

She knew that the decision was illogical, that she would be returning nothing at all if she didn't get a new body, and yet she still found herself tucking the holographic card against her torso and turning away. Which was when she realized that she had nowhere to go, and besides, she wouldn't make it very far. She spotted the used android dealer down the way, and a darkness settled in her vision, washing all the color away entirely.

Her treads clattered as she started back through the crowd.

"Wait."

Pausing, she spun back to face the mechanic, who was rubbing her fingers against her temple again, leaving a dark smudge on her skin.

"You remind me of a friend of mine. Iko, also an android," she said. Then she added, gesturing to the card, "Plus, my little sister really loves that guy. So . . . here, I think I might have something. Hang on."

Pulling herself from the chair, she headed toward the back of the booth. Mech6.0 waited as Linh Cinder shuffled miscellaneous bits of machinery.

"Well, she's not a huge improvement," she said, "but I do have this." She emerged from behind a towering shelf with the body of a girl draped over one arm. Shouldering aside a toolbox, she dropped the girl on the table with a thud. A limp arm splayed out toward Mech6.0 and her scanner picked up on precisely trimmed fingernails, the natural curve of her fingers, the faint blue veining beneath her skin.

And then she spotted the near-invisible imprint across the girl's wrist. A barcode.

She was an escort-droid.

"She's almost thirty years old," said Cinder, "and in pretty bad shape. I was really just keeping her around for spare parts." She adjusted the head so Mech6.0 could see her face, which was beautiful and convincingly lifelike, with dark irises and sleek black hair. With her empty gaze and a rosy flush to her cheeks, she looked like she was dead, but only recently so.

"If I remember right, something was wrong with her voice box. I think she'd gone mute and the last owner didn't want to bother with replacing it. She was also prone to occasional power surges, so you might want to look into replacing her wiring and getting a new battery as soon as you can." Cinder brushed some dust off the escort-droid's brow. "And on top of that, with her being so old, I don't really know how compatible she's going to be with your personality chip. You might find that you experience some weird glitches. But ... if you want her ..."

In response, Mech6.0 held out the holographic card.

"SO ... YOU'RE AN ELECTRICIAN?" SAID TAM SOVANN, SCAN-ning her profile on his portscreen.

Mech6.0 nodded, smiling as she had seen humans do. It had taken her nearly two weeks to set up a net profile and manage to steal some proper work clothes that fit her, even though it went against everything her android code told her. Still, she had done it and she had made her way back to the shipyard and she was here, with a humanoid body and a convincing identity and Dataran's locket snapped snugly in her pocket.

"And you specialize in classic podships and cruisers, particularly the luxury lines . . . impressive." He glanced up again, as if trying to decide if the profile could be believed.

She kept smiling.

"And you're . . . mute."

She nodded.

He squinted suspiciously for a moment before going over her profile again. "Well, we certainly do work on a lot of luxury lines like these . . ."

Which she knew.

". . . and I have been faced with a high turnover of electricians lately."

Which she also knew.

"I'd have to start you at a base salary, until you prove you can do the work. You understand that."

She nodded. Having never received a salary before, she did not even know what she would do with that measly base pay.

"All right. Well. Let's give it a shot," he said, as if he couldn't quite believe he was saying it. Mech6.0 wasn't sure if it was her muteness that had him unconvinced about her, or the fact that her escort body was startlingly attractive, even in her drab work clothing. "And what was your name again?" he said, before flinching at her patient smile. "Right, sorry, uh—" He scanned through her profile again. "Hoshi . . . Star."

Mech6.0—no, *Hoshi Star* nodded.

His eyes narrowed suspiciously, but then he shrugged. "If you say so. Well then. Welcome aboard, Hoshi-mèi. I have a project that I think will be perfect for you. This way."

She braced herself before rising off the chair. Her personality chip hadn't synced quite right with the outdated escort body, and Linh Cinder was right—it had caused a peculiar glitch that manifested itself whenever she walked. The effort caused pain to shoot through the wires from her legs to her chest, burning into her synapses. The first time it had happened, she had gasped and collapsed onto the sidewalk and sat trembling on the ground for close to an hour while blinding light flooded her senses.

Pain.

She had never known pain before—androids should not have been able to experience it at all. But she had no doubt that's what it was. Just as the human brain used pain to recognize when something was horribly wrong, her processor was warning her that this body was not hers. That this combination could not last.

The third time it had happened, she had considered going back to the market and pleading with Linh Cinder to take the body away, but she had ultimately refused to do that, not before she saw Dataran again. With time, the pain was becoming more bearable, even if only because she was learning to compartmentalize it away from the rest of her sensory input.

Clenching her teeth, she pushed herself to her feet and followed Tam-shìfu out into the shipyard.

She began searching for him the moment she stepped into the massive hangar. Her eyes darted from human to human, searching for a graceful frame and an easy smile. She'd been worried ever since she'd left, terrified that he hadn't fully recovered from the fall into the oil, terrified that she hadn't gotten to him in time.

Though her gaze darted from one corner of the yard to the other as they walked, there was no sign of the young engineer.

"Here we are," said Tam, gesturing to the space yacht, the Orion Classic. Over the past two weeks, the exterior had been nearly completed, but Star could guess that the interior still had plenty of work to be done. "This is for one of our premium clients, and he doesn't want to spare a single expense. But of course, he's on a tight schedule, as they always are. I'll track down some electrical blueprints for you. And—ah! You'll be reporting directly to Wing-jūn here. Dataran, come meet our newest electrician."

He came around from the front of the ship, a portscreen in his hand and a stylus tucked behind one ear, and a surge of electricity coursed so fast through Star's body she thought for a moment she would experience an actual meltdown. But she didn't, and when he politely bowed his head, she remembered to politely bow hers as well.

"It's nice to meet you," he said. "You'll be working on the Orion Classic with us?"

She smiled, but Tam was already waving his hand. "That's right, she says she's an expert with the classics. Keep her busy. Let's see what she can do, all right?" He glanced at the port. "I have to check on the racer. Dataran, do you mind showing her the ropes?"

"Not at all, sir."

Tam was gone almost before he'd finished talking, and Dataran was chuckling after him. "Don't take it personally. He's like that toward everyone."

His kind smile made the pain of standing recede almost fully from her thoughts, and Star beamed hopefully back.

"I'm sorry, I didn't get your name."

Lashes fluttering, she opened her lips, but of course there was nothing. Flinching, she patted a hand against her throat. Dataran frowned. "Did you lose your voice?"

She shrugged. Close enough.

"Oh. Then, um. Should I call you . . ." He frowned, not able to come up with anything appropriate on the spot.

Perking up, she grabbed his sleeve and dragged him back toward the front of the ship, where she gestured up at the name that had been freshly painted on its side. *Child of the Stars.*

"Uh—Stars? Star?"

When she beamed again, he laughed. "That wasn't so hard. It's a pleasure to meet you, Star."

She tried her best to speak through her eyes, her stretched lips, her trembling fingers, which had released his sleeve and were too afraid to reach for him again. *It's me*, she thought, willing him to understand. *I'm the one who rescued you. I'm the one who found your locket. It's me, it's me, it's me.*

But Dataran just jerked his head toward the landing gear. "Come on, I'll show you the engine room and how far we've gotten in the wiring so far—which isn't much. We could definitely use your help."

Before he turned away, he glanced up toward the cockpit windows one level up, and his mouth quirked fast to one side.

Star followed the look.

Ochida Miko and her father were sitting in the cockpit. He appeared to be teaching her something, gesturing at the different controls, but Miko had spotted Dataran outside and didn't seem to be listening.

Star had a sense that Miko's bashful smile had not been intended for her, or Miko's father, to see.

"OH, IT'S BEAUTIFUL!" SAID MIKO, SITTING ON DATARAN'S other side.

Star knew that she was talking about the ship that was about to leave the hangar—a sleek, flashy thing that had been commissioned for the annual Space Race to Neptune (which everyone knew was a fallacy—the race officially ended at Jupiter, but the sponsors claimed that didn't have the same ring to it). It *was* a beautiful ship, with its elongated thrusters and needle-sharp nose. The painters had outdone themselves, creating a very realistic montage of New Beijing's skyline across its frame.

But Star did not care so much for the ship. Her attention had gone back up to the ceiling as it pulled back to reveal the endless sky. Although her new life as a human had given her the opportunity to gaze up at the night sky as often as she wished, her eyes never tired of it. The sense of vastness and eternity, the yearning to see what else the universe had to offer, even for one as small and unimportant as she was.

She didn't think that Miko had glanced up at all since the ceiling had lifted to allow the ship an exit. Of course, *she* had already been to space countless times. Would be going again as soon as the Orion Classic was finished—another two or three weeks at the most. Ochida-shīfu had been growing more and more impatient, urging them to tighten the schedule, to work longer hours, to finish early.

Miko and Dataran, on the other hand, seemed to become more and more miserable as each step of the rebuild was completed. If anything, Dataran's pace had slowed as the ship's deadline loomed.

Star pulled her attention away as Dataran was explaining the different features of the racer, gesturing at the elegant curve of its back, the power behind the rocket boosters, and on and on. Star was more interested in the sound of his voice than his words. The subtle inflections. The careful pronunciation of very technical terms. The way he talked faster when something struck him as ingenious. Listening to him felt like being plugged into a power dock, feeling the gentle current of electricity warm and enliven her.

She glanced over at him, and the contented smile fell from her lips.

Dataran had laced his fingers with Miko's and was holding her hand on his knee while his other hand drew explanatory pictures in the air.

Something flashed in Star's chest—a spark, maybe, or a power surge. Her fingers curled into fists, tightening with the urge to reach across Dataran and rip their hands away from each other. To shove Miko aside. To wrap her own fingers around Miko's neck.

Grimacing, she turned away and waited for the flood of white to fade from her vision.

It was not the first time such horrible thoughts had come into her head. Generally, she found that she enjoyed Miko's company. She was a smart girl who talked just enough to keep Star from feeling strange that she couldn't participate in the conversation, and who had insisted that Star take the occasional walk with her in a nearby park when she deemed that Star had been working too hard lately.

But when they were with Dataran, which was more often than not, Star found herself withdrawing away from Miko's friendliness and discovering a darker part of her programming. She figured it had to be another glitch, this strange desire to hurt a human being, which seemed to emerge only when Dataran found some subtle way to touch Miko. Just placing a hand on her elbow or brushing a lock of hair off her shoulder.

These little moments made Star feel like she was disintegrating inside.

Maybe the malfunctions were getting worse. Maybe a new processor would help. Had she earned enough money now to afford one? She wasn't sure, and she needed to weigh it with her need for a power source that didn't threaten to die near the end of every workday.

"Star? Are you all right?"

Prying her eyes open, she forced herself to look at Dataran. A quick glance confirmed that their hands remained entwined, but she still forced her lips to curl upward and her head to bob up and down.

The concern lingered in Dataran's gaze, but then a cheer rose up from the audience and the racer was taking flight; Dataran and Miko shifted their giddy attention back to the spectacle.

Star tried to focus on the ship, or even the starry night sky, but she couldn't get the image of her own pale fingers around Miko's neck to fade from her thoughts. It disturbed her, that her processor was capable of imagining something so horrific, and the shipyard mechanic's words flashed through her head.

The fact is, an unpredictable android is a dangerous one.

Was she unpredictable?

Was she dangerous?

She felt the shudder along her wires as soon as the ship lifted up off the ground to another uproarious cheer.

Her energy was running out.

She switched her internal settings to power-saving mode, and the world dulled to shades of gray, the sound in her ears a jumbled hum as her audio receptors stopped sorting and cataloging the input.

She set a hand on Dataran's shoulder and climbed to her feet. The movement came with a jolt of pain that threatened to cripple her. She grimaced and waited a moment before waving good-bye.

"Where are you going?" Dataran pointed at the ship. "It will only be another few minutes. We can take a hover together."

Her fan whirred faster. On her third day at the shipyard, she had made up a home address that was near to his and they often left together when the workday was over. Sometimes Miko joined them too, and Star thought she and Dataran might have plans that didn't involve her, and yet they were always so good to not suggest she was an unwanted intruder.

Those hover rides, simply listening to Dataran talk and laugh, were some of the best moments of her short existence.

But this time, she shook her head. She needed to find a charging dock, and quickly.

He did not expect her to explain, an unexpected benefit of being mute, and so he simply nodded, still frowning, and let her go.

But Star had not gone a dozen steps before she felt the power drain from her legs. Warnings pounded into her consciousness, but they were too late—she was falling. Her head crashed into the hard floor and she lay there with her arms twitching so hard she worried they would pull themselves right out of her shoulder sockets.

She picked out Miko's and Dataran's yells even from the chaotic roaring in her ears, and then they were above her, tenderly turning her onto her back. She scanned their faces, recognizing shock, fear, panic, uncertainty. Dataran was speaking but she couldn't comprehend. Miko was pressing a hand against her forehead.

Her processor began to flicker back to life, programs gradually rebooting themselves. Though she still had no control over her legs, she could once again make out Dataran's concerned questions, raining down on her like shooting stars.

Then Miko laid a hand on Dataran's arms and said, with calm authority, "Bring her some water."

With a frantic nod, he pushed himself to his feet. When he had gone, Miko sighed, her gaze full of sympathy as she tucked a lock of Star's hair behind an ear.

"The fit seems to have passed, but just lie still."

Star withered from embarrassment to know that Dataran had seen her like this.

"I'm sorry if I offend you by asking this," Miko whispered, glancing in the direction Dataran had gone, "but ... are you an escort-droid, Star-mèi?"

Eyes widening, Star tried to sit up, only succeeding when Miko tucked an arm beneath her shoulders and lifted her. She realized the thought of Miko knowing her secret terrified her, but Miko's smile was kind. "Don't worry. I don't think Dataran has noticed anything, and I won't tell anyone. You are very ... convincing." Her lashes dipped, and she murmured, "But like recognizes like."

Star scrutinized her. *Like recognizes like.* The words repeated in her head, but she couldn't seem to compute them.

Then Miko reached a hand for the back of her neck, where Star had noticed that strange dark spot a dozen times since her return, always hastily covered up. "I'm not an android," she said, shaking her head. She cleared her throat and dared to meet Star's gaze again. "But I am a cyborg."

Cyborg. The definition was in her database, but Star doubted its accuracy. Miko? Lovely young Miko?

Miko glanced around to make sure no one was near. They had been sitting near the paint booth, which offered a good view of the ship's takeoff without all the crowds, and no one was paying them any attention.

Sitting back on her heels, Miko pulled up the wide sleeve of her silk kimono. Star watched, mesmerized, as Miko dug her fingers into the flesh of her elbow and began to peel the skin back. A perfect, thin layer of flesh rolled down her am like a tightly knit sleeve, and beneath the skin was a finely crafted arm made from lightweight carbon-fiber polymer, the same material Star's body was constructed from.

As soon as Star had seen, Miko rolled the skin back into place, rubbing at the synthetic until the edges had merged seamlessly back together.

Gaping, Star pointed to where Dataran had gone.

"He knows," said Miko. "I told him as soon as . . . well . . ." She stared down at her prosthetic hands, now clutched together in her lap. "As soon as I realized that I was falling in love with him. I thought for sure it would put an end to it all. That he wouldn't want anything to do with me once he knew. But . . . he isn't like that, is he?" A happy flush bloomed across her cheeks, but was smothered as she glanced out toward the rows of ships in all stages of incompletion. And down the lane, the *Child of the Stars.* "Not that it matters. As soon as the ship is done, we'll be leaving, and nothing will change my father's mind. I know he thinks it's for my own good, but . . ."

Star listed her head, urging her to continue.

"We're leaving the Commonwealth because he's afraid that I'll be selected for the cyborg draft if we stay. I know it's by random selection, and the odds are so small, and yet he's convinced that the draft skews toward female cyborgs, and young ones at that. I don't know how he got this into his head, but ... That's why he bought the ship, why he's so insistent that they finish it as soon as possible. And when it's done ... I'll have to say good-bye."

Star thought she detected a shimmer in Miko's eye, but it was gone just as fast. "I should be grateful. I know that. He's going through so much trouble to keep me safe. But I can't help but feel that I would rather take my chances with the draft, if it means being with Dataran."

Star looked away. She knew that feeling so well. The pain that jolted through her vertebrae when she walked. The torture of seeing how his eyes latched on to the bright-colored *obi* that wrapped around Miko's body. How agonizing it was, this life of silence and yearning.

Yet how very worth it when his eyes found hers, and she could still recall the look of disbelief and gratitude and curiosity that had passed over him when she'd pulled him from the oil tank.

"Here, I usually keep a portable charger with me," said Miko, pulling her handbag toward her. "Dataran will be back soon, and it will be difficult for me to explain why you aren't drinking any water unless you seem recovered. Is the receptacle in your neck?"

Star nodded and tried her best to be grateful as Miko opened the panel beneath her ear and inserted the charging cord, but there was something dark lingering still, making her dig her own fingertips into her thighs. An impatience with Miko, a throbbing irritation with her presence.

Ever since she'd returned to the shipyard, Star had thought of Miko's departure as an ending—and a beginning—and that feeling grew stronger by the day. She was only biding her time until Miko was gone. Then she would buy a new body that didn't rebel every time she walked, and she would return the locket that contained the whole galaxy to Dataran and explain everything to him. She would tell him that something in his smile had changed her, back when it shouldn't have been possible for her to be changed. She would tell him that she was the one who had saved his life, because something about him made her unpredictable, and maybe dangerous, and she couldn't exist in a world without him.

STAR DRAGGED A FINGER ACROSS THE SCREEN EMBEDDED IN the wall, and the lights of the cockpit went dark. She swirled it clockwise; they gradually brightened again. Counterclockwise; they dimmed darker. A tap here to raise the temperature, here to lower it. She tested every command: play music, adjust the air filtration system, seal the cockpit door, heat the cockpit floor, place an order for a beverage through the automated beverage service.

Confident that everything was working just as it should, she shut the panel of wiring beneath the screen and gathered up the tools that she'd used, hooking them neatly into her tool belt. She then paused, preparing herself to walk, before heading toward the ship's main exit. Her body screamed at her as she walked, and she knew that the exertion was beginning to take its toll on her system. For weeks she had done her best to ignore the pain and the knowledge that sooner or later, her escort-droid body would rebel and reject the installed personality chip altogether, and there were times when she felt she was holding her body together through sheer willpower.

It wouldn't be long, though, before she could afford a new body. Just a little while longer.

A voice made her foot catch and she paused on the exit ramp. *Dataran.*

Turning, she peered into the common room that divided the front of the ship from the living areas. An assortment of comfortable seats, accented with silk pillows and cashmere throw blankets, were arranged around a gurgling aquarium that reached from the floor to the tiled ceiling. The brightly colored fish had been brought to their new home a few days before and seemed content to float mindlessly among their artificial coral reef.

Star crept toward Miko's rooms, her back against the wall, aware that this was not something she would have done when she was Mech6.0. Spying, sneaking, eavesdropping. Androids were not made to be curious.

And yet, there she was, standing beside the doorframe and listening to the hiccupping sounds of a girl crying.

"If we could just talk to your father . . . show him how much we love each other . . ."

"He'll never agree to it. He doesn't think you could keep me safe."

Dataran released a disgruntled sigh. "I know, I know. And I couldn't stand it if anything happened to you either. I just need time . . . I can get us a ship. It may not be anything like this, anything like what you're used to, but . . ."

"That doesn't matter. I would go"—she sobbed—"anywhere with you. But Dataran . . ."

"But what?"

Her crying grew louder. "Do you really want to live—your whole life—with a cyborg?"

Star dared to inch closer, shifting her weight so she could peer through the crack between the lavish mahogany doors. These rooms were completed. The ship was almost finished, but for some last detail work in the front end.

Scheduled departure was in two days.

She spotted them standing near Miko's netscreen desk, and Dataran was embracing her, one hand cupping the base of her head as she buried her face into his shoulder.

Memorizing the pose, Star brought her hand up to the back of her neck and dug her fingertips into her own hair. Tried to imagine what that must be like.

"Miko, please," Dataran whispered. "Your arms could be made out of broom handle for all I care."

Star adjusted her audio interface, so loud that she could hear the rustle of fabric, his breathing, her sniffles.

"All I care about is what's in here."

He pulled far enough away that he could slide his hand around and place it over a chrysanthemum flower painted onto the silk of her kimono. Right below her collarbone.

Star followed the movement. Felt her own chest, her own

hard plating, with the slightest bit of softness from her layer of synthetic skin. But no heartbeat, no pulse.

"You're perfect, Miko, and beautiful, and I love you. I want to marry you."

The words, spoken so quietly, were like a gunshot in Star's head. She flinched and stumbled backward, pressing a hand over one ear. But it was too late. Those words, still smoking, were burned into her database.

Miko gasped and they pulled apart, spinning toward the door.

Dataran was there in a moment, whipping the doors open, and relief crossed over them both when they saw her.

"Oh, stars," whispered Miko, placing her own artificial hand over her very real beating heart. "I thought you were my father."

Faking apology, Stars took a step toward them and gestured at the lights that ran around the room, then at the control panel on the wall. She raised her eyebrows in a question.

It was a lie. She had checked all these rooms the day before, and she knew there was a time when she wouldn't have been capable of the falsehood, even an implied one.

"Oh—yes, yes, everything seems to be working perfectly," said Dataran, stringing a hand through his hair.

He seemed flustered, while Star felt broken.

"I should finish packing," mumbled Miko, sounding no more enthusiastic than if she were moving into a prison cell, not the lavish yacht. Ducking her head, she shuffled toward the door. "So many more cases to bring in ..."

"Miko, wait." Dataran grabbed Miko's wrist, but then glanced at Star. She turned to inspect the electronics control panel. "I have to try," he whispered, lowering his head toward Miko. "I have to at least ask him ..."

"He won't say yes."

"But if he did ... if I could convince him that I would take care of you, that I love you ... Would you say yes?"

Star absently punched her fingertips against the screen.

"You know that I would," Miko responded, her hushed voice breaking on the last word. She sniffed and cleared her throat. "But it doesn't matter. He won't say yes. He won't let me stay."

Then her soft footsteps padded out toward the ship's exit.

Daring to glance over her shoulder, Star saw that Dataran had pressed his forehead against the wall, his fingers dug into his hair. With a heavy sigh, he dragged his palms down his face and looked up at her. She noted darkening circles beneath his eyes and a paleness that seemed all wrong on him.

"Ochida-shìfu ... he's worried for her safety ..." he said, as if in explanation, then looked away. "And I am too, to be honest. But if she leaves, I might never see her again. If I just ... if I had a ship of my own, but ..." Shaking his head, he turned so that he could lean his back against the wall, like he might collapse without its support. "I was actually saving up for one. Have been for years. And I almost had enough, along with this antique holograph locket that should have been plenty to make up the difference, but I lost it in that stupid oil tank."

Star pressed a hand against her hip, where the locket sat snugly in her pocket. She'd kept it, waiting, expecting there to be a perfect moment to give it back to him, but the time never seemed right. And in the evenings, when she was alone, she would open it up and let herself get swallowed up by the stars, and think about what life would be like when Miko was gone. There would be so many chances, so many opportunities . . .

"I'm sorry, Star. I shouldn't talk about my problems like this. It's not fair, when you can't tell me about yours."

He met her gaze again and she pulled her hand away from the pocket, curling her fingers into a fist. Miko would be gone in two days. Only two more days. And then . . . and then . . .

Dataran smiled, but it was exhausted and missing all the warmth that had so often interrupted the flow of electricity to her limbs. "Do you have any problems you wish you could talk about, Star?"

She nodded.

"Maybe you could write them down. I would read them, if you wanted me to."

Dropping her gaze, she shook her head. Out in the common room, the aquarium bubbled and hummed, the sound that was meant to be calming now taking up the entire ship and drowning her.

"I understand," said Dataran. "I probably haven't shown myself to be the best . . . listener, since we met. But I do wonder what goes on in that head of yours sometimes. Miko likes you, you know. I think . . . she hasn't said it, but I think you might be the only friend she has."

Star looked away. Clenched her fists. Then, daring to meet his gaze again, she lifted a hand and tapped a finger against her hollow chest. Dataran was watching, but uncertain. He didn't understand.

Star took a step toward him and tapped the same finger against his heart.

He blinked and opened his mouth to speak, but Star leaned forward and kissed him before he could. Just a peck, but she tried to put every unspoken word into it. *It's me, it's been me all along, and I may have saved your life, but I would be nothing if it wasn't for you. I would be just another mech-droid, and I wouldn't know what it's like to love someone so much I would give up everything for them.*

But when she pulled away, he looked shocked and horrified and guilty, and she knew he didn't understand. She left the room before Dataran could speak. He didn't call her back, and he didn't come after her.

Star fled from the ship and kept going until she was out of the hangar, out of the shipyard, a single lonely android beneath an enormous morning sky, before she reached into her pocket and wrapped her fingers around the locket and a universe that meant nothing to her without him.

UNLIKE THE *TRITON'S* LAUNCH, THE LAUNCH OF THE *CHILD OF the Stars* was a private affair. Some of Ochida-shìfu's old coworkers and acquaintances had come out to wish them a safe journey, along with the shipyard staff, but that was all. No friends of Miko's. Maybe Dataran was right and she didn't have any, which made

Star wonder if it was because she was rich and sheltered, or shy, or because she was cyborg.

Star couldn't take her eyes from Dataran, standing sunken-shouldered in the crowd, his eyes haunting the ship as its engines rumbled and the lifter magnets beneath the hangar's floor hummed with life. He was probably hoping to catch a glimpse of Miko through the windows, although all but the cockpit windows were so small it was an impossible hope. Star wondered if they had seen each other at all since she had stumbled upon them two days before. The words she'd overheard still bounced around in Star's head, and she ached from the memory, almost as much as she ached from the kiss.

She had not seen Dataran since that morning. She'd been avoiding him. Unable to stand his sorrow over losing Miko, and whatever kind, sensible things he would say to explain why Miko was the one he loved, and why Star would never be, even after Miko was gone.

As she stared, the crowd shifted around Dataran. A figure moved gracefully between the bodies.

Star cocked her head and squinted. Staring. Waiting.

Dataran gave a start, then whipped his head around. His gaze fell on Miko, who was wearing plain coveralls, and he drew back in surprise. Her smile was shy but bright as she pressed up closer to him and whispered. She lifted her hand and something small glinted from her palm. Though Star was too far away to see, she knew it was the locket. Her locket. Her galaxy.

Dataran shook his head in disbelief and glanced back toward

the ship. Then, on the verge of a smile, he took Miko into his arms and kissed her.

Star pressed her fingertips against her own lips. Imagining.

Her arm weakened and she let it fall to her lap. It wouldn't be long now. She could feel her body beginning to rebel. It was in the pain that was almost constant now, a stabbing sensation that tore through her legs even when she was only sitting. It was in the frequent loss of control in her twitching limbs. It was in the blackness that clouded in around her vision, and how she always thought this would be the last time, before, after a long, agonizing moment, she returned to consciousness again.

Footsteps thumped in the common room and paused in the doorway. Star turned her head away.

"One minute to takeoff," said Ochida-shìfu. "Do you want to come sit with me in the cockpit?"

She shook her head and adjusted the sleeve of the silk kimono so that he was sure to see the metal plating of her arms. The synthetic skin had been easy to remove, and though seeing her android insides was disconcerting, the limb reminded her of the three-fingered prongs from her Mech6.0 body, and there was a comforting familiarity in that.

Ochida sighed heavily behind her. "I'm doing this for *you*, Miko. It's better this way. And he's just a boy—you'll get over this."

When Star didn't respond, he huffed and withdrew from the doorway.

"Fine. Be angry. Throw your tantrum if you have to. Just put your skingraft back on before you snag that material. Whatever point you're trying to make, it isn't working. The reminder of what you are just further convinces me that I'm making the right decision."

Then he was gone.

Star returned her gaze to the window, the hangar, the crowd. Hundreds of mech-droids lined up against the charging wall. Miko. And Dataran.

Not minutes had gone by before she heard the magnets engage and felt the ship rise off the ground. The crowd cheered. Dataran wrapped his arms around Miko and she was beaming. Though Star didn't think Miko could see her, she felt almost like they were looking at each other in that moment, and that Miko knew precisely the decision that Star had made. And she, too, knew it was the right one.

Then the thrusters engaged, and the ship was climbing up out of the hangar, over the glittering, sprawling city of New Beijing. And Dataran was gone.

Suddenly weary, Star leaned her head against the window. Her audio input dulled to a faint, distant hum as the *Child of the Stars* speared through the wisps of clouds and the sky turned from bright blue to blushing pink and pale orange.

Her fan was struggling inside her torso, moving slower and slower …

Then, so suddenly she almost missed it, space opened up before her. Black and expansive and endless and filled with more stars than she could ever drink in. More stars than she could ever compute.

It was so much better than a holograph.

Her wires quivered as the last dregs of power sizzled through them. Her fingers jolted and twitched and then lay still.

She was smiling as she imagined herself as one more star in the sea of millions, and her body decided it had had enough, and she felt the exact moment when her power source gave up and the hum of electricity extinguished.

But she was already vast and bright and endless.

The Mechanic

THE HOVER WAS WAITING OUTSIDE THE PALACE'S NORTHWEST
gate. Kai feigned nonchalance as he made his way through the
garden's path, Nainsi's lightweight android body tucked under
one arm and a pack carrying a hooded sweatshirt slung over his
opposite shoulder. He didn't hurry, but he wasn't meandering,
either. He pretended that he was unconcerned about being noticed. It wasn't like he couldn't be tracked. He had not one but *two*
identity chips hidden beneath his skin, and his security team were
experts at keeping tabs on him.

It wasn't a secret that he was leaving.

But he didn't want it to be public knowledge either.

The day was hotter than it had been all week and the humidity
made his hair cling to the back of his neck. The garden gate opened
without a sound, though he could feel the security camera overhead following his movements. He ignored it and approached the
hover with the same straight-spined confidence he'd learned
to do every task with, no matter how trivial. He waved his
ID-embedded wrist over the hover's scanner and the door whis-

pered open, revealing a spacious interior behind the tinted-glass windows. Hidden speakers emitted the soothing notes of a flautist. Though the air inside had been cooled to a pleasant temperature, an ice bucket in the corner was still slick with condensation. It displayed an assortment of flavored waters and cold teas.

Kai pushed Nainsi in first before settling onto one of the upholstered benches. The door shut, and he realized that, despite the tranquility of the hover's interior, his heart had started to pound.

"Good afternoon, Your Imperial Highness. What is your destination?" the hover asked in an artificially feminine voice.

He rubbed away a bead of sweat before it could drip down his temple. "The market at city center."

The hover lifted off the street and glided away from the palace, taking the looping drive around the protective exterior wall before dipping down the hill toward New Beijing. Through the dark-paned glass, Kai could see his city shimmering with waves of heat, the windows and metal structures glinting beneath the afternoon sun.

He loved his city. He loved his country.

He would risk anything to protect it.

Inhaling sharply, he unclipped the portscreen from his belt and pulled up the net. The profile he'd looked up days ago greeted him on the main page.

LINH CINDER, LICENSED MECHANIC

LOCATION: NEW BEIJING WEEKLY MARKET,

    BOOTH #771

480 RATINGS; 98.7% CLIENT APPROVAL

There was no picture of the mechanic or the shop, but Linh Cinder had a reputation of being the best mechanic in the city, and the approval rating was higher than anyone else Kai had looked up. He'd first heard of Linh Cinder from one of the mechanics at the palace who was charged with keeping the royal androids well maintained. When they had failed to properly diagnose Nainsi after running the basic tests, Linh Cinder's name had come up as the best chance for fixing the android.

Of course, they had all thought Kai was crazy for being so invested in an android.

We'll order up a new one, they said. *Run it through the palace budget. Standard procedure. She's just a tutor android, after all, programmed with a few assistant apps. Easily replaced, Your Highness. Not for you to worry about.*

But they were wrong. Nainsi was not easily replaced. The information she had—or that Kai *hoped* she had—was not easily replaced at all.

He returned the portscreen to his belt and pulled the android toward him, peering into the sensor light that had been black for days. Once again, he sought out the minuscule power button. Once again, nothing happened.

He sighed, though he'd long given up hope that Nainsi would just wake up and spill all her secrets. Her power cell was fully charged, and according to the diagnostics tests, everything was working properly. No one could figure out what was wrong, and the timing couldn't have been worse.

"We're so close," he whispered to himself. Leaning back against the bench, he dragged a hand through his hair. Frustration had been growing behind his rib cage for weeks now, ever since that Lunar thaumaturge, Sybil Mira, had come to visit for her "ambassadorial mission." She was a witch. A creepy, mind-controlling witch. Just knowing that she was in the palace set Kai's teeth on edge. It was like he could feel her eyes following him, or sense her breathing down the back of his neck, even when she wasn't in the same room. He didn't know if it was his own paranoia or some Lunar trick, but he did know that he couldn't wait for her to leave him and his family and his country alone.

Then his father had become ill.

No, not *ill*. His father had the plague. His father was dying, and there was absolutely nothing Kai could do to stop it.

And now this. Nainsi malfunctioning right when he was *sure* she'd found something useful, something priceless.

Something regarding the whereabouts of Princess Selene.

He knew it was a risk. If Sybil Mira, or any Lunar, learned that he was trying to find the lost princess, it could lead to a political catastrophe between Earth and Luna. He knew that Queen Levana wouldn't be quick to forgive the fact that Kai was adamantly attempting to usurp her.

But it was a risk worth taking. Finding Selene and putting her back on the Lunar throne was his best chance—and possibly his only chance—of ridding himself of Queen Levana and her threats toward the Commonwealth. Threats of war. Threats of mass enslavement.

Almost worse—threats of a *marriage* alliance.

It could not be allowed. He had to find the true Lunar heir before it was too late.

He and Nainsi had been researching for months, and though there had been countless false claims and dead ends, lately he'd been sure they were getting somewhere. Nainsi had heard about a Lunar doctor who was suspected of having an involvement with the lost princess's disappearance, and also a potential relationship with an Earthen woman years before.

It was a thin hope—the thinnest of hopes—but Kai's instincts told him there was more to it. He'd ordered Nainsi to find out as much information as she could on the doctor and this Earthen woman and then, two days later—nothing.

Nainsi was dead to the world.

It was enough to make him want to put his head through the hover car's control board.

"Approaching the city center," lilted the robotic voice, snapping Kai from his thoughts. "Where would you like to deboard?"

He glanced out the window. The streets were cast in shadow from the high-rise buildings in every direction. Storefronts sparkled with netscreen advertisements and pristine escort-droids modeling the latest fashions and gadgets. A block away he could see the edge of the market, all tight-squeezed booths and bustling crowds.

"Here is fine," he said, reaching into the pack and pulling out the gray hooded sweatshirt he'd smuggled from the palace—the most discreet item of clothing he owned.

The hover swooped to the edge of the street. The magnets hummed as it lowered itself to the ground. "Shall I wait here for your return?"

"Please," he said, threading his arms through the sleeves and tugging up the zipper. "I shouldn't be long."

He considered giving a specific time—*If I'm not back in an hour, then I've probably been cornered by paparazzi and screaming girls and you should send the royal security squad after me.* But even thinking it made him feel melodramatic, so he just pulled the hood over his brow and stepped out of the hover, dragging Nainsi's pear-shaped body after him.

He hadn't gone far when his senses were assaulted by the chaos of the market. The smell of lemongrass, ginger, and sizzling meat. The sounds of laughing children and roaring shopkeepers and chiming sales announcements. The sweltering heat that, even in the shade, soaked straight through his sweatshirt and wrapped him in a suffocating cocoon. He unzipped the sweatshirt slightly as he walked, but dared not take down the hood. The last thing he wanted was to draw attention to himself.

And the problem with being the crown prince was that he *always* drew attention.

Crown prince, and soon-to-be emperor.

No, he couldn't think of that now. It would cripple him. The thought of losing his father, and to the same devastating plague that had taken his mother years ago. The thought of ascending to the throne. The thought of all the people who would be relying on him to do the right thing, to make the best decisions. It was too much. He wasn't ready. Not yet. Maybe not ever.

He swallowed the rising bile in his throat. He had only one

prerogative today: confirm that Linh Cinder was capable of fixing Nainsi.

Once Nainsi was repaired he could proceed with his search for the princess.

He let out a slow breath, and when he inhaled again, he let the aromas of street food and incense ground him back in the market. He dared to lift his head enough to get his bearings. Though his mother had brought him to the market sometimes when he was young, it had been years since he'd been there, and it took him a moment to pick out the faded booth numbers stenciled on canopies and metal frames. He turned to the right and weaved through the crowd, past barrels of rice and tables of mangoes, handwoven rugs, and bargain-price netscreens and portscreens—likely name-brand imitations.

Finally, he saw it. He knew it was the mechanic's booth even before he checked for the stenciled number: 771. A labyrinth of storage shelves filled the space, cluttered with rusted android prongs, dented hover car panels, bins of bolts and screws, and a thousand different tools whose uses Kai couldn't even fathom. A table sat across the booth's entrance, draped in a grease-covered cloth and scattered with an assortment of wires and screwdrivers. A small metal foot, for an escort-droid, or maybe even a cyborg, sat amid the mess. It seemed so unexpected and random that Kai almost laughed.

His amusement was tempered by disappointment, though.

Despite the rolling door being wide-open, there was no one tending the booth.

Frowning, he dropped Nainsi onto the table with a loud thud.

He heard a gasp and another *thunk*, then a girl appeared from beneath the table, rubbing the top of her head. She looked up at Kai, her expression dark with annoyance.

Then she froze.

He could tell the precise moment when she recognized him.

His smile was instinctive. A little bit apology, a little bit politeness. And a little bit of charm because, of all the things he'd expected to come from his trip to the market, meeting a cute girl with messy hair and dirty work gloves had definitely not been one of them.

"I'm sorry," he said. "I didn't realize anyone was back there."

She gaped at him for another heartbeat, then two, then three, before launching herself to her feet and lowering her head in an awkward bow. "Your Highness."

Grimacing, Kai glanced behind him at the milling crowd. No one else had recognized him yet. He hastily turned back and tilted toward the girl. "Maybe, um"—he drew his fingers across his lips—"on the Highness stuff?"

She nodded, but there was still that baffled expression on her face, and he wasn't entirely sure she had grasped the importance of his remaining incognito.

"Right. Of course. How—can I—are you—" She paused, pressing her lips tight, and lowered her gaze to his chest. He could tell she was embarrassed by her own reaction, but she wasn't blushing. At least, not yet.

"I'm looking for a Linh Cinder," said Kai, still feeling bad for startling her. "Is he around?"

She fidgeted with the hem of her left glove. He thought she was going to take the gloves off—they must have been as hot and uncomfortable as his sweatshirt—but she didn't. "I—I'm Linh Cinder."

Kai's eyebrows jumped in surprise. That couldn't be right. Maybe he'd misheard. Maybe Linh Cinder was a family name, taken from her mechanical-minded uncle or some such.

This girl was *maybe* Kai's age, but he guessed she was even younger.

He settled a hand on Nainsi's head, shifting forward. "*You're* Linh Cinder?"

"Yes, Your High—" She hesitated again, biting her lower lip to stifle the royal title. That small, embarrassed gesture was surprisingly charming.

"The mechanic?"

The girl—*Cinder*—nodded. "How can I help you?"

Kai stared at the top of her head.

Linh Cinder.

The renown. The reputation. The approval rating.

New Beijing's best mechanic was . . . a teenager?

Kai was intrigued. He was amused, but more than that, he was *impressed.* After all, he still needed help installing the software every time he upgraded to a new port. Meanwhile, this girl ran her own mechanic business.

Kai had always been curious about people in general. Torin said it was one of the qualities that would someday make him a strong emperor. And now he was eager to know more. How did she get into this business? Where did she learn to do all this? How old *was* she?

But Linh Cinder, ignorant of his astonishment, was still staring at his chest. Still gnawing at her lower lip.

Kai leaned down, putting himself directly into her line of sight, and forced her to meet his eyes. Only when he was sure she would see it did he smile at her again. He meant it to be friendly, even comforting, but by the way her eyes widened he thought it might have served to startle her even more.

At least when he straightened again, her gaze stayed on him.

Her hair was pulled into a ponytail high on her head, with un-kempt bangs feathered over her brow and ears. She looked like she hadn't given a passing thought to her hair or clothes that day, maybe ever. She was pretty, but not exceptionally so. Not *noticeably* so, until you bothered to look.

Kai realized, with some surprise, that he was looking.

Which was how he noticed a splotch of grease on her brow, half covered beneath her bangs.

Another laugh caught in his lungs.

It was so endearing, and such a far cry from the perfectly coiffed and bejeweled girls who he normally met, that it made his fingers itch to reach across the table and rub it away.

He scolded his fingers. He scolded himself. He needed to pull himself together.

"You're not quite what I was expecting," he said, hoping she didn't pick up on what an enormous understatement that was.

"Well, you're hardly—what I—um." Cinder cleared her throat and dropped her gaze again, this time to Nainsi. She pulled the android toward her. "What seems to be wrong with the android, Your Highness?"

Kai's shoulders fell slightly and he wasn't sure if it was due to disappointment or relief or a little bit of both. Nainsi. He had come here for Nainsi. And Princess Selene. And saving the blasted world from Queen Levana and her entire cruel, hateful race.

"I can't get her to turn on. She was working fine one day, and the next, nothing."

Cinder turned the android around on the table. "Have you had problems with her before?"

"No." Tearing his gaze from the mechanic, Kai glanced back down at the table. His attention caught again on the small mechanical foot, and he picked it up. "She gets a monthly checkup from the royal mechanics, and this is the first real problem she's ever had."

The foot was petite—shorter than his hand from palm to fingertips—and looked like it should have been thrown into a trash compactor ages ago. The joints were stiff and squeaky as he fidgeted with the toes, and the seams between the plating were packed with grease. A cluster of baffling wires erupted from the ankle cavity, and he couldn't help wondering what each of them did. How could a handful of wires mimic small motor skills? It amazed him every time he thought of it, though if he were being honest, he hadn't given it all that much thought before.

He noticed a fingerprint smudge on one side of the foot and rubbed it away with his sleeve, then realized that Cinder was watching him.

He froze, unsure why he felt like he'd been caught doing something he shouldn't be.

But instead of telling him to leave her stuff alone, Cinder said simply, "Aren't you hot?"

He blinked. He'd almost forgotten the heat and humidity, but her words brought it rushing back. He could feel the sweat on the back of his neck, his hair clinging to his neck.

"Dying," he confessed. "But I'm trying to be inconspicuous."

After a moment in which he thought she might say more, Cinder looked down at Nainsi again and opened the panel on her back. "Why aren't the royal mechanics fixing her?"

"They tried but couldn't figure it out. Someone suggested I bring her to you." Kai set the foot back on the table, then let his focus travel over the shelves that filled up the booth behind her. So many tools and pieces and parts. So many mysteries. "They say you're the best mechanic in New Beijing. I was expecting an old man."

He sort of meant it as a joke, but she didn't laugh. "Do they?" she said, without removing her attention from Nainsi's innards. He wanted her to say something, to give some indication as to how she had managed to earn such a reputation so quickly, but she just said, "Sometimes they just get worn out. Maybe it's time to upgrade to a new model."

It took him a second to realize she was talking about Nainsi.

Kai shook his head, but she wasn't looking at him. "I'm afraid I can't do that. She contains top-secret information. It's a matter of national security that I retrieve it … before anyone else does." He wanted to sound mysterious. He wanted to sound *witty*, even if it was the truth.

Cinder looked up, speculation scrawled across her face.

He aimed for nonchalant as he continued, "I'm just joking. Nainsi was my first android. It's sentimental."

Her brief silence was disconcerting. "National security. Funny."

It was the most deadpan compliment he'd ever heard. She wasn't amused. If he didn't know better, he'd think she knew he was lying.

Maybe, a small voice whispered in his head, he wanted her to think he was lying. He wanted her to believe he had some life-or-death agenda that required her assistance. Maybe he was trying to impress her, at least a little.

Which was absurd.

He was a prince.

He was *the* prince.

Perhaps the title itself didn't count for much, but Kai had spent his life making it more than just a title. He had studied his country's history and politics, sat in on state dinners, and quizzed his father's cabinet members on aspects of public policy. He'd watched his father's speeches over and over until he could write a perfectly crafted speech of his own—it wasn't until he was a teenager that he'd realized his father had speechwriters to do that for him. He had long ago determined that he would not let his birthright go unearned, that the history texts would not condemn him as an unworthy emperor. And while he may still have been plagued with doubts every single day, he knew, deep down, that he was doing his very best.

And it had been a long, long time since he had met someone who wasn't impressed by that.

It had also been a long, long time since he had cared.

"Tutor8.6 model," said Cinder, reading off Nainsi's panel. "She looks to be in pristine condition."

Kai opened his mouth to agree, but before he could, Cinder raised a fist and brought it hard against the side of Nainsi's spherical head. Kai jumped in surprise. The android began to topple off the table, but Cinder caught her easily and set her back on her treads. She seemed almost—*almost*—sheepish when she said, "You'd be surprised how often that works."

Kai laughed, a little awkwardly. He was no longer sure exactly who was trying to impress who . . . or if either of them were succeeding. "Are you sure you're Linh Cinder? The mechanic?"

A high-pitched voice interrupted them, along with the crunch of android treads on the street. "Cinder! I've got it!"

Kai turned to see a servant android rolling toward them, its blue sensor light flashing excitedly.

The android slammed a second robotic foot onto the table, its plating shiny and clean compared with the old one's. "It's a huge improvement over the old one, only lightly used, and the wiring looks compatible as is. Plus, I was able to get the dealer down to just six hundred univs."

The mechanic grabbed the new foot and dropped it behind the table. "Good work, Iko. Nguyen-shìfu will be delighted to have a replacement foot for his escort-droid."

"Nguyen-shìfu?" said the android. "I don't compute."

With a nervous smile, Cinder tilted her head toward Kai. "Iko, please pay your respects to our customer . . . His Imperial Highness."

The android tilted back her bulbous head. Though androids didn't have genders, many personality chips were programmed to identify more male or female, and it was clear from the high voice that this was a she. It was an easy connection for Kai to make—after all, this Iko had a similar body style to Nainsi, who he'd always thought of as a *she* as well.

The android's sensor flashed as she scanned Kai's face. "Prince Kai," she said, her voice taking on the unexpected tinge of a sigh. "You are even more handsome in person."

Kai laughed—a sudden, uncontrollable laugh that burst out of him before he could reel it back.

"That's enough, Iko," said Cinder. "Get in the booth."

The android obeyed, ducking under the tablecloth.

Still grinning, Kai leaned against the sturdy frame of the booth's rolling door. "You don't see a personality like that every day. Did you program her yourself?"

Cinder started to smile, too, and though it had a sardonic edge to it, Kai felt like he'd won something. "Believe it or not, she came that way. I suspect a programming error, which is probably why my stepmother got her so cheap."

"I do not have a programming error!" Iko's irate voice screeched from behind one of the towering shelves.

Kai chuckled again. Cinder caught his eye for a brief moment before she looked away.

Back at Nainsi.

The reason he was here. The oh-so-important reason.

Why was he so distracted?

He lowered the zipper on his sweatshirt a hair. The heat was becoming unbearable. His shirt would be drenched with sweat by the time he got back to the hover, and he was grateful that it hadn't yet seeped through the sweatshirt.

"So what do you think?" he asked.

"I'll need to run her diagnostics. It will take me a few days, maybe a week." Cinder pushed a strand of hair behind one ear and lowered herself into a chair.

Only then did Kai realize that she'd been trembling a little. Maybe she was dehydrated.

He thought of offering to go get her some water, but then remembered that she had an android assistant to do those things for her. So instead, he held up his ID-implanted wrist and asked, "Do you need payment up front?"

Cinder was waving away the suggestion almost before he'd finished. "No, thank you. It will be my honor."

He opened his mouth to protest, but hesitated. This wasn't un-common when he was dealing with small business owners—they seemed to think that his patronage was payment enough, or maybe the publicity that would be gained from it. Arguing over a payment generally led to the vendor feigning offense and him feeling like a braggart.

He lowered his hand and shifted his attention to Nainsi again. "I don't suppose there's any hope of having her done before the festival?"

"I don't think that will be a problem," said Cinder, shutting Nainsi's control panel. "But without knowing what's wrong with her—"

"I know, I know." Kai hooked his thumbs on his sweatshirt pockets and rocked back on his heels. Ever since he'd started searching for Princess Selene it had been his dream to announce her survival and imminent reclamation of her throne at the annual ball. It was, after all, a celebration of world peace. He could think of no greater gift to his country than ridding them of Queen Levana, their sneakiest and most deceitful enemy. "Just wishful thinking."

"How will I contact you when she's ready?"

"Send a comm to the palace." Kai paused, remembering Sybil Mira—the Lunar Queen's own minion. Remembering how important it was that she never suspect he was searching for the missing princess, or doing anything else to undermine Levana's rule. Quickly, he added, "Or will you be here again next weekend? I could stop by then."

Iko's voice chirped from the back, "Oh, yes! We're here every market day. You should come by again. That would be lovely."

Cinder winced. "You don't need to—"

"It'll be my pleasure."

It wasn't a lie. Not only would this allow for him to keep the transaction discreet, but it also meant that he would be picking up Nainsi in person, rather than having her dropped off with some nameless assistant at the palace. It meant he was sure to see Linh Cinder again.

Maybe he could learn more about her then.

Maybe he'd make her smile. A *real* smile.

Maybe . . .

Maybe he needed another hobby.

He nodded a farewell to her. She returned the nod, but didn't stand or bow—all professional politeness, without much of the royal courtesy he was used to. It was sort of refreshing.

Pulling the hood over his face again, he turned and slipped back into the bustling crowd.

He felt lighter than he had in days as he made his way back to the hover car. He knew that nothing was resolved, not yet. His father was still dying, his country was still in danger, and Nainsi was still unable to share her secrets.

But there was something about Linh Cinder. Something capable and confident, even if she had been a little nervous to be talking to him. There was something about her that went beyond an unexpected reputation.

The knot in his chest loosened, just a little. Linh Cinder was going to solve this problem. He knew it. She was going to fix Nainsi, and then he would be able to retrieve the lost information about the princess. He would find Selene and, for the first time in generations, Earth would have a true ally in Luna.

He was optimistic as he left the weekly market behind. More optimistic than he had been in weeks.

That mechanic was going to change everything.

Something Old, Something New

CINDER SQUEEZED THE SUITCASE SHUT WITH A SIGH OF FINAL-
ity. Iko had been pestering her all week about what she was and
wasn't going to pack, insisting on a variety of gowns and uncomfortable shoes and rolling her eyes at Cinder's constant reminders
that they would be spending most of this trip on a *farm*. With cows
and chickens and mud.

"Just because you're not a queen anymore," Iko had said, her
hands fisted on her hips, "doesn't mean you get to go back to looking like you just rolled out of an engine compartment."

Together they had finally agreed on a few pairs of comfortable
pants and lightweight blouses, plus a simple emerald-green
cocktail dress—"Just in case," Iko had insisted.

Cinder stepped back and looked at the suitcase with some
trepidation, trying to determine what she'd forgotten, but she
knew the nerves writhing in her stomach had nothing to do with
what she would wear or the possibility of leaving something
behind—after all, they had shops on Earth.

No, she was nervous to be leaving.

For the first time since her official abdication, she was leaving Luna.

She had been back to Earth only once since she'd reclaimed her place upon the Lunar throne. She had kept to her promise and been Kai's date to the Commonwealth's ball last year, and it had been . . . terrifying. But also extraordinary. The people of Earth still weren't sure what to do with the fact that one of their beloved leaders was not so secretly dating a Lunar, and a cyborg Lunar at that. There had been protests. There had been countless comedy skits taking jabs at a romance that most of the world deemed unconventional, even offensive. There had been jealous, hateful glares from the other guests, and live newsfeeds that criticized everything from Cinder's gown to her posture to her sarcastic (i.e., *tasteless*) sense of humor.

She would have been humiliated, or possibly furious, if it hadn't also been for the amazing things that had come from that trip.

Iko had been one of the stars of the ball—the first android to ever receive an official invitation.

Dozens of kids had asked Cinder to autograph their portscreens, calling her a role model and a hero.

There had been her elation at seeing her friends again.

There had been all the Earthens who *weren't* against her. In fact, her critics were in the minority, at least according to Iko's frequent updates and reminders. There were plenty of people who defended her against the outcry, reminding the world that she was the girl who had saved them from Levana and done nothing but show loyalty to Earth and display bravery worth commending.

And, of course, there was Kai. The way he had looked at her when she first stepped off the spaceship and onto the platform at New Beijing Palace had been encapsulated in her memory. She had long felt a homesickness for Earth. Despite how hard she'd fought to rescue the country she knew so little about, Luna had never felt like home, not even after two years of living here. She'd thought she was homesick for New Beijing, even though her life with Adri hadn't felt like much of a home, either.

It wasn't until that moment, seeing Kai's smile and being wrapped up in his arms—both of them ignoring the fact that the world was watching—that she realized *he* was the home she'd been missing.

In the months since then, relations with Earth had grown stronger, and it seemed the Eastern Commonwealth citizens were gradually coming to terms with their emperor's unusual romantic choice. Cinder's abdication hadn't hurt. From the moment she'd announced her plan to dissolve the Lunar monarchy and host elections for a democratic ruling system, the people of Earth had rejoiced. To them, it was the ultimate political statement. The promise that there would never again be a Queen Levana.

Lunars hadn't been quite as enthusiastic about her choice, but once nominations ensued and election campaigns were under way, the mind-set of the country shifted. There was a potential to this system that hadn't been there under royal rule: Every one would be represented, and any of their children could grow up to be a leader. It was a new way of thinking, especially for those in the outer sectors, and Cinder had been immensely relieved when her plan gained traction. When the ballots were released, almost every single citizen had cast a vote.

She had never been so proud of an accomplishment, not even the revolution that had ended Levana's reign.

A knock thumped at her door and Iko entered, bouncing like a kangaroo. "They're here! I just got the comm from port security—the Rampion has arrived!"

"Good," said Cinder, with a firm nod at her suitcase. "I'm ready to go."

Iko paused and took in the suitcase with a disbelieving frown. "Is that all you're bringing?"

"That's it. Why? How many suitcases are you bringing?"

"Three, and that was after I pared it down." She placed a hand on Cinder's arm. "Don't worry. If you run out of clothes, I'll lend you some of mine. Kinney?" Iko glanced back. "Would you be a dear and take Ambassador Linh-Blackburn's luggage down to the docks?"

Cinder followed her look. Liam Kinney was hovering in the doorway, arms folded over his chest. Kinney had been one of the royal guards who had sided with Cinder during the revolution, and she'd come to consider him a friend since then. He was no longer a *royal* guard—there wasn't any *royalty* to protect—but he had been keen to take the position of protecting the new Grand Minister and his parliament of elected representatives, and Cinder had been happy to recommend him.

"With pleasure," Kinney deadpanned. "In fact, I was hoping that if I came to see you off, I would be asked to do manual labor."

Iko shrugged. "If you don't want to do any heavy lifting, then stop having such impressive muscles."

Cinder stifled a laugh as Kinney stepped forward to haul the suitcase off her bed. Though he was pretending to scowl, she could detect redness around his ears. "At least yours is about half the weight of Iko's," he said, casting Cinder a grateful look.

"I had only your comfort in mind," said Cinder. "Thanks, Kinney."

He gave her a bow, a habit that had been impossible to break him of. "My shift starts in an hour, so I won't be at the dock to say good-bye, but I wanted to wish you both safe travels."

"Try to keep that new Grand Minister out of trouble while I'm gone."

"I'll do my best." He headed back for the door, and a smile so quick and secretive passed between him and Iko that Cinder almost missed it. Iko didn't take her gaze from him until he was gone.

"He could have come with us, you know," said Cinder, glancing around the room one last time.

Iko shook her head. "He has a painfully strong work ethic. It's one of his more annoying characteristics."

Cinder chuckled. "Well, nobody's perfect."

"Speak for yourself." Iko spun back to her and clapped her hands excitedly. "Are you ready? Can we go?"

Cinder sucked in another breath. "Yes, I think so." She frowned. "You don't think it's a mistake to leave, do you?"

"Mistake?"

"It's just . . . the new parliament only took office six weeks ago. What if something goes wrong? What if they need me?"

"Then they can send you a comm." Iko settled her hands on Cinder's shoulders. "You're an ambassador to Earth now, Cinder. So it's time you got yourself to Earth and started doing some ambassadorizing."

Cinder cocked her head to one side. "That's not a word."

"It should be. Besides, the Grand Minister has had more assistance and transition into his gig than you had when you took the throne. He'll be fine." She locked her elbow with Cinder's and dragged her toward the door. "Now, come on. Paris awaits!"

"We're not going to Paris."

"It's close enough for me."

Cinder set aside her resistance as she and Iko made their way through the palace-turned-government-headquarters. The white marble. The towering glass windows. The sea of stars in the black sky beyond.

She couldn't decide if she was sad or thrilled to be leaving. Iko kept up enough enthusiastic chatter that her worries began to calm, and she was right. Though Cinder had been heavily involved in the transition to the new governmental system—advising the elected leaders as much as she could once they'd taken office— her role was already becoming moot. It had been decided early on that she would continue to be involved in Lunar politics, but as an advisor and ambassador, like Winter. She was in a unique position to continue smoothing the relations between Earth and Luna, after all, and . . .

Kai.

She was desperate to see Kai again. To kiss him. To be in his arms. To laugh at his ironic jokes and watch his eyes crinkle when he laughed at hers.

It was easy for Cinder to justify the desperation because—unromantic as it may have been—she knew that together, she and Kai had the power to do more for the prejudices between their people than any amount of political discussions could hope to accomplish.

When she and Iko entered the spaceship docks that were located beneath the palace, the Rampion was the first thing she saw. It was enormous compared to most of the small royal pod-ships lined up in neat rows. Its metal plating was beat-up and dingy, its cargo-toting body almost cumbersome when compared to the sleek designs that surrounded it. But it was beautiful, and its lowered cargo ramp was more welcoming than any red carpet.

Thorne and Cress were waiting for them at the bottom of the ramp, and when Cress and Iko spotted each other they shared a squeal. Thorne and Cinder shared a cringe, and then they were all smiling and embracing as if they hadn't seen each other in years—even though they still got together with some regularity. Thorne and Cress's role in distributing the letumosis antidote to Earth brought them to Artemisia every time there was a new breakout, and it was those intermittent moments of easy friendship that had helped to keep Cinder sane as she struggled to grasp the intricacies of Lunar transportation systems, trade policies, and educational mandates.

With his arms draped over Cinder's and Iko's shoulders,

Thorne guided them up the ramp. "How does it feel to be a layperson again, Miss Linh?"

"Wonderful," she said. "I never want to hear the words *Your Majesty* ever again."

"Never? Never ever?" Thorne quirked an eyebrow at her. "What if there was an *Imperial* thrown in between them? Would that change your mind?"

Cinder clenched her jaw, glad that his teasing couldn't rile a blush from her. With a sharp elbow jab to his side, she extricated herself from beneath his arm. "How's the ship been holding up?"

"Nice dodge," said Thorne, dropping his other arm from Iko and hooking a thumb over his belt. "But as your question is pertinent, I'll allow it. There's actually been a rattle in the compression system for the past month or so."

Cinder glanced up at the ceiling of the cargo bay, even though she couldn't hear anything with the systems powered down.

"I told him to take it to a mechanic when we were in Dublin last week," said Cress.

"And I told her that I already have a mechanic," said Thorne, pointing at Cinder.

Cress shrugged apologetically.

"It's fine," said Cinder. "I kind of miss the work, actually. I'll check it out when we're in the air."

Thorne clapped his hands. "Great, then let's get this diplomatic envoy started. Ship, raise the ramp! You all just sit back and relax and we'll be on Earth in no time." He turned to head for the cockpit, adding over his shoulder, "I've been practicing takeoffs, by the way. I think you'll be pleasantly surprised."

As soon as he was out of earshot, Cress turned back to Iko and Cinder with a grimace. "He hasn't really gotten any better," she whispered. "Let's go back to the crew quarters. There's more to hold on to back there."

Cress took the lead, walking the narrow corridor of the Rampion with the air of a hostess welcoming important guests into her home. Cinder grinned at her back, thinking of what a change it was from the first time Cress had been aboard the Rampion—all meek and awkward and barely able to say more than two words without hiding behind Thorne.

She took them to one of the small crew quarters—a room long left empty. In fact, as Cress was opening the door, it occurred to Cinder that this had been *her* room for the brief time she'd sought sanctuary on the ship. She stepped inside with a sense of nostalgic awe . . . and promptly began to laugh.

The room was full of white crepe paper and tulle, unburned candles and glass lanterns, streamers and small silk bags overflowing with sugared almonds.

Iko gasped and trailed a finger over an enormous tulle bow. "Is this all for the wedding?"

Cress nodded, but her expression was worried as she looked around at the scattered decorations. "Wolf told us to bring whatever we thought might be needed, so we stopped at a wedding supply store in the Republic and just about cleaned out their stock." Chewing on her lower lip, she glanced back at Iko. "Once we got it all piled in here, though, I started to wonder if it was maybe all a bit on the gaudy side?"

Iko shrugged. "We can work with gaudy."

The Rampion began to rumble. Cress and Iko each took a spot on the lower bunk bed that took up one wall of the cabin, but Cinder made her way through the jumble of rose-petal-stuffed baskets and empty glass vases and stacked ivory linens until she came to the round window at the back of the room.

Cress was right. Thorne's takeoffs were still horrendous. But Cinder didn't move away from that window until the white city of Artemisia was nothing but a glint of light on the moon's cratered surface.

THE LANDING WAS BETTER, MAYBE BECAUSE CINDER WAS SO entertained by Iko's bubbling monologue about European wedding traditions that she hardly noticed the rocks and sways of the ship. While in space, she had fixed the loose fitting that had caused the rattle and spent the rest of the long flight catching up with Thorne and Cress, learning of all the sightseeing and adventures they'd had in between antidote runs. Thorne, it seemed, had made it a personal goal to ensure that Cress got to see and experience everything she'd ever dreamed of seeing and experiencing, and it was a personal goal he was taking seriously. Cress didn't seem to be complaining, though it was clear from the way they leaned into each other that it was his company, more than the museums and monuments, that really mattered to her.

"How often have you been to visit Wolf and Scarlet?" Iko asked, kicking her feet against a storage crate in the cargo bay as Thorne powered down the ship's engines.

"A few times a year," said Cress. "Scarlet finally built us a landing pad beside the hangar so Thorne would stop flattening her crops." She glanced toward the cockpit. "I hope he didn't miss it."

They could hear Thorne's growl from the cockpit. "I didn't miss it!"

The ramp roared and creaked as it began to lower, and Cinder stood, surprised at how her heart started to thunder.

First there was the sky—a strip of impossible blue along the ramp's edge. Then her first full breath of air. Air that came from trees and plants, not a recycling tank, and it was coupled with the aroma of fresh-churned earth and sweet hay and not-so-sweet animals. There were so many noises, too, distantly familiar. Birds chirping. Chickens clucking. A breeze whistling through the opening the ramp had created. And also . . . voices. A cacophony of voices. *Too many* voices.

It wasn't until the ramp was halfway lowered that Cinder saw them. Not Wolf and Scarlet and their friends, but . . . *journalists.*

"It's her! Selene! Your Majesty!"

Cinder took a step back and felt her serenity slough away, leaving behind the same tension she'd lived with for two long years. That feeling of being in the spotlight, of having responsibilities, of needing to meet *expectations* . . .

"Why did you abdicate the throne?" someone yelled. And another: "How does it feel to be back on Earth?" And "Will you attend the Commonwealth ball again this year?" And "Is the upcoming Lunar-Earthen wedding a political statement? Do you want to say anything about the union?"

A loud gunshot blared across the gravel driveway. The journalists screamed and dispersed, some cowering behind the Rampion's landing gear, others rushing back to the safety of their own hovers.

"I'll give you a statement," said Scarlet, reloading the shotgun in her arms as she marched toward them. She sent a piercing glare at the journalists who dared to peek out at her. "And the statement is, Leave my guests alone, you pitiful, news-starved vultures."

With a frustrated huff, she looked up at Cinder, who had been joined by the others at the top of the ramp. Scarlet looked much the same as Cinder remembered her, only more frenzied. Her eyes had an annoyed, bewildered look to them as she gestured haplessly at the farmland behind her.

"Welcome to France. Let's get you inside before they send out the android journalists—*they're* not as easy to scare off."

SCARLET RELEASED A GROAN AS SHE SHUT THE FRONT DOOR behind her guests. "They started showing up two weeks ago," she said. "They tried camping out in the sugar beet fields, like they owned the place! I've had to call the police four times for trespassing, but honestly, I think the police are about as dumbfounded by all this media attention as I am." She sighed and slumped against the door. "I wanted a quiet, intimate wedding, not a *circus.*"

Thorne leaned against the staircase rail. "It's the first known

Lunar-Earthen wedding in generations, the groom is a bioengineered wolf-human hybrid, and you invited the emperor of the Eastern Commonwealth *and* an ex–Lunar Queen. What did you expect?"

Scarlet glared at him. "I am marrying the man that I love, and I invited my *friends* to celebrate with us. I expected a little bit of privacy."

"I'm sorry," said Cinder. "We should have tried to be more discreet with our plans."

Scarlet shook her head. "It's not your fault. Kai's travel schedule is pretty much public knowledge, so there was no stopping this, I'm afraid." She snorted. "Just be glad you weren't here to see the hoard of screaming girls when *he* arrived."

Cinder stood straighter. "He's here already?"

Scarlet nodded. "He arrived last night. And Winter and Jacin flew over from Canada this morning. Everyone's here, so now I just need to survive the next three days of chaos until the wedding, and then it will all be over." She massaged her brow. "At least, that's assuming the bloodsucking heathens out there don't try to crash the ceremony. You know, the worst part of it is that they keep trying to make this out to be some big political statement. 'Earth and Luna, united at last!' 'Earthen girl tortured by Levana agrees to marry Lunar soldier!' It's revolting." She sighed before adding, "He's not *here*, Cinder."

Cinder snapped her attention back to Scarlet, realizing she'd been ignoring most of her diatribe while she peered through the doorways into the kitchen and sitting room and tried to listen for footsteps coming from the floor above. "What?"

Iko tittered, but Scarlet buried her annoyance with an understanding smirk. "Wolf took them for a tour of the farm. They'll be back soon."

"Right. Sorry. I wasn't—"

Scarlet waved her away. "It's fine. Besides, if anyone understands what it's like for their relationship to be treated like a political stunt, it's you."

Cinder lowered her eyes, not sure if that was meant to make her feel better.

"Hey, Cinder," Thorne said, pacing to the opening that separated the entryway from a humble sitting room. "Remember when we were here before? When we were just two crazy fugitives, on the run from the law?"

"You mean when we discovered the secret lair under the hangar where I'd been kept comatose for eight years of my life, then turned into a cyborg by some mystery surgeon before being given away to a family who didn't really want me? Yeah, Thorne, those were the good old days."

Thorne winked. "I was actually referring to that cute blonde who found us and nearly had a heart attack. Hey, is she going to be at the wedding?"

"Her name is Émilie," said Scarlet, "and yes, she is. Please try not to flirt with her in front of your girlfriend. I have enough drama to deal with this week as it is."

Cress shrugged. "It doesn't really faze me much anymore. Besides, he probably already told her he loved her, so what else can he say?"

Thorne cast his gaze to the ceiling in thought. "It's true. I might have. I honestly don't remember."

Cress rolled her eyes, but if she was harboring any resentment, Cinder couldn't detect it. She opted not to tell them that Thorne *had* in fact claimed love at first sight when Émilie had fainted at the farmhouse's front door.

Hinges squeaked from the back of the house, followed by thumping footsteps and Winter's dreamy voice flowing through the house's narrow halls.

"But I will have a chance to milk her before we go? I've never milked a cow before. I think I'd be good at it."

"Of course you would," said Jacin with a chuckle. "She'll just stare at you dumbfounded the whole time like all the other animals that fall under your spell."

"What spell?" said Winter, knocking her shoulder into Jacin as they rounded the base of the stairway. "I'm not a hypnotist."

"Are you sure?"

They froze when they spotted everyone in the foyer.

"You made it!" cried Winter. She flung herself at Cinder, giving her a brief squeeze before embracing Thorne, Cress, and Iko in turn.

Wolf had come in with them, too, showing a full row of sharp teeth as he grinned at the new arrivals. And beside him . . .

"I told them that was the dulcet roar of a Rampion's engines," said Kai, "but they all insisted it was just another media hover flying over." His hands were tucked into his pockets and he was dressed more casually than Cinder was used to seeing him—a cotton button-down shirt with the sleeves rolled to his forearms and dark denim jeans. She had never imagined that farm life might suit him, but he looked as comfortable here as he did anywhere.

Cinder crossed her arms over her chest. "You're an expert on the sound levels of spaceships now, are you?"

"Nah," said Kai. "I've just been waiting to hear that sound all day."

She smiled at him, feeling the hummingbird flutter of her own pulse. He smiled back.

"Aces," said Thorne with a low groan. "They haven't even kissed yet and they're already making me nauseous."

His comment was followed by a pained grunt, but Cinder didn't know which of her friends had smacked him. Kai rolled his eyes, then grabbed Cinder's hand and yanked her toward the back hallway. It was only a few steps. Not even a wall or door separated them from the others, but within moments it felt like they were alone.

Covertly, blissfully alone.

"How was the flight?" Kai whispered, standing so close she imagined she could feel the vibrations of his heartbeat in the air between them.

"Oh, you know," Cinder murmured back. "Thorne was flying, so it was a constant stream of near-death experiences. How's emperor life?"

"Oh, you know. Press conferences. Cabinet meetings. Adoring fans everywhere I go."

"So also a constant stream of near-death experiences?"

"Pretty much." He'd inched closer to her as they talked. Cinder was nearly pressed against the wall, standing between a wall peg holding heavy overalls and a stack of muddy boots on the floor. "Is that an acceptable amount of small talk?"

"Acceptable to me," said Cinder, digging her hands into his hair and pulling him to her.

BREAKFAST SERVED IN 20 MINUTES.

Cinder grumbled under her breath at the message scrolling across the darkness of her eyelids. She squeaked her eyes open and peered into the dim sunlight that filtered through the room's tiny window. The familiarity of the Rampion surrounded her, a far cry from the luxury of Artemisia Palace, yet more comfortable to her even now. The gurgle of a water tank through the metal walls. The aromas of steel and recirculating air. The too-firm mattress on the bunk bed's lower cot.

However, the sensation of an arm thrown over her waist was something new.

She smiled and shut her eyes again, ushering Scarlet's comm away. She and Kai had stayed up far too late—rays of sunlight were appearing on the horizon when they'd finally fallen asleep. They'd wandered the endless crops, their hands interlaced, content that all the journalists had finally gone to bed. They'd sat on the stoop of the farmhouse, staring up at the moon in a near-cloudless sky. They'd ended up in the crew quarters that Kai had slept in during his stint aboard the ship, cuddled on the lower bed and talking, talking, talking, until the words had turned gummy in their mouths and their eyelids had been too heavy to keep open.

It was almost like they'd never been separated at all, and Cinder couldn't help feeling relieved to know that his presence was as reassuring to her now as it ever had been. She felt like she could tell him anything and, judging from the fears and pet peeves and frustrations he'd shared with her, she sensed he felt the same way.

With a heavy sigh, she eased onto her back. Kai groaned in protest and shifted his weight to press his face into the pillow beside her head.

"Scarlet's making breakfast," she told him. Her voice was scratchy from the hours of talking and laughing.

"Time is it?" Kai mumbled into the pillow.

Cinder checked the clock in her head. "Almost nine."

Kai groaned again. They couldn't have slept for more than four hours. She guessed that Wolf and Scarlet had been up since dawn, tending to the farm. They had probably just missed each other.

"Come on," she said, reaching for Kai's arm. "It's a big day."

Kai jerked in protest when her metal hand touched him, and Cinder recoiled.

"Stars, that hand gets cold," Kai murmured. Rolling onto his back, he took the prosthetic hand in between both of his palms, warming it as he would warm icy fingers on a winter's day. Cinder sat up and looked down at him. His eyes were still closed. He could have fallen asleep again, but for his palms rubbing over her metal hand. His shirt was rumpled, his hair tousled against the sheets.

"Kai?"

He grunted in response.

"I love you."

A sleepy smile curved across his mouth. "I love you too."

"Good." Leaning over, she kissed him fast. "Because I'm taking the shower first."

THE HOUSE WAS TOO SMALL TO ACCOMMODATE THEM ALL, SO while Winter and Jacin had taken the one spare bedroom, the others stayed aboard the Rampion, and they made their way across the drive together once they'd all showered and dressed. The journalists were out in force again, screaming their questions and snapping their pictures, but Wolf and Jacin had erected a simple rope barrier the evening before and, for now at least, the journalists were content to stay behind it rather than risk Scarlet's wrath.

Cinder tried to ignore them, but their presence made her a hundred times more aware of the warmth of Kai's hand pressing against her lower back.

The house smelled of bacon and strong coffee when they entered. Jacin was sitting at the round table in the kitchen, peeling apart a croissant, while Scarlet, Wolf, and Winter bustled around him in an assortment of patterned cooking aprons—even Wolf had blue-checkered fabric tied around his waist.

"Grab a plate," Scarlet ordered, pointing at a stack of plates on the counter with a wooden spoon. "We're going to eat in the sitting room. It's too crowded in here."

Cinder did as she was told, helping herself to a cinnamon pastry, some bacon, a casserole of potatoes, onions, and peppers, and a cluster of garnet-purple grapes. Then she retreated to the sitting room, where Iko was waiting with one leg thrown over the arm of a rocking chair. She sighed when Cinder sat on the floor beside her.

"I don't want to hear one word about how delicious that is," said Iko.

"It's terrible," said Cinder, biting a piece of bacon in half. After swallowing, she added, "Especially the bacon. You would *hate* bacon."

The others filed in, taking over the sofa and nearly every available spot on the worn rug. Wolf and Scarlet came last.

"One of you had better be planning on making lunch," said Scarlet, untying her apron as she claimed the last spot on the sofa. Wolf handed her a plate of food, then sat between her feet, draping one arm over her knee as he gobbled down his own food.

Thorne lifted his fork. "I'll make a run for takeout?"

"Deal," said Scarlet, clinking the side of her fork against his.

Iko stopped rocking in her chair and leaned forward. "So tell us what's in store for your big day. Have you had fun planning it? What are you most excited about?"

Scarlet leaned her head against the sofa. "I'm most excited for it to be over, and for all those stupid media people to leave so we can have our lives back."

Wolf petted her knee and kept eating.

Cress frowned. "Aren't you excited to be married?"

"Oh, sure," said Scarlet. "That part will be nice. But I never wanted to have a big wedding, and I certainly didn't expect it to turn into this jamboree." She straightened again. "Not that I'm regretting inviting you guys," she added, looking pointedly at Kai and Cinder, with an extra glance at Winter. "Obviously, I want you here. It's just . . ." She heaved a big sigh.

"We understand," said Kai, picking apart the sections of an orange. "Having lived with paparazzi my whole life, I would never wish it on anyone."

"You don't really think they'll interrupt the ceremony, do you?" asked Iko.

Scarlet shrugged. "I hope they have more integrity than that. Although it is tradition for the bride and groom to walk to the ceremony through the streets of town and cut through ribbons that the children are supposed to have prepared for us. But I can't even fathom walking down my own driveway with those goons out there, so I don't know if that's going to happen."

Cinder cleared her throat. "Is that tradition . . . important to you?"

Scarlet scoffed. "The only tradition that I care about is saying *I do.*"

There was an almost visible sigh of relief around the room and Cinder flinched, sure it would be obvious to Scarlet, but she was buttering a slice of bread and didn't seem to notice anything unusual. Kai caught Cinder's eyes and mimed wiping sweat from his brow. She buried a laugh.

"Tell us more," said Winter. "I know very little about your Earthen customs, and it could come in useful for my role as cultural ambassador someday." She cupped her cheek with her hand, nearly obscuring her scars. "But mostly, I want to know what traditions Scarlet Benoit-Kesley deems important."

"Oh, I don't know," said Scarlet. "We'll exchange rings and say some vows, but you do that on Luna too, don't you?"

Winter nodded. "Will you carry a bouquet?"

"Probably. I thought I'd pick whatever looked good in the garden that day."

"Do you have a color scheme?" asked Iko.

Scarlet hesitated. "Um . . . white?"

"Will there be cake?" asked Cress.

Scarlet grinned. "Of a sort. Émilie is bringing *croquembouche*, which is a big stack of doughy pastry balls drizzled with caramel. It'll be delicious."

"I heard of a tradition," said Thorne, "where the guests are supposed to make a bunch of raucous noise outside of the bridal chambers on the wedding night, until you give us candy and send us away."

Scarlet glared at him. "Yeah, please don't do that."

"How many people will be there?" asked Kai.

Another groan from Scarlet. "The whole blasted town, from what I can tell. I'm not sure how that happened—I certainly didn't invite everybody. Small and intimate, I kept saying. Only close friends, I told them. But in a small town, I guess everyone just assumes that *they* fit under that umbrella. If it was up to me, it would just be the people in this room." She paused. "Well, and Émilie. Because, again, she's bringing the dessert."

Wolf stood up and began gathering everyone's empty plates to be returned to the kitchen. After he had gone, Iko leaned forward and clapped her hands. "I know! Why don't you show us your dress? I'm *dying* to see it."

Scarlet cocked her head. "You can't wait two more days?"

"Absolutely not. Please?"

With a careless shrug, Scarlet pulled herself to her feet. "Come on, it's upstairs." She left the room, with Iko close on her heels. Cinder made to follow, but hesitated, glancing around at the guys.

"You can handle this?" she asked.

Thorne saluted her. "No problem. Just distract her for as long as you can."

Wolf reappeared from his trip to the kitchen and settled an enormous hand on Cinder's shoulder, so heavy it made her jump in surprise.

"Don't let her come down here without the Something Old," he whispered.

"Something Old?"

He nodded. "She'll explain. She didn't mention it before, but I know it's one of the traditions that is important to her."

"Better hurry up," said Jacin, nudging Winter, Cinder, and Cress toward the staircase. "You're in our way, and evidently we have *decorating* to do."

He didn't try to hide his disgust at the idea, and Cinder snorted at the mental image of Jacin decorating anything.

She turned and hurried up to the second floor, but paused halfway up the staircase. Cress crashed into her, nearly knocking Cinder to her knees, but she grabbed the rail and steadied herself.

"What is it?" asked Cress.

"Nothing," said Cinder, trying to shake off the wave of memories that was accosting her. She had climbed these stairs once before, when she and Thorne had come to the farm searching for Michelle Benoit. When they'd come searching for answers to Cinder's past. "It's just weird being here again," she said, as much to herself as to Cress and Winter. "Being here, and not feeling hunted or afraid." She glanced back and shrugged. "It's a big difference from the last time I was here."

With a smile she hoped looked cavalier, she vaulted up the rest of the steps.

The second floor held a small corridor and three doors—two of which were shut. The open door revealed a bedroom with blankets in disarray, sun-bleached curtains, and a large tuxedo hanging from a hook on one wall. Iko was sitting on the mussed bed with her knees drawn up to her chest, watching as Scarlet wrestled with a garment bag. No sooner had Cinder and the others filed in than Scarlet spun toward them with a pronounced "Voilà!" and held up the dress for them to see.

A mutual gasp arose from Iko, Cress, and Winter, followed by a round of giddy *oohs*. Cinder couldn't help chuckling at the drama of it all.

The dress *was* beautiful, though, and uniquely Scarlet. A simple white cotton dress, with a sweetheart neckline accented with sheer fabric that continued to her neck and was finished with white piping. A full skirt that would hang just below Scarlet's knees. A bright red sash around the waist was tied in a simple bow, matching the red vest and bow tie of the tuxedo.

"It's perfect!" said Iko, scrambling off the bed to touch the dress. She ran her fingers adoringly over the sash and down the full gathering of the skirt. "Simple and lovely—just like you, Scarlet." She sighed dreamily. "You *have* to try it on for us."

Scarlet waved away the suggestion. "You'll see it on me in a couple of days."

"Oh, please," gushed Cress, tucking her clasped hands under her chin. She was joined by pleading doe eyes from Iko, but Scarlet just shook her head and made to put the dress back into the garment bag.

"I don't want to risk spilling something on it," she said.

"It's good luck!" Winter said suddenly, her eyes bright with mischief.

Scarlet paused. "What's good luck?"

"On Luna," said Winter, folding her hands as if she were reciting from a wedding etiquette guide, "it's considered good luck for the bride to don her dress for at least an hour for each of the three days leading up to the wedding. It symbolizes her commitment to the marriage. And as your groom is Lunar, I think we should follow some of his traditions, don't you?"

"An *hour?*" said Scarlet. "That's really pushing it, don't you think?"

Winter shrugged.

With a drawn-out sigh, Scarlet said, "Fine, I'll go put it on. But I'm not going to stay in it for an hour. I still have chores to do." She slipped out of the bedroom carrying the dress, and a moment later they heard the click of the bathroom door in the hall.

"I've never heard of that tradition before," said Cress.

"That's because I made it up," said Winter.

Iko beamed at her. "Well done. Now, quick." She hurried to the tuxedo and pulled it off the peg, passing it to Cress, who passed it to Cinder. "Get that down to Wolf before she comes back."

Cinder rushed it to the staircase and hissed. Within seconds, Kai appeared in the foyer below with a garland of ribbon and roses draped across his shoulders. Cinder smirked. "Having fun down there?"

"Surprisingly, I sort of am. Turns out Thorne has a weird knack for this wedding thing. He says it's because Cress has been poring over wedding feeds for the past few months, but . . . I think he's secretly enjoying it."

Thorne's voice came booming from the sitting room: "Don't mock a guy for having good taste!"

"Here, give this to Wolf," said Cinder, lowering the tuxedo to Kai. He flashed her a thumbs-up before retreating.

Hearing the click of a door, Cinder pivoted around to see Scarlet emerging from the bathroom, wearing the white dress. "I need someone to zip it up," she said, pulling her curls over one shoulder and turning her back to Cinder.

"Er, we should let Winter do it," said Cinder, coaxing her back into the bedroom. "You know my tendency to leave grease stains on every pretty thing I touch."

The other girls were anxiously anticipating Scarlet's return, and her appearance brought on another chorus of swoons. Winter pulled up the zipper and Scarlet gave a half turn, letting the full skirt swish around her legs. It was the girliest thing Cinder had ever seen her do, and even Scarlet was beaming when she caught sight of herself in the full-length mirror in the corner.

"Oh, Scarlet," Cress sighed. "You're getting *married*. It's all like a dream."

"I guess it sort of is," Scarlet agreed, her cheeks flushing pink around her freckles.

Iko petted the edge of the bed. "Sit down and let me do your hair."

"My hair? What are you going to do to my hair?"

"I'm not sure yet, which is why I need to practice for the big day."

With Scarlet's back turned, Iko winked at Cinder, who alone knew that Iko had been researching popular wedding styles and practicing on the palace maids for weeks.

Scarlet groaned. "How long will this take?"

"Why, you have somewhere else to be? Stop whining and sit down. Cinder, you have those hair accoutrements I told you to hold on to?"

"Oh. Right." Cinder had forgotten all about the brush, clips, bobby pins, and curling iron that Iko had ordered her to stash in the hollow compartment of her cyborg leg before they'd left Luna. She sat down and pulled them out.

Scarlet's jaw dropped. "You're frighteningly prepared," she said, pushing a fingertip through the pile of bobby pins that Cinder set on the bed. "What if I told you I just wanted to wear my hair down, like normal?"

"Then I would use my powers of persuasion to change your mind." Iko grabbed the sides of Scarlet's head and forced her to face forward. "Now hold still."

The others sat down to watch Iko work. She'd just finished teasing the hair at the crown of Scarlet's head when Scarlet asked, "Why is Wolf's tuxedo missing?"

Cinder traded looks with the others. "It ... um ... we were ..."

"Thorne came up and took it," interrupted Cress. "When you were changing."

Scarlet frowned. "What for?"

"Because ... he wanted to ..." Cress swallowed. "Um ... compare it to his own tuxedo. To make sure they were, uh ... matching?" Her gaze darted to one side as she realized how implausible that sounded, even for Thorne.

"She means," interrupted Cinder, "that Thorne was concerned that he and Wolf might have purchased the same tuxedo, which I guess is considered a big faux pas. You know how Thorne is about that sort of thing. Can't be seen in the same tux as the groom! How *embarrassing*, right?"

Scarlet opened her mouth to speak again, her brow furrowed, when Iko asked, "What shoes are you going to wear?"

Scarlet moved to turn her head, but Iko grabbed it and faced her forward again. She huffed. "I don't know. Winter said she had a pair I could borrow."

Winter snapped and hopped to her feet. "Right. They're still packed away. I'll go get them." She darted across the hall into the guest room, rustled around for a moment, then returned carrying a pair of red heels, almost the exact color of the dress's sash.

The appearance of the perfect shoes were met with another round of *ahh*s, and this time Cinder couldn't contain a chuckle and shake of her head. Winter sat cross-legged in front of Scarlet and pushed the shoes onto her feet. "How do they feel?"

"Not bad." Scarlet turned her ankle back and forth. "If I can keep from tripping and breaking an ankle in them, this wedding will be a smashing success."

Iko snorted. "They're barely a two-inch heel."

"Which is two inches taller than I'm used to."

A crash from downstairs made them all jump.

"What was—" Scarlet started to push herself off the bed, but Iko held firm to a lock of hair and tugged her back down.

"What part of 'hold still' don't you understand?" she scolded.

"I'll go see what it was," said Cinder, slipping into the hallway and darting down the stairs. Jacin was sitting at the bottom, hunched over something and working intently.

"That was Thorne," he said, without glancing up at her.

"What did he do? Knock down a wall?" Cinder stepped past Jacin, but hesitated when she saw the vase of white flowers on the floor at his feet. He was meticulously pulling the flowers out of the water, one by one, and wiring their stems together. His brow was knotted in concentration.

"Are you making a bouquet?" she asked incredulously.

"Shut up." He held the cluster in one hand and turned it a few different directions, before plucking out a white hydrangea and adding it to the mix.

Shaking her head, Cinder turned away and glanced into the sitting room. It was already transformed—flowers and garlands and tulle bows draped over every surface. It was beautiful, if also a bit chaotic.

Wolf was nowhere to be seen—probably changing, she thought—but Thorne and Kai were each standing on chairs and hanging a swath on the wall above the fireplace mantel as a part of their makeshift altar.

"What's going on?" Cinder asked. "What was that noise?"

"Iss all unner control," said Thorne through a mouthful of tacks.

She looked at Kai, who shrugged sheepishly. "We had a disagreement with a bookshelf, but Thorne's right. We've got this."

Cinder opened her mouth to demand more information, but hesitated and glanced around the room again. Nothing seemed irreparably damaged.

"How much more time do you think we have?" Kai asked.

"Iko is doing her hair right now. Maybe . . . half an hour?"

He gave her a nod, and Cinder turned and rushed back up to the bedroom.

"Nothing to worry about," she said as she let herself back in. Iko had almost finished with a complicated-looking braid that wrapped around Scarlet's head like a halo, leaving the bottom half of her hair loose and curly around her shoulders.

"But what was it?" asked Scarlet.

Cinder gaped at her, scrolling quickly through a list of potential logical responses. "Uh . . . they knocked over a chair. When they were . . . wrestling." She flinched on the inside, surprised that her internal lie detector didn't go off on herself. She could see the suspicion deepening in Scarlet's face, but she smiled and said, "That looks really great, Iko."

"I still need to touch up her natural curls," said Iko, turning on the curling iron. "And tuck some of these pearls into the braid."

Scarlet laughed. "This is just for practice, Iko. Don't waste your time."

Iko made a clicking sound in her throat—akin to a subtle *tsk*. "How else are we going to get the full effect? Dress, shoes, hair, everything. It all has to work together."

Scarlet sighed. "You're all acting weird. Is there something going on that I should know about?"

A chorus of highly incriminating *No*s and *Not at all*s flurried around her. Scarlet scoffed.

"Why don't you tell us about . . . something old?" said Cinder, sitting beside Winter.

Scarlet frowned. "Something old?"

"Yeah. Um. Wolf had said something about a tradition . . ."

"Oh!" Scarlet fluffed her skirt, keeping out the wrinkles as much as she could. "There's an old, old wedding tradition, in which the bride should wear something old, something new, something borrowed, and something blue. So, for me, my dress is new." She gestured at the dress. "The shoes are borrowed. And my something old is right over there." She pointed.

Cress turned and picked something small and shining off the top of the dresser. She held it toward Scarlet, who nodded before showing it to the others.

It was a brooch. A yellow gemstone was at its center, set into a five-pointed star, with two golden wings stretching out to either side. Cinder's retina display recognized it almost immediately, informing her that it was a pilot pin from the European Federation military, circa 81 T.E.

"It was my grandmother's," said Scarlet, holding out her palm. Cress set the pin into it. "It was given to her when she became a pilot. She gave it to me years ago, and . . . I thought it would be like having a part of her with me. I thought I'd pin it to the bouquet or something."

"Don't be silly." Winter rose up onto her knees and scooted closer to Scarlet. Taking the brooch from her hands, she leaned forward and pinned it through the fabric of the white bodice, right over Scarlet's heart. "This is clearly where it belongs."

Scarlet was smiling as she looked down at the brooch. "You don't think it clashes with the outfit?"

"Oh, it definitely clashes," Iko said from behind her.

"But do you care?" added Winter.

Scarlet shook her head. "Not really."

"I figured as much."

"Done!" Iko leaned back. "Get up and show everyone."

"When did you become so bossy?" Scarlet said, chuckling, as she stood and straightened the dress. She gave a twirl, then stopped and let everyone admire Iko's handiwork. Her hair fell in large spiraling ringlets—still curly and wild, but neater than she usually wore it, and topped off with the elegant, pearl-studded braid. She went to look at herself in the mirror.

After a long, silent moment, she swallowed and placed a finger against her grandmother's brooch. She sniffed, then tilted her head way back and inhaled deeply in an attempt to keep tears from falling. After a second, she laughed again and lowered her head.

"I wish she were here," she murmured, and no one had to ask who she meant. "She would have loved him so much." There was another sniff, and she turned around, swiping at her eyes. "She would have loved all of you, too. I think . . . I think she was a little concerned that I never made very many friends." She swept her arms in no particular direction. "And now look. I have so many friends, I need a cargo ship to keep you all in."

Winter stood and wrapped her arms around Scarlet's waist. "She's in the stars," she whispered. "Jacin and I saw her when we were in the sky, and she was smiling down at you, and so very, very proud."

Scarlet shook her head even as she sank into the embrace. "I thought you weren't crazy anymore."

Winter grinned. "I never made any promises," she said, lifting her chin high. "And I believe it, besides. She is watching you, Scar, and she is proud."

With a nod, Scarlet rubbed at her eyes one more time. "This is good," she said. "It's better to get all of this out of the way so I'm not a mess during the actual wedding, right?"

Cinder looked down, but she could still sense the awkward glances shared between Cress and Iko before Cress cleared her throat and asked, "What about the something blue? You didn't tell us what that was going to be."

"Oh, that." Scarlet extricated herself from Winter's arms. "I couldn't really think of anything, so I thought I'd skip that part. It's just a silly tradition, anyway."

Winter jolted, her eyes gleaming. "It's not silly at all, and I know just the thing. Do you have any blue thread?"

Scarlet peered at her uncertainly. "There's a sewing kit in the top drawer over there."

Winter hurried to the dresser, found the kit, and within moments had threaded a needle with cobalt blue thread. "Sit down again."

"Now what are you doing?" Scarlet asked with some trepidation as Winter folded up the hem of her dress, revealing the silky lining underneath.

"Don't worry. I taught myself how to embroider years ago." She lowered her head to concentrate, her thick spiral curls curtaining her face.

Scarlet sighed, but didn't argue. "How long is *this* going to take? Maybe someone should go tell Wolf to water the flower beds before it gets much later?"

"I'll go," said Cress. She was out of the room in a blink, shutting the door softly behind her.

Apparently tired of avoiding wrinkles in the dress, Scarlet sighed and lay back on the bed, letting Winter do whatever she was doing to the lining. Cinder tried to peer over Winter's shoulder, but her hair blocked the needlework, so she gave up and joined Iko on the bed, leaning against the headboard.

She pulled up the commlink screen on her retina display and jotted off a quick message.

ANYTHING WE'RE FORGETTING?

Iko glanced at her. They rarely communicated using their internal computer interfaces anymore—using portscreens instead made them *both* feel more human—but being cyborg and android still had their conveniences.

CRESS IS SUPPOSED TO BE HANDLING THE MUSIC, came Iko's reply. I JUST SENT HER A COMM REMINDING HER.

Cinder nodded and folded her arms over her knees. "Are you nervous?" she asked.

Scarlet turned her head. She was probably destroying that braid, but no one said anything. "No," she said. "At least, not about getting married. I'm a little nervous at the idea that this has become an international spectacle and there are people who don't know me or Wolf who are going to take it on themselves to judge our wedding, but ... no. I'm not nervous about getting married, or being married. It's Wolf. It feels ... right." Her eyes turned hazy as she stared at some insignificant spot on the wall over Cinder's head. "There was never a time when it didn't feel right."

Cinder swallowed and couldn't help thinking of Kai. Had there ever been a time when it didn't feel right?

There had been difficult times, certainly.

When she'd first started to fall for him but had been too scared to tell him she was cyborg.

When he'd learned that she was Lunar, and thought she'd brainwashed him into having feelings for her.

When she'd kidnapped him, undermining his attempts to end a war and obtain the letumosis antidote.

And, oh, that one time when he'd married her tyrannical aunt.

She couldn't very well say that their relationship had ever been *easy*, but then, neither had Wolf and Scarlet's.

But had it always been *right*?

Her pulse hummed at the question.

It must have been, she thought, even way back when everything was so wrong. She couldn't have fought so hard for him otherwise.

She wasn't sure how much time had passed with her lost in thought when a subtle knock sounded at the door and Cress re-entered. "The flowers are taken care of," she said, and winked at Iko. Luckily, Scarlet had her eyes shut and didn't notice the blatant code word, if that's what that was supposed to be.

"I'm almost finished," said Winter.

"I can't wait to see what you've done to my beautiful dress," said Scarlet, although she didn't sound overly concerned.

"You will love it." Winter tied a knot into the thread and bent over, using her teeth to cut off the long strings. "There."

Scarlet sat up as the others crowded around.

This time, when Cinder saw what Winter had done, even she couldn't prevent a joyful gasp from escaping her.

In the beautiful blue thread, into the silk lining of Scarlet's wedding dress, Winter had embroidered a single word in simple, elegant script: *Alpha.*

"You're right," said Scarlet, rubbing her thumb over the word. "It's . . . perfect."

"It's something blue, at least," said Winter.

Cress cleared her throat. Cinder looked up to see that she had her portscreen with her, and she was entering some command. She had an excited, beatific smile on her face.

"What now?" said Scarlet, her suspicious tone returning.

The only response, though, was the sound of string music echoing up from the floor below, loud enough to fill the whole house.

Scarlet pulled herself off the bed and let her uncertain glare travel from one friend to the next. "What's going on?"

Cress pulled open the door, letting the music spill into the room.

Scarlet took a hesitant step toward the door, but Iko stopped her and made a few quick adjustments to her hair before nudging her forward. They all filed behind the bride as she emerged on the landing and peered down the narrow staircase. Since Cinder had been out before, the banister had been wrapped with white crepe paper and finished with an enormous tulle bow. The doorway below, which separated the foyer from the sitting room, was hung with fine white streamers. The whole house smelled of roses.

Scarlet turned back. "What have you done?"

They all stared with close-lipped, secretive smiles.

Shaking her head, Scarlet made her way down the stairs in her red-heeled shoes. When she turned into the sitting room, she was greeted by Jacin, holding out an expertly crafted bouquet. She took it from him, her mouth hanging open, and stepped through the fluttering streamers.

Then she began to laugh.

Cinder hurried to join her, eager to see what the boys had done. But when she stepped into the sitting room, it was not the decorations that caught her attention first, but Wolf, standing in front of the fireplace altar in his formal black-and-red tuxedo. Though it had been made especially for him, the jacket still stretched across his broad chest and shoulders, and the red bow tie was almost humorous against his fierce features and lupine bone structure.

Almost.

Despite everything Levana had tried to do to him, Cinder had to admit that he was still handsome, with his olive skin and vivid green eyes and unkempt hair. Most of all, though, it was the look he was giving Scarlet, which would have taken away the breath of any girl.

Kai and Thorne were there, too, each of them standing with their hands in their pockets, rocking back on their heels with supremely smug looks on their faces, like they were daring anyone to suggest it wasn't the most beautiful impromptu wedding ever created.

And they had done a marvelous job—much better than Cinder would have expected. The turmoil from before had somehow been tweaked and massaged into a picture-perfect scene, with flower garlands over the tables and ivory fabric draping the windows and pillar candles flickering around the room.

There was also Émilie, Scarlet's friend and the girl who had once been deathly afraid of Cinder, back when she was a wanted fugitive. Now, Émilie was beaming and standing next to a small table that held a towering pyramid of golden pastries.

"What," Scarlet breathed, clutching the bouquet, "is this?"

Wolf smiled around his canine teeth. "You are the most beautiful sight I have ever laid eyes on."

Scarlet cocked her head. "And *you* look like you're about to get married." There was blatant amusement in her tone.

Wolf's eyes dipped once to the carpet, but he didn't stop smiling. He paced across the room and took Scarlet's hands in his, so that their palms engulfed the wrapped flower stems.

"Scarlet," he said, "I know how frustrated you've been with the ... attention our wedding has brought, and how much you hate what it was turning into. And on our wedding day, all I want is for you to be happy and content. I don't want you thinking about journalists or cameras or newsfeeds. You didn't sign up for any of that, and it isn't fair to you. So ... I thought ... I wondered if you might marry me now, *here*, instead."

Scarlet tore her gaze from him and let it wander to everyone else in the room. "You were all in on this."

"Wolf had the idea a few weeks ago," said Kai, "when he noticed you were getting ... upset about the media. That's why he wanted us all to come early."

Scarlet blinked tears from her eyes. "I . . . this is . . . it's perfect, but I think you might have forgotten one important element." She turned back to Wolf. "There's no officiant here. Who's going to marry us?"

Wolf's grin widened, and he glanced at Kai.

Scarlet followed the look. "Seriously?"

Kai shrugged. "I've never done it before, but it is within my powers as the emperor of the Eastern Commonwealth to marry people. It will be perfectly legitimate and binding."

Wolf took a step closer so that he towered over Scarlet, creating what could have been a moment of intimacy if the room hadn't been so crowded. "So? Will you marry me?"

Scarlet started to smile.

"Wait. Before you answer that," said Thorne, gesturing around the room, "you should know that the store where we got all this stuff doesn't take returns."

Casting her gaze skyward, Scarlet said, "Well, in *that* case. Yes. Yes, of course I will." Her eyes glimmered as she draped her arms over Wolf's shoulders. His hands spread out across the sash at her waist and he bent toward her—

But just before their lips touched, Thorne thrust his hand in between them, receiving dual kisses on his fingers. Wolf and Scarlet jerked back.

"Slow those rockets," said Thorne. "I'm no expert, but I'm pretty sure we're not to the kissing part yet." He pried Scarlet away from Wolf, who growled low in his throat, and ordered, "Places, everyone!"

Cinder gladly claimed one of the wooden chairs that had been brought in from the kitchen, and Émilie took the seat beside her, whispering, "Aren't they the most beautiful couple? I introduced them, you know."

Cinder cast a frown at her. "You did?"

Émilie shrugged and flashed an impish grin. "Well . . . sort of."

Kai and Wolf stood at the makeshift altar, while Winter and Jacin took the remaining dining chairs. Thorne led Scarlet back out to the foyer, and Cinder could hear him whispering hasty directions before coming to sit beside Cress and Iko on the sheet-draped sofa.

After Cress punched a new command into her portscreen, the music changed to a classic wedding march. The change was affecting, sweeping away the frivolity of the decorations and Thorne's humor and filling the house with a sense of intent.

Scarlet waited a moment, allowing the music to permeate the ceremony, before she glided through the wall of streamers. Her eyes were locked onto Wolf's as she took one meaningful, patient step after another.

Émilie sniffled and raised a handkerchief to her nose. "I love weddings."

Grinning, Cinder glanced toward Kai and found him smiling back at her. If he was nervous to be playing such an important role on such a momentous occasion, he didn't show it.

Scarlet stopped beside Wolf, and Cress lowered the music's volume, letting it fade pleasantly into silence. There was another sniffle in the room—*Winter*, Cinder guessed.

"Dear friends," Kai began, "we are gathered today to witness and to celebrate the union between Wo—er, Ze'ev Kesley and Scarlet Benoit. Though we are a small gathering, it's clear that the love we feel for this bride and groom would span to Luna and back." His copper-brown eyes passed fondly from Scarlet to Wolf. "Of course, we know that the world sees this wedding as a historical event. The first recorded marriage union between a Lunar and an Earthen since the second era. And maybe that is important. Maybe the love and compassion these two people have for each other is symbolic of hope for the future. Maybe this wedding signifies the possibility that someday our two races will not only learn to tolerate each other, but to love and appreciate each other as well. Or, *maybe...*" Kai's eyes glinted. "...this relationship has absolutely nothing to do with politics, and everything to do with our shared human need to find someone who will care for us as much as we care for them. To find a partner who complements us and teaches us. Who makes us stronger. Who makes us want to be our best possible self."

Cinder heard yet another sniffle—this time from Iko, and she nearly choked. Iko, like her, couldn't cry, but that had never stopped her from faking it before.

Kai continued, "I think that when every person in this room looks at Ze'ev and Scarlet, they don't see a Lunar and an Earthen. We don't see an agenda, or two people trying to make a statement. I think we see two people who were lucky enough to find each other in this vast universe, and they weren't going to let any boundaries of distance or race or even physiological tampering get in the way of a happy life together."

Cinder listed her head thoughtfully. *Distance. Race. Physiological tampering.* It was almost as if Kai wasn't just talking about Wolf and Scarlet. He could just as easily have been talking about their own relationship. She squinted at Kai, newly suspicious, but his eyes never darted toward her, and she began to feel self-absorbed for thinking it. This was Wolf and Scarlet's moment, and Kai respected that.

But when he was writing this speech, the similarities must have occurred to him. Right?

She held her breath, listening a little more closely to Kai's words, wondering if he'd intended a meaning that went beyond this one ceremony.

Kai reached into his pocket and pulled out two golden rings. He handed one to Wolf, then took the bouquet from Scarlet and gave her the other.

"In preparing for this ceremony," Kai said, setting the bouquet on the mantel behind him, "I did some research and learned that the word *Alpha* has held many meanings across history."

A chuckle moved through the room. They all knew of the "alpha mate" relationship that Wolf and Scarlet had, and over the years it had developed into an inside joke among them. But Cinder also knew it was a joke founded on a deeper truth. Wolf and Scarlet took the designation seriously, in a way that even Cinder could admit was painfully romantic.

"*Alpha* can refer to the first of something," said Kai, "or the beginning of *everything*. It can be attributed to a particularly powerful or charismatic person, or it can signify the dominant leader in a pack of animals, most notably, of course, wolves." His serious expression tweaked briefly into a teasing smile. "It has meanings in chemistry, physics, and even astronomy, where it describes the brightest star in a constellation. But it seems clear that Ze'ev and Scarlet have created their own definition for the word, and their relationship has given this word a new meaning for all of us. Being an Alpha means that you'll stand against all adversity to be with your mate. It means accepting each other, both for your strengths and your flaws. It means forging your own path to happiness and to love." He nodded at Wolf. "Now I'll have you place the ring on your bride's finger and repeat after me."

Wolf took Scarlet's hands into his, as tenderly as he would pick up an injured butterfly, and slid the band onto her finger. His voice was rough and wavering as he recited—"I, Ze'ev Kesley, do hereby claim you, Scarlet Benoit, as my wife and my Alpha. Forevermore, you will be my mate, my star, my beginning of everything." He smiled down at her, his eyes swimming with emotion. Scarlet returned the look, and though Wolf's expression teetered between proud and bashful, Scarlet's face contained nothing but joy. "You are the one. You have always been, and you will always be, the only one."

Scarlet took the second ring—a significantly larger version of the same unadorned band—and pressed it onto Wolf's finger. "I, Scarlet Benoit, do hereby claim you, Ze'ev Kesley, as my husband and my Alpha. Forevermore, you will be my mate, my star, my beginning of everything. You are the one. You have always been, and you will always be, the only one."

Wolf folded his hands around hers. From where she sat, Cinder could see that he was shaking.

Kai grinned. "By the power given to me by the people of Earth, under the laws of the Earthen Union and as witnessed by those gathered here today, I do now pronounce you husband and wife." He spread his hands in invitation. "You may kiss your—"

Wolf wrapped his arms around Scarlet's waist, lifting her off the floor, and kissed her before Kai could finish. Or maybe she kissed him. It seemed mutual, as her hands wound through his disheveled hair.

The room exploded with cheers, everyone launching to their feet to congratulate the still-kissing couple. Scarlet had lost one of her red shoes.

"I'll get the champagne," said Thorne, heading toward the kitchen. "Those two are going to be thirsty when they finally come up for air."

CINDER COLLAPSED ONTO THE STAIRS AND LEANED AGAINST the rail, where the crepe paper wrappings had come unstuck and were slowly unwinding themselves as the night went on. She was exhausted. Her right foot was throbbing and her left leg felt like it was filled with lead. She'd never danced so much in her life, not even at last year's ball, when she'd been too self-conscious about everyone staring at her to spend more than a handful of songs on the ballroom floor. But this felt different. Cress had somehow compiled the perfect list of songs, and every time it seemed the party was dwindling, a song with just the right beat would come on and everyone would be up again, laughing and spinning. Kai and

Winter had even taught the others a few basic waltz steps, and Iko had made it a point to steal multiple dances with every person in the room. She, of course, was tireless. Even Émilie had been folded easily into their festivities.

There had been feasting, too, though mostly on the *croquem-bouche*, which had so far contributed to both the lunch and dinner of the day, and was probably going to become a late-night snack as well.

And there was laughter. And teasing. And nostalgic remembrances of their many adventures, and the times when most of them had been crew members aboard the Rampion.

Kai appeared before Cinder, running a tired hand through his hair, and slumped down on the stair beside her. "Well? How do you think we did?"

She settled her head on his shoulder and watched Iko and Jacin waltz across the foyer, not really sure who was leading who. "I'd call it a brilliant success. All those journalists are going to be so disappointed when they find out they missed it."

"They'll have plenty to report on still. They don't need to intrude on Wolf and Scarlet's privacy anymore in order to do it."

"Are you going to hold a press conference in place of the wedding in a couple days? Tell the world about your first foray into matrimonial officiating? Wax poetic about the historical importance of such a union?"

He turned his head and smirked down at her. "Nope. But I might tell them what an honor it was for me to be able to marry two of my closest friends, who happen to love each other very much."

Her grin widened. "That won't satisfy them at all."

"I know. That's half the appeal."

Cinder took Kai's hand and squeezed it. "There's something I want to show you. Do you think anyone would notice if we slipped away for a bit?"

He raised an eyebrow at her. "Given that we make up a full quarter of the guest list, I would be a little insulted if they didn't notice."

"It was a rhetorical question."

"Then by all means, lead the way."

She stood and headed for the back door.

Darkness had fallen and the fields were lit only by the moon and the stars, casting the world in a wash of silver-blue. Cinder paused on the short porch, listening for the sounds of voices or footsteps or android treads, but it seemed the paparazzi had gotten bored with waiting for their prey to emerge from the farmhouse and retreated for the night.

Still holding Kai's hand, she led him across the drive to the enormous hangar that housed Scarlet's podship. Not wanting to turn on the hangar's light and alert someone to their presence, she shut the door and turned on the flashlight in her cyborg finger, letting the thin beam of light guide them around the podship and a cluster of toolboxes stacked up on the floor. She found the cabinet at the back of the hangar, just where it had been the last time she'd been there. Releasing Kai's hand, she crouched down and felt around the floor of the cabinet until her fingers brushed against the latch she knew was there. She yanked it upward, revealing an eerie blackness and a series of plastic rungs set into the concrete wall, disappearing into the shadows below.

Kai grunted in surprise. "You have my attention."

Cinder shone the flashlight down into the hatch to see where she was heading before she grabbed the first rung and lowered herself down. Kai followed fast behind.

As soon as she heard his feet hit the ground, Cinder said, "Lights on."

A generator started to hum, and overhead lights flickered to life, brightening the space that was as large as the hangar above, but intended for a much different purpose. Cinder swallowed as she looked around. Nothing had changed since she and Thorne had discovered this place two years before. She wondered if Scarlet had ever come down here to see the room her grandmother had kept a secret for so long—if she was curious, or willing to let it lie abandoned and forgotten for eternity.

There was the suspended animation tank where she had rested for most of her childhood.

There was the operating table where she had been transformed into a cyborg.

There were the machines that had kept her alive and stimulated her brain and monitored her vital signs, all while she went on sleeping her dreamless sleep.

The silence that engulfed her and Kai was as thick as the metallic-scented air of the secret room until Kai brushed past her and went to stand beside the empty tank. A blue gel in its base still showed the faint imprint of a child's body.

"This is where she kept you," he murmured.

Cinder licked her lips and glanced around. Part of her thought of the room as a sanctuary—the one place in the world that could have kept her safe for so long. But another part of her couldn't help picturing it as a dungeon. "I was down here for eight years."

"Do you remember any of it?"

"No, I was unconscious until the very end. I do have one faint memory of climbing up that ladder and leaving the hangar. It's pretty hazy, though. If Thorne and I had never come here, I would have always thought it was a dream."

Leaving the tank, Kai paced around the room, taking in the tools made for attaching cyborg prostheses and integrating complicated wiring into the human nervous system. The bright lights, now turned off, that hovered like octopus tentacles over the operating table. He scanned the netscreens on the wall, but didn't try to turn them on. After making a complete circle around the room, he paused and said, "Imagine how proud she would be."

"Michelle Benoit?"

He nodded. "She'd be so proud of Scarlet, and of you. I can only begin to imagine the sacrifices she made to keep you safe, and all so one day you could face Levana and end her tyranny. You not only succeeded, but you signed the Treaty of Bremen and dissolved the Lunar monarchy. You've changed the course of history in ways that I'm sure she never could have predicted, and now . . ." His mouth quirked to one side as he glanced up in the direction of the farmhouse. ". . . Now her granddaughter is married to a Lunar.

Openly. *Happily.* When just a few years ago, that wouldn't have been possible." His smile turned to melancholy. "I'm sorry I never got to meet her."

"Me too," said Cinder.

Lacing their fingers together, Kai lifted the back of her hand to his mouth. "Was there any reason in particular you wanted to show me this?"

"I'm not sure. I figured you know all about my biological family and the world I was born into, and you've of course had the great pleasure of meeting my adoptive family on numerous occasions, so this was the last piece of the puzzle." She waved her free arm around the room. "The missing link to my past."

Kai looked around one more time. "It's pretty creepy, actually."

"I know."

After another moment of reverent silence, Kai said, "I'm surprised Thorne hasn't asked if he can start leading guided tours down here. I bet you could charge a hefty admission fee."

Cinder snorted. "Please don't plant that idea in his head."

"Scarlet would never allow it anyway. Come on." He started heading back toward the ladder. "It's my turn to show you something."

They could still hear music spilling out from the farmhouse, but Kai passed by it and headed into the fields that surrounded them. They hadn't gone far before the mud from recent sprinklers sucked at their feet. They walked for a long time, stepping over the rows of sugar beets, letting the moonlight guide them. After a while the sound of music disappeared in the distance, and another sound took its place—the melodic burble of a small creek.

At the end of the field, the land dipped down into a narrow ravine that the creek had carved over time. There were a few trees scattered along its banks, the roots sometimes emerging from the tiny cliff side before plunging down into the soft silt. Kai found a grassy spot where they could watch the subtle glint of moonlight off the foaming water, and they sat beside each other. His arm wound its way around Cinder's waist.

"All right, I give up," said Cinder. "How did you know this was here?"

"Wolf mentioned it last night when he was showing us around the farm. The creek marks the end of their property. That side belongs to the neighbor."

"It's very nice," she said somewhat haltingly, "but ... why are you showing me a creek?"

"We're not looking at the creek." He pointed up. "We're looking at the stars."

She laughed and tilted her head back. The moon had begun to dip toward the horizon, three-quarters full and surrounded by swirls of stars that could never be seen from a metropolis like New Beijing.

"Also very nice," she said. "But believe it or not, I've actually seen these stars before."

"Well, aren't you hard to impress," he said wryly.

"Sorry. What I meant was, this is *breathtaking.*"

"Thank you. I thought it would be nice to look up at the night sky with you beside me for once, rather than just wishing you were beside me."

Cinder felt a pang of guilt for being so flippant before, when the truth was ...

"I do that too," she said. "I'll look out at the stars and pretend you're with me, or wonder if you're looking at the same constellations that I am, maybe at that same moment." She nestled her body against his and smiled when Kai kissed the top of her head. It felt so natural. Like they'd done this every night for years, rather than having been separated for most of that time.

"I have a confession," Kai mumbled into her hair.

She tilted her head to peer at him. "Careful. There could be paparazzi hiding behind these trees. Any confessions might end up on tomorrow's newsfeeds."

He pretended to consider this for a moment, eyes twinkling, before he said, "I could live with that."

She sat up straighter so she could turn to look at him. "Out with it, then."

"When I was figuring out what to say for the wedding, I kept thinking about you and me."

Cinder jolted. "I knew it!"

Kai's eyebrows shot upward.

"I mean, there seemed to be a lot of overlap," she added. "Especially that part about defying race and distance and physiological tampering."

He cocked his head, grinning as he inspected her. "Actually, I was referring more to the part about finding someone who complements you and makes you stronger. And being with someone not because you have some political agenda, but because ... you love them."

She gazed at him, and he gazed back for a long, long moment, until finally Kai shrugged and admitted, "And, fine, what you said too."

"Thank you."

"Cinder." Kai pulled one leg onto the bank, turning his body so they were facing each other. He took her hands between his and her heart began to drum unexpectedly. Not because of his touch, and not even because of his low, serious tone, but because it occurred to Cinder all at once that Kai was *nervous*.

Kai was never nervous.

"I asked you once," he said, running his thumbs over her knuckles, "if you thought you would ever be willing to wear a crown again. Not as the queen of Luna, but ... as my empress. And you said that you would consider it, someday."

She swallowed a breath of cool night air. "And ... this is that day?"

His lips twitched, but didn't quite become a smile. "I love you. I want to be with you for the rest of my life. I want to marry you, and, yes, I want you to be my empress."

Cinder gaped at him for a long moment before she whispered, "That's a lot of wanting."

"You have no idea."

She lowered her lashes. "I might have some idea."

Kai released one of her hands and she looked up again to see him reaching into his pocket—the same that had held Wolf's and Scarlet's wedding rings before. His fist was closed when he pulled it out and Kai held it toward her, released a slow breath, and opened his fingers to reveal a stunning ring with a large ruby ringed in diamonds.

It didn't take long for her retina scanner to measure the ring, and within seconds it was filling her in on far more information than she needed—inane words like *carats* and *clarity* scrolled past her vision. But it was the ring's history that snagged her attention. It had been his mother's engagement ring once, and his grandmother's before that.

Kai took her hand and slipped the ring onto her finger. Metal clinked against metal, and the priceless gem looked as ridiculous against her cyborg plating as the simple gold band had looked on Wolf's enormous, deformed, slightly hairy hand.

Cinder pressed her lips together and swallowed, hard, before daring to meet Kai's gaze again.

"Cinder," he said, "will you marry me?"

Absurd, she thought.

The emperor of the Eastern Commonwealth was proposing to her. It was uncanny. It was *hysterical.*

But it was Kai, and somehow, that also made it exactly right.

"Yes," she whispered, "I will marry you."

Those simple words hung between them for a breath, and then she grinned and kissed him, amazed that her declaration didn't bring the surge of anxiety she would have expected years ago. He drew her into his arms, laughing between kisses, and she suddenly started to laugh too. She felt strangely delirious.

They had stood against all adversity to be together, and now they would forge their own path to love. She would be Kai's wife. She would be the Commonwealth's empress. And she had every intention of being blissfully happy for ever, ever after.

Long before she was the terror
of Wonderland—
the infamous Queen of Hearts—
she was just a girl who wanted to fall in love.

HEARTLESS

Turn the page for a special bonus excerpt from
Marissa Meyer's first standalone novel, *Heartless*,
coming in Fall 2016.

CHAPTER ONE

THREE LUSCIOUS LEMON TARTS glistened up at Catherine. She reached her towel-wrapped hands into the oven, ignoring the heat that enveloped her arms and pressed against her cheeks, and lifted the tray from the hearth. The tarts' sunshine filling quivered, as if glad to be freed from the stone chamber.

Cath held the tray with the same reverence one might reserve for the King's crown. She refused to take her eyes from the tarts as she padded across the kitchen floor until the tray's edge landed on the baker's table with a satisfying thump. The tarts trembled for a moment more before falling still, flawless and gleaming.

Setting the towels aside, she picked through the curled, sugared lemon peels laid out on parchment and arranged them like rose blossoms on the tarts, settling each strip into the still-warm center. The aromas of sweet citrus and buttery, flaky crust curled beneath her nose.

She stepped back to admire her work.

The tarts had taken her all morning. Five hours of weighing the butter and sugar and flour, of mixing and kneading and rolling the dough, of whisking and simmering and straining the egg yolks and lemon juice until they were thick and creamy and the color of buttercups. She had glazed the crust and crimped the edges like a lace doily. She had boiled and candied the delicate strips of lemon peel and ground sugar crystals into a fine powder for garnish. Her fingers itched to dust the tart edges now, but she refrained. They had to cool first, or else the sugar would melt into unattractive puddles on the surface.

These tarts encompassed everything she had learned from the tattered recipe books on the kitchen shelf. There was not a hurried moment nor a careless touch nor a lesser ingredient in those fluted pans. She had been meticulous at every step. She had baked her very heart into them.

Her inspection lingered, her eyes scanning every inch, every roll of the crust, every shining surface.

Finally, she allowed herself a smile.

Before her sat three perfect lemon tarts, and everyone in Hearts—from the dodo birds to the King himself—would have to recognize that she was the best baker in the kingdom. Even her own mother would be forced to admit that it was so.

Her anxiety released, she bounced on her toes and squealed into her clasped hands.

"You are my crowning joy," she proclaimed, spreading her arms wide over the tarts, as if bestowing a knighthood upon them. "Now I bid you to go into the world with your lemony scrumptiousness and bring forth smiles from every mouth you grace with your presence."

"Speaking to the food again, Lady Catherine?"

"Ah-ah, not just any food, Cheshire." She lifted a finger without glancing back. "Might I introduce to you the most wondrous lemon tarts ever to be baked within the great Kingdom of Hearts!"

A striped tail curled around her right shoulder. A furry, whiskered head appeared on her left. Cheshire purred thoughtfully, the sound vibrating down her spine. "Astounding," he said in that tone he had that always left Cath unsure whether he was mocking her. "But where's the fish?"

Cath kissed the sugar crystals from her fingers and shook her head. "No fish."

"No fish? Whatever is the point?"

"The point is *perfection*." Her stomach tingled every time she thought of it.

Cheshire vanished from her shoulders and reappeared on the baking table, one clawed paw hovering over the tarts. Cath jumped forward to shoo him back. "Don't you dare! They're for the King's party, you goose."

Cheshire's whiskers twitched. "The King? Again?"

Stool legs screeched against the floor as Cath dragged a seat closer to the table and perched on top of it. "I thought I'd save one for him and the others can be served at the feasting table. It makes His Majesty so happy, you know, when I bake him things. And a happy king—"

"Makes for a happy kingdom." Cheshire yawned without bothering to cover his mouth and, grimacing, Cath held her hands in between him and the tarts to protect from any distasteful tuna breath.

"A happy king also makes for a most excellent testimonial. Imagine if he were to declare me the official tart baker of the kingdom! People will line up for miles to taste them."

"They smell tart."

"They *are* tarts." Cath turned one of the fluted pans so the blossom of the lemon-peel rose was aligned with the others. She was always mindful of how her treats were displayed. Mary Ann said her pastries were even more beautiful than those made by the royal pastry chefs.

And after tonight, her desserts would not only be known as more beautiful, they would be known as superior in every way. Such praise was exactly what she and Mary Ann needed to launch their bakery. After so many years of planning, she could feel the dream morphing into a reality.

"Are lemons in season this time of year?" asked Cheshire, watching Cath as she swept up the leftover lemon peels and tied them in cheesecloth. The gardeners could use them to keep pests away.

"Not exactly," she said, smiling to herself. Her thoughts stole back to that morning. Pale light filtering through her lace curtains. Waking up to the smell of citrus in the air.

Part of her wanted to keep the memory tucked like a secret against her chest, but Cheshire would find out soon enough. A tree sprouting up in one's bedroom overnight was a difficult secret to keep. Cath was surprised the rumors hadn't yet spread, given Cheshire's knack for gossip-gathering. Perhaps he'd been too busy snoozing all morning. Or, more likely, having his belly rubbed by the maids.

"They're from a dream," she confessed, carrying the tarts to the pie safe where they could finish cooling.

Cheshire sat back on his haunches. "A dream?" His mouth split open into a wide, toothy grin. "Do tell."

"And have half the kingdom knowing about it by nightfall? Absolutely not. I had a dream and then I woke up, and there was a lemon tree growing in my bedroom. That is all you need to know."

She slammed the pie safe shut with finality, as much to silence herself as to prevent further questions. The truth was, the dream had been clinging to her skin from the moment she'd woken up, haunting and tantalizing her. She wanted to talk about it, almost as much as she wanted to keep it locked up and all to herself.

It had been a hazy, beautiful dream, and in it there had been a hazy, beautiful boy. He was dressed all in black and standing in an orchard of lemon trees, and she had the distinct sensation that he had something that belonged to her. She didn't know what it was, only that she wanted it back, but every time she took a step toward him he receded farther and farther away.

A shiver slipped down the back of her dress. She could still feel the curiosity that tugged at her chest, the need to chase after him.

But mostly it was his eyes that haunted her. Yellow and shining, sweet and tart. His eyes had been bright like lemons ready to fall from a tree.

She shook away the wispy memories and turned back to Cheshire. "By the time I woke up, a branch from the tree had already pulled one of the bedposts full off. Of course, Mama made the gardeners take it down before it did any more damage, but I was able to sneak away some lemons first."

"I wondered what the hullabaloo was about this morning." Cheshire's tail flicked against the butcher block. "Are you sure the lemons are safe for consumption? If they sprouted from a dream, they could be, you know, *that* kind of food."

Cath's attention drifted back to the closed pie safe, the tarts hidden behind its wire mesh. "You're worried that the king might become shorter if he eats one?"

Cheshire snorted. "On the contrary, I'm worried that I will turn into a house should I eat one. I've been minding my figure, you know."

Giggling, Cath leaned over the table and scratched him beneath his chin. "You're perfect no matter your size, Cheshire. But the lemons are safe—I bit one before I started baking." Her cheeks puckered at the sour memory.

Cheshire had started to purr, already ignoring her. Cath cupped her chin with her free hand while Cheshire flopped deliriously onto one side and her strokes moved down to his belly. "Besides, if you ever did eat some bad food, I could still find a use for you. I've always wanted a cat-drawn carriage."

Cheshire opened one eye, his pupil slitted and unamused.

"I would dangle balls of yarn and fish bones out in front to keep you moving."

He stopped purring long enough to say, "You are not as cute as you think you are, Lady Pinkerton."

Cath tapped Cheshire once on the nose and pulled away. "You could do your disappearing trick and then everyone would think, My, my, look at the glorious bulbous head pulling that carriage down the street!"

Cheshire was fully glaring at her now. "I am a proud feline, not a beast of labor."

He disappeared with a huff.

"Don't be cross. I'm only teasing." Catherine untied her apron and draped it on a hook on the wall, revealing a perfect apron-shaped silhouette on her dress, outlined in flour and bits of dried dough.

"By-the-bye." His voice drifted back to her. "Your mother is looking for you."

"What for? I've been down here all morning."

"Yes, and now you're going to be late. Unless you're going as a lemon tart yourself, you'd better get on with it."

"Late?" Catherine glanced at the cuckoo clock on the wall. It was still early afternoon, plenty of time to—

Her pulse skipped as she heard a faint wheezing coming from inside the clock. "Oh! Cuckoo, did you doze off again?" She smacked her palm against the clock's side and the door sprang open, revealing a tiny red bird, fast asleep. "Cuckoo!"

The bird startled awake with a mad flap of his wings. "Oh my, oh heavens," he squawked, rubbing his eyes with the tips of his wings. "What time is it?"

"Whatever are you asking me for, you doltish bird?" With a harried groan, Catherine ran from the kitchen, crashing into Mary Ann on the stairwell.

"Cath—Lady Catherine! I was coming to . . . the Marchioness is—"

"I know, I know, the ball. I lost track of time."

Mary Ann gave her a fast head-to-toe glance and grabbed her wrist. "Best get you cleaned up before she sees you and calls for both of our heads."

CHAPTER TWO

 ARY ANN CHECKED that the Marchioness wasn't around the corner before ushering Cath into the bedroom and shutting the door.

The other maid, Abigail, was there already, dressed identical to Mary Ann in a demure black dress and white apron, attempting to swat a rocking-horse-fly out the open window with a broom. Every time she missed, it would nicker and whip its mane to either side, before flying back up toward the ceiling. "These pests will be the death of me!" Abigail growled to Mary Ann, wiping the sweat from her brow. Then, realizing that Catherine was there too, she dropped into a lopsided curtsy.

Catherine stiffened. "Abigail—!"

Her warning was too late. A pair of tiny rockers clomped over the back of Abigail's bonnet before the horse darted back up toward the ceiling.

"Why, you obnoxious little pony!" Abigail screeched, swinging her broom.

Cringing, Mary Ann dragged Catherine into the powder

room and shut the door. Water had already been drawn in a pitcher on the washing stand. "There isn't time for a bath, but let's not tell your mother that," she said, fiddling with the back of Catherine's muslin dress while Cath dipped a washcloth into the pitcher. She furiously scrubbed the flour from her face. How had she managed to get it behind her ears?

"I thought you were going into town today," she said, letting Mary Ann peel off her dress and chemise.

"I did, but it was fabulously dull. All anyone wanted to talk about was the ball, as if the King doesn't have a party every other day." Taking the washcloth, Mary Ann scrubbed Catherine's arms until her flesh was pink, then spritzed her with rosewater to cover up the lingering aroma of pastry dough and oven fires. "There was a lot of talk about a new court joker who will be making his debut tonight. Jack was bragging about how he's going to steal his hat and smash the bells as a sort of initiation."

"That seems very childish."

"I agree. Jack is such a knave." Mary Ann helped Catherine into a new chemise before pushing her down onto a stool and running a brush through her dark hair. "I did hear one bit of interesting news though. The cobbler is retiring and will be leaving his storefront empty by the end of this month." With a twist, a dish full of pins, and a touch of beeswax, a lovely chignon rested at the nape of Catherine's neck and her face was haloed by a cluster of jovial curls.

"The cobbler? On Main Street?"

"The very one." Mary Ann spun Cath around, her voice

dropping to a whisper. "When I heard it, I immediately thought what a fine location it would be. For us."

Cath's eyes widened. "Sweet hearts, you're right. Right next to that toy shop—"

"And just down the hill from that quaint white chapel. Think of all the wedding cakes you'd be making."

"Oh! We could do a series of different-flavored cobblers for our grand opening, in honor of the shoemaker. We'll start with the classics—blueberry cobbler, peach cobbler—but then, imagine the possibilities. A lavender-nectarine cobbler one day, and the next, a banana-butterscotch cobbler, topped with graham cracker crumble and—"

"Stop it!" Mary Ann laughed. "I haven't had supper yet."

"We should go look at it, don't you think? Before word gets out?"

"I thought so too. Maybe tomorrow. But your mother . . ."

"I'll tell her we're going shopping for new ribbons. She won't mind." Cath swayed on the balls of her feet. "By the time she finds out about the bakery, we'll be able to show her what a tremendous business opportunity it is and even she won't be able to deny it."

Mary Ann's smile turned tight. "I don't think it's the business opportunity she's bound to disapprove of."

Cath flitted away her concern, although she knew Mary Ann was right. Her mother would never approve of her only daughter, the heir to Rock Turtle Cove, going into the men's world of business, especially with a humble servant like Mary Ann as her partner. Besides, baking was a job fit for servants, her mother would say. And she would loathe the idea that Cath planned on using her own marriage dowry in order to open the business herself.

But she and Mary Ann had been dreaming of it for so long, she sometimes forgot that it wasn't yet reality. Her pastries and desserts were already becoming renowned throughout the kingdom, and the King himself was her grandest fan, which might have been the only reason her mother tolerated her hobby at all.

"Her approval won't matter," Cath said, trying to convince herself as much as Mary Ann. The idea of her mother being angry over this decision, or worse, disowning her, made her stomach curdle. But it wouldn't come to that. She hoped.

She lifted her chin. "We're going forward with or without my parents' approval. We are going to have the best bakery in all of Hearts. Why, even the White Queen will travel here when she hears word of our decadent chocolate tortes and blissfully flaky currant scones."

Mary Ann bunched her lips to one side, doubtful.

"That reminds me," Cath continued. "I have three tarts cooling in the pie safe right now. Could you bring them tonight? Oh, but they still need a dusting of powdered sugar. I left some on the table. Just a teeny, tiny bit." She pinched her fingers in example.

"Of course I can bring them. What kind of tarts?"

"Lemon."

A teasing smile crept up Mary Ann's face. "From your tree?"

"You heard about it?"

"I saw Mr. Gardiner planting it under your window this morning and had to ask where it came from. All that hacking they had to do to get it unwound from your bedposts, and yet it seemed no worse for wear."

Catherine wrung her hands, not sure why talking about her dream tree made her self-conscious. "Well, yes, that's where I got my lemons, and I'm certain these tarts are my best yet. By tomorrow morning, all of Hearts will be talking about them and longing to know when they can buy our desserts for themselves."

"Don't be silly, Cath." Mary Ann pulled a corset over Cath's head. "They've been asking that since you made those maple–brown sugar cookies last year."

Cath wrinkled her nose. "Don't remind me. I overcooked them, remember? Too crisp on the edges."

"You're too harsh a critic."

"I want to be the best."

Mary Ann settled her hands on Cath's shoulders. "You are the best. And I've calculated the numbers again—with the expected costs attached to Mr. Caterpillar's shop, monthly expenses, and the cost of ingredients, all measured against our planned daily output and pricing. Adjusted to allow some room for error, I still think we would be profitable in under a year."

Cath clapped her hands over her ears. "You take all the fun out of it with your numbers and mathematics. You know how they make my head spin."

Mary Ann sniffed and turned away, opening the wardrobe.

"You have no trouble converting tablespoons into cups. It's not all that different."

"It is different, which is why I need you on this venture. My brilliant, oh-so-logical business partner."

She could almost feel Mary Ann's eye roll. "I'd like to get that in writing, Lady Catherine. Now, I seem to recall we had chosen the white gown for tonight?"

"Whichever you think." Stifling the fantasy of their future bakery, Cath set to clipping a set of pearls to her earlobes.

"So?" Mary Ann asked as she pulled a pair of drawers and a petticoat from the wardrobe, then urged Cath to turn around so she could adjust the corset laces. "Was it a good dream?"

Cath was surprised to find that she still had pastry dough beneath her fingernails. Picking at it gave her a good excuse to keep her head lowered, hiding the blush that crept up her throat. "Nothing too special," she said, thinking of lemon-yellow eyes.

She gasped as the corset tightened unexpectedly, squeezing her rib cage. "I can tell when you're lying," said Mary Ann.

"Oh, fine. Yes, it was a good dream. But they're all magical, aren't they?"

"I wouldn't know. I've never had one. Though Abigail told me that once she dreamed about a big glowing crescent shape hovering in the sky . . . and the next morning Cheshire showed up, all grinning teeth hovering in the air and begging for a saucer of milk. Years later and we still can't seem to get rid of him."

Cath grunted. "I'm fond of Cheshire, yet I can't help but hope that my dream might portend something a bit more magical than that."

"Even if it doesn't, at least you got some good lemons out of it."

"True. I shall be satisfied." Though she wasn't. Not nearly.

"Catherine!" The door swung open and the Marchioness floated in, her eyes saucer-wide and her face purple-red despite having been recently powdered. Catherine's mother lived her life in a state of constant bewilderment. "There you are, my dear darling! What are you—not even dressed yet?"

"Oh, Mama, Mary Ann was just helping me—"

"Abigail, stop playing with that broom and get in here! We need your help! Mary Ann, what is she wearing?"

"My lady, we thought the white gown that she—"

"Absolutely not! Red! You will wear the red dress." Her mother swung open the wardrobe doors and pulled out a full gown overflowing with heavy red velvet, an enormous bustle, and a neckline that was sure to leave little unexposed. "Yes, perfect."

"Oh, Mama. Not that dress. It's too small!"

Her mother picked a waxy green leaf off the bed and draped the dress across the covers. "No, no, no, not too small for my precious little sweetling. This is going to be a very special night, Catherine, and it's imperative that you look your best."

Cath traded a glance with Mary Ann, who shrugged.

"But it's just another ball. Why don't I—"

"Tut-tut, child." Her mother scurried across the room and framed Cath's face in both hands. Though her mother was bony as a bird, there was no sense of delicacy as she pinched and squeezed Cath's face. "You are in for such a delight this evening, my pretty girl." Her eyes glimmered in a way that made Catherine suspicious, before she barked, *"Now turn around!"*

Catherine jumped and spun to face the window.

Her mother, who had become the Marchioness when she married, had that effect on everyone. She was often a warm, loving woman, and Cath's father, the Marquis, doted on her incessantly, but Cath was all too familiar with her mood swings. All cooing and delighted one moment and screaming at the top of her lungs the next. Despite her tiny stature, she had a booming voice and a particular glare that could make even a lion's heart shrivel beneath it.

Cath thought by now she would have been used to her mother's temperament, but the frequent changes still took her by surprise.

"Mary Ann, tighten her corset."

"But, my lady, I just—"

"Tighter, Mary Ann. This dress won't fit without a twenty-two-inch waist, although just once I'd like to see you down to twenty. You have your father's unfortunate bones, you know, and we must be vigilant if we're to keep from having his figure too. Abigail, be a dear and bring me the ruby set from my jewelry cabinet."

"The ruby set?" Catherine whined as Mary Ann undid the corset laces. "But those earrings are so heavy."

"Don't be such a jellyfish. It's only for one night. Tighter!"

Catherine pinched her face together as Mary Ann tugged on the corset strings. She exhaled as much air as she could and gripped the side of the vanity, willing away the sparkles dancing before her eyes.

"Mother, I can't breathe."

"Well then, next time, I hope you'll think twice before taking a second helping of dessert like you did last night. You can't eat like a piglet and dress like a lady. It will be a miracle if this dress fits."

"We could—wear—the white one?"

Her mother crossed her arms. "My daughter will be wearing red tonight like a true . . . never you mind that. You'll just have to go without dinner."

Cath groaned as Mary Ann cinched the corset one more time. Having to suffer through the bindings was bad enough, but going without dinner too? The food was what she looked forward to most during the King's parties, and all she'd eaten that day was a single boiled egg—she'd been too caught up with her baking to think about eating more.

Her stomach growled in its confinement.

"Are you all right?" Mary Ann whispered.

She bobbed her head, not wanting to waste any precious air to speak.

"Dress!"

Before Catherine could catch her breath, she found herself being squashed and wrangled into the red velvet monstrosity. When the maids had finished and Catherine dared to peek into the mirror, she was relieved that, while she may have felt like an encased sausage, she didn't look like one. The bold color brought out the red in her lips and made her fair skin appear fairer and her dark hair darker. When Abigail settled the enormous necklace onto her collarbone and replaced her pearls with dangling rubies, Catherine felt, momentarily, like a true lady of the court, all glamour and mystery.

"Marvelous!" The Marchioness clasped one of Catherine's hands in both of hers, that peculiar, misty-eyed look returning. "I'm so proud of you."

Catherine frowned. "You are?"

"Oh, don't start fishing now." Her mother clucked her tongue, patting the back of Cath's hand once before dropping it.

Catherine eyed her reflection again. The mystique was quickly fading, leaving her feeling exposed. She would have preferred a nice, roomy day dress, covered in flour or not. "Mama, I'll be overdressed. No one else will be so done up."

Her mother sniffed. "Precisely. You look exceptional!" She wiped away a tear. "I could scatter to pieces."

Despite all her discomfort, all her reservations, Cath couldn't deny a hot spark behind her sternum. Her mother's voice was a constant nag in her head, telling her to put down the fork, to stand up straight, to smile, *but not that much!* She knew her mother wanted the best for her, but it was oh so lovely to hear compliments for once.

With one last dreamy sigh, the Marchioness mentioned checking on Cath's father before she fluttered out of the room, dragging Abigail along with her. As the door to her chambers closed, Cath yearned to fall onto her bed with the exhaustion that came from being in her mother's presence, but she was sure she would rip an important seam if she did.

"Do I look as ridiculous as I feel?"

Mary Ann shook her head. "You look ravishing."

"Is it absurd to look ravishing at this silly ball? Everyone will think I'm being presumptuous."

Mary Ann pressed her lips in apology. "It is a bit of butter upon bacon."

"Oh, please, I'm hungry enough as it is." Cath twisted inside the corset, trying to pry up some of the boning that dug into her ribs, but it wouldn't budge. "I need a chocolate."

"I'm sorry, Cath, but I don't think that dress could fit a single bite. Come along. I'll help you into your shoes."

Thank you for reading this FEIWEL AND FRIENDS book.
The Friends who made

possible are:

Jean Feiwel
publisher

Liz Szabla
editor in chief

Rich Deas
senior creative director

Holly West
associate editor

Dave Barrett
executive managing editor

Kim Waymer
production manager

Anna Roberto
associate editor

Christine Barcellona
associate editor

Emily Settle
administrative assistant

Anna Poon
editorial assistant

Follow us on Facebook or visit us online at mackids.com.

OUR BOOKS ARE FRIENDS FOR LIFE